Praise for *Meet M*

"*Meet Me at the Starlight* is a delightful multigenerational novel. I was fully invested in these memorable characters who are as colorful as the iconic Starlight's neon sign. This story will have you flipping pages well past midnight as the community fights for their local treasure, and the ending will renew your faith as good prevails."

—Nancy Naigle, author of *The Shell Collector*

"In a charming story set across three generations, Hauck introduces readers to a delightful town, Hollywood stars, a royal mystery, and the Starlight skating rink at the heart of it all. While *Meet Me at the Starlight* wraps you in a twentieth-century fairy tale, its themes of forgiveness, trust, second chances, acceptance, and love carry the day and will leave you grinning at the last page."

—Katherine Reay, bestselling author of *Dear Mr. Knightley* and *The Printed Letter Bookshop*

Praise for *The Best Summer of Our Lives*

"Hauck's exploration of friendship, second chances, and faith is tender and often emotionally nuanced. It's an undeniable heartwarmer."

—*Publishers Weekly*

"Bestselling, Christy–winning Hauck presents a powerful inspirational tale of friendship that touches on two horrific real crimes of the 1970s and charts a rocky path to redemption and love."

—*Booklist*

"Themes about the endurance of friendship and the ability to come home give readers plenty to think about, and those nostalgic for childhood summers will enjoy this novel."

—*Library Journal*

"In true Rachel Hauck fashion, *The Best Summer of Our Lives* blends faith and hope into a story about the seasons of life, the seasons of friendship, and the seasons of love. A journey that will warm your heart and make you yearn to reconnect with old friends."

—Lisa Wingate, *New York Times* bestselling author of *The Book of Lost Friends*

"Rachel Hauck sets the gold standard in inspirational fiction. *The Best Summer of Our Lives* is a nostalgic novel of friendship, romance, and the choices that define a life."

—Brenda Novak, *New York Times* and *USA Today* bestselling author

MEET ME *at the* STARLIGHT

BETHANY HOUSE BOOKS BY RACHEL HAUCK

The Best Summer of Our Lives

Meet Me at the Starlight

MEET ME *at the* STARLIGHT

a novel

RACHEL HAUCK

BETHANYHOUSE
a division of Baker Publishing Group
Minneapolis, Minnesota

Published by Bethany House Publishers
Minneapolis, Minnesota
BethanyHouse.com

Bethany House Publishers is a division of
Baker Publishing Group, Grand Rapids, Michigan

Printed in the United States of America

Library of Congress Cataloging-in-Publication Data
Names: Hauck, Rachel, author.
Title: Meet me at the starlight / Rachel Hauck.
Description: Minneapolis, Minnesota : Bethany House, a division of Baker Publishing Group, 2024.
Identifiers: LCCN 2023049983 | ISBN 9780764240980 (paperback) | ISBN 9780764243042 (casebound) | ISBN 9781493446490 (e-book)
Subjects: LCGFT: Christian fiction. | Novels.
Classification: LCC PS3608.A866 M44 2024 | DDC 813/.6—dc23/eng/20231103
LC record available at https://lccn.loc.gov/2023049983

This book is a work of fiction. Names, characters, places, and incidents are the product of the author's imagination or are used fictitiously. Any resemblance to actual events, locales, or persons, living or dead, is coincidental.

Cover design by Faceout Studio, Jeff Miller

Baker Publishing Group publications use paper produced from sustainable forestry practices and postconsumer waste whenever possible.

24 25 26 27 28 29 30 7 6 5 4 3 2 1

For Robbi and Trudy

1

TUESDAY

JUNE 1932
SEA BLUE BEACH, FLORIDA

The sight of the Starlight just on the edge of her kitchen window eased her lingering regret over her fight with Leroy last week.

Even though she deserved an answer, she hated his pained expression as she called him a scallywag, declaring how he'd let her and their boys down. *"I've never been more disappointed. Where do you go each week? Tell me now."*

More disappointed? Those words were not true. Tuesday Knight had been disappointed plenty in her life. Leroy was least of them all.

Still, after three years of his clandestine activity, she had a right to know, didn't she? He must work hard at whatever he was getting up to because he brought home cash, enough to pay the grocer and keep the lights on. And in these lean times, that was saying something.

Ever since the Crash and the Depression sat down on everyone, Leroy Knight had changed. Her hero, her knight in shining armor, a Great War soldier with chest full of medals, had become *way* too friendly with the Memphis and Chicago gangsters passing through their beloved Sea Blue Beach.

Wiping her hands on a stained dish towel, she stepped onto the porch and into the humid evening heat of Florida summer. At six o'clock, the day remained summery bright, with a bit of the Starlight's neon light in its ribbons.

"It's been too long since I visited you with my skates." She'd been speaking to the rink as a friend ever since she was a girl. Shoot, the rink was her *family* before Lee and the boys.

The Starlight gave her comfort. Skating helped her think through things. And she needed to *roll* her way through this turmoil with Leroy.

"Why can't I know where you go every week? I'm your wife, the mother of your sons. Is that too much to ask?"

"Well it is, Tooz, so drop it. I'm here now, aren't I?" He'd pulled a few greenbacks from his pocket. *"This ought to square our account with Old Man Biggs at the grocery store. There's a bit more here to stock up on what you need."*

"I won't touch a penny of that until you tell me where it came from. 'Cause if it's blood money or from running booze—"

"It ain't blood money. Holy shamoly, Tooz, can't a man provide for his family without the third degree?"

That's when he'd left without a by-your-leave. Since they didn't have a phone, he couldn't call. And Leroy was not one for writing letters. So she had no idea if he'd return home as usual this Friday.

"Beg pardon, Tooz." She glanced around to see Drunk Dirk, as everyone called him, coming up the shell-and-sand driveway.

"Dirk. What can I do you for?"

Not much older than Leroy, Dirk was also a Great War veteran who played the Wurlitzer at the Starlight. It was a darn shame his reputation, lovely wife and two sons, along with his touted musical ability, was eclipsed by his drunkenness. Lord only knew where he got the hooch in the first place. Sea Blue Beach was a dry town.

"I's just wondering if Lee was around. You seen him lately?"

"Sure haven't." Giving Dirk the once-over, she wondered if it was her husband supplying Dirk's habit. Another second passed before she pointed to the kitchen's screen door. "Care for some dinner?"

"Naw, naw, Tooz, but thanky. I got a hankering for . . . something else." He sloughed off without another word, tripping as he entered the street, turning left, then right toward the Starlight.

That's it, Drunk Dirk, get to the Starlight. That'll soothe your soul. Maybe help you to stop drinking. Besides, the evening session started in an hour, and Dirk was scheduled to play.

Back in the warm kitchen, Tuesday removed the pork and beans from the old potbelly, which glowed with burning logs and turned the whole house into an oven. She set the table and stirred up a pitcher of iced tea, using the last bit of ice from the icebox. She'd have to make up a list, send Leroy Junior to Biggs tomorrow.

Speaking of LJ, where was he? And Dupree? Her old dinner bell had blown away during some storm or another. Back out on the porch, she looked toward the horizon for signs of her boys, thirteen and eleven, respectively. They'd probably lost track of time.

Well, she'd wait. Tuesday sat on the old stone step and faced the beautiful, beautiful Starlight—she would love that place till the day she died—and wondered if Dirk had made it to the organ.

He had to know, as she and everyone in Sea Blue Beach, that no town in all of America, maybe the world, had a skating rink as grand and lovely as the Starlight. After all, it was built by a prince—Prince Rein Titus Alexander Blue, or Prince Blue as they called him—from faraway Lauchtenland, a tiny North Sea nation.

Tuesday hoped to go there one day, see where Prince Blue had lived before he crashed on their North Florida shore. He'd built the Starlight on the very spot, on the bedrock that held everything together—the sand and shells, the dirt and grass, trees, maybe even the Gulf itself. Certainly all of Sea Blue Beach.

"Ma, Ma." LJ, tall and lanky, sprinted down the driveway. Trailing behind was Dupree, pumping his still-short legs to keep up.

"Can we skate tonight at the Starlight? Mr. Hoboth ain't there, but Burt says we can skate for free if we help clean up."

"That was kind of him."

Jud Hoboth, along with Burt, had managed the rink ever since Prince Blue left to command a Lauchtenland regiment during the Great War. Hoboth was a nice man, if not temperamental, with one foot out the door, always talking about adventures out west or down Mexico way. But what would happen to the Starlight if he just took off?

"Go on inside, wash your hands. Dinner's on."

"Can we go, huh? All the kids are going tonight."

"When have I ever said no to the Starlight? I might go too."

The house rattled as the boys ran up the stairs and fought to be first at minuscule bathroom sink. When they came down, their faces were washed, their hair combed and slicked back, and their shirts soaking wet.

Tuesday loved her boys.

She served them bowls of pork and beans, corn bread slathered in butter, and cold milk. "What'd y'all do today?"

In the summer, she let them tear all over God's green earth after morning chores. Growing boys needed to use up their energy. They came home to dinner stained, filthy, and full of stories, then scampered back outside until dark. Then it was bath time, followed by popcorn and their radio program, Jack Benny or Eddie Cantor, ever since baseball banned broadcast of their games.

"We went fishing on the beach," LJ said, dipping his corn bread in his bowl.

"We helped Cap'n Tatum unload a fresh haul." Dup gulped down his milk. "He gave us fifty cents, so we went to Biggs for candy. Got a milkshake at Alderman's too." He handed Tuesday his bowl for seconds.

"Then we got up a game of kickball with the fellas," LJ said. "We lost, thanks to Dup."

"Did not."

"Did so."

Tuesday returned Dup's bowl, steamy and full. "I thought two young men in this house wanted to go to the Starlight tonight."

That shut them up. Worked every time. The forty-five-year-old rink was loved by the entire Knight family. Even Leroy.

"I'm going to skate on a racing team when I get bigger," Dup said.

"Ah, you're not fast enough." LJ reached around and yanked Dup's hat from his head. "You're at the table."

"I am too fast enough. Take it back. Ma—"

"You'll be fast when you need to be." Tuesday gave LJ a side glance. *Be nice.*

When they finished eating and the boys had washed the dishes—which always included flinging Super Suds at each other—Tuesday said, "Get your skates. Bring mine as well."

It had been a splurge, more than they could afford, to buy everyone Richardson boot skates for Christmas. But last year Leroy played the big shot, telling Tuesday to order whatever she wanted from the skate catalog. He brought home a money order from the bank, and she put the whole kit and caboodle in the mail the day after Halloween. The skates arrived a week before Christmas. Lordy, how the boys shouted when they unwrapped their boxes.

While Tuesday loved her skates—which she'd not trade for anything—she remained a bit vexed that she still cooked on a wood-burning stove. Sakes alive, it was 1932, and no matter how many hints she dropped to Leroy, he never clued in. She might just have to take matters into her own hands. Or flat out say, *Lee, I need a new stove*. But he was stubborn. Sometimes the more a body wanted something from him, the more he resisted.

While the boys thumped around upstairs, Tuesday got to work on tomorrow morning's bread, then hurried to freshen up.

"Can we get some popcorn, Ma?" Dup dropped into his usual seat at the table, clutching his skates.

"Don't see why not." Tuesday set the dough aside, then reached for the cannister on the pantry's top shelf. "Maybe a soda pop too." The can contained the fun money she earned from helping Mr. Hoboth at the rink. "I can hear Dirk firing up the organ as we speak." She took her pocketbook off the hook by the door and stuffed two dollars inside. "LJ, what are you doing?" She called up the stairs. "Get a move on. Don't forget to bring my skates. Dup, go see what your brother is doing."

His skates clattered to the floor, and he started yelling before he left the kitchen, "LJ, Ma says hurry up."

Now where was her lipstick? Caught in the torn lining of her purse, that's where. Tuesday leaned toward the windowpane, using it as a mirror, when she heard, "Am I invited too?"

She whirled around to see Leroy at the door, his broad shoulders filling the frame. He gave her a sheepish grin, hat in his hand. Fifteen years together, and he still made her knees weak.

"Lee, what are you doing here? It's only Wednesday." She capped her lipstick and ran into his arms. "About the other day . . . I didn't mean what I said."

"Sure you did, and I deserved it." He pressed his lips to hers, drawing all the blood in her veins to her heart. "I'm sorry, Tooz. I didn't mean to pop off and leave without a word."

"I'm sorry too, and I'm so glad you're home." She brushed aside his dark bangs and searched his blue eyes. Too handsome for anyone's good, she'd fallen in love with him the moment he asked her to skate.

He'd just returned from the war, and her friends whispered, *"He's trouble."* But Tuesday Morrow did *not* care. If he was trouble, let her sink in deep. Beneath his cotton shirt beat the heart of a warrior.

"The boys and I took a run near here." He released her as he gazed toward the stove and tossed his hat onto the table. "I thought I'd pop in to see my favorite gal. My beautiful wife."

"Well, my *boys* and I were about to go skating." She took a step back. She hated that he referred to his crew as "the boys."

LJ and Dupree were his boys. The others were junior thugs of some sort.

"Don't start, Tooz." He opened the icebox. "Can you heat up some supper?"

"Why don't you come with us and buy a hot dog?"

He frowned. "All I ever eat is diner fare. I'd like some home cooking."

"Home cooking? You think I made pot roast and potatoes, with an apple pie for dessert? We live on beans, corn bread, sourdough bread, eggs, cereal, and milk, Lee. If you want a bowl of beans, stir up the stove and grab a pot. And if you're tired of diner fare, well, that's all on you." Tuesday braced for his reply, but the boys—*their* boys—clambered down the stairs and into the kitchen.

"Pa!" LJ dropped his skates and fell against him. Dup clung to Lee's arm. "You're home. Golly gumdrops. Can you skate with us?"

LJ poised for a dash upstairs to retrieve Lee's Richardson skates, the ones he'd worn only once in the last six months.

"Um, well, I suppose." He glanced at Tuesday, longing in his eyes for something besides dinner, which made her burn through and through, wanting him more than the Starlight. At least for now. He tipped his head toward the ceiling. *Can't we . . . ?*

"Get your father's skates, LJ," Tuesday said. Lee would just have to wait. "We'll have a much-needed family outing."

LJ retrieved his pa's skates, then shot out the door after Dupree and raced down the drive to Sea Blue Way and the Starlight.

Tuesday was about to follow when Leroy spun her around for a kiss, moving his warm lips from hers down to her collarbone.

She refused to surrender, no matter how much she wanted to take his hand and head up the stairs. "The boys will expect us."

"Tooz, don't punish me."

"Punish you? Why would I when it means punishing myself? But your boys—your *sons*—need time with you. Now let's go so's you can put your skating talent on display."

He sighed and searched her eyes. "Look, I don't want to open the can of worms again, but I want you to know this is not the life I dreamed for us."

"Well, we have that in common." Tuesday clung to her skates. The stove fire had died, but the kitchen seemed warmer than ever. "Just what did you dream for us? And why aren't you doing it?"

"I sort of am, I reckon. Don't you see? I'm setting us up, giving LJ and Dupree a better future. You think I can buy you nice things, like those skates you're holding onto for dear life, or send the boys to college by working on a fishing vessel? Or breaking my back logging? I was a soldier, Tooz. A fighter. I earned medals. Do you see me clerking at the bank or stocking shelves for Biggs?" He pointed to water stains on the ceiling and the tired wallpaper curling away from the corners. "This place . . . it's a dump and I aim to find a way to change our station."

"How? By doing what? Where does a soldier go for a job? Don't tell me you're back in the army."

"I tried the army," he said softly. "They thanked me for my service but didn't have anything for a man my age."

"Lee, I'm sorry." Tuesday pressed her hand on his. "Just so you know, I love this house. I gave birth to our sons in this house."

"Never mind the army. You wouldn't have wanted the army life anyway, Tooz. Can you see yourself leaving Sea Blue Beach or the Starlight?" Lee leaned out the door and gazed toward the changing horizon. "Don't you want to move across the street to one of the new cottages they're building on the beach? Three bedrooms, two baths, a sunroom, solid wood floors, and a roof that don't let in the rain. How about new furniture and a bed that don't creak when we . . ." Her man blushed. Sure enough.

"Not if it means you leaving every week to do God only knows what. Lee, I don't want much in life. I'm the unwanted child of an unmarried sixteen-year-old girl who was so delirious with pain that she named me Tuesday 'cause she thought the midwife asked what day it was."

"I still want to know why a midwife would ask a laboring mama to tell her the day of the week."

"I'd love to ask more than that, but since I've never even met her. . . ." Every now and then, if she spoke of her mama, the tears bubbled up. And she resented it. Margie Lou was a rebel who wanted nothing to do with her family or her newborn daughter. "Then Mamaw and Gramps raised me as a cousin, though everyone knew I was Margie Lou's daughter. I looked just like her. Then Gramps died, and Mamaw sold up and moved to Tampa with Aunt Marcy, leaving me here all by myself at fifteen." She gripped his shirt. "But you know all of this. You know this town and our family are everything to me. I want our boys to come home to a loving mother *and* father every night. But lately, they only have me."

"I want everything you want and more." He hooked a strong arm around her. "I *am* your family, Tooz, and I'm doing my job to provide and make a better life. Dream a little with me, will you?"

"You know what I'm dreaming, Lee?"

"Tell me."

"That I wake up one day to find an electric stove and refrigerator right here in this kitchen."

"Golly mo, Tooz, you dream of appliances?"

"I'm more practical these days. It's 1932, and I cook on an ol' potbelly and keep our food in an icebox." He laughed and hugged her close. "But, Leroy Knight, hear me now, I don't mind none of it if it means you hang your hat on that hook"—she pointed to the largest nail by the door—"every evening."

"One day, I promise, Tooz. I'll be home. We just got to get through this government mess. Ol' FDR and his henchman Hoover has messed us up something fierce, but—Oh, wait, I got a surprise for you. How could I forget? It's the reason I'm home. Shoot fire, your kisses got me all confused."

"Oh hush, now what are you talking about?"

"When I proposed, I promised one day I'd buy you the biggest, brightest diamond to wear on your finger."

"How could I forget? My warrior is also a big talker." She didn't want him to buy her a ring if it meant him running all over who-knows-where, but oh, wouldn't it be lovely to have a symbol of belonging? A sensation she'd never had growing up. Until Mamaw left and Prince Blue took her in, gave her a room at the Starlight along with a job.

"I mean to keep that promise, Tuesday. But for now, I wondered if this would do." Lee stepped onto the porch and took a rolled document from his worn travel bag and tossed it to the old, scarred table. "Read it." He puffed up like he'd done something extraordinary.

Tuesday set her skates on the floor and reached for a parchment-like document. "It's a deed . . . to the Starlight." She peered up at him. "Lee, what is this? I don't understand."

"I got you the Starlight, Tooz."

"You . . . you *bought* the Starlight?" She scanned the ornate deed with gilded edges and calligraphed inscriptions.

Prince Rein Titus Alexander Blue, of the House of Blue, to Miss Tuesday Morrow, on this day, the twelfth of June 1916 AD.

The prince's titled signature, in his lovely penmanship, stretched across the bottom of the parchment.

"It's signed by the prince."

"Yeah, ain't that something? Anyway, I'd heard Hoboth decided to scratch his itch to see the world. You know running a skating rink weren't his idea of a good time." Leroy shrugged, leaving Tuesday to figure out the rest of her husband's noble deed.

"Goodness, I figured he'd leave one day, but we were just talking last week about how Mrs. Elkins made me the most delicious silk cake for my birthday. He said, 'How old are you now?' I said thirty-two, and he got this smarmy expression and said he had something to do." She read the parchment again. "Leroy Knight, you best not be joshing me. This doesn't look like a county deed. And my married name isn't on it."

"Got me, Tooz. I handed him money and he handed me that-there deed. Maybe he forgot your married name."

"The date is 1916."

"Hoboth is missing a few, if you know what I mean." Lee tapped the bottom of the document. "But it says whoever's name is on this piece of paper is the pure and true owner of the Starlight. That's good enough for me. But ask the boys at county records when you file the deed."

"Where did you get the money? How much did it cost?"

"Listen, doll, when a man gives his wife a gift, he doesn't tell her how much it cost. Do you like it? Are you happy?"

"Leroy Knight, you almost make me sorry I badgered you about never being home. This . . . this is the greatest thing anyone has ever done for me. I feel like. . . a princess. With her own little kingdom."

"I promised you a diamond ring, but—" Leroy tugged her curves against him. "How about a little starlight for now?"

2

HARLOW

MARCH 1987
MANHATTAN, NEW YORK CITY

About a month ago, she'd started referring to herself in the third person. *Harlow Hayes should do something about her life. Harlow Hayes should take a shower. Harlow Hayes should get a haircut. Harlow Hayes, Harlow Hayes, Harlow Hayes.*

That's when she realized something had to change.

But how? She had become a joke. To the world. To herself. Friends pitied her. Comedians made her a punch line for their late monologues. Last month, *Saturday Night Live's* Victoria Jackson played Harlow Hayes while wearing a ridiculous wig and some sort of fat suit.

But when the love of her life crushed her without so much as an "I'm sorry," Harlow Hayes gave up and gave in.

Maybe living in the third person wasn't so bad. And the dark "cave" in which she dwelt most of the time was comforting. Her small, narrow bedroom—which was probably once a Gilded Age butler's pantry—allowed no expectations and thus no failures. No letdowns. No feckless laughter from late-night audiences.

But it's all sticks and stones, right?

Harlow flicked an empty box of Cheez-Its to the floor, ignoring the few crumbs that scattered over the small rug. She'd clean it up later. On her twin bed, she tried to sleep while Jinx—make no mistake, this was her apartment—blasted the six o'clock news.

Chuck Scarborough's smooth news voice reminded America that presidential candidate Gary Hart withdrew from the race due to his affair with Donna Somebody, and then recapped the aftermath of a Belgium ferry capsizing, killing 193 passengers and crew.

She shivered with the cold of the news as well as her room. The old window in the exterior wall allowed in the heat and the cold. But Harlow didn't care as long as she had a place to escape, a place to sleep, and let's be honest, a place to eat.

When she moved in six months ago—her last landlord, also a friend and fellow model, had kicked her out to move her boyfriend in—Harlow had asked Jinx for a space heater.

"No, you'll asphyxiate yourself or wake up in a fiery blaze." She'd bent down to pick up the Hayes Cookie wrapper on the floor. *"And burn us all down."*

Not true, but just in case, Harlow didn't press the issue. Burrowing under the blanket she'd purchased in Egypt two years ago, she considered how *that* Harlow Hayes knew who she was, where she was going, and what she wanted.

Two years ago, her life of photo shoots, haute couture fashion shows, and one small part in a romantic comedy made sense, because every road led to Xander Cole, the gorgeous Gilded Age heir, financier, and almost billionaire. She'd been named the Most Beautiful Woman in the World and one of the first models to earn the moniker "super."

Muffled voices seeped through the thin apartment wall.

Mom?

Harlow pressed her ear to the wall. A door clicked. Muted footsteps struck the hardwood, then landed on the carpet. Glasses clinked.

"Thank you . . . darn plane was late . . . rain . . . Atlanta . . . should've hired a car . . . cab driver . . ."

What was Mom doing here? Did Jinx call her? Well, no surprise there. Those two were tight. Jinx, a former model turned Icon Agency scout turned executive for CCW Cosmetics, founded by the illustrious Charlotte Coral Winthrop.

But Jinx had discovered Harlow twelve years ago when she was barely seventeen—much to Mom's delight. Then Icon took a slow approach to Harlow's career—much to Mom's consternation—until a photographer friend asked her to pose for a poster. Ka-boom!

"I think we do, Jinx. Get her going. Moving forward. Kick in . . . keister."

Mom. Such a southerner. No one said *keister* in Manhattan in 1987.

"I can prescribe something."

A third voice? Harlow slipped on her fuzzy slippers and, gathering the gaps in her too-tight pajama top, she schlepped from her dark hovel into the bright living room lights.

"Well, look who's up." Mom held Harlow by the shoulders and kissed her cheek. "Still wearing those same wool pajamas, I see." Her gaze swept Harlow up and down. "A bit tight but still rather darling."

"What are you doing here, Mom?" Harlow retrieved a glass and filled it with milk, which would be spectacular with a large squeeze of Hershey's chocolate syrup. But considering her current audience, she'd refrain. "You brought the shrink along?"

"We're here to help, Harlow." Dr. Tagg had a smooth and not quite but almost condescending tone.

"Help me do what?" Harlow worked her way through the crowd for the sofa. Jinx's apartment was a one bedroom, one bath, with a square living room and minuscule kitchen, along with Harlow's "closet." Two was a crowd. Four was a throng.

"Figure out your life, darling," Mom said.

"Well, if you don't mind . . ." Harlow sat on the sofa and reached for the VCR remote. "I fell asleep during *All My Children* today. Thank goodness I have it recorded. Angie and Jesse are in a real battle for their marriage."

"And you are in a battle for your life, Harlow Anne. We want to talk to you." If Mom added, "young lady," Harlow would be out. Literally. Through the door in her too-tight pajamas.

"Can't you berate me in the morning?" she said.

Mom grabbed the remote to shut off the TV, but a picture of Xander popped on the screen as Mary Hart opened *Entertainment Tonight*.

"We open with happy news. Xander Cole"—Harlow shrank back and cradled her milk—"and his ex-wife Davina will be tying the knot *again*, in style on the Coles' private Caribbean Island." A clip played of Xander and Davina standing on the sandy shore of the beach, their Frank Lloyd Wright–style home looming in the background.

"Did you know about this?" Harlow glanced at her guests as Mom shut off the TV. "Is that why you're here, Mom? Because they've announced their wedding?"

"Of course not. How would I have even known? If he called, I'd have given him a piece of my mind." Mom's disgusted tone was offset by her lilting southern charm.

"Oh please, you love him. If he came back to Harlow Hayes, you'd be buying bridal magazines."

"I beg your pardon. I would—"

"Anne, Harlow, let's talk about why we are all here." Jinx sat on Harlow's right, while Mom sat on her left. Dr. Tagg perched on the coffee table, clicking her pen in an annoying rhythm, prescription pad in hand.

"Are you committing me to a psych ward?" Harlow pointed to

the prescription pad. "Don't even think about it. You're all aware of the Studio 54 scene. Drugs kill. Listen to Nancy Reagan, if not me. 'Just Say No.'"

"This is different," Mom said. "This will help you get over this slump . . . this depression."

"Is that what you call a broken heart?" Harlow set her glass on the coffee table next to the good doctor and tried to squeeze out from between Mom and Jinx.

"Let's review the last two years," Jinx said, holding onto Harlow's arm.

"Must we?" She'd been trying to forget the past two years. But when a supermodel gains something like forty pounds—she'd not stepped on the scale in a year—she loses her career.

"I'd like to point out *two* key words." Mom's lilt came with a verbal highlighter. "*Two. Years*. Harlow, it's been *two years* since Xander went back to Davina. It's time to move forward. Write a new future. Xander is getting married, yet you sit here—"

"Wallowing?" Harlow freed herself from the sofa's confinement. "News flash, Mom, Jinx, Dr. Tagg. I've loved every minute of it." Not true, but she had to fight back somehow. "The End. Film at eleven." She leaned over Dr. Tagg. "Don't you have something for these two? Help *them* leave me alone?"

"I really think losing your money sent you over the edge." Mom frowned.

No, losing the love of her life sent her over the edge. Discovering her financial advisor—recommended by Xander, of all people—absconded with her small fortune was the cherry on top.

All she had left after being Felix Unger'ed from the penthouse she'd shared with her fiancé and future husband was the savings Dad insisted she set aside for a rainy day. Or, in her case, a deluge.

All of her hard work—the early days of go-sees, of running from one catalog shoot after another, of sleepless nights in Milan during fashion week, and years of being primped and plucked—vanished in an FBI white-collar crime raid.

She imposed on the generosity of friends, sleeping on their couches and in their guest rooms. When her fellow models were on location, she fed their cats in exchange for living quarters. Somewhere in the madness, food became her solace. Maybe it was her first bite of Lombardi's Pizza, or that thick burger with a side of fries. Or maybe her first bag of Hayes Cookies—which she spotted at a Broadway tienda—that she'd consumed with a chocolate shake from a mom-and-pop diner.

Snap. Years of disciplined eating ended. Junk food was marvelous. Comforting. And something that was all hers.

Around her, Jinx, Mom, and Dr. Tagg talked as if she wasn't there. Mom mentioned something about Harlow's famous poster, the one that launched her career.

"If you had royalties from that thing, you'd be in better shape." Mom had never forgiven Jinx for letting Harlow go to the shoot without a contract in play.

"He was a friend," Jinx said. "Asking a favor. How was I to know it'd become a worldwide phenom?"

"In my view," Dr. Tagg weighed in, clicking her pen, "you've given Xander too much authority. What right does he have to kill your spirit because he went back to his ex?"

"Exactly. Where's our girl who wowed everyone on the set of *Talk to Me Sweetly*?" Mom switched from fretter to cheerleader. "Everyone thought you were amazing, and it was your first movie."

"HH got the stuffing kicked out of her." Harlow took a big gulp of milk, then tugged on her pajama top where her middle pushed against the buttons.

She'd met Xander—he was one of the executive producers—on that movie set, where she'd also been given the nickname *HH* because she was so businesslike.

"I know, sweetie." When Jinx pulled Harlow down to the couch next to her, one of her pajama buttons popped off and landed on Dr. Tagg's prescription pad. Okay, that was embarrassing. "But it's time to get to work. Your mom is here because I have good news. Charlotte Winthrop wants you to be the new face of CCW Cosmetics."

Dr. Tagg discreetly set the button in the coffee table ashtray.

"Why me? Trace Sterling is their face."

"Her contract ends in August." Jinx's expression was bright, like a parent about to tell their kid he's getting a puppy or a pony. "And she asked me to get you." Ta-da. She spread her arms wide, smiling big. Expectant.

"Okay, but when? Not now." August was only five months away. She'd have to starve herself to get down to her modeling weight, and frankly, she didn't have the heart for it. Five-eleven, a hundred-and-thirty-two just didn't seem feasible for a grown woman.

"She wanted to meet right away, but I put her off until September. Charlotte likes to launch new faces over the holidays. So, do you think you could, well, pull yourself together by then?" Jinx squeezed her hand. "CCW is willing to shell out big bucks to get you, Harlow. Like *never*-before-seen money."

"Harlow, darling, isn't that marvelous?" Mom carried Harlow's glass of milk to the kitchen sink and dumped it out. "You've always wanted to work with CCW, and here they are coming for *you*."

"To be honest," Jinx said, "I think Charlotte hired me away from Icon for the express purpose of bringing you in one day."

"I don't know." Harlow gathered her pajama top, missing the popped button. "CCW *has* always been a goal. Harlow Hayes likes their brand, history, and products." She flipped to third person seamlessly. "Are you sure they don't want Kim Alexis or Christie Brinkley?"

"It's all you, sweetie. They believe your time away from the scene will make you all the more intriguing when they roll out their new campaign."

Hmmm, this put a wrinkle in her wallowing. If she couldn't have what she really wanted, had *always* wanted—a husband and kids with the house and sprawling yard, white fence, dogs and cats, a hamster on the wheel, and eventually the PTA and a mommy carpool—why not get back to work? Sign with CCW? She'd given her life to modeling. Trimmed the edges of her education, even friendships, to go along with Mom's grand scheme of creating *the* Harlow Hayes, *supermodel*.

In that moment, the clouds parted, and she realized if she let her hard work go to waste, continued to give Xander Cole power over her, she was denying her very being.

On the other hand, she'd become accustomed to sleeping in, eating whatever she wanted, whenever she wanted, and parking on the couch from one to four every afternoon for *All My Children*, *One Life to Live*, and *General Hospital*.

"I can prescribe diet pills." Dr. Tagg clicked her pen.

"No way, Dr. T." Harlow moved around the small space to think, to stretch.

"There's more," Mom said, nearly as expectant as Jinx had been. "Icon called and—"

"Icon fired me."

"They want you back. Designers are asking for you, missing your focus and work ethic."

"I'll go to Wilhelmina or Ford before Icon."

"I knew you still had some fight in you." A giddy Anne Hayes launched into full cheerleader mode. *S-u-c-c-e-s-s, that's the way we spell H-a-r-l-o-w.* "Darling, let all this with Xander go, and get back to work. You're Harlow Hayes, the Most Beautiful Woman in the World."

Yeah, about that . . . The title was almost four years old, and she'd been eclipsed by Jaclyn Smith, yet every time her name was mentioned, the moniker tagged along. And she was proud of it. She'd worked hard at her craft, and the world took notice.

"I don't know if I was ever the most beautiful, but I did work hard."

"Exactly," Jinx said. "So don't lose all your hard work over a *man*."

Dr. Tagg nodded as she doodled faces on her prescription pad.

She'd done that through most of Harlow's sessions last year. While she was grateful to talk to someone, Harlow never really gained any power over her troubles. The best part of each session was the subway ride afterward to Lombardi's for a slice or two. Food was more than her solace. It was her late-in-life rebellion.

"One last thing," Jinx said. "You can't keep living in my closet. I was fine when you landed here last fall, but that room is not safe for you physically or emotionally. Not to mention it's the only closet in the apartment."

Harlow sank down to the nearest chair. "I figured this day would come sooner or later."

"Darling, you're coming home with me," Mom said. "We can work on getting in shape together."

"I'm not going to Atlanta, Mom."

"Whyever not?"

"Because I'm not seventeen. I'm almost thirty. I'll find a place. A room to rent." It would deplete the last of her savings, but she was squandering her money anyway, one takeout at a time.

However, if she signed with CCW, she'd be in the black. "How big of a contract, Jinx?"

"Let's just say *I'll* be asking to room with *you* at your Park Avenue penthouse."

"That's it, you're coming home with me." Determination powered Mom's words. "We'll do this together, Harlow. It would make me *so happy* if you—"

"Anne, don't. Harlow is not responsible for your happiness." Dr. Tagg said what Harlow couldn't. What she wouldn't.

"I resent that, Dr. Tagg. I only have my daughter's best—"

"Harlow, you're right. You don't need a prescription." Dr. Tagg scooped up her Coco Chanel coat and matching bag. "You need to get off your duff, take control of your life, and stop letting someone else drag your heart around." She glared at Mom. "I'm sending you the bill for this one."

"Well, that was rude," Mom said when the door closed behind

the good doctor. "And what was that look she gave me on her way out?"

"What look?" Harlow said, feigning ignorance. She may have mentioned once or twice during her sessions with Dr. Tagg how she lived to make her mother happy.

Still, through all the pain and humiliation, she'd managed *not* to tuck her tail and run to Atlanta. She saw no reason to give in now. Yet how many options did a broke, overweight supermodel have?

A firm knock rattled the quiet room.

"Dr. Tagg must've forgotten something." Jinx opened the door to find a messenger standing on the other side.

"Delivery for Harlow Hayes."

The plain white envelope had no markings, only the letter inside along with a deed to a property in Florida. "It-it's from Xander."

"What does he want?" Jinx leaned to read over Harlow's shoulder.

"Did he finally apologize?" Mom squeezed in for a look.

"No, he's, um, he's giving me the cottage we bought and renovated in Sea Blue Beach, Florida." She'd secretly wanted the cottage when they separated but never had the chance to ask.

"Now?" Mom said. "Where's this been the last two years? Read his note, Harlow."

"Can you back up?" Harlow shrugged off Mom and Jinx. "Give me a minute."

Harlow, see enclosed. Sincerely, Elmar, Assistant to Xander Cole. A second note fell to her lap, with a key taped to the plain, thick stationery.

Enjoy the house, H. I mean it. Please.—X.

"Well?" Mom hovered five feet away with Jinx.

"He said to enjoy the cottage." She reread the deed with her name and buzzed with a bit of excitement.

"Why now?" Jinx said. "Can you accept it? What if there's some sort of lien attached, or the police just discovered a murdered body?"

"Murdered body? Geez, Jinx, your one episode on *Kojak* really messed with you." She'd played a murder victim during her modeling days. Slept with a night-light ever since.

Harlow reread Xander's brief note. This was classic Xander Cole. He was equal parts scumbag and good guy.

"Tell him no thanks and come on home," Mom said. "I think that's best and—"

"Harlow Hayes is going to Sea Blue Beach." She headed for her room. "It may be two years late, but this is his apology. And I accept. Jinx, I'll write a check for my half of the utilities. Mom, thanks for coming."

"You're leaving now?" Mom said. "It's almost eight o'clock."

"Perfect. Traffic will have died down. I can drive all night."

"Don't you want to sleep? To think about it?"

"I've been sleeping for two years, and for the past hour, you've been telling me to get myself together, so here I go. This is it. Harlow Hayes is heading down the main line. Off to Margaritaville. I am woman, hear me roar."

"Any more song lyrics in there?" Jinx said, laughing, approval in her voice.

"So you'd rather live in a house your ex-fiancé bought for you than come home with me?"

"I renovated that house, Mom. It's all me—well, almost, except the ghastly chandelier Xander insisted on—and frankly, he owes me. One for recommending that lousy financial advisor, and two for . . . for *everything* else."

"Go get 'em, girl. The beach will do you good," Jinx said. "Fresh air, sunshine, and sand. You'll be in shape for CCW in no time."

Maybe. Maybe not. But for now, Harlow Hayes was *doing* something with her life.

3

SEA BLUE BEACH

Welcome to Sea Blue Beach. Founded by Prince Rein Titus Alexander Blue in 1882.

He landed on our dark shores with the pieces of his wrecked yacht as a storm raged in the Gulf. Malachi Nickle, a young, freed slave, found him alone, half drowned, and gave him shelter. Together, they built Sea Blue Beach. The prince built the Starlight so Sea Blue Beach would never be dark or lonely again.

We've quite a history, you see. Besides a prince and freed slaves, we've hosted rumrunners and gangsters, hobos and drifters, families looking for a warm meal, families on holiday, and kids on spring break, all the while nesting our hometown folks in sunbaked cottages on sunbaked streets.

Look, there's Harlow Hayes. We'd have put up a sign for her, but we didn't know the supermodel was coming. It's been a while since she graced our shores. Three years, perhaps, since she sailed down with Xander Cole on his fancy yacht.

So we whisper to Dale Cranston, owner of the Midnight Theater, to show *Talk to Me Sweetly*, Harlow's movie with our very own hometown boy, Matt Knight. Yes, sir, an A-list actor grew up here.

After a run of horror flicks and B-cop movies, Dale needs to change the marquee anyway. Folks on a beach holiday want a comedy or love stories.

Harlow parks in front of 321 Sea Blue Way. We've kept our eye on that place for years. It's special. The first and only home of our prince. When he left for the Great War, he sold it to Malachi and his wife, Ida, for a song. They passed it down to their son, Morris, and his wife, Harriet.

When the Beauty and the Billionaire bought the place and sent in men with hammers and saws, we hoped they wouldn't turn all of our memories to sawdust.

While things are peaceful in town, something is afoot. A contingent of men in fancy suits are gathering at the town hall with the mayor.

In the last year, we've heard whispers. Change is coming. But know this, every little town has a secret. Sea Blue Beach is no different.

4

MATT

MARCH 1987
SANTA MONICA

Ugh. What time was it? By the angles of sun on the floor, it was midmorning. A hundred yards away, the ocean waves refreshed the southern California shore as seagulls circled, calling for breakfast.

Someone had opened the French doors out to his balcony, letting in the sounds of the street—a car door slamming shut, masculine voices tangling in tight conversation.

"Matt, bro, you got coffee?" A bare-chested man stood in the doorway, his jeans slung low, his hair standing on end.

"In the pantry. Coffee maker is on the counter." *And you are . . . ?*

Matt was no stranger to strangers in his place, but in the last year, his open-door policy had gotten wider and wider. What started as an intention to be gracious and helpful had turned into destruction. What started as trying to redeem himself by being a friend to many ended with strangers, looters, and squatters ruining his place. He'd replaced doors, windows, bathroom fixtures, carpet, tile, and at least four mirrors. He'd painted and repainted the bare walls and replaced the bare cupboards—bare because his housekeeper, Golda, hid all of his carefully curated art, fine china, flatware, and Egyptian cotton linens.

As Matt reached for his jeans, his brain sloshed against his skull in searing protest. Oh, man, what happened last night? He breathed through a wave of nausea and disgust, catching visions of a drag race.

What day was it? Sunday?

Last night, he'd dined at the Beverly Hills Hotel with the beautiful, sexy Cindy Canon. They'd been cast in a new romantic comedy *Date for My Daughter*, and through table reads and rehearsals, they'd discovered their sultry chemistry.

But that was on set as Mitchell and Clementine. So Matt invited her to dinner to test their *personal* chemistry. Why not? She was gorgeous, with expressive eyes and full pink lips. He was, well, *the* Matt Knight.

During the evening, they sipped wine and talked about how her career took off after her second film and how she was shedding her small-town Mississippi ways and the rules of her father's house and church.

"*Jesus, Jesus, Jesus,*" she said with a cute Elvis-like flip of her lip. "*Dad, there's a world out there to be lived, you know? To* explore. *Like, time to loosen the religious tie, old man.*"

She laughed a lot, which made Matt laugh, which he'd not done very much of in recent memory. Laughter inoculated him from the general sense of unease he always carried with him.

After filming a World War Two version of *Top Gun*, called *Flight Deck*, which had him in Europe and on rolling seas for five months, Matt came home exhausted and ready to par-tay.

He and his co-stars, Rob Stone and Steven Hilliard, had become superstars when the movie eclipsed last year's flyboy flick. Sorry, Tom Cruise.

So he was ready for a rom-com with someone fun, spunky, lively.

Cindy was great, but he knew they had no future. Once, just once, he'd fallen for a co-star, but she'd fallen for the billionaire producer.

Making his way to the en suite, he brushed away last night's death smell with Colgate, then studied the bruises around his knuckles. Matt didn't need the mirror to know he was an unshaven thirty-two-year-old man with bloodshot eyes, bed head, and a body in need of a shower.

Think, man, what happened? After dinner, Cindy clung to his arm—which he liked—as they left the hotel, discussing where to go next. They decided on Whisky a Go Go, where they ran into Steve and Rob, who were in a *Flight Deck* frame of mind.

After the first round of tequila shots, it was pedal to the metal and somewhere along the way, he lost Cindy, perhaps took a swing at someone and . . . the rest of the night was a blur.

Out of his room, he ran into another interloper, wrapped in a sheet. "I found this in the bathroom." She passed him a letter before disappearing in the last bedroom on the left. Man, he *really* had to get a hold of his life.

The envelope bore the familiar pinched handwriting of Booker Nickle, former best friend.

This was his third letter in three years, and the third one Matt tossed, unopened. He didn't know why Booker was writing, but he lacked the courage to find out. Their *final* words eight years ago lived in his soul.

Stuffing the letter in his hip pocket, Matt leaned over the second-floor balcony to assess the living room. It was littered with people, empty whiskey bottles and drug paraphernalia defacing the glass top of his custom coffee table. The sight was all too familiar.

When he spotted his Porsche keys on the carpet under an end table, he bound down the wide curved staircase and snatched them up with a vague memory of Steve dragging down Sunset Strip. If the cops didn't knock on his door to arrest him for reckless endangerment or for public intoxication, he'd repent of his ways—for real this time—and find a way to live right.

In Hollywood, Matt Knight was a giant. The lucky kid who came to play football at USC but ended up "in the pictures," as Granny would say. Everyone wanted to be him.

Yet in real life, he was nothing like the characters he portrayed on the silver screen—heroic, larger than life, defender of truth and justice—and, yeah, the contradiction ate at him.

Stepping over bodies and bottles, Matt grabbed the small gong purchased somewhere in Manhattan while promoting a rom-com he did a few years back with Hazel Rosen and supermodel Harlow Hayes.

"All right, let's go, let's go. Everyone up and out, out, out!" He hammered the gong and kicked at a guy under the coffee table.

In the kitchen, the bare-chested dude looked up from where he nuzzled the neck of a disheveled brunette. "What about that coffee, man?"

"There's a diner down the street. Let's go, let's go." Yelling made his head pound, but he wanted the evidence of last night—and of so many, many, *many* similar nights—out of sight. No less than twenty or thirty people filed out of his seven-bedroom, six-thousand-square-foot house on the Santa Monica coast. He recognized no one.

When he was alone, he locked the door and surveyed the damage. *Why, Matt? Why do you do it?* His beautiful place, the one he paid hundreds of thousands of dollars to decorate with one-of-a-kind pieces, was being destroyed. Last time Golda came to clean, she informed him she might not be able to scour away the perpetual reek of sweat, booze, and vomit. But she'd try.

He reached for the portable phone. "Golda, hey, it's me. Can you come clean the place? It's a mess. Call me." She'd charge him double for a Sunday, but he didn't care. He'd pay triple just to have last night Cloroxed away.

Shoving open the glass doors to the lanai, a salty bite of the Pacific breeze cleared his head a bit, and his stomach growled for breakfast. The aforementioned diner served a mean omelet and good coffee.

He showered and dressed in his last pair of clean jeans and pulled a T-shirt from a bureau drawer—one a stranger had clearly rifled through. The dirty jeans, he tossed in the laundry, and the letter? He hesitated. Why was Booker writing? To say once again, *"You ruined my life, man."* Was this a new tradition? An annual tribute to remind Matt of his failings? Maybe he should gather up some courage and read it. Yet another moment ticked by, and he dropped the envelope in the trash.

Next, he stripped every bed in the house and dumped the lot in the laundry room. Forget triple. He'd be paying Golda quadruple for this mess.

The front doorbell rang, and Matt dashed to answer. "Golda, darling—"

"It's Amelia, darling, and why are you still here?"

"I live here. What are *you* doing here on a Sunday morning?" He stepped aside to let her in.

"I knew it. You forgot." Amelia, his public relationship guru, had handled his press since he earned his SAG card. "You're supposed to be at a luncheon in Beverly Hills." She stood in the grand foyer, glaring at him with disdain. "You *promised* me you'd be there, and now I'll be covering your backside *once again* as well as mine. I know you pay me the going rate of a babysitter, but I'm not your *nanny*, I'm your publicist." She cut the air with a swipe of her hand. "No, I *was* your publicist. I quit, and oh my gosh, why does the house smell like a sewer?"

"Amelia, I'll go. Right now. I promise." He reached for his car keys. "Call them, say I had an emergency but I'm on my way. And you can't quit."

"Watch me. And put your keys down, it's too late. By the time you arrive, they'll be on the golf course. But that's the good news." She moved to the living room and looked around. "Where can I sit without contracting a disease?"

"You'd better stand until Golda comes. What do you mean that's the good news?"

"Last night is all over the papers and radio. Were you really dragging down Sunset Strip?"

"My car, yes. Steve was driving."

"And you got in a fight with a fan?"

Matt flexed his hand. "I don't know. Maybe."

"I can't stand it. You rich man-boys. Matt, you've got to grow up, honey." Barely in her mid-thirties herself, Amelia was "Mama" to all her clients. "It's biting you in the butt. The drag racing is one thing, the fighting another. But, darling, you left Cindy Canon behind. You abandoned her at some seedy bar. She was terrified."

"Abandoned? Come on, that's not . . . like me." It certainly *was* like him.

"She's furious. Her agent called me at three in the morning. Do you know how much I hate to be pulled out of a good dream to be yelled at? Do you know how often I have *good* dreams?" Amelia leaned to see something moving on the carpet, made a face, and jumped to the lanai doors. "Matt, you're one of my favorite clients, but, sweetheart, you've got to stop sabotaging yourself. You're taking me down with you."

"Amelia, I'm sorry. Truly. We were, shew, um, I remember there were tequila shots and—why did her agent call you and not Cosmo?" Cosmo Gilcrest, agent to the stars, all but discovered Matt twelve years ago.

"Oh, he called Cos too." Amelia inhaled a deep breath. "Matt, you're thirty-two years old. Stay out of the clubs. You're fine for months on end, even years, then bam! You blow all your goodwill in a weekend. You're not a drinker, Matt. Shoot, you're not really a partier. Stop this nonsense because it's not killing whatever's eating you."

"Nothing's eating me."

"How little we know ourselves." She smiled, patted him on the cheek, wished him luck in his future endeavors, and left. He stared after her, trying to find the words to explain how a single letter riled up so much inner strife.

Grabbing a trash bag and a pair of work gloves from his immaculate garage—he may have to live there while the house was fumigated—he gathered discarded clothing, bottles, and carryout bags stained with grease. He'd give Amelia a few days, then call her and repent. And he wasn't above begging.

He shoved a ratty T-shirt that had been thrown over his answering machine into the trash bag. It blinked up at him. He had a message?

Matt pressed play. The first voice was from Tom Cruise, back when *Flight Deck* surpassed *Top Gun*. Matt hit delete, unsure why he'd even saved Cruise's humble response to Matt's gloating and taunting.

Matt, be better.

Next was a message from Cosmo, but they'd talked since then, so . . . delete.

The next voice was so sweet, so familiar, so emotionally stirring. Granny. "Matty? Can you call me?"

The recording ended abruptly, with a time signature from twenty days ago. *Twenty days?* Then a second message played from ten days ago.

"Matty, I think the Starlight is in trouble. We need you."

What? How could the Starlight be in trouble? The old rink was the heart of his hometown.

Another beep, and Dad's voice played from the machine. "Matt, it's Saturday night so you're probably out but don't ignore your grandmother. Call her."

I will, I will. How did he miss her messages? He was about to dial Granny when Cosmo rang in.

"Hey, is this about last night?" Matt asked. No use beating around the bush.

"Are you sitting down?"

"That bad?"

"You're off the movie with Cindy. She didn't appreciate being left alone, and I quote, 'at a dark cave with werewolves and vampires.' She was scared, and in her mind, made to look a fool."

"Werewolves and vampires?"

"Her metaphor, Matt. But did you hear me? You're off the movie."

"Yeah, I heard you. Isn't that a bit drastic? Cindy and I are great together. She's just mad. I'll send her twelve dozen roses, apologize, and promise to never do it again."

"Amelia tells me you missed the Beverly Hills luncheon."

"I overslept."

"We worked hard to get you a spot at that luncheon. The producers of the new action film *Die Hard* were there. Which, by the way, John McTiernan, the director, just called. He's going with Bruce Willis."

"The guy from *Moonlighting*? He can't be serious."

"Matt, you work like a dog on set. No one can challenge you there, but every now and then your personal life turns into a freak show. I don't get it."

"Cosmo, you can't throw a rock in LA and not hit a freak show. And what's wrong with a guy blowing off steam?" He glanced around his trashed place. "Or helping out a few down-and-outers?"

"If you wanted to help those less fortunate, start with yourself. Look, Cindy doesn't want you in her movie. The screenplay was written for her. She's the star. She has the producer's ear and probably his heart. So she gets her way. Besides leaving her to fend for herself, you also told her she needed to work on her craft or you'd upstage her. You also insulted the director, saying he didn't know his head from—"

"I get it, Cos." When would he learn? Alcohol lured every thought from his head and through his lips. "I'll apologize." He'd gotten good at apologies. Except for the one that mattered most. "And for the record, Roger Woods is a brilliant director."

In twelve years, he'd done twenty films, half of them rom-coms, several with Roger, and they'd all been huge successes. Except for the one about the alien monsters, but it was early in his career, so Matt didn't count it.

"I'll pass that along. Just so you know, I'm on your side, Matt," Cosmo said. "But you have to figure out why you do this. Maybe filming and promoting *Flight Deck* took it out of you. Why don't you take some time off? Go to Club Med or Greece or Australia."

"I think the Starlight is in trouble."

"Actually, I'm going home. See what's happening in Sea Blue Beach."

"Excellent idea. You can disappear from the news for a while. Make people miss you."

"Thanks, Cosmo. I mean it. Sorry for all the trouble. If you need me, I'll be at my dad's."

Matt took ten minutes to pack and call Golda to tell her he was going out of town. "I'll leave you a check on the kitchen counter. Close the place up when you're done. I don't want anyone crashing here while I'm away."

Then he threw his bag in the Porsche and headed east through the evening shadows toward the Starlight.

5

TUESDAY

1987

The weight of carrying the Starlight was almost too much for her old shoulders. At eighty-seven, she needed to slow down a bit. Years of physical labor were taking a toll. She had help from Spike Chambers, who was on his third career after sacking groceries at Biggs, then joining the army. He took over the rink's concession services years ago. Called it Spike's Concession at the Starlight.

He didn't have to help with the rink, but she'd never known a soul more kind than Spike.

She had her youngest, Dupree, who wasn't so young anymore, who would help if she asked. But he owned a construction company, which kept him hopping. And to be honest, Dup's love for the Starlight was chilly at best. She suspected he secretly agreed with the town council's plan. She was too scared to ask.

But now that Matty was here, a bit of her burden lifted.

"Start from the beginning," he said, munching on the hot dog Spike handed him, along with a tall soda. He'd arrived at Dup's last night in his fancy car. After sleeping in, he came to the rink.

"Harry and the town council want to tear down the Starlight," Spike said. "Eminent domain, which I never heard of until the *Gazette* wrote up a big piece on it."

Just the idea of tearing down her precious Starlight gave Tuesday's old heart palpitations.

"What are they going to do with the land?" Matt said.

No sooner had he spoken than Mayor Harry Smith himself strolled in for his pre-lunch snack from Spike's Concession—popcorn and a Coke.

"Harry, just in time," Tuesday said. "My movie-star grandson has some questions."

"Matt, good to see you." Harry extended his hand.

Matt hesitated before he shook it. "What's this about the Starlight?"

Harry popped some fat kernels in his mouth. "Matt, we're near the end of the twentieth century, staring down the barrel of a brand-new millennium, and it's time to bring Sea Blue Beach into the modern era."

"Love it. What about all the land west of town?"

"We got plans for that too, but it begins right here. In the heart of things. How can we have a modern town with this monstrosity of a skating rink? Looks like a runaway circus tent." Harry slurped his Coke.

Tuesday made a face. Harry wasn't a bad man, generally speaking, and rather nice-looking, which helped him win elections. And she'd known him his whole life. But, at the moment, she'd label him a selfish prig. To think his daddy was Drunk Dirk, who got born again and became Dear Dirk because Tuesday let a traveling revival use the rink for a week. Dirk got drunk in the Spirit and everything changed.

Harry leaned back in his chair. "The Starlight is old, Matt. Built by a prince who died in the first war. The Royal Blue family probably don't even know it's here. If they did, they'd have made overtures. I doubt they want to bother with an old relic on American soil." He gave Tuesday a soft look. "You can't deny the popularity of skating has waned. We're a beach town, for crying out loud. No one wants to be inside roller skating on a day like today. In these modern times, folks are on the Beachwalk, Rollerblading or riding bikes. They grab a soda from the Soda Gal trailer or basket of fries from the Beach Eats truck. Janelle Samson just purchased a beignet business and will have a trailer up next month. The Blue Plate Diner is expanding into the old yarn shop and widening their outside deck. Mr. Chin's Chinese also wants to expand. The rink is just not who we are anymore."

"Yet you still come in every day for popcorn and Coke," Tuesday said. "What about the business Spike runs out of here?"

"I can get popcorn and a Coke from Biggs," Harry said. "Spike can open his own food truck. The sooner the better, I'd say. You know the town will compensate you, Spike."

From the office's front corner, Spike listened, arms crossed, expression pinched.

"Harry Smith, you're just saying things to sound official." All this talk riled Tuesday. "The Starlight is *exactly* who we are. It's the heartbeat of Sea Blue Beach. The first building. The first shelter from a storm. Where we've gathered for large parties and holiday fun since the nineteenth century, where every little kid has learned to roll before he could walk. You can't undo the Starlight's history with a stroke of a Bic pen. The Starlight has survived hurricanes and mobsters, harbored the downtrodden, fed the hungry." She shuffled the papers in front of her to keep from bursting into tears. "Granted, roller skating has changed, but the Starlight still stands. We're in the black." Barely, but Harry didn't need to know the details. "We're busy every weekend. Never mind we're doing a service to the United States Air Force. The boys from Eglin *love* to blow off steam wearing a pair of skates."

The eloquence of her speech did not quell her inner doubts. Just last week, as she was trying to fall asleep, the Starlight's neon sign buzzed and flickered, threatening to go out. Darned if it didn't feel like an omen.

Then with a loud ca-chunk, it burned bright, giving her profound relief. If the Starlight died in any way, shape, or form, she'd go right along with it. The rink was more than the town's heartbeat. It was *hers*.

"There's more to it, Tuesday." Harry gave Matt his attention. "The prince knew what he was doing when he built the Starlight. It sits on the highest point in town, smack on the main bedrock running through this stretch of Florida. The potential developer, the Murdock Corporation, owns some of the land west of here, and we own a bit. Even Dupree owns a long stretch of land. But it starts here, on the rock of the Starlight. Have you seen the plans, Matt? No? They're splendid. We'll make Niceville look like a cow pasture. We've a new road coming in as well as a park with a pavilion, and one of those newfangled splash pads for kids and pets to play in. An official auditorium for town events. We'll expand parking for the downtown as well as the new shops to the west. We've wanted to do this for decades, but no one had vision for it until I met the folks from Murdock. However, the Starlight is standing in the way." Harry's look of sympathy didn't sway Tuesday one bit. "I'm sorry, but the Starlight has to go."

Had he forgotten she'd taught him to skate after hours so he could impress his friends? Or how she coached him on the Starlight's championship race team of 1950? How she brought around food for him and his mama, sister, and brother when Drunk Dirk went on a bender? It was Harry's days at the Starlight that gave him confidence to go to college, start a business, run for mayor.

But the Starlight was so much more. *Roller Skating News* magazine had featured the rink a dozen times over the decades. The high-pitched roof was held up by octagon-shaped walls. The panels painted with skaters from the last century, smiling up at the image of a man the prince called Immanuel, were an artistic wonder. The prince spared no expense, bringing over an Italian master to bring his vision to life.

In the skating heyday of the '30s, Betty Lytle performed at the Starlight, along with Fred "Bright Star" Murree and Gloria Nord. During the war years, Tuesday entertained troops and introduced live bands to serenade the skaters. Post war into the '50s and '60s, the Starlight sponsored figure-skating competitions and racing teams.

Every kid in town had at least one birthday party at the Starlight. Some kids had a skating party every year. Tuesday organized anniversary celebrations, family reunions, and fundraisers. The Starlight's history was the town's history.

Harry had forgotten how she decorated for Valentine's Day, St. Paddy's, Fourth of July, Halloween, celebrating every holiday with something special—an All-Night Skate or Skating for Lovers. The rink was the town gathering for Thanksgiving and at Christmas, when Santa gave away gifts from baby Jesus. New Year's Eve? The Starlight hosted the biggest and brightest party on the North Florida coast.

Sea Blue Beach was the place to be *because* of the Starlight. Now Harry was declaring it an eyesore and in the way of progress.

"To be honest, Harry," Tuesday said, "the shortness of your memory is astounding."

"I'm not short of memories, Tuesday. I'm just not letting sentiment get in the way of what I was voted to do. The next generation needs jobs and opportunity more than they need roller skates."

Why not just spit in her eye, then?

"I'd like to see these plans, Harry," Matt said. "I bet you can do what you want without knocking down the Starlight. Seems kind of drastic to me."

"I see, did you play a civil engineer in a movie, Matt? Now you think you know more than we do?" Harry stood, adjusting his slacks and tie, smoothing back his hair. "We're discussing the plans tonight at the town council meeting. Seven o'clock." Harry tossed his popcorn container and soda cup in the garbage. "Come early. It'll be a packed house." At the door, he turned back to Tuesday, Matt, and Spike. "We'll purchase the Starlight and land at a fair price. You're eighty-seven, Tuesday. Time to retire, go visit Matt in Hollywood. Maybe you'll get a part in a movie."

"Not unless you can guarantee Cary Grant. Can you, Matt?"

"He died last year, Granny."

"There you have it, Harry."

"What about the Starlight's sign, Harry?" *Good one, Matty.* "The fishermen look for it on a dark night. The neon red, blue, and green is the town streetlamp from one end to the next, and way out into the Gulf. You can see it for miles."

"Murdock offered to put the sign on top of the first condominium they build." Harry tapped Matt on the shoulder. "Talk some sense into her, will you?"

"I'd rather talk some sense into you."

Matty is full of beans this morning!

"I need to go, but I'll see you at the meeting." Harry paused at the door. "One last thing before I forget. Do you have the deed to the rink, Tuesday? We were looking in the records and—"

"Of course I do. What are you implying, Harry?"

He shrugged. "I'm not implying anything, Tooz. We just need to verify you're the real and rightful owner. You know, red tape and all. If we're paying compensation, we want it to go to the right people."

Matt shot to his feet, knocking over his chair. "First you threaten to take the rink and now you imply Granny's not—"

"Simmer down, Matt." Harry grinned and patted him on the shoulder. "We've got the purchase price in the budget. All we're asking is for help dotting the i's and crossing the t's. It's in your best interest, Tuesday. See you at the meeting."

"Granny, where's the deed?" Matt said when Harry had gone and Spike went to receive a delivery at the back door. "Let's not give him any excuses to flat out steal the Starlight."

"He doesn't need the deed, not with this eminent domain. But if he tries to take the Starlight without compensation, he'll have a riot on his hands." Tuesday opened the cupboard and pulled out her old Richardsons. "I think I'll do a bit of skating before we open. Matt, put on some Glenn Miller, will you?"

6

TUESDAY

NOVEMBER 1934

On Tuesday nights, when everyone had gone, Tuesday Knight skated alone to music from a phonograph.

It was her special night with the Starlight—when she attempted a new figure-skating move or skated as fast as she could without fear of running over a little munchkin and getting ejected by the floor guard. Yes, they ejected her too if she broke the rules.

It was also when she communed with the soul of the rink—if she was allowed to believe such things—and regained any peace of mind robbed by day-to-day troubles.

She'd been a girl when the artist from Italy stood on scaffolding and painted children from every walk of life—all skating toward that pivotal image of a giant man wearing a hat and long duster, his golden brown hair curling into his collar. His eyes, such a vibrant color, seemed alive. She'd looked at him every day since she moved into the rink at fifteen, and without fail, something flipped inside her each time.

"Immanuel," the prince called him.

The panels were a novelty in 1887, able to roll up and allow the sea breeze to cool off warm skaters. The floor was made from the finest teak, the kind used to build Prince Blue's yacht. Some parts of the floor were from the shipwreck that brought the humble royal to the southern American state.

The Starlight had been his life's work. Then it became hers.

Tonight, like every Tuesday night, she'd sent LJ and Dupree home with strict instructions—wash up, brush their teeth, and go to bed.

Of course they goofed around, went home the long way, first walking down the beach, then cutting up through the seagrass to look for treasure. She knew from neighbors that they snuck between houses, tossing pebbles at the bedroom windows of friends

Then they would head over to the Nickles' place on 321 Sea Blue Way, being as their son Abel was LJ's best friend, creep into Harriet's kitchen—Morris never believed in locked doors—and snatch a handful of her molasses cookies.

Finally heading home, they'd peek through the dark windows of the closed shops until they arrived at the Knight house, end of the street and one block south. They'd raid the icebox and eat the last of the pie or cake from the Good Pickens Bakery. They'd wrestle on the floor while listening to the radio, then before the end of the program, Tuesday imagined LJ would say something like, *"Off to bed,"* to which Dupree would respond, *"You're not the boss of me."*

Eventually they'd push and shove up the stairs to see who washed first. They'd leave wet towels and water on the black-and-white linoleum for her to step in later.

You're missing it, Leroy. The best part of their lives.

On this particular night, she skated until her heart was full, then cleaned the skates' wooden wheels and stored them in the original box. She tidied the office, locked the money bag in the safe, and shut off the lights.

The back door rattled with a fervent knock.

"Hello, anyone there? Mrs. Knight?" A man's voice pressed through the side door.

"Yes? Who is it?" She settled her hand on the derringer tucked inside her pocketbook.

"Um, ma'am, we're weary travelers. Sorry to bother you so late, but we saw the lights. . . . Folks at the Blue Plate said you could help us."

Tuesday worked the lock and leaned out. In the glow of the Starlight's sign, a young family hovered in the chill—husband, wife, and three little ones.

"Please, come in." She reached for one of the large, battered suitcases and carried it with her across the rink floor and through the blue door under the organ loft. Down a short, narrow hall, she entered a rather large room with storage cabinets, a double bed, and a bath. It wasn't fancy, but it was enough. After all, this had been her home for four years until Leroy married her.

"Sorry for a bit of clutter." Tuesday set down the suitcase and moved aside a large box of concession supplies. One day, she planned to sell off the food portion of the business.

"It looks like a palace to me." The wife's eyes brimmed with tears.

"The bed is comfy," Tuesday said, retrieving extra blankets and pillows. "You can make pallets for the children. Fill the tub with hot water, I don't mind." She smiled at the little ones. "There are plenty of towels on the bathroom shelves."

Tears streamed down the woman's dirty cheeks. She looked to be no more than twenty-three or four. "What can I do to repay you?" She spoke so earnestly. "I do washing and ironing. Ain't a woman alive who wouldn't give over her ironing. Maybe some mending?"

"She's good with needle and thread." The husband was gangly, with long limbs and an awkward stance, but Tuesday reckoned she'd never seen such kind eyes. There was a sadness too. Folks probably took advantage of him. Eyes do reflect the soul. "I can do any sort of mechanical work. I noticed the worn floorboards as we passed your lobby. . . . Get me some lumber and I can have those fixed right up for you."

"He can, Mrs. Knight. He can fix just about anything."

"Please call me Tuesday."

"Tuesday?" The man sounded amused. "Y-your name is Tuesday Knight?"

"It's my married name, but I guess the good Lord thought I needed a sense of humor and a bit of humility." Tuesday pressed her hand on his arm. "How about a hot bowl of my famous bean soup, some bread and butter, and hot chocolate?"

The wife laughed. "Sounds like a feast for a king."

The husband cleared his throat. "Thank you, ma'am. Much obliged. We're Norvel and Elise Brandley. This here's our boy Mikey, our daughter Sissy, and baby Elias."

Outside the room, Tuesday fell against the wall and pressed her hand over her nose and mouth, muffling a soft sob. But for the grace of God—

"Tooz?" She glanced through her tears to see Leroy coming her way. "What's the matter?"

"Goodness, Leroy. You startled me." She wanted to run into his arms, but his long absence frosted her affection. "So you finally decided to stop in, say hello?" She avoided him as she started across the rink toward concession, to the small kitchen with a two-burner hot plate, refrigerator, and popcorn machine.

"Don't bust my chops, babe. I've been working."

"A phone call wouldn't go amiss, Lee." She'd installed a phone at the rink last year. "Or a letter. You do know how to write a letter, don't you?" She'd stopped counting the months since she'd heard from or seen him. Was it May or June? Every year, he wandered farther and farther away from home.

"You get my bank drafts, don't you?"

"Money. It's always about money with you."

"Excuse me, but I don't understand this complaint. I'm doing my job, supporting my family."

She swung around in the middle of the rink. "You're never home, Lee. That's my complaint. I'm raising our boys alone. They're fifteen and thirteen—the age they need their daddy to teach them to be men." She gestured to the Man's image looking down on them from the other side of the rink. "Though I thank Immanuel you're not around to teach them to be like you." She started toward the kitchen again but paused with another thought. "Is there someone else? Hmm? Tell me. Do you have a woman on the side? Maybe other children?"

"Ah, for pity's sake, Tooz, you think I'm crazy?" He reached for her hand, but she tucked it behind her back. "I value my life too much. I know you'd knock me into eternity if I ever stepped out on you."

"So you're not messing around? A young, virile man like you isn't finding *comfort* in some other woman's bed? Because you sure aren't finding it in mine."

"Your bed is the only bed I want to lie in, Tooz. But I'm here now and you're fighting me."

"I'm having my say. Besides, you're only here cause your hoodlums, your so-called 'boys,' need a meal and a bed, or some doctoring." She jammed her finger into his chest. "You can't just roll in and out of here whenever you want, Lee. We're not your puppets or pets, we're your family. I'm your wife. I have a say in how things go in this *relationship*."

"You don't think I know that, Tuesday? I'm scared of you half the time. My crew won't even come in here."

"Best thing you've ever said to me." She stormed toward the concession in the corner of the rink and plugged in the hot plate. While the soup heated up, she scooped butter from the tub into a small bowl for the corn bread.

"Fill that pot with milk, will you?" She pointed to the copper pan hanging from a hook under the cabinet. "For hot chocolate."

"Can you make some for the boys—er, fellas I got with me?"

"Fine, but they sleep outside. I don't want them bothering that sweet family."

"It's cold, Tooz. The wind off the water is bone chilling. How about they sleep in our barn?"

"There's no hay." It'd been two years since they kept cows for milk and meat. Without Leroy, the chores became too much for her and the boys.

"Can you spare a couple of blankets and pillows?"

"You're vexing me, Lee." Tuesday sighed as she stirred the soup. "I'll look when I get home."

She still knew very little of her husband's business. She'd suspected rum-running and bootlegging, but with the end of prohibition, she guessed he'd moved on to gambling and money laundering, maybe thugging for some mob boss. She peeked at his knuckles. They were scarred and bruised.

Leroy confessed nothing other than he "worked for a good firm" out of Memphis. But she read the papers, heard the rumors.

Leroy set the pot full of milk on the second burner. "Why were you crying back there?"

"Who said I was crying?" Tuesday reached for the Our Mother's Cocoa can and the sugar canister.

"You had your face buried in your hands." Leroy wrapped her in his arms and rested his chin on top of her head. "I heard you. Talk to me."

"Just some old memories coming up is all." She pulled away to retrieve paper cups from the upper cabinet. Fisherman Joe, who came in once a quarter and roller-skated until he had blisters on his feet, introduced her to this new invention—paper cups and plates—and she'd never looked back.

"From your mamaw?" Lee said. "What a wicked woman. Baby, those days are behind you. You're with Leroy Knight now. You own the Starlight." He tried to hold her again, but she busied herself with setting up the food tray. "You'll never be homeless again."

"I was only homeless for a week before the prince put me up." Though it felt like an eternity. "And the Starlight is good company. However—" She looked him in the eye. "I married you for better or worse, Lee, and I mean to keep my word, but it seems the better is long gone and the road ahead is nothing but worse."

Leroy sighed and whispered something about checking on the fellas. By the time he returned, Tuesday was ladling the bowls and cups with soup and steaming cocoa. From the cookie tin, she selected five of Harriet's best and added them to the tray. "Let me get this to my guests. You tend to your people."

"They're good men, Tuesday. Just trying to make it in these hard times."

She glanced back at him. "Might as well take them some cookies too."

She caved whenever he came around. She'd spend months brewing up a fight, but without fail, love eventually calmed her storm.

In the back room, the kids splashed in the tub. The wife had washed her face and the husband had shaved. He took the tray as Tuesday entered.

"We'll clean up, I promise," he said.

"I know you will. You can stay the week. That's all I allow. Tomorrow, I can arrange one long-distance call for you if that will help."

"That would be—" The couple exchanged a glance. Then Norvel said, "I'll find a way to repay you."

"When you're on your feet again, help someone who's like y'all are now. That's all I ask."

"Everyone was right, you know," the wife said. "When we came into town asking for work or any sort of help, everyone—down to the man or woman—said, 'Go see Tuesday at the Starlight.'" Her eyes glistened. "'She'll help you. She's the nicest woman around.'"

"I've been in your shoes. I know what it feels like to be desperate and have a kind soul offer more than you could imagine."

Lee was gone when she came out, so she unplugged the hot plate, tidied the concession, and locked up her office, then the rink.

In the cool night, she walked home, the neon light of the Starlight behind her. In the distance, a foghorn called to passing vessels. At the end of Sea Blue Way, she turned south on to Third Street, where a single light drifted from her barn, along with a low hum of male voices.

In the kitchen, Tuesday hung her sweater and pocketbook on her hook by the door. Up the stairs, she peeked into the bathroom. The floor was dry, the sink clean, and the towels neatly hung. She found Lee stretched out on their bed in his undershirt, reading the paper.

"You picked up the bathroom." She slipped from her low-heel oxfords and worked the buttons of her dress, noticing the thin material under the sleeves before hanging it in the closet.

Out of her slip and stockings, she tugged on a cotton nightgown that was once a brilliant blue, knowing Leroy only pretended to read the paper. He was watching her.

"What do you want, Leroy?"

"You." He patted the bed beside him.

"What am I to think? You return home only when you can't take it any longer? You think I don't have needs when you're away, Lee?" She grabbed the pouch storing her toothbrush and private toothpaste, a little pleasure she allowed for herself.

In the bathroom, she regarded her reflection. At thirty-four, she wasn't bad-looking, with a nice natural wave to her brunette hair. Her green eyes were nice—set too close for her taste—but the flecks of gold made her feel special. She was no great beauty like Greta Garbo or Claudette Colbert, but she'd earned a whistle or two in her time.

She liked being an ordinary girl. Felt it was enough to get her a loving husband and family. Which was all she'd ever wanted, and Lee had given it to her.

Oddly, he'd also taken it away.

By the time she returned to the bedroom, Lee had cut out his lamp and rolled over to face the wall. When Tuesday shut off her light and slipped under the covers, he didn't stir. The hush in the room, along with Lee's weight next to her, made her heart thump and her breath weak.

"I love you, Tooz." The bed bounced as he moved onto his back. "I'm sorry it has to be this way."

"Then we've nothing else to say." Yet the warmth of his skin stirred all her desires, and despite their differences, she wanted his love. "You leave me no choice."

A beat of silence ended when he asked, "Is the Starlight deed in the house?"

She sat up and clicked on her light. "You touch the Starlight and it's over, Lee. I mean it. All you've been saying about love and finding a way to better our lives will be for nothing."

"Simmer down, Tooz. It's not what you think."

"What do I think?"

"It's just Mr. Trudeau over at the bank asked if we'd filed the deed. He couldn't find it in the county records."

"When did you see Mr. Trudeau? Why was he looking? Why ask you instead of me?"

"Guess he saw me first." Lee grinned. "You look so pretty in the lamplight."

"I filed the deed, Lee. I pay my taxes." Her lie felt justified given his query. In her mind, the county had no business with her ownership of the Starlight. If she filed the deed, they might challenge her maiden name, or the prince's signature. Even the date. They might ask questions about Hoboth—who'd not been heard from in two years.

Would the county consider her deed a fraud? Did Hoboth have a different deed on record? Did he hand Leroy a forgery? Would he reappear one day, the wanderlust from his bones, and demand the return of the Starlight? These questions plagued her on the nights she couldn't sleep.

More than anything, if she filed with the county, Tuesday feared they'd raise her taxes and require Leroy's name on it too. Which would grant him access to the rink for collateral in his business shenanigans.

Well, not while she breathed the sea air. No, the Starlight deed stayed with her, in a box she'd hidden under a kitchen floorboard.

"Okay, don't get so riled. I was just asking. But, Tooz, you should put that fancy deed in the county records. It will protect you if anyone tries to come after it."

"Like who? You?" Tuesday shut off the lamp, and in the dark, she fluffed her pillow and straightened the covers, speaking to her husband without words, fighting the draw of his masculine presence.

"I won't touch the Starlight, Tooz."

"Thank you." She wiped a tear from the corner of her eye.

It felt so strange to lie beside him in bed, three inches and a world apart. "Can I kiss you good night?" he whispered.

"Yes, please, Lee, kiss me. Kiss me now."

7

MATT

"Can I stay here for a bit?" He sat on the back porch steps next to his father.

"Why ask? Your stuff is already in your room." Dad peeled off a slice of the orange in his hand and passed it to Matt. "And this is your place too, Hollywood."

Dad called him *Hollywood* before Tom Cruise and *Top Gun* had a naval aviator with that call sign. Matt could never quite discern Dad's tone when he used the word. Was he proud or just being sarcastic?

"How was work?" Matt popped the orange slice in his mouth and flicked a touch of juice to the ground.

"Busy." Still in his dusty jeans, plaid shirt, and worn leather work boots, Dad seemed more weary than the last time Matt was home. Which was . . . a year ago? Two years? Dad handed over the last two orange slices.

"You sound tired. Why don't you let your crew do more of the heavy lifting? You're sixty-six, Pop."

"Which means what? I'm old? No thanks. I lead by example." Leaving his work boots on the back porch, along with his hard hat, Dad picked up his metal lunch box with its large green thermos and headed inside. "I don't have anything for dinner. How long you in town this time?"

"I'll pick up a pizza from Tony's." Tony's made the best pizza—which was saying something, considering all the pizza Matt tasted around the world. "And, um, I think I'll stay for a while, if it's okay. Got a break in my schedule. What do you want? Pepperoni?"

"Sounds good."

"Got anything to drink?" Matt opened the fridge to find milk, iced tea, and beer. Good enough.

Dad washed up at the sink like he'd done Matt's whole life. Matt watched as he wiped down his lunch box, rinsed the coffee from his thermos, and knocked the crumbs from his sandwich container. He tossed a couple of baggies and a wadded napkin into the trash before storing the whole kit in the pantry—everything in the Knight house had a place.

Dad was still lean and muscled, with a thick head of silverish hair. Matt had inherited Dupree Knight's good looks and his mother Mimi's flair for the dramatic.

"The mayor came by the rink today." Matt shut the kitchen door against the heat. "Are you for this thing the town wants to do? Tear down the rink?"

"I'm not one way or the other," Dad said. "Granny's eighty-seven, Matt. I know she believes Jesus is going to meet her at the Starlight and skate with her on a rainbow through the pearly gates, but it's more likely she's going to fall and hurt herself. She still skates every Tuesday night after closing. If she fell, we'd never know it. I told her to call me when she gets home, but she never remembers."

"Telling her to slow down or retire isn't the same as smashing the Starlight with a wrecking ball, Dad."

"No, I reckon not." He leaned against the counter, towel still in his hands. "One of the fellas on the job today told me you cut up pretty good out in Hollywood. Said his wife read about you in some column. You were in a fight and dragging your Porsche down Sunset Strip?"

"I don't remember the fight, and Steve was behind the wheel of the Porsche."

"I'd think you'd had enough drag racing for one lifetime. You wrecked your Cuda—"

"Booker wrecked it."

"Can't imagine what you're like all spiced up. You had a few beers as a teen and told everyone—"

"Don't." Matt stood in the opening between the kitchen and dining room, facing the opposite window, flexing his bruised hand. "I know what happened. Never mind my agent and publicist, who quit by the way, already read me the riot act."

"Seems to me, Matt, you're still letting things eat at you." Dad draped the towel over the stove handle to dry. "Is it your mom?"

"You've been reading those pop psychology articles at the barber shop again."

"You know my pa wasn't around much when I was growing up. Then World War Two came. I know what it feels like to wonder if you're loved."

"Mom loved me. She just died before I really knew it. Besides, Granny loved both of us enough for three or four people."

Mimi Knight drowned in the Gulf when he was two. While he had no memories of her, sometimes a soft, feminine voice hummed through his dreams.

"You and Granny did a good job." Matt held his dad's gaze for a moment, but mushy stuff had never felt natural between them. The ticking of the grandfather clock ten feet away in the living room filled the silence. "It's not your fault I do dumb stuff now and then."

"That so?" Dad reached out, grabbed Matt in for a hug, and gently slapped the side of his head. "Then I expect you to come home more than every other year, Lieutenant Striker."

"Aha, you told me you hadn't seen the movie."

"Of course I have. The guys wouldn't let me live it down if I didn't go to opening night."

"Is that the only reason you saw it?"

Dad started down the hall. "I'm hitting the shower."

"Did you like it?" Matt called after him. "It was based on real events. Some of the men who survived that air battle were on set."

Dad paused. "Your Uncle LJ would've been proud."

"What about my dad?"

"He's proud too. He just doesn't want you to get a big head."

Matt laughed and reached for the phone, dialing the number that was burned into his memory for all eternity, and ordered two large pepperoni pizzas, plus a garden salad, which he called the guilt eliminator.

Leaning against the counter, he decided on pickup instead of delivery, wanting to take in the town, see what had changed. But more than not, he wanted to see what remained the same. Maybe he was getting older or maybe he was sick of his LA routine, but Sea Blue Beach was beginning to feel like home again.

When he hung up from Tony's, the phone rang. Cosmo.

"You're still fired from the movie," he said. "But never fear, I'm working some other angles."

"Are you? Really?" Hollywood was a fickle town. One day you're on top of the world, the next you're begging for money by your star on the Walk of Fame. Was Matt losing his touch? His charm?

"Well, I'm trying," Cosmo said. "Everyone thought you were doing the rom-com. Don't worry, though, this town has the attention span of a gnat. Relax, enjoy Sea Blue Beach. You've earned some time off. You certainly don't need money."

True. Matt had managed his earnings well. But according to his shrink—who he'd not seen in ages—he had a high need for acceptance, which meant he never stopped working.

As he hung up the phone, Dad returned to the kitchen in a clean white T-shirt and a pair of shorts, his wet hair smoothed back.

"Who was that?"

"Cosmo. I got fired from a rom-com, and an action flick I wanted went to Bruce Willis."

"Who?"

"Bruce Willis. The guy on *Moonlighting*."

"On what?"

"Dad, do you watch *any* television?"

"*The Rockford Files*."

James Garner as Jim Rockford was undeniably appealing. "If I ever play a suave PI like Rockford, you'd better watch." He glanced at the time. "I'm going for the pizza." He paused at the back door. "Dad, are you going to side with the town council tonight? Are you for tearing down the Starlight?"

"I don't feel the same about the Starlight as you and Ma." He grabbed a broom and swept away some imaginary dirt. "Growing up, I enjoyed the perks of being the son of the owner, I won't lie. But the Starlight and LJ were her favorites."

"Which she would deny."

"She relied on him to be the man when Pa wasn't around. I got in my mind the darn place was more curse than blessing." He returned the broom to the small utility closet. "It's sad, but if it has to go to make room for a better Sea Blue Beach, then we'll have to suck it up. Besides, what's she going to do with the rink when she dies? Take it with her? I don't want it. Do you?"

"Maybe."

"Come on, Matt." Dad gave him the all-seeing eye. "You have a career in Hollywood. Never mind you only come home once a year, if that. You can't manage the Starlight two thousand miles away."

"You make me sound shallow." Which was probably true. "I wanted out of Sea Blue Beach, but so did you."

Matt had heard Granny say it a hundred times. "*Your daddy wanted adventure, to see the world, but after the war . . .*"

"I had an all-expenses-paid tour of Europe, thanks to Hitler," Dad said. "Then the University of Florida."

Dad graduated, married his hometown sweetheart, and waited ten years to have a son. When she drowned. . . end of story. Dad never left Sea Blue Beach for greener pastures. Never fell in love again.

"You know, I *could* keep the Starlight." Matt pulled his car keys from his pocket. "Hire a good management team, oversee things from LA. Come back a few times a year."

Dad grabbed a beer from the fridge. "You'll come back for a skating rink but not your Pa and Granny?"

"Maybe I'm rethinking my values."

"Matt, even if it was an option for us to take over for Ma, the rink would still be up for demolition. This has nothing to do with Granny or this town's history. It's about the future. The Murdock offer is huge. Do you know what it takes to get development green-lighted? Between the architectural plans, environmental studies, state and county regulations, and surveys?"

"Dad, if they take the Starlight, you might as well dig Granny's grave."

"I thought I'd bring her out to LA when it all begins. I can take a few weeks off."

"And then what? Bring her back here to see a condo going up in its place? There's probably not a day in her life where she didn't look out her windows at the Starlight sign. It's her center, her purpose, her life."

"Harry's taking the town through the motions, but this is all but a done deal. I've looked at the plans, the approvals, talked to the city council. They're dead set on it. Eminent domain gives them complete autonomy." He lifted the lid from the cookie jar and took out a twenty-dollar bill. "Will this cover dinner?"

"Pizza's on me, Dad." Matt waved off the money with a renewed sense of purpose. "I'm going to fight the city council with Granny. Save the Starlight. It should be her own son fighting with her, but whatever."

"Watch yourself, Matt." Dad's face flashed with a bit of anger. "I've been on Granny's side my whole life. When there was no one else, I was here. So don't tell me you're the Lone Ranger propping her up. If she was smart, she'd take the money and run. Travel. Go to Lauchtenland and see where Prince Blue was born, tour Perrigwynn Palace. Murdock will give her a good deal on one of the condo units, which will be a heck of a lot nicer than the rattletrap she's been living in since the twenties."

"If she wants to go to Lauchtenland, I'll take her, and she can come to LA for as long as she wants. But she's not giving up that house and you know it. Especially if she loses the Starlight."

"I wish you'd seen her back in the day, Matt." Dad softened with a chuckle and looked out the kitchen window toward the rink. "She was a fighter. I gave her guff, but I respected the heck out of her. Shoot, the whole town is tied up with memories of Ma and the Starlight. Remember the first time I put skates on you?"

"I fell backward and cut my head open."

"But you still wanted to skate."

Matt laughed softly, then sobered. "She asked me to help her, Dad. I'm going to do what I can."

HARLOW

In the five days she'd been in Sea Blue Beach, Mom had called fifteen times.

"What's the plan?"

"How's it going?"

"I sent you a Richard Simmons workout video. I think you'll enjoy it."

"I found an aerobics studio in a town called Niceville. How far is that from you?"

Jinx called once. "*CCW still wants you, so . . .*"

Harlow Hayes felt the pressure. The resurrection of her career and the overthrowing of Xander's power depended on her returning to her former self. Was it even possible to be a hundred-and-thirty-two pounds again? Or even one-thirty-five? It was one thing to be the thin teenager maturing into womanhood. It was another to shove her womanly female self back into a teen body.

She'd been so in love with Xander, enjoying her life with him and planning the wedding, she'd gained seven pounds before the breakup. But now she wasn't in love, wasn't enjoying her life, and her habits were hurting her more than Xander.

That was the trouble with rebellion. The rebel suffered the most.

Last night, while trying to figure out the best window covering to keep the light from the big neon sign across the street—*Starlight*—out of her living room, Harlow assured her mother she was working a diet plan, even spouted off details of her daily routine. She simply left out the part about it being fiction. She intended to do everything she said. Didn't that count for something?

What caused her delay? For starters, the Blue Plate Diner. It would take Harlow Hayes a month to work through the breakfast options alone. Then there were seafood-and-steak platters and sides like fried green tomatoes and fried pickles. How could she resist? She wasn't sure she wanted to.

Growing up, she'd never been allowed the luxury to eat what she wanted.

Biggs Market, one of the oldest grocery stores on the coast, sold the thickest cut of steak she'd ever seen, perfectly marbled, and oh my word, send-you-to-heaven delicious.

And what about the ice cream shop, the Tasty Dip, and the half dozen food trucks along the Beachwalk? They all served items from French fries to hot dogs, beignets to sub sandwiches, and her favorite, the one-serving cinnamon rolls, which could be washed down with the creamiest chocolate shake.

Then there was the bakery, Sweet Conversations, which sold the best sourdough and Tuscan bread. Harlow already had more loaves than she could eat in a month. But she couldn't resist the aroma of freshly baked bread.

Yesterday, when she stopped by for an apple fritter, the girl behind the counter told a curious tourist that the shop was named in honor of the movie *Talk to Me Sweetly*. What a small world. She was tempted to step up and say, *I'm Harlow Hayes. I played the other woman*. But when she caught her reflection in the large paned glass, she left without a word. Or the apple fritter.

So far, no one around town had recognized her, for which she was grateful. Besides gaining weight, Harlow Hayes had let her famous golden hair fade to bronze, and without makeup, she looked nothing like the airbrushed girl on the cover of *Glamour* or *Allure*.

But of all the places she loved in Sea Blue Beach, Tony's Pizza had won her heart. Coming from New York City with the world-famous Lombardi's, she never expected to find the best pizza *ever* in this little town.

Pizza with a glass of wine and the TV tuned to Superstation WTBS had quickly become one of Harlow's favorite pastimes. The heady taste of dough, tomato sauce, and cheese along with the black-and-white reruns of *Leave It to Beaver* and *The Andy Griffith Show* restored her hope in mankind.

So, on this particular sunny afternoon, with the light cascading through the skylights, wearing the pink summer dress she'd ordered from Sears, Harlow Hayes finalized her grocery list before heading out.

In her BMW, she cruised through the pretty little town toward Biggs, barely shifting into third gear before turning into the parking lot. The late-March temperatures were leaving winter behind, and before she reached the sliding door, she was perspiring. She welcomed the freezing temps of the store as she grabbed a shopping cart and started toward the produce section.

Whispers buzzed around her.

". . . look . . . Harlow Hayes?"

"No, no, can't be. In Sea Blue Beach?"

". . . cover of *National Enquirer*, and she does *not* look good."

So, she'd been found out. Harlow snatched a beach hat off a rack as she passed, letting the price tag dangle Minnie Pearl–style. In Manhattan, she ordered groceries to be delivered. If she ventured out, she covered herself with long loose clothes. Winter wear made it easy to hide. But in Sea Blue Beach, winter wear made her stand out.

You're here to get in shape for work, Harlow Hayes. True, true. *Thank you, inner voice, for reminding me.*

Grapes, bananas (though she recently read somewhere they caused cancer), apples and oranges, eggs, broccoli, carrots, celery, lettuce, tomatoes, light salad dressing, three cases of Diet Coke, chicken breasts (she passed on the steak, though it almost killed her to do so), cream cheese, cottage cheese, skim milk, a case of SlimFast . . .

At the checkout line, she kept her chin low, only glancing at the cashier when she said, "Fifty-two eighty-nine, please."

"Did you get the hat?"

"I got the hat."

She paid and as she headed to her car, a group of teenage girls approached. "Hey, lady, wait up. Are you—" The blonde asking the question peeked at her friends. "*Her?* Harlow Hayes?"

"Me?" Harlow Hayes feigned a laugh. "As if. . . . Sorry to disappoint." She smiled, then remembered it was one of her main identifiers and toned it down. "I get that a lot, though."

"See, I told you."

"Wait until I see Susie. She swore it was her."

From now on, she'd have to pay attention. She wasn't so incognito in a small town.

At home, Harlow had every intention of grilling a nice piece of chicken for dinner and tossing a garden salad. She'd dine on the back porch with the wind in her face and a good book in her hand.

Yet instead of prepping the chicken, she flashed on an image of the girls wondering if she was Harlow Hayes. Why had she lied to them? They might have been excited if she'd said, *Yes, I am*. Instead, she'd denied herself, afraid they'd laugh at her. How ironic that one of her first commercials was for a body spray with the tagline *Because it's wonderful to just be you*.

That's it. Prada handbag slung over her shoulder, the Biggs' hat still low on her head, price tag swinging, she headed to Tony's. Pizza for one, please.

You be you, girl.

She ordered and paid under the name Glenda, then stepped aside.

Fifteen minutes later, she was back in her Beemer, blasting the air. She was about to shift into reverse when the aroma of pizza coming from the passenger seat made her whole body tingle.

Have a slice! It was intoxicating to eat whatever she wanted when she wanted. She'd never, ever had such freedom, even for a day, until she was twenty-seven years old.

Harlow grabbed a napkin from the Tony's bag, added some parmesan cheese to her selected slice, and bit into the hot, tangy, savory cheese and pepperoni.

Know what? *This* could be her true self. Why not? She'd never intended to be a model her whole life anyway, let alone a supermodel or the Most Beautiful Woman in the World. Titles come and go. Beauty fades. But pizza . . .

Eyes closed, she rested her head against the seat and savored the crispy dough, the garlic and oregano, the creamy mozzarella.

She was about to take another bite when one high-pitched scream, followed by another, caused the slice to slip from her hand and plop against her dress. Well, shoot. As she reached for more napkins, she glanced out the window. Was everything okay? She didn't see anything except the girls from Biggs clustered around a tall, broad-shouldered man with a shock of black hair over a smooth, chiseled face.

Harlow squinted through the windshield. He looked a lot like —oh my word—Matt Knight.

Suddenly, he snapped around, glancing her way, as if he heard her thoughts or sensed her presence. Harlow's hat tumbled off as she shot down in the seat, shoving her legs beneath the steering wheel. Did he see her? *Please, please, please. . .*

Her head rested against the seat back and angled her chin toward her chest. A hot drip of sauce splashed against her skin, above the scoop neckline. She wiped it away with her finger, and waited, listening.

The girls' voices mingled with Matt's. He had such a great timbre. It had wooed her on the set of *Talk to Me Sweetly* . . . until Xander. Handsome, charming, and fifteen years her senior, he had practically won her with a glance.

Not knowing how long Matt would chat with his adoring fans, she remained put, despite the growing crick in her neck. Might as well fold her pizza slice in half and finish it off. What was Matt Knight doing in small, tiny Sea Blue Beach? Wasn't he filming a rom-com with Cindy Canon?

Harlow had just finished the last bit of crust when a shadow fell over her and *the* Matt Knight stared down at her through the windshield.

"Harlow?"

"H-h-hey, *yooouuu* . . ." She sat up, working her legs out from under the steering wheel, noticing her stained and soiled dress was hiked up to her underwear.

"Girl, what are you doing?" He moved from the windshield to her door. "You need help?"

Matt . . . No, no, no . . . Do not open . . . the . . .

Door. He opened the door.

"Look. At. You," she said with a squirm and a he-he, ha-ha, tugging her dress over her knees, hoping Matt had not seen her rubbed-red thighs. "Opening my door like, like a . . . gentleman." She should've locked it.

"What are you doing in Sea Blue Beach?" He knelt down to see her face, his blue eyes sparkling with that famous twinkle.

"Well, um, I—" Forcing herself to act natural, like talking to Matt Knight from her previous awkward position while wearing a tomato-stained dress was exactly what she intended. "Enough about me. W-what are *you* doing in Sea Blue Beach?" Was that a plop of sauce on the steering wheel?

"I grew up here. Came to see Dad and Granny. Here, let me—" Matt grabbed the napkin crumpled in her hand and wiped the marinara from the wheel. "Seriously, HH, what are you doing here?"

Could Harlow Hayes just drive into the Gulf right now and live with the fish? Who would miss her, really?

"I-I live here. Sort of."

"In Sea Blue Beach? Since when?" Now he leaned against the side of the car, one arm propped on the door handle, his gaze melting her more than the Florida heat ever could.

"Since last Monday, I guess." She'd missed *All My Children* on move-in day, and thus a pivotal point in Jesse and Angie's relationship. She'd been out of sorts ever since.

"How long are you staying?" The clean notes of Matt's cologne and soap mingled with the fragrance of pizza. "And where?"

"Through the summer, I think. And I own 321 Sea Blue Way."

"The old Prince Blue and Nickle place? Really? How did I not know? I grew up running in and out of that house."

"So this is Matt Knight's hometown."

"Born and raised. Wow, what a small world." Too small at the moment. "What made you come down, H?"

Matt had been the first person to call her by her initials. The cast and crew picked it up during filming, and by the time they went on a press junket, everyone called her by her initials. Even her dad called her H or HH now and then.

"Well, since Xander and I . . ." Tears often chose the most inopportune time.

"Right, right. Say no more."

"He recently gave the house to me. Guilt offering, I suppose."

"Xander's a dip wad, HH. He'll be sorry he let you go."

"Let's not do the cheerleader routine, Matt. He's back with Davina." Even with a pizza stain on her dress, talking to Matt Knight was easy. "So, you came home to see family?" Harlow gestured to the spot where he'd been surrounded by the girls. "Meet your fans?"

"Yes, all six of them." She'd always loved his laugh. "I came to help my grandmother with something, and it seemed like a good time to get out of LA."

"Aren't you filming a rom-com with Cindy Canon?"

"I was, yes."

"Past tense. What happened? Wait, you don't have to tell me."

"It's not a secret, H. But I'm touched that you don't know. Just more bad-boy antics. Not on purpose. Just being stupid. I don't do well when I'm not working. Anyway, then my granny called, and I came running. She owns the Starlight skating rink, and we need to save it."

"The big hexagon-shaped place is a skating rink? It's breathtaking. I can see the light from the sign shining in my bedroom window."

"That's the Starlight. It was built by a prince a hundred years ago. The same prince who built your house, by the way. A Prince Rein something, something Blue. Around here he's just Prince Blue. He co-founded this town with freed slaves. Legend has it he landed on the beach after his yacht broke apart in a storm. The night was pitch black except for a single star cutting through the darkness." Matt had a sincere way of telling a story. "He thought he was going to die, until this mysterious man walked out of that starlight and changed his life. Then Malachi Nickle, a freed slave, came along." He laughed softly. "That was more than you wanted to know."

"Actually, I love it." She resisted the urge to touch his arm.

"Sounds like the town has a special history. Who was the mystery man?"

"A man called Immanuel. I think it's Lauchtenland folklore, but Granny seems to think it's real—that he's real. You should come to the Starlight. There's a beautiful painting of him on the wall."

"I will. But why do you have to save the Starlight? Sounds like a Matt Knight, Lieutenant Striker, heroic move."

"The town wants to knock it down. Eminent domain. Dad says it's futile, but you never know until you try." His gaze lingered on her for a moment. "I'm really glad to see you, H." His genuine tone nearly undid her. "What's your plan while you're here?"

"Same as you." She looked over at the pizza box. "Attempt to do something futile."

8

SEA BLUE BEACH

City hall is packed. Standing room only. A man in a white shirt, pleated slacks, and power tie enters with a large black portfolio under his arm. Everyone whispers that Luke Murdock will bring Sea Blue Beach into the modern era. A long line of folks study his drawings and nod their approval.

We like the look of him. Handsome in a stuffy sort of way, but will he have the town's best interest at heart? Or merely his own?

Some folks whisper the Midnight Theater should be torn down and a new one built, but Dale Cranston sits on the town council, so his theater remains safe. And truth be told, the movie house doesn't sit on the bedrock.

Tuesday Knight just left the rink for the town hall. We consider her one of our greatest citizens. A few of us watched her grow up from a sweet babe to an abandoned teen—oh, her mamaw, Irene Morrow, was an ugly soul—to a beautiful wife and mother, a fighter if ever there was one.

She watched the rest of us grow up. Taught us to skate. Everyone loves her. And the Starlight. Harry Smith does too, if he allows himself to think about it, but he has dollar signs for pupils.

From the sound of things, the meeting is starting. . . .

TUESDAY

She was nervous as she sat between son and grandson, with Spike on the other side of Dupree, in an overflowing town hall. By the time Harry banged his gavel and spoke into the microphone, she felt a bit faint. Was this it? The end of it all?

"It's good to see so many in support of Sea Blue Beach's future." Harry introduced the council members, to which Tom Caster called out, "We know who you are, we voted for you. Move along, Harry."

So the mayor turned everything over to Luke Murdock, the man of the hour, vice president of Murdock Development. He was young, handsome, and modern. Tuesday felt old, wrinkled, and from an age gone by.

Mr. Murdock gave a rousing speech about how proud they were to partner with Sea Blue Beach, the gem of the North Florida coast, with the white-sand beaches, blue-green waters, and inlets for fishing, kayaking, boating, and swimming.

He showcased the drawings of their future—condos and hotels, shops and restaurants—declaring that families, vacationers, honeymooners, and tourists from all over the world would be clamoring to visit Sea Blue Beach. The local business owners would see tremendous growth. Why, they'd all be millionaires by the year 2000. Lah-de-dah.

Okay, so he didn't say that, but he sure implied it. Tuesday would be a hundred years old in 2000. What did she need with millions? She just needed her Starlight.

"If you want to be a leader in the new century," Murdock concluded, "you must prepare now."

The gallery burst into applause. Oh, this guy was good.

Tuesday glanced at Dup, who listened intently, then at Matt. She was losing them both, she could feel it. Spike, on the other hand, sat with his thick arms folded over his chest, frowning. He sniffed malarkey when it was being shoveled.

"So you bring in more tourists. How does this impact us?" Audra still wore her Blue Plate Diner apron and chef's beanie. "Sea Blue Beach is run by mom-and-pops. We don't even have a McDonald's. Will the Sea Blue Beach of the future be littered with chain restaurants and businesses? That will kill us locals."

"Great questions . . ." Luke glanced at Harry, who whispered Audra's name. "Audra. As of now, Murdock has no plans to bring in competing businesses. As far as we're concerned, the shops and restaurants of Sea Blue Beach will service all its visitors."

"That remains to be seen," Hank said. He was the general manager at Biggs and a regular at the Starlight with his kids. "It will be harder for us to maintain a larger demand. Next thing we know, you're bringing in chain stores who will undercut our costs, and we'll be closing our doors."

"Hank, Hank, why so doom and gloom?" Now Harry was the snake-oil salesman. "*Eventually*, of course, we'll want new business. But there will be plenty to go around."

Luke tugged on his tie as he pointed to the new downtown. "The park with the splash pad and the additional downtown parking will go here." He circled a pretty-looking park adjacent to an enormous condominium that would replace the Starlight and cast a shadow over the whole downtown.

"Can I bring my Bessy to the splash pad?" Fred Martin always had the oddball question. "She loves water."

"Bessy?" Luke said. "Certainly. Children as well as adults will be welcomed."

"Bessy is his cow, Luke." Harry hammered the gavel. "Fred, you cannot bring your cow to the town square. Folks, let's take this seriously, all right?"

"Let me get this straight, Murdock." Matt stood. "You're destroying the beautiful Starlight, the most unique and historic roller-skating rink in the country, for a run-of-the-mill condo, a parking lot, and a splash pad?"

"And a *park.*" Luke slapped his hand against the rendering. "Don't forget the park."

"Well, of course not the *park*. The one right next to a gorgeous white-sand beach that already has pavilions for picnics and family gatherings."

"Wait a minute, you look familiar," Luke said. "Are you—"

"He is," Harry said with a sigh. "Matt Knight. Don't let his star power distract you."

"Not at all, Harry. Matt Knight, everyone, the great Lieutenant Striker from *Flight Deck.*" Luke started a round of rousing applause. "Harry, you never said you had a celebrity in your midst. This will maximize Sea Blue Beach's success." He pulled a small white card from his shirt pocket and stretched over the front row, handing it to Matt. "Let's talk. Do you have a restaurant or any business here? We've got retail spaces available."

Murdock was schmoozing her grandson. Right in front of her. *Back off, Murdock. He's here for me.*

Matt took the card out of sheer courtesy, naturally, but Tuesday snatched it from him and crumpled it against her palm. She was eighty-seven. She could do what she wanted.

"I appreciate your *kind* words, Murdock." Matt knew a thing about schmoozing too. "Except I'm here to defend the Starlight. Though you *are* amusing." He turned to the room. "He's a better actor than I am."

Tuesday patted his back. Bravo. Then Dup leaned around and said in a hushed tone, "Sit down, Matt. Hear him out."

She knew it. Her youngest son was for this new Sea Blue Beach and against the Starlight.

"Here's our proposal for the town square." Luke switched to a different drawing. "We expand Sea Blue Way to manage increased traffic."

"You're taking out all those old fishing shacks?" The question came from the left side of the room.

"The seller was more than happy to let them," Harry said.

"About time. Those were an embarrassment."

Consensus was starting to build. People liked the idea of progress, of updating the older, less appealing part of town.

Luke bragged how the Blue Plate Diner and other businesses along Sea Blue Way would be able to expand, since the new parking lot required reengineering that section of the beach. The Starlight's parking lot would be torn up for the road improvements and public parking. The sewer system would be upgraded as well—a benefit to all. Even the quaint old Sands Motor Motel could get rid of the broken cistern and hook up to city water. And of course new residents and vacationers will fill their "big, beautiful high-rise."

When Luke finished, folks were smiling. Whispering and nodding.

". . . good for Sea Blue Beach."

". . . been wanting to expand my shop for years."

". . . tax dollars finally put to good use. More revenue for us all in the long run."

". . . high school needs a new gym."

". . . the condo blocks all the light. I don't like it."

Tuesday had heard enough. "I'd like a word." She planted her hand on Dup's shoulder and pushed to her feet. "Seems to me the only business that gets destroyed is mine."

"The Starlight stands on the bedrock that holds this town together," Harry said. "We need that land going forward for the expansion."

"Which says to me that *the Starlight* holds us all together. It's a picture of our history." She turned to face her peers. "Remember when we all said, 'Meet me at the Starlight,' and we'd skate until midnight?" Back to Harry. "Why can't you just use the bedrock the Starlight isn't sitting on?"

"We plan on it, but the Starlight is the bottleneck. It will take some engineering to do all we want, so in order to get things going, Murdock wants to build the first condominium." The room began to rumble. "The money from one building alone could increase our revenues by thirty percent. Murdock predicts each new hotel, condo, and business will do the same—if not more."

"Thirty percent? I smell skullduggery." Tuesday gave Murdock a sharp glance. "What we'll get is a bunch of high-rises blocking the sun, new business that steal from the old, and a splash pad full of sand, 'cause that's where folks will rinse off after a day at the beach."

"And no Starlight," someone shouted from the back of the room.

A chorus of "Hear, hear" followed.

"Tuesday, we all love the Starlight, but we can't stop progress." Another voice declared from the back with the corresponding "Hear, hear."

"Is skating even all that popular anymore?" Dale Cranston spoke up. "We have the Beachwalk. Folks can Rollerblade outside."

"Then we don't need a movie theater, Dale." Tuesday scooted past Dupree into the aisle. "The Starlight was the port in the storm for so many while Prince Blue and Malachi Nickle built this town. Some of us in this room hunkered down at the Starlight during the Great Hurricane of 1935. During the Depression and beyond, anyone who needed a place to lay their head was welcomed. It didn't matter from where they hailed. The Starlight was the first church, the town hall, even the jail for a short while—and always a place for families to have fun together. A place to sing and laugh with other folks. Why, the first moving picture was shown at the Starlight." She made the claim without looking at Dale.

"The prince loved this town. He loved roller skating, said it brought folks together. 'Best way to cast off your cares is put on a pair of wheels and go round and round under Immanuel's eyes,' he'd say. He put his own wealth, sweat, blood, and tears into this town and that rink. Same as Malachi. They were men of honor and integrity. Why, Harry, Malachi taught you to fish when your daddy was known as Drunk Dirk, and if memory serves, you kissed your first girl in the Starlight's concession."

The room hooted with laughter.

"Cecilia," Tuesday went on, "Spike gave you your first job, and Paul, you're a banker now, but who showed you how to count cash and make change?"

Harry banged his gavel. "Tuesday, this is all well and good, but it's the past. It's my opinion, and the town council's, that the prince and Malachi would want Sea Blue Beach prepared for the future. They were visionaries, and we"—he motioned to the council—"carry their heart."

"Harry, why can't we put this to a town vote?" Dion Jackson, who ran Jackson Landscaping, presented a fair question. "You can still be a visionary without throwing out the traditions and history that unite us."

"A vote? That's not how it works, Dion. You voted for us to make these decisions on behalf of the citizens. Now we—"

"We can start a petition," someone said.

"The town charter allows us a special referendum." Millicent Bakewell taught history at the high school. "If five percent of the population signs a petition, we'd have a referendum for a vote. That's about three hundred folks. We got half that in here right now."

"No, no, no." *Please, someone take that gavel from Harry.* "The town council decides."

"I think we're onto something," Dion said. "Who can work on a petition?"

Mary, who owned the Tasty Dip, raised her hand. Tyler Neal from the Copycat Print Shop joined in, said he'd work with Mary.

"Count me in," Matt said. "I'll throw my *celebrity* into the ring just like Luke here suggested."

Well, it got a bit wild after that, with folks talking at once, yelling and pointing at one another. Tuesday sank down to her seat.

"Look what you started," Dupree whispered.

"I've protected the Starlight for over fifty years. I'm not about to give up now."

Up front, Luke argued with Harry, saying something to the effect of, "If you're going to back out over a stupid skating rink, we'll go on down the road."

The cry for the vote swelled. "Vote, vote, vote, vote."

"Quiet!" Harry jumped onto the table like a madman, shouting, "I'm the mayor of this town, and I will make the decisions, along with my town council. Now—"

"We want a special referendum, Harry. We want a vote on this here progress." Dion's voice echoed in the hall.

Paul Minor was new to the town council and the first to cave. "It's in our charter, Harry. You have to let them try. And as I told you, I'm not convinced about this expansion, especially if it means swinging a wrecking ball through the Starlight."

"I don't mind putting it to the town either," Cecilia said. "It's a big decision."

Tuesday squeezed Matt's hand. They were going to win. While the council deliberated on the timing of the petition and subsequent vote, Tuesday asked Matt to help her stand on her chair.

She whistled with her fingers like old Burt from her younger Starlight days taught her. "Everyone interested in helping with the petition and referendum, meet me at the Starlight tomorrow morning at nine."

9

MATT

A grand total of five people gathered in Spike's Concessions on Wednesday morning. Granny, Matt, Spike, Mary from Tasty Dip, and Tyler from Copycat. Dion said he'd try to make it, but he had a lot of work on his schedule. *"But count me in,"* he'd promised.

Matt doctored the cup of coffee Spike handed him, and when he looked to the huddled group, all eyes were on him.

"What's our marching orders, Captain?" Granny said. "We have six weeks to get three hundred and fifty signatures."

The town council gave them until Thursday, April 30, to collect signatures, which initially seemed like ample time, but this was Sea Blue Beach. The referendum of 1964 took six months to get half as many. And Matt felt sure Harry, infuriated how he'd been outmaneuvered, would start a campaign of his own.

"I'm not sure we need a captain, but"—Matt surveyed the crew and sipped his coffee—"where do we start?"

Spike retrieved a thick folder. "I went by town hall this morning and asked Leslie for copies of our original charter and constitution." He handed the folder to Matt. "We can put forth the petition and call for a vote but—"

"Federal and state law gives Harry and his council the right to invoke eminent domain for the good of the town." Matt flipped through the documents. "We need to start a campaign, get as many signatures as we can—more than we think we need. You know Harry and his crew will find a way to remove a few during the verification process."

"Can we really stop them from tearing down the Starlight?" Mary said.

"We can try. If enough people vote to keep it, then maybe the town council will capitulate," Spike said. "Petitions can only be posted at the courthouse and post office." He pointed out that detail on the papers Matt held. "We can't go door to door, but we can pass out flyers and such."

"Harry will be a stickler for this to be done by the book." Matt passed the folder back to Spike. "I'll see about getting a story in the *Gazette*. And some ads. Tyler, can you design a flyer?"

"Already got something in mind," he said.

"Great," Matt said. "Also, Rollo on the Radio always wants me on, so I'll reach out."

"Why isn't the rink a historical landmark?" Mary said. "Or some sort of House of Blue or Lauchtenland artifact? It was built by one of their princes."

"I can answer that," Granny said. "In the state's mind, the Starlight has done nothing significant for history and does not qualify to be a historical landmark. As for the royal family, I've no clue."

"Should we reach out to them?" Mary certainly had lofty ideas. "You're a celebrity, Matt. Don't you know people?"

"Not from the House of Blue. Lauchtenland's royal family is very private. We've not heard a word about them since Princess Catherine's twenty-first birthday. They don't go for celebrity attention." Matt eyed his small posse. "Let's just focus on what we, the people of Sea Blue Beach, can do."

"What about Malachi Nickle, a freed slave?" Spike said. "He helped build this place. Doesn't that qualify the Starlight as an historical landmark?"

"He helped build the town," Granny said. "The prince built the skating rink, while Malachi built the sawmill, which does qualify as a historic landmark. It was used heavily during both world wars."

"Matt, talk to your dad," Tyler said. "Is there any other part of town for Murdock's development?"

"Good point. I'll ask."

Mary was a member of a half dozen clubs and committees, and experienced with the red tape of town hall, so she volunteered to file the proper papers. She'd also present the Starlight's case to those who liked fighting for causes.

Another meeting was scheduled in three days to kick off their campaign. With high fives and bolstered declarations of courage, the small committee dispersed.

Spike pulled Matt aside. "Got a second for me to show you a few things?"

Starting with the main area, Spike pointed out the scuffed and battered walls, the stained and threadbare carpet, and the duct tape holding a set of speakers together. There were worn places on the skate floor, and a rotting section of the balcony railing begged for a lawsuit. All of the wooden benches bore the marks of kids-in-skates for the last few decades.

The Wurlitzer organ worked but barely. It needed major repair if Granny wanted to keep it. Matt pressed one of the keys, and it never released. As far as he could remember, Granny had played music from a sound system. But the antique organ was part of the Starlight's original magic.

"Dirk could sure play the whiz out of this thing," Spike said. "You'd think Harry would appreciate that his daddy got born again in this place and was forever changed. From drunk on booze to drunk on the Spirit. That's what he always liked to say. From Drunk Dirk to Dear Dirk."

"Harry seems bent on his own legacy—not his daddy's, not Granny's, not the Starlight." Matt looked at Spike's clipboard. "What else?"

"Follow me, my brother."

Several bathroom toilets and sinks leaked above chipped or broken floor tiles. The back room—with a single bed and battered chest of drawers—was loaded with things Granny wanted to "store."

"She don't need any of this. It's just a bunch of old papers and records." Spike opened one box to reveal a bunch of broken skates. "The last five years she's become a pack rat." He opened another box full of accounting ledgers.

Matt reached for one dated 1952. "We can deal with this room sooner rather than later, but the rest will take time."

"I'll take the benches to my workshop. Start refinishing them up one at a time. If we fail in our mission, she can sell them in an auction."

Matt tossed the ledger into the box. "Do you think we have a chance, Spike?" He didn't believe his celebrity would carry much sway. Who cared what Matt Knight wanted when he lived in California?

"There's always Immanuel." Spike walked out of the room and down the side of the rink, past the battered benches, and stopped under the murals.

"Spike, he's a painting. A fairy tale told by a brokenhearted, shipwrecked prince." The image of the man looming over the rink had scared Matt for most of his childhood. Maybe even a little bit right now. Under his wide-brim hat, his eyes seemed to watch. To see.

"He's more than a fairy tale to your granny. I might also point out the murals are ninety years old and are as beautiful as the day they were painted. You know, with a fancy Italian artist's name attached to these panels, they'd go for a pretty penny at auction." Spike moved on to the sound booth. "In here, some of the equipment was damaged when the roof leaked. I think Tooz spent all her reserve fixing it. Nora made up this tip sheet for the DJs when things don't work." Spike held up a stained yellow pad with curling edges.

Turn off and turn back on.

Take off old duct tape, put on new.

Pound the receiver gently! (circled in heavy ink) *Smack on top, center.*

"Dad didn't step in to help with the roof?" Matt scanned the rest of the list.

"By the time he'd heard, she'd already hired the crew and paid the money."

"Were they fair?"

"I hate to tell you this, Matt, but just about everyone these days takes advantage of your granny—from the kids she's hired to Mayor Harry Smith. I try to watch out for her but . . ." He motioned for Matt to follow him to the ticket booth. "This cash register is from before the war. Probably dates back to the thirties. With no sales tape, skimming a fiver or tenner from the till is easy as pie. Who would know? Tuesday counts on their honesty."

Spike continued the tour to the booth room, where Granny caught up to them. "What are you two doing? Snooping?"

"Just showing Matt what's what, Tooz. I told you things need fixing up around here."

"I told you I run a tight ship," she said. "Nothing some paint, mop, and broom won't fix."

"You think so?" Spike picked up a skate and jimmied the trunk loose from the boot. "This ain't safe. Also, Tooz, that kid Kenny lets his buddies in for free. I watched him do it all week, then heard a couple of them bragging about it in concession. Bunch of heathens."

"Kenny? Are you sure? Both of his parents worked here as teens. They were great kids."

"Well, he's a cheat. Don't get me started on Chondra."

"Now what's wrong with her? She's a hardworking gal."

"How about I step in, lend a hand for a while?" Matt roped his arm around her. "I'll work with Spike to get a few things fixed up while we promote our petition. Then, when we win, I'm investing in the Starlight. If Harry demands Sea Blue Beach moves into the future, let the Starlight lead the way."

"Well, I feel I should protest," Granny said. "You work hard for your money, Matty. But if this life has taught me anything, it's always to accept a lending hand."

"Consider it payment for eighteen-plus years of breakfast, lunch, and dinner, taking care of me while Dad worked, and buying me clothes *and* my first car."

A '70 Cuda. Wrecked by Booker. Which created a domino of events. For Booker. For Matt.

Matt followed Granny toward the rink, her chin up, shoulders back, striking a pose in her pale pink blouse, dark slacks, and brown oxfords. Her white hair was still thick and holding the curl from her weekly wash-and-set at Brenda's Beauty.

"The Starlight and I survived the Depression and the war, never mind the ill intentions of your grandpa's mob friends. Now I got teenagers robbing me? Maybe Harry and the council are right," she said, looking surprisingly defeated. "Maybe the days of the Starlight are over."

10

HARLOW

The package on the porch came from Buckhead, Atlanta. Mom. Harlow plopped the box on the kitchen table, along with bags from Lloyd's Hardware, Weldon's Five & Dime, the Haberdashery, and Biggs Market.

While the beach house was beautifully decorated and stocked with the best cookware, cutlery, flatware, dishes, and linens, it lacked the real essentials. Band-Aids, Scotch tape, dish soap, laundry detergent, scissors, bottle and can openers, bathroom soap . . . the list was long.

She'd been here over a week, and it was time to *move* in. She wore her beach hat, without the price tag now, hoping no one would recognize her. Especially Matt Knight. Three days had passed since their meet-cute at Tony's. Did he say how long he was in town? If she was lucky, he'd been called back to Hollywood.

Removing her hat, she fished her new scissors from the hardware bag and cut open Mom's package. Did she even want to know what was inside? The phone rang, giving her a momentary reprieve.

"Did you get my package?"

"Hello to you too, Mom. I'm opening it now."

"Well?"

"Well, what?"

"Do you like them? I talked to Jane Fonda's people, and they recommended—"

"Mom, do not talk to *people* about me."

Of all Mom's antics, this one bugged her the most. She had a ridiculous habit of sharing Harlow's business with everyone. Nothing was sacred.

"Why not? You're my daughter, and you need help."

"I do not need help." *Oh*, she needed help.

"I thought new workout clothes would inspire you. I bought one size too small and—"

"You don't know my size, Mom."

"I have an eye for these things." True. She did. "The leotards will be tight at first, but when you lose ten pounds or so, they'll be comfortable. Then I'll get the next size down. I wish I could see you. The blue will be stunning."

Harlow cradled the receiver and sliced open the box with the edge of the scissors. Sure enough, it was packed with blue spandex.

"They're really nice, Mom. Thank you."

"Anything for my girl. How's it going?"

"How's what going?"

"Harlow—"

"It's going."

And it was. During the day, she faithfully ate salads and grilled chicken, even though she yearned to work her way through the menu at the Blue Plate Diner. But at night, when the small town of 6,981 settled down, Harlow's pulse thumped in her ears. If only she had the sounds of the city or the anticipation of Jinx's key in the door to drown out her thoughts.

Sea Blue Beach was quiet. And she was alone. A deadly combination for a girl trying to forget her heartbreak and move on.

The worst part was she'd convinced herself the house on Sea Blue Way had no memories of Xander. But it did.

Xander guiding her down the sidewalk for a surprise, his broad hands over her eyes.

Bubbling up with tears when she saw the house for the first time.

The scent of Xander's skin as he wrapped her in his arms and painted an idyllic picture of their life at 321 Sea Blue Way.

His kiss as he carried her over the threshold.

The remodel debate. Laughing at their very different tastes. She was minimalistic but elegant. Xander was maximalist and gaudy. He'd spent too many summers at his grandmother's Newport cottage—a mansion filled with decades of inherited heirlooms. The giant chandelier now hanging from the vaulted ceiling was exhibit A. Seriously, if it fell for any reason, she'd have to redo half the downstairs.

She'd forgotten those moments until she began living here, and it made her wound fresh again.

Harlow put away her purchases, then carried the Jane Fonda–approved workout clothes upstairs, where she folded them neatly into her dresser drawer.

Harlow Hayes had already picked out an exercise getup—a pair of old sweats she'd cut into jogging shorts, with an oversized T-shirt from Jinx's ex-boyfriend. She cut the collar and sleeves *Flashdance* style and planned to start jogging in the morning. Which morning remained to be seen.

Maybe if she dressed for exercise, she'd actually exercise. Harlow exchanged her sundress for the sweats and T-shirt, then tied on her new Adidas. Back in the kitchen, she retrieved the salad she'd been munching on for two days—in exchange for eating a whole Tony's pizza Monday night and going to the Blue Plate yesterday. One of these days, she was going to weigh herself on the big green scale at Biggs. Promise.

Plopping on the sofa, she reached for the VCR remote. The familiar theme of *All My Children* played as she stabbed at her wilted salad.

Things were heating up in Pine Valley. Julie just discovered she was given up for adoption because her mother was a prostitute. Cue dramatic music!

A soft knock interrupted the opening scene of Erica Kane in one of her scheming dialogues, with her classic narrowed gaze and curled lip.

"HH, it's me, Matt."

"Matt Who?" *Girl, come on. You know who*. She set aside her salad with one eye on the television. What did Erica Kane just say?

"Matt Knight."

"Oh, hey." *You fool no one, H*. "W-what are you doing here?"

"I wondered if you wanted to grab a bite at the Blue Plate Diner."

The Blue Plate? *Matt, what are you doing to me?*

"Now?" She checked her reflection in the gilded mirror next to the door. Well, the sweats and cut up T-shirt were a step up from her pizza-stained dress. Her ponytail was cuter than hat head.

"Yes now. It's lunchtime. Are you going to open up or just keep talking through the door?"

"I, um, just . . . " Why was she nervous? ". . . came in from a jog." *No, you didn't*. "Give me a sec." *You are certifiable.* Grabbing her deflated salad, she ran to the kitchen, tossed it in the trash, then for some unknown reason, splashed her face, her shirt, and her hair with water. Ridiculous, meet stupid. "Matt, why don't I just meet you there? Give me fifteen?"

"I can wait. I'm curious to see what you did with this place." He knocked again. "I thought we'd walk over together. Harlow?"

Somewhere between splashing her face and hair, she heard herself call out, "Come on in," as if they were back on the set of *Talk to Me Sweetly*, running in and out of each other's trailers between takes.

The door opened, and Matt strolled in, wearing jeans, a white pullover, and a pair of Pumas.

Not going to lie, she swooned a little.

Matt smiled. "How was your *jog*?"

"Cut the pretense. You know I didn't go."

"But you were planning to?"

"Yes. No. Maybe. One day." She pointed to the stairs. "Give me fifteen."

She showered, again, for no *freaking* reason other than to continue the charade, toweled off, slipped into a sundress and sneakers, braided her hair, mascaraed her eyelashes, then finished it off with a swipe of pink lip gloss.

Matt stood when she came down, his gaze resting on her longer than she deserved. "You clean up nice."

The vibe between them was delicious *and* disrupting, like being on a first date. Not that she'd had many first dates, but it only took one or two to understand the zingy-yet-nervous undercurrent.

However, anything reeking of romance was not an option. Not after Xander. Besides, Matt was just being nice. It was who he was, despite his bad-boy rep.

She clicked off the television. She'd catch up with her people tonight. God bless the man who invented the VCR.

"Sorry about the fake jogging story," she said.

"You almost had me." He opened the front door. "But sweat doesn't usually gather in a single spot in the middle of your chest. Or only the *ends* of your hair."

"So you're a sweat expert? There's no end to your talents." She walked out with Matt, closing the door behind him.

The connection they had on the set of *Talk to Me Sweetly* had not faded. Even after everything wrapped, and she was in love with Xander, they sent each other funny cards and talked on the phone about once a month.

Matt started down the sidewalk. "I love Sea Blue Beach in the spring."

"Do you have a house here?" she said.

"I'm not home enough to warrant my own place so I just bunk in with my dad. But I'll be here awhile in order to save the Starlight. Hey, you should help us out. We need three hundred and fifty signatures to get a referendum to put the town's development plans to a vote."

"How can I help? I just got here." But she warmed at the idea of belonging to this town. Her *own* town. She'd never really had anything that was just hers before.

"You're a property owner. You can register to vote, sign the petition, ask others to do the same."

As they walked, he brought her up to speed on the town council meeting. "They're using eminent domain rules, but those of us who love the Starlight want to put *progress* to a vote. If we get enough signatures, maybe we can turn this ship around."

"Matt Knight, oh my gosh, it's Matt Knight." A group of tourists across the street ran toward him. Matt grabbed her hand and dashed for the diner.

Harlow Hayes had never been one for exercise, but her current physical state gave out-of-shape new meaning. She gasped for every breath.

Matt, however, never gulped air once. "Table for two, Blaire," he said to the hostess. "In the back."

"Follow me." Blaire batted her eyelashes at him. Her long hair and teased bangs suffered from too much Sun-In, but she was pretty. Pleasant.

"What'll y'all want to drink?" She passed out the menu with a second glance at Harlow. "Hey, I know you. You were in yesterday. Pitcher of sweet tea, right?"

"Unsweet for me," Matt said, reading the menu.

"I'll have the same." *Now go away.*

Yes, she'd been in yesterday because the fried fish platter tempted her away from her resolve for salad. Of course it had to be paired with sweet tea.

Now Harlow glanced toward the Sweet'N Low. She'd been on artificial sweeteners since she could remember. She was sick of them.

"You have quite the fan base in Sea Blue Beach," she said.

"Hometown boy and all."

"Or good-looking superstar who's made so many great movies and won a Golden Globe."

"Definitely not that." He looked so adorable trying to hide his smile as he read the menu. "You think I'm good-looking?"

"Please, the whole world thinks you're good-looking. Especially that hostess."

"I don't know. I've never been named Most Handsome Man in the World."

"I do believe you were once dubbed Most Eligible after Xander and I got engaged."

"He scooped you up before I had a chance."

"I'll add flatterer and liar to your talents. Keep it up and I'll rescind my apology about the fake jog." She leaned over her menu. "Matt Knight, why *are* you so eligible? What happened with you and Francesca Bianchi? She should've been named Most Beautiful over me."

"We had different ideas about love."

"I know the feeling." She studied the menu because looking up was an invitation for Matt to ask questions. While it felt good to talk about Xander, there were things she'd never shared. Not even to her parents, or Jinx, or Dr. Tagg. What happened that day in the penthouse lobby, or those that followed, was her secret.

Blaire reappeared with a fresh swipe of bright red lipstick. "Are you ready to order?" She snapped her gum and glanced down at Harlow, her pen poised over the order pad. "You want the fish platter again?"

"The garden salad with grilled salmon looks good." Matt handed over his menu.

"I'll have the same, dressing on the side." Said like a bona fide salad-ordering pro, which Harlow Hayes was, in a different life. But in this moment, she was a fraud because she most definitely wanted the fish platter. Why was she faking it? What did she have to prove? Matt had already seen her at her worst.

"So, what have you been up to?" he said after Blaire left.

"Mostly watching soap operas and thinking about jogging. What about you? What happened with Cindy Canon?" Harlow heard pieces of the story on *Entertainment Tonight*.

"I sort of ditched her at some seedy bar so Steve could drag my car down the Strip."

"Why'd you ditch her for Steve and Rob?"

"Unless you're Lucy and you've hung up your *Shrink Is In* sign, let's move on."

"Okay, Charlie Brown."

Their laughter intermingled, picking up where they left off after *Talk to Me Sweetly* wrapped.

"So . . ." Matt leaned toward Harlow. "I have a proposition for you."

"Already?" But yes, whatever, she'd do it.

"Come work at the Starlight. Granny needs to fire a few people, and I want to hire people I trust. You said you were here all summer, so how about it?" He paused. "Wait, are you working? Do you have any jobs coming up?"

"Matt, come on, you know I'm not working. You know I don't have any jobs coming up."

"Then come work at the Starlight."

"Doing what?" She reached for her napkin roll, remembering her upcoming salad with a sting of disappointment. "I don't know how to skate."

His smile melted some of her icy places. "Can you count money? Wash a window? Take out trash?"

"How much trash?"

He stuck out his hand. "You're hired."

"Wait, wait, wait. Let's talk money, Mr. Knight. I'm a skilled model. Harlow Hayes can sit at your ticket counter and stare at nothing for hours."

"So the girl negotiates. All right." He thought for a moment. "How about . . . now, this is not your typical HH money . . . minimum wage? Three thirty-five an hour."

"Matt, hey—" Blaire returned with members of the diner's crew and a Polaroid camera. "Sorry to barge in, but can we get a picture? Please?" She handed the camera to Harlow. "Could you?"

"You might want her in it too, Blaire," Matt said. "You know she's the Most—"

"Amazing photographer." Harlow pointed to the front window. "This is not the best place for a light. It's better over there." She'd learned a few things about lighting and photography over the years. Though it was anyone's guess what a Polaroid would spit out.

The crew clustered around Matt, with Blaire tucking herself under his arm. Matt's party-boy reputation always puzzled Harlow. On set, he'd been so focused and serious. Devoted to his craft. Kind and generous with everyone. For their first scene, he'd rehearsed with her for over an hour, coaching her, giving her tips, putting her at ease. At the end of filming, Matt bought brand-new cars for two of the crew members, then denied it when asked by the press.

"Everyone ready?" Harlow said. "Say cheese." She aimed and clicked, waited for the film to slide from the box, then shot a couple more. She set the prints on a table to dry and handed the camera to Blaire, who gave her a lingering look.

"Say, you do look familiar. How do you know Matt?"

Thankfully, a strong female voice bellowed from the kitchen. "I got food to be cooked and tables to be served, so if y'all aren't back to work by the time I count to two, every last one of you is fired. One,"—The crew scattered—"two."

Back at their booth, Matt said, "You were a sport, taking the pictures without saying anything."

"I didn't need to say anything. Besides, I like being on the other side of the camera. Working with photographers like Richard Avedon and Irving Penn taught me to appreciate the art of photography."

"I worked with Avedon a few times," Matt said. "He was so creative."

"He shot my first *Vogue* cover and sealed my success. Yet if you ask my mother, she's the . . ." She sighed. "Never mind. Let's not go there."

Their salads arrived, and Blaire topped off their tea while giving Harlow another good look before flirting with Matt again.

"Are you going to ask her out?" Harlow said when she'd gone.

"I was thinking of asking you out."

Harlow choked on her first bite of salmon and lettuce, washing it down with a swig of unsweetened tea. "Very funny."

"Why's that funny?"

Their gazes locked while she fished for a clever reply. Was he serious? Didn't he see she wasn't *the* Harlow Hayes anymore?

"You can't ask me out. You just became my boss. No fraternizing."

"Then I guess I'll have to fire you."

"Too late. I've accepted the job." She stabbed at her salad. Was he teasing her? *Having her on*, as her British friend Tippy would say.

"If you're not doing anything this afternoon, meet me at the Starlight. I'll show you around."

"All right, but I'm warning you—no skates."

The grilled salmon salad was delicious, even familiar in a good way. Maybe she'd missed a little bit of Peter Rabbit food.

A customer paused at their table to tell Matt she had his poster on her wall during high school, and another asked for his autograph. He graciously signed and chatted with her.

When he tried to pay, Blaire told him Audra comped his lunch. "Rollo on the Radio announced you were here, and now folks are lined up down the block."

"Who's Rollo on the Radio?" Harlow asked.

"Local DJ. Good guy. A few years ahead of me in high school. Can you get us out of here, Blaire? And tell Audra she owes me more than a lunch for dropping my name to Rollo."

Blaire escorted them through the kitchen to go out the back so folks wouldn't know he'd left. Laughing, they ran toward the beach, and Harlow was grateful when he stopped at the Beachwalk. Despite the cool spring breeze, certain parts of her dress were dark with perspiration.

"Thank you, Matt."

"For what?"

For being nice. For being her friend. For treating her like she mattered. "If you don't know, then forget it, but—"

"Maybe I do, maybe I don't. But you'd do the same for me."

She peered up at him, a bit of the Starlight's neon light on his face. "Yes, I probably would."

11

TUESDAY

DECEMBER 1936

"Ma!" LJ thundered into the kitchen, with Dup following and the screen door slapping behind them. "You got to come. Now." He tugged on her arm so hard she nearly knocked over a huge pot of chili.

"LJ, mind yourself. What are you all riled about?" She sampled the chili. Fair to middling, seeing how this was her umpteenth batch and she'd run out of salt. Tonight was Christmas at the Starlight, which was free to all, and she needed a lot of chili. In about an hour, the place would be bustling with volunteers to decorate and prepare for Ol' St. Nick to arrive, along with the baby Jesus, of course.

Over at the Nickle place, Harriet baked up a mountain of corn bread, while her sisters Jubilee and Rosalie baked so many pies Tuesday could smell the sweetness all the way to her corner of town.

Everyone turned out for Christmas at the Starlight. This year, a newcomer, Mr. Giovanni Esposito, volunteered all the gelato they could eat. Such a treat. Then, last night, Mr. Milner delivered so many oranges the volunteers stuffed two into every child's stocking.

The Depression lingered along the Panhandle, but with the Works Progress Administration and some ingenuity, the citizens of Sea Blue Beach prospered, sharing from their abundance, or perhaps their lack, but thriving all the same.

All week long, folks passed on the street, calling out to one another, "Meet me at the Starlight on Christmas Eve," their arms laden with packages from the shops and the post office.

"Ma, you have to come. Now." LJ tugged on her again.

"I thought I was the mother around here. Dupree, hand me that crock by the door. LJ, did you do like I asked and pick up the dishes from Miss Harriet's church? Is Burt at the rink? He'll need to let folks in."

"Ma!" Dupree shoved the crock into her arms, his man-boy voice amplified in the small space. "It's Pa. He's hurt bad."

"What? Your pa?" She handed the crock back to Dupree. "Fill this with chili." *Leroy, what have you gone and done now?* "LJ, stoke the stove. We don't need no sparks burning the place down."

The wet December chill felt good on her skin, while the hammer of her heels against the pavement sent vibrations through her limbs and around her heart. One block, two blocks, three blocks . . . yet the Starlight seemed farther away. When she gasped for a breath, the air's icy edge cut up her lungs.

She burst through the back door into a cluster of men in work trousers and suspenders hovering against the wall, hats in hand.

"You Tuesday?" One of the men pointed to the closed room. "In there. Doc's with him."

She shoved into the room, where stacks of presents, and a mountain of stuffed stockings, awaited the evening's festivities. And where another family down on their luck had recently vacated. A relative came through with a job and wired money for them to drive home for Christmas.

Leroy lay on the floor, his shirt soaked with blood, a strap of leather between his teeth as a man with a knife worked his shoulder, using a candle for more light.

"Nearly there." He gingerly sank the tip of the knife into an open wound. Leroy writhed in pain, and Tuesday fell against the chest of drawers, clinging to it as her vision began to fade. "Mac, bring a couple of the boys in to hold him steady. Sorry, Lee, but this is the only way. You Mrs. Knight? I need antiseptic."

"W-what?" She tried to gather some strength.

"Antiseptic." Doc sank the knife deeper in the wound, and Leroy swooned. "I'll need bandages as soon as I get this bullet out."

"Bullet?" she whispered.

LJ burst into the room. "Is he dead? Is he? Ma?"

"LJ, get the antiseptic." She grabbed his shoulders and turned him out. "In the office . . . Medicine cabinet."

Leroy remained unconscious, thank goodness, while Doc worked. After a minute, or maybe an eternity, he rose up with a small piece of metal in his hand. "Got it." He wiped his knife with the edges of Leroy's torn shirt. "We need clean bandages, Mrs. Knight."

"Of course." But she was a statue, unable to move from the bureau. When LJ returned with the bottle of Listerine, she told him to run to the house and get a set of clean sheets. She'd taken the ones she used for the Starlight's guests home to wash.

Doc poured a generous amount of antiseptic over the wound, using Leroy's shirt to mop up the excess and the blood. Lee stirred with a moan.

"You want him in here?" Doc tipped his head toward the bed. "To recuperate?"

"No, no, take him to the house. After you've doctored him."

"You going to be able to take over?" He regarded her for a long moment as if deciding Tuesday's competency. He was handsome, with salt-and-pepper hair, hazel eyes with flecks of green, and an intense scar down his right cheek. "I can show you what to do."

Tuesday swallowed and nodded. "I-I can." She resented feeling weak, resented the residue of the scared fifteen-year-old girl standing on the side of Gulf Road South as her mamaw, the only mother she'd ever known, drove off in a loaded wagon, leaving her behind.

"Can't take you with, Tooz. The town folks will tend to you. Go to school and behave yourself."

"Ma?" LJ shoved a set of sheets against her middle. "These the right ones?"

"Um, no. Yes. They'll do. Thank you." She clutched the linens like a life vest before handing them to Doc. LJ brought her good sheets. The ones she'd purchased from Montgomery Ward after saving for two years. Now they'd soak up her husband's blood. "I'll get the scissors."

She crossed the rink in a haze. *Don't you die on me, Leroy Knight.*

At the top of the rink, a band warmed up with a song from the latest Fred Astaire and Ginger Rogers movie.

Burt met her as she came out of the office with the shears. "Where're you going with those, Tooz? I thought you was home cooking chili."

"I was—I am. We had a . . . never mind. Burt, who is that band and why are they here? Where's Dirk?" If asked right now, she may not know her own name.

"The high school band, Tooz. They're practicing. You invited them to play for Christmas Eve."

"And Dirk? Where's he?"

"Don't know. Why?"

"Call around, see if you can't find him. He's the organist for singing the carols, and I want him here. See if he's . . ." Had he been with Lee? Was he shot as well? "Just find him."

"Tooz, what's going on? Why you so jittery? Don't tell me Lee's gone and done something again." Burt had never approved of Leroy's ways and never shied away from expressing his opinion.

"Just find Dirk, will you?"

Back in the room, fragrant with sweaty men and drying blood, she cut up her precious sheets until Doc said he had enough. Even then she continued because she didn't know what else to do.

"Take these home, LJ." She looped the extra strips around her son's neck, her gratitude and anger beginning a tug-of-war.

"Mrs. Knight?" Doc said. "We're carting him to your home."

"Fine." She watched as five men carefully loaded Lee onto a flatbed truck.

"Care to ride?" The lanky one with dark, close-set eyes offered his hand.

"No, thank you. I-I'll walk." She steered LJ toward the truck. "Ride with them. Show them where to go."

She'd started to depend on her firstborn too much, yoking him to manhood before he'd shed all the innocence of childhood. He ran errands, worked at the Starlight, discussed money and provisions. He chopped wood for the fireplace and cookstove, did his share of the washing and ironing, and even tried to teach Dup the ways of a man—which he barely understood himself. He was tall and muscular, disciplined, finishing his homework by lantern after Tuesday cut out the lights to save on the electric bill.

Curse you, Leroy, for doing this to us.

"Can I walk with you, Mrs. Knight?" Doc asked.

"Yes, but you must call me Tuesday." She returned the scissors to her desk and met the man called Doc out front, along with the crew bringing tonight's Christmas tree. The volunteers would show up any minute to start the decorations. Then to bring the wrapped presents and prepared stockings out of the same room where Leroy's blood soaked the rag rug. "Go on in, Mr. Warren," she called. "Thank you so much. Burt's inside, he'll help. Oh, and could you ask him to clean up the back room right away? Please."

"Sure will, Tooz. You all right?"

"Well, of course." She struggled to smile. "It's Christmas Eve. May I introduce Doc? A friend of Lee's."

The day was cold, despite the brightness of the midmorning

sun. Tuesday wrapped her arms about her torso and walked a block with Doc before either of them spoke.

He went first. "Guess you figured Lee was shot."

The damp Gulf air sank into her bones, making her shiver. "The big question is, who shot him and why?"

"I can't say."

"Can't or won't?"

"Maybe a little of both."

"He's running booze, isn't he? Why else would he be gone so much or need a crew of 'boys'?" Boys, ha. Hoodlums, every last one of them. Except maybe Doc here. He felt out of place with the others. Had an air of sophistication about him. "What else? Gambling? Women?"

Even with prohibition over, the bootlegging continued. Where there was a flow of booze, one could count on gambling and whoring.

"He loves you, Mrs. Knight . . . Tuesday. Talks about you all the time."

"Is that my consolation prize? He's never around, and he's engaged in things that get him shot, but I should feel lucky that he talks about me."

"He's trying to be a good man."

"Then Leroy Knight and I will have another come-to-Jesus meeting, because I didn't marry him so I could live alone and raise my sons without a father."

"We live in hard times, Tuesday. A man can't find a job worth more than the shirt on his back. I believe Leroy is doing his best to provide for his family."

"Is getting shot part of the plan? What about the WPA? Plenty of men make money on President Roosevelt's program." Tuesday slowed and turned toward him. "I don't buy into this notion of thieving and robbing because a good job just don't pay enough. Honesty is worth far more than a dollar, Doc. I'd a-soon he washed fish guts off the boats or picked oranges than run with folks who get him shot. The next bullet might not miss his heart." She brushed a cold tear from her cheek. "Besides, I can't remember the last time he showed up with any cash."

"Like I said, times are rough."

"Tell me, are you a real doctor?"

"I studied but never finished. My father died, and I had to take care of my mother and siblings. By the time my youngest brother left the house, I was thirty years old and ready for adventure. I worked my way across the Atlantic on a merchant ship. Got a job in London as a doctor's assistant. By some miracle, I married a beautiful, charitable English heiress and had two stunning daughters."

"How do they feel about you running around with hoodlums?"

"They're dead." Said so succinctly she almost didn't believe him except for the grief in his eyes.

"I'm so sorry."

"My wife was from a long line of lords and ladies. One of her uncles was a British general during our Revolutionary War. Her family, the great Traffords, had people in New York and wanted my wife to bring our daughters over for the summer Season. That way, when they made their American debut, they'd have made the right acquaintances."

"Seasons and debuts," Tuesday whispered. "Sounds like a Jane Austen novel."

"My wife booked passage for the spring, and I was to follow a month later. After all, I was still a working man. Once I arrived, we'd spend a month with my family and sail home together. I stood on the dock, watching them board the HMS *Titanic*."

"Doc." Tuesday grabbed his arm. "Weren't they rescued?"

"Betsy, my wife, was the most generous soul. She had gone to steerage to help a sick family. So like her, my Bets." He sighed and walked on. "The girls woke when the ship started listing and tried to find her, probably ended up belowdecks or trapped somewhere. They were eleven and nine."

"I cannot imagine," Tuesday said with a shiver against the chill.

"Yes, that's the thing, isn't it? What we imagine. I had some relief when the wife of the couple in the stateroom next to my girls wrote to me, told me what she believed happened." Doc gazed toward the sound of the waves. "Two years later, when the Great War broke out, my wife's uncle recruited me for the Royal Army Medical Corp. I was forty years old. My two brothers died in 1918. The Battle of Belleau Wood. My mother succumbed to the Spanish flu, and my sister married and moved west. In the blink of an eye, I was utterly alone. I sailed back to the States, sold the family home, and hopped a train. Found a life on the rails, hoboing, doing odd jobs, doctoring folks who might not want a real doctor or hospital to know what they'd been up to. Helped a few gals in trouble, who got in the family way."

"Doc—"

"I am not proud. Not at all." He glanced at her. "How'd you meet Lee?"

"At the Starlight. I worked there. Lived there too, in that very room where you fixed him up. My mother was sixteen and unmarried. My grandparents raised me, but Mamaw was done raising kids after seven of her own. My mother was the youngest. Probably why she got in trouble. When Gramps died, Mamaw packed up and left. Prince Blue at the Starlight saved me. Then I met Leroy."

"Lee was real proud when he gave you the rink."

"You knew him then? Did he tell you what I really wanted was a diamond ring?" She smiled softly. "But the Starlight is a marvelous substitute. Incomparable, really."

"Can I give you some advice?" Doc waited for her answer, a somberness about him.

"Go on."

"Leroy may not be living up to what he promised you as a young man in love, but sometimes love requires taking it as it comes and in the manner it's given. You can choose to accept or reject it. I've lived a good many years, Tuesday, and my advice is to see Leroy's love as he gives it. Then, like the rest of us, do what you must to fill the cracks."

12

HARLOW

When her alarm buzzed at five in the morning, she rolled over and slapped the off button. Yeah, this jog was *not* happening.

She'd never been athletic, let alone a jogger. When she shot a sneaker commercial in the early eighties, they hired a coach to help her move like an athlete.

Burrowing under the covers, the memory of that job resurrected the reality that so much of her life was fake. She was airbrushed, dressed, and posed to look like an image in someone else's mind. A corporate view of beauty.

The only thing she'd ever earned—a word she used loosely—was the title of Most Beautiful Woman in the World. Producers, editors, and fashion industry folks around the world decided each year's Most Beautiful. When they named her, it was humbling. She attributed most of her success to Mom, good luck, and good genes, but her hard work and dedication earned her the Most Beautiful title.

However, that was then, and this was now. Time to get her day going. Stop stalling. She had to punch in at the Starlight later today. Well, in that case, she should really sleep in. Cuddling her pillow, she'd just drifted off when a startling knock rattled her door.

"H, you up? Let's go."

Matt? What was he. . . ? No, surely not. He wasn't that insane. Though she had mentioned a five a.m. jog to him as she left the Starlight yesterday.

"Harlow Hayes, wake up!"

She grabbed her robe and headed downstairs. "You're rude, you know that?"

"You're not ready?" He clapped his hands as he came inside, spilling the light into the dark morning. "Let's go, let's go." He wore shorts, a *Flight Deck* T-shirt that fit his muscled chest, and a pair of Adidas.

"Remember when I said Harlow Hayes doesn't skate? She also doesn't jog. It only sounds like a good idea. I see people jogging and think, 'That might be fun.' But that's the whole of it, Matt."

"It is fun. Come on, H, you've got the legs for it."

"Had, Matt. Had."

"How about we go around the block once? You can do it."

"I don't know." She tightened the belt of her robe and leaned against the sofa. "I feel like . . ." Should she just say it? Be honest? "I feel like I'd be the first elephant to jog in Sea Blue Beach."

"H, please. You are not an elephant. Second, a carnival came through a few years back and their elephant escaped. Ran right down Sea Blue Way."

"I'm going to need photographic evidence." But he made her smile.

Matt leaned next to her. "Okay, maybe a carny elephant never ran through town, but tell me why you want to start jogging. Why'd you try to fake me out the other day?"

"Because—" She peered at him. "CCW wants me as their next It Girl. I have to lose weight."

"Do you want to lose weight? Be their It Girl?"

"I'd like to be more of my former self, prove all the mess with Xander no longer has power over me. I've not aimed for much in my career, but CCW is a job I've always wanted. However, I ate my way out of one job after another because that yahoo broke my heart."

It was easy to be vulnerable in the predawn hours.

"Then get dressed. Let's go. One trip around the block. Hey, you can be the first Most Beautiful Woman in the World to jog in Sea Blue Beach."

"That's not me anymore, Matt. I'm the punch line of comedy sketches and the cover girl for tabloids."

"H, look at me. I've been in LA a long time, and I know real beauty is about more than what you look like. It's about who you are. Do you want to make some improvements? Great. We all do. But don't define yourself by a few pounds. Now, go change. Didn't you say you wanted the CCW job? Wanted to prove Xander doesn't have power over you?"

"Fine." Nothing like talking to a guy who made sense. Who used her own words against her. "Give me five."

Once she was in her cut-up sweats and T-shirt, Matt led her through a few stretches, then started a slow pace down the street through the dawning morning, where late winter's thinness lingered in the spring air. She was halfway down the street before she realized every limb, every muscle, ached.

"Doing great, H." Matt stopped at the end of Sea Blue Way. "Let's cross and go up the other side, then back to your house. A half mile."

"A half a mile?" If Harlow Hayes learned anything through modeling, it was perseverance.

"Are you looking forward to your shift at the Starlight?" Matt said without so much as a huff or puff.

"Yeah." Gasp, huff, puff, gasp, gasp. "Tired of . . . cooped up . . . house. Bored."

By the time Matt jogged up her sidewalk, she was a sweaty mess, and the pain in her side might require a trip to the ER. Matt joined her on the concrete steps to cool down.

"Don't run tomorrow. Just walk," he said. "Pick up running the next day. Try to go a little farther."

"I take it you're not going to bang on my door at five."

"Maybe." She felt his smile all the way to her backbone and down to her toes. *Harlow Hayes, careful. He's out of your league.* "I know you said you don't skate, but it's great exercise. Easy on the joints."

"Harlow Hayes is going to need this face for CCW. Can't risk skidding across the rink floor." She patted him on the shoulder and started inside. "HH is going back to bed. See you this afternoon, boss."

"One o'clock. Punch in on time or I'll have to dock your pay."

MATT

The Save the Starlight group reconvened the last Saturday in March. Dion was able to join this time, so their ranks swelled to six. Got to say, Matt was disappointed more townspeople didn't show, especially on a weekend morning. Granny deserved better from her fellow citizens.

Gathering folks to help the petition campaign was the one place Matt had counted on his celebrity power—after all, fans traveled to California from around the world for a chance peek of him. But in Sea Blue Beach, he was just Tuesday's grandson and Dupree's kid.

However, Mary and Tyler, Spike and Dion, and even Granny, assured him folks were eager to save the Starlight.

"Where are we on the petitions?" He looked at Tyler. "And the flyers?"

"Sorry, Matt, I had a big job come in from the high school for prom and graduation. My crew has been working overtime."

"Understandable. Can you get to it this week? Mary, what about the petition? Did you file the paperwork?"

"Got busy myself. I'll file on Monday. Remember, forms can only be posted at city hall and the post office."

Okay, the Save the Starlight team was fumbling a bit.

To be honest, he was a bit distracted himself with Harlow Hayes crossing his mind at random intervals. Last night, he set his alarm to wake up for a jog, then fell asleep thinking about her.

He never let women sneak up on him, get into his head and dreams. But the supermodel was not just any woman.

"Did you talk to Dup, Matt?" Spike asked. "Did he have any ideas of alternate locations for expansion?"

"He said there's land west of town. In fact, another developer is building a gated community."

"A gated community?" Granny puffed up. "In Sea Blue Beach? We don't gate up our neighborhoods. We share things around here."

"Welcome to the future. Dad said Murdock has plans to do the same."

"I don't mean to throw a wrench in the works," Dion said, a seriousness in his southern drawl, "but have y'all seen Harry's flyers? He's launched his own campaign."

No one was surprised, but Dion's words lit a fire under them. Tyler said he'd start on the flyers today, before his son's baseball game. Mary pledged to start calling her committees and clubs, but first—

"Who was the beautiful woman you were with at the diner?" Mary smirked at Matt.

Matt made a show of looking down at his clipboard. "I'm sorry, that's not on the meeting agenda."

"I move to add Matt's lunch date to the meeting agenda," Mary said.

"Second." *Granny, you traitor.*

"All in favor, say aye." A rousing affirmation followed. "The ayes have it."

"Spike, Tyler, way to turn on a guy. Dion, I thought you'd have my back."

"I'm an old romantic at heart."

"She's just a friend," Matt said with no amount of affection, ignoring the silly flutters thoughts of Harlow inspired. "She owns 321 Sea Blue Way. Now, can we get to work on saving the Starlight?" *And remove me from under the spotlight?* Small-town life . . . sheesh.

Ten minutes later, with everyone committed to their assignments, Matt called the *Sea Blue Beach Gazette* from Granny's office.

"I'm not so sure I'm on your side, Matt." Rachel Kirby, editor-in-chief, had inherited the newspaper from her grandfather, who inherited it from his father and grandfather. Besides growing up in a journalism family, Rachel developed her reporter chops in Tallahassee and Jacksonville, and once on assignment in London for the AP. Her husband ran the printing press. They had three dogs and lived in the big house "up the hill" from the Starlight on Salty Sea Way. With no children, the *Gazette* was their baby.

"You're a journalist, Rachel. Tell both sides. But you have to remind people about the history and importance of the Starlight."

"You got me there, Matt. Okay, I'll assign a reporter to the story."

"Thank you. Now, how do I buy ad space?"

"I'll connect you to our sales director. We're more than happy to take your Hollywood money."

The ad director was out, but his second-in-command sold Matt a full-page color ad for the Sunday *Gazette* and a black-and-white half page for the weekdays and scheduled it to run through the end of April. For Granny. For the Starlight.

When he hung up, Matt wandered toward the rink floor, feeling satisfied with the committee's morning efforts. The ten o'clock session for the fifty-five-plus crowd was in full swing.

Granny wore the floor guard whistle around her neck while skating backward, talking to Belinda Miracle, a woman from her school days. Take away the gray hair and wrinkles, Granny and Belinda looked like your average teens chatting about books, or school, or boys.

Suddenly, Granny stumbled, and as Belinda reached to steady her, Matt ran to catch Granny before she brought Belinda down on her.

"How about I take the whistle?" he said when he'd gotten Granny upright and Belinda stable.

"No . . . no . . . Matty, I'm fine." Nevertheless, her voice trembled. "Just got tangled up."

"Well, I'm sitting down. My heart's beating like a jackrabbit's." Belinda patted Matt's arm and headed for the benches.

Granny slowly handed Matt the whistle. "Guess I do have a new shipment of brownies to inventory."

"New skates? When did you order those?"

"A while back. Before I knew Harry intended to destroy the Starlight."

Matt helped her off the floor with a growing sense of Granny's fragility. Losing the rink might do her in.

He'd settled her in her office when he ran into Dale Cranston coming from Spike's Concession with a Coke and bag of popcorn. He eyed Matt, grinned one of *those* kinds of grins, and kept going.

What are you up to, Dale Cranston? You think your team has won? That the rink will be smashed, leaving more business for your sticky-floor theater?

The senior session ended at noon, and Harlow arrived a little before one for the first afternoon shift. This was her third day, and she was already better than Chondra and Kenny combined.

"Long time no see," she said, sticking her large designer bag under the ticket counter.

"Good run this morning," he said. She'd been waiting for him on the porch when he arrived a little after five. Together they circled Sea Blue Way again, thus securing Harlow Hayes as a permanent fixture in Matt's thoughts.

"Really? I almost tripped on a flat sidewalk with no cracks." She greeted the couple coming in with their skates dangling over their shoulders. "How you are doing, Mr. Danvers, Mrs. Danvers?" The Danvers were longtime Sea Blue residents. Longtime Starlight skaters. They skated every afternoon, avoiding the senior session because the "old people" were too slow.

"Matt," said Mrs. Danvers, "we're counting on you to save this place. We had every one of our kids' birthday parties at the Starlight from age five to eighteen. Forty-two parties. The Starlight is family to us."

Next, a group of lobster-red spring breakers arrived, claiming they needed shelter from the sun. When Harlow handed them their tickets, the lot of them froze and stared.

"Right in there." She pointed around the corner. "To get your skates."

"You're . . . *you're* Harlow Hayes, aren't you?" The girl with the permed and poofed brown hair and red cheeks was in awe.

"I'm your hostess for this skating session. Enjoy."

Matt tried not to laugh as they walked away furiously whispering, wondering if the woman who sold them skate tickets was a world-famous model.

"You can't keep this up forever, you know," he said.

"I can if I want. I noticed you didn't introduce yourself. Hello, how many? Five? That'll be fifteen dollars. The skates are around the corner. Matt, can you get us going with some music?"

In the sound booth, he loaded *Nora's Perfect Afternoon Session* CD and pressed play. The melody of "Strawberry Letter 23" filled the rink.

Skaters of various skill levels hurried to the floor, talking and laughing, singing. The Danvers continued to couple skate—as they would all session no matter what the song—displaying their skill with a practiced routine.

Matt paused by the ticket booth before heading to the back room, where he'd been cleaning and purging. So far, Granny missed none of it.

"Can I buy you dinner between sessions, H?"

"Maybe. But not as a date, right? You *are* my boss."

"Totally platonic. Five thirty?"

He'd just hauled a large garbage bag to the dumpster when Dad walked in with a studious man swinging a large briefcase.

"Matt, this is Gordon Vale, property appraiser. Gordon, go on back and get yourself set up. I'll be along in a minute."

"Property appraiser?" Matt said. "Dad, this will crush Granny. Bringing him in here is all but admitting defeat."

"It's called being prepared. Harry's not going to just let you work up the town to vote against his proposals. Trust me. And I want Ma to get a fair price."

"You think he's that determined? That the town will go with him?"

"You saw him at the meeting, Matt. Sea Blue Beach may be small, and we may know everyone's name, but politics is politics. Harry is chomping at the bit to wield his elected authority. We need to do our homework." Dad started to walk toward the office. "You home for dinner?"

"Going to the Blue Plate with Harlow."

"I see. Is there something you need to tell me?" Dad, oh Dad.

"Yeah. I drank the last of the milk."

13

HARLOW

A sense of normalcy settled over Harlow as she jogged down Sea Blue Way with Matt the first Wednesday of April, a growing ease in her movement.

In the almost three weeks she'd lived in Sea Blue Beach, she'd developed a routine. Jogging Monday, Wednesday, and Friday. Then chores and errands in the morning before punching in at the Starlight. Last week, when the cute Tony's pizza delivery boy, Simon Caster, mentioned how he had to part the grass to make it up the walkway, she hired him to mow her lawn and trim the hedges.

At the end of the street, Harlow crossed over with Matt and headed toward the Starlight, where they circled the rink once, then cut through the parking lot toward Pelican Bay Way before heading home.

This morning, Matt picked up the pace as they rounded the Starlight, as if working out his own tensions. Harlow struggled to keep up. By the time they arrived at her front steps, she was breathless and wiping the sweat from her eyes.

"You want water? I need water."

When Harlow returned with two glasses, Matt said, rather out of the blue, "I stole my first kiss on this porch. Patti Evans. I was sixteen."

"At some wild Sea Blue Beach rave?"

"Hardly. Granny's friends, the Nickles, lived here. They were holy people, king and queen of hospitality. They loved to throw parties and host picnics. Half the town came out. If the party wasn't at the Starlight, it was the Nickles' place. Grandpa Morris smoked beef and pork that melted in your mouth. He and his brothers had a bluegrass band, pickin' and grinnin' long before *Hee Haw*." Matt gulped down his water. "I kissed her just as the Fourth of July fireworks started exploding over the beach." He laughed. "Metaphor, anyone?" He slapped the concrete step. "Kissed her right here. Wonder what she's up to these days? So, HH, what about you?"

"Me? I didn't even know Patti Evans, let alone kiss her."

"Your first kiss, goofball."

"Oh, that. Hmm, Logan Howard. My first and last crush until Xander." Except for those first weeks on *Talk to Me Sweetly*, when the presence of Matt Knight made her quiver. "I was a junior, and he was a senior with gorgeous hair and a motorcycle. Dad liked him. Didn't bat an eye when I rode off to the movies on the back of his bike. Mom was out shopping, so Dad shooed me out the door quickly. If Mom had seen me on the back of that motorcycle, she'd have chased us down. We saw *Gone in 60 Seconds*."

"Love that movie."

"Afterward, at the Dairy Queen, Logan ordered a milkshake, and I ordered a Sprite. But when he went to say hi to friends, I switched my order to water and pretended it was a soda."

"Sounds boring."

"Or crazy. All my life Mom regimented my diet. When modeling jobs started rolling in, she doubled down. Especially after we met Jinx and she talked of bringing me into Icon. Want another little secret? I'd never even had a milkshake until after, well, everything."

"Never? Not even as a kid? Or at a party?"

"Not that I recall. I started modeling around Atlanta when I was seven. Until two years ago, I'd never tasted Halloween candy or Christmas cookies, ice cream or pizza. In a blind taste test, I couldn't have told you a Hayes Cookie from an Oreo. I honestly believed if I had anything forbidden, I'd balloon up overnight. And Mom would know the moment I walked through the door. Anne Hayes is one of the original Jedis, you know. She kept a close tab on me. But I didn't mind, really. My modeling career made her happy, and I *loved* making her happy."

"Sheesh, H. But to never have had a milkshake . . . I mean . . . How could you stand being so controlled?"

"I thought we were talking about first kisses."

"So we were. All right, you rode off like *Easy Rider* with Logan, man of great hair. Did he kiss you good night?"

"He did." Her cheeks warmed at the memory. "We lingered at the door, and as much as I wanted him to kiss me, I was terrified. Then he put his arm around me and looked into my eyes. I'll never forget how his lips felt—cool and soft."

"Like a chocolate shake."

She laughed. "Maybe. I was puckered with goose bumps. A real 'Dear Diary' moment. I floated inside, ready to tell my parents everything, but they were in Dad's study, talking, and Mom was crying." Her mother's tears were Harlow's kryptonite. "She'd seen me arrive home on the back of the bike. It terrified her. She was saying things like 'I'm losing her' and accused Dad of undermining her plans for my career. Then Dad said, 'Isn't it more your career, Anne? You're still mad at me about everything.' I never even knew Mom had a career. She met Dad in college. They married after he graduated. I crept upstairs and put Carole King on the record player. Two months later, she said Jinx wanted me in New York and whisked me away."

"Why did you *love* to make your mother happy?"

"Back to first kisses." Harlow gulped the last of her water. "I never kissed Logan again. Apparently you never kissed Patti again."

"Nope."

Their laughter mingled. "Oh, to *not* be sixteen again," Harlow said.

"I'd be sixteen again if it meant I could meet you. Keep you from Xander Cole."

"You met me two weeks before Xander." She peered at him through the dappled light breaking through the leaves. "I don't regret Xander, Matt. I loved him more than anything. He loved me, or so he said. But Davina had a hold on him he couldn't break. She broke his heart. Broken things want to be mended. If Xander came waltzing into Sea Blue Beach and said, 'I love you and want you back,' I'm not sure what I'd do."

Matt squeezed her hand. "Promise you'll call me if he does."

"They've gone public with their wedding. I won't be hearing from him."

"Remember when we went out to dinner? The first week of filming?"

"Of course I remember. You were charming."

"As were you."

"We laughed a lot, drank too much wine."

"Talked over each other half the night because we liked all the same things."

"You held my hand across the table."

"You kicked me under said table when I didn't see a hovering fan." Matt feigned a wince.

Harlow laughed. "Oh, that's right. She was all of sixteen. So cute and sweet."

"She asked for my autograph . . . for her grandpa."

Harlow hadn't laughed this easily in two years.

"I'm sorry we lost touch, H," Matt said.

"Well, we're in touch now, aren't we?"

Grinning and casting side glances at each other, they lingered in silence and the beauty of the morning. Harlow felt a bit giddy and lighthearted, more than she cared to admit, by being in Matt Knight's presence.

"I should get going. I need to pick up a few things from Biggs before work." She gathered their empty glasses. "My boss is a tyrant."

"I've heard he's a real piece of work." Matt stood, stretched, and started down the walk. He paused and turned back. "I'm just going to say it. I like you, Harlow, and I want to know your story. Can I ask you about Xander or your parents or your career?"

"Is this a two-way street, Matt Knight?"

He made a face, the one that enchanted female moviegoers the world over. "With a few red lights, yes."

She laughed. "You can ask, Matt. Doesn't mean I have to answer. But there's a part of me that wants to leave it all behind. Even though things went wrong between me and Xander, I'd like to believe our years together had meaning."

At last, she'd found a few words to make sense of it all. Right there, on the porch of her Sea Blue Beach home, in the shadow of the Starlight.

In the kitchen, she gulped another glass of water and watched Matt jog through her backyard toward his dad's place. She grabbed some grapes from the fridge, frowning at the number of takeout cartons on the shelves. Leftovers never got eaten. She collected the lot and tossed them in the trash.

What would life be like if her *one* dinner date with Matt had flamed into more? What if Xander had never shown up on set? Because from the moment he introduced himself, she was trapped in his orbit and had no choice but to fall in love.

After her run, she showered, fell asleep catching up on her soaps, and woke up in a sun-soaked room. Now she was running late. Mom called as Harlow headed out on her errands.

"How's it going?" No "hello" or "how are you?" Just *"How's it going?"*

"Did I tell you I have a job at a roller-skating rink?"

"You don't skate."

"I sell tickets, count money, wash windows, take out the trash."

"Harlow, you're an international beauty. Why are you working at a roller rink? How's the diet? How much have you lost?"

In moments like these, Harlow wondered about her mother's love. Matt's comment on Mom's controlling ways was nothing new. Half the modeling world had made the same observation.

To be sure, their relationship was complicated. Beyond the typical mother-daughter angst. Anne and Harlow Hayes needed each other somehow. For Mom, Harlow seemed to fill an unseen void. For Harlow, it was a profound need to please the woman who'd given her life.

"I'm not sure."

"You've been down there a month, Harlow. Time is of the essence if you want the CCW job. You're—"

"Mom, please, stop. What about you? How are the vacation plans with Dad?"

"I'm sending you a book on the Atkins diet." The woman didn't know the meaning of the word *stop*. "It's supposed to help shed pounds quickly. I tried a few recipes. I think you'll like it. Vacation is postponed. Maybe after you sign with CCW, we can all go."

"Me? I'll be working. Mom, is everything—" Dare she ask? Prod into her parents' marriage? Harlow softened. Despite being a complicated woman, Mom loved her family. "Hey, thanks for calling. I've got some errands to run before work."

Walking down her front sidewalk toward Biggs, Harlow felt at home with the sights and sounds of Sea Blue Beach. She passed the Tasty Dip with resolve and entered the grocery store's ice-cold atmosphere. Usually after a Mom call, she reached for *comfort* in the form of pralines and cream. Today, *comfort* was the face of the big green scale.

Glancing around to ensure the coast was clear, Harlow Hayes kicked off her Keds as a trio of ladies entered, glancing at her with a sense of curiosity and sympathy.

For the first time in her life, Harlow felt a part of the general womanhood. She was down with them in the struggle. No longer one of the beautiful people who appeared to have it all together.

"Hello," she said tentatively. "Do you know if this scale is accurate?"

"I have never stepped on that thing," the tall one said.

"I've not stepped on a scale in twenty years," the second lady said, patting Harlow's arm. "They're such liars."

Harlow laughed, while the third woman gave her the once-over. "You look familiar." But she didn't wait for an answer. Just pushed her squeaky-wheel cart into the store. "Let's go, y'all."

Well, that was fun. Harlow faced Big Green. Liar or not, she had to get a handle on things if she wanted the CCW job. She cringed as the needle swung far—very far—to the right. Oh. Wow. She had no idea. If this scale lied, it lied big!

She felt punched and, frankly, sad. Not because she'd eaten all the forbidden foods of her childhood or rebelled against the standards of her mother and the modeling world, but for giving Xander and her emotions so much power.

Grabbing a shopping cart, she crossed several things off her list—pint of ice cream, peanuts, chocolate syrup—and aimed for the produce section, her confidence from the morning with Matt waning.

Maybe Mom was right. Harlow Hayes needed her.

"Hey, H, are you following me?" Matt strolled toward her with his silver-screen smile. She felt nervous, as if Big Green had plastered her weight on her forehead. But Matt's attention and smile faded as he noticed the cashier. "Trinity. Hello. I didn't know you were back in Sea Blue Beach. It's been a long time since—"

"Let's not reminisce and pretend, Matt." Trinity took Harlow's check, then jotted down her driver's license number without a blink at her name, cashed her out, and handed over the short receipt. "Have a nice day."

Harlow exited the register lane with a glance between Matt and the slender woman with even features and tawny skin.

"What's the story behind that icy exchange?" she whispered.

"Nothing. Look, I need to cash a check. The line at the bank was too long. Wait for me?"

Harlow rested against the end of a closed cash register, the number on the big green scale running through her mind. If she was serious about CCW, she'd have to lose at least forty pounds. After the meeting, they'd ask for another ten. Even then, she'd be fifteen pounds above her supermodel weight.

Did she want to rejoin the grind? Get back into the world of haute couture, rabbit food, and protruding bones? Yes. Because it seemed to be the best way to break Xander's hold on her.

At customer service, Matt chatted with the man behind the counter and Harlow Hayes wondered what it'd be like to lean against Matt's thick chest.

She startled when the magazine vendor stocking the aisle dropped the most recent issue of *People* at her feet. Xander and Davina were on the cover, alongside the headline, *The Coles' Amazing Wedding Plans. Page 21*.

Harlow squinted at the image, bending for a closer look. Oh my gosh, Davina was wearing Harlow's Van Cleef & Arpels Amoureux diamond watch. The one Xander gave her on their first anniversary. *"Magic,"* he'd said. *"We're magic together."*

When he *finally* talked to her after the breakup, he told her it was lost.

Air. She needed air.

"Matt, I'll see you later, okay?" She started for the exit, feeling nervous and full of her failures, but slowed when she heard the familiar whir of a camera shutter.

Paparazzi? In Sea Blue Beach? She scanned the front of the store for a photographer. Listened for more shutter sounds. Except for Matt signing a few autographs, the magazine vendor, a cashier stocking gum and candy, and Trinity, who was cleaning her register, the store was empty.

"Harlow, wait." Matt jogged toward her. "Is everything okay?"

"Xander and Davina are on the cover of *People*. I was on the cover with him once. 'The Billionaire and the Beauty.' I don't get it, Matt. Of all the things he told me about her, I can't believe he . . . well, they were high school sweethearts. It's hard to compete with that kind of history." Now that she started talking, Harlow couldn't stop. "Did you see a photographer anywhere? I thought I heard a shutter click. Next week I'll probably be on the cover of *National Enquirer*." She was shaking, fighting tears.

"Hey, hey, Harlow, it's going to be all right. Don't let Xander get to you. He's a putz. So is she." Matt wrapped her in his arms, as if he'd done so a thousand times. "Let's get your stuff home and then have a little Blue Plate therapy."

"Thanks but no thanks." She freed herself and headed for the exit. "I just stepped on the big green scale, so I won't be eating until 1988."

"Very funny, H. You have to eat to lose weight, and this isn't about food. Where's your car? Did you walk?" He retrieved her bags from the cart and pointed to his Porsche. "We'll drop these at your place, then go to the Blue Plate for a Diet Coke or iced tea."

"Why are you so nice to me, Matt? And I should remind you that you're my *boss*."

"Okay, let's drop the boss business." He closed the trunk and walked around to the passenger door. "Why wouldn't I be nice, H? Besides, it's time to shed my bad-boy ways." He glanced at her. "I'm not that guy."

"Thank goodness you've come to that revelation." Matt held her hand as she folded into the passenger seat. "And you're nice to me because the former Most Beautiful Woman in the World is a mockery. A punch line."

"Are you? 'Cause I'm not laughing."

14

MATT

The diner was quiet, waiting for the lunch rush. Miss Beulah, a friend of Granny's, manned the Blue Plate's hostess stand today, making napkin rolls.

"Well, bless my eyes! Look who's here." She ruffled Matt's hair and leaned toward Harlow. "I remember him when he was running around town in his underdrawers."

"Really? Do tell."

"I was three," Matt protested.

"Now he's a big star. Tuesday's so proud." Miss Beulah clutched a couple of menus against her ample chest and walked toward the large Gulf-facing pane window. "A booth in the back?"

When she passed out the menus, her gaze lingered on Harlow. If she said anything about her looking like Harlow Hayes, Matt planned to announce, "*Because she* is *Harlow Hayes.*" She couldn't hide forever.

Miss Beulah took their drink order. Matt ordered a Coke and

Harlow a Diet Coke. When he opened his menu, she shoved hers aside.

"I can't keep doing what I'm doing. Not if I want to move on from Xander and win the CCW job." She stared off for a moment. "Some ladies walked in as I was about to step on the scale. One of them told me the scale was a liar." She smiled softly. "I don't think it lied today."

"Did you want it to lie?"

"Actually, no. It feels good to be honest with myself. Matt, when I saw those women, I felt like one of them. Not some prima donna with an unrealistically thin body, walking the runway in a ten-thousand-dollar dress." She leaned toward him. "So, what's the deal with you and that cashier?"

"Oooh, sorry, you've hit your first red light."

"I see. She's the one that got away? Ooo, is she the girl you kissed? Patti What's-her-name?"

"No. She's the sister of my best friend. Former best friend."

"Former is very telling."

Should he confess? Just say it? *"I ruined my friend's life, Harlow."* Instead, he said, "For the record, I like you as you are, Harlow."

When she smiled, the dark, cold spot in the core of his being at the mention of Booker Nickle warmed a little. "You are so good at changing the subject."

"So are you."

"And you don't have to say you like me as I am now. No one else does."

"Who cares? Do you like yourself?"

"I like who I am now, sitting with you in this booth."

"Me too. Because I see the in-command girl I met on set. HH, head of the boardroom, walking in like a boss."

"That girl was terrified. Her confidence was fake. She wanted people to believe she belonged there. That she'd earned the part."

"We did believe you. I watched you, and your confidence was

not fake. And don't credit Xander for any of your success. You knew who you were the first day."

Miss Beulah set down their sodas, and Harlow took a long sip. She ordered a house salad with oil and vinegar. Matt ordered the same.

"When I was asked to audition for *Talk to Me Sweetly*, I felt like I'd earned that on my own. Not because Mom knocked on the right door, which she miraculously, mysteriously did when we first went to New York. But the part of Bryn was all me—well, that and being named Most Beautiful. Which I'm proud of because I think my hard work earned me the title. But if you ever tell anyone, I'll deny it."

"My lips are sealed. Hang onto the feeling," Matt said. "You'll earn the CCW job too, if it's what you want. Do you? What does HH want for her life?"

She fiddled with her napkin roll. "Honest?"

"Honest," he said.

"Don't laugh." She peered at him. "Harlow Hayes wants to rep CCW. But little ol' me wants to be a wife and mom. Not very modern, is it?"

"Don't look now, but Matt Knight wants to be a Hollywood superstar, but little ol' me wants to be a husband and father." Their laughter mingled and roped another piece of him. "Is that what happened with Xander? He didn't want a family?"

"He wanted a family as much as I did. On our very first date, we talked about kids and where we would raise them. It was like we were already engaged."

"So it was true love?"

She smiled softly. "Pretty much."

Miss Beulah arrived with their salads. "A bird couldn't live on this, but I suppose you know what you're doing."

Matt reached for the oil and vinegar after Harlow sparingly dressed her salad. "So what happened? All I heard was you mutually decided to go your separate ways."

"According to Xander's press agent." She stabbed at her salad without taking a bite. "I've never told anyone the whole story. Not Mom or Jinx or my therapist."

"You don't have to tell me, Harlow."

"It's just so humiliating and painful. How could someone I loved, who said he loved me, treat me the way he did?"

"Matt, Matt, Matt." Dale Cranston's pear-shaped shadow fell over the table. "How long are you in town?"

"We're in the middle of a conversation here, Dale." Matt sat back, guarded.

"My apologies." Dale shifted the toothpick in his mouth from one side to the other. "You're not going to win on this eminent domain thing."

"And here I was expecting to see your John Hancock on the petition for a vote."

Dale removed the toothpick as he laughed. "Hollywood made a dreamer out of you. I'll tell you what, though, the prince knew what he was doing when he built the rink on the rock. That's why we're reclaiming the land. With the rink out of the way, we can move forward, embrace progress, do what needs to be done. Can't live in the past, Matty."

Dale had always been an arrogant blowhard. Even when Matt worked for him at the theater, he'd kept a running dialogue against Granny and the Starlight. Of course, Matt reported back to her. The only reason he worked there was because Granny made him.

"I made the mistake with your pa and uncle of leaning on them too much for the Starlight. You go work for someone else. It'll be good for you. Besides, I prefer the title of Granny, not boss."

"We're not trying to live in the past," Matt said. "We're all for progress. Just not for destroying the best part of this town."

"You're David, and we're Goliath," Dale said. "Can't fight city hall, you know."

"Dale, Goliath lost."

"Whatever. Matt, be realistic. Tuesday is too old and decrepit to run the rink. Are you going to give up your career for the Starlight?" He held out his hand to Harlow. "Dale Cranston, Matt's old boss at the Midnight movie theater. This boy ate his weight in popcorn, but I like to think the Midnight is the reason he fell in love with the movies."

Harlow offered her hand, which Cranston held too long.

"Have we met?" He stepped back to glance at Harlow up and down. "I've seen you before. Where have I seen you?"

"Dale, this is Harlow Hayes. She played Bryn in *Talk to Me Sweetly*. Which you just showed at the Midnight."

"By golly, I heard you blimped up, but dang, girl." Dale scrunched up his face. "Is this why that millionaire dumped you?" He puffed out his cheeks and held his arms wide to indicate an expanded girth. "You were gorgeous in the movie, but wow—" He swatted Matt on the arm with the back of his hand. "Guess she's pretty enough for a tumble or two, am I right?"

Son of a—

Matt threw the first punch as he slid from the booth, then finished Dale with an uppercut, and cross. The rube movie theater owner and city councilman tumbled backward into a waitress loaded down with dirty dishes. Food and white porcelain went everywhere as the two of them Geronimoed into the adjacent table. Audra and the staff spilled out of the kitchen, demanding to know what was going on.

Matt apologized, dropped a wad of cash on the table, and grabbed Harlow's hand. "Let's go."

15

TUESDAY

MARCH 1937

"You serve a mean pot roast, Tuesday." Doc shoved his plate forward and patted his belly. "I'd ask for your buttery potatoes with gravy as my last meal."

"Don't flatter her, Doc." Leroy lit a cigarette and shot her a wink. The knife scar down the side of his cheek was new. Longer and deeper than the one Doc bore. More evidence of his dangerous games. "Tooz already knows she's worth a million smackeroos."

How would he know when he was never around? After being shot, Leroy hadn't changed. He came and went just like before, only now appearing with a knife wound.

At night, he nuzzled her with kisses, wearing down her resistance until she gave into him and pretended things were as they used to be. Afterward, he'd fall asleep with a lit cigarette dangling from his full lips.

Sleep never came easy for Tuesday on those nights when she

still buzzed with his love. She'd take his cigarette downstairs, stand by the window facing the Starlight, and finish the last few puffs.

The neon light atop the roof anchored her when it felt as if life was out of her control.

"Pie for dessert?" Tuesday gathered the dishes with a glance at Doc and Lee, then called to the boys, who'd been excused to the living room. "LJ, Dup? Blueberry with a dollop of ice cream?"

"Pie? I want pie." Dup ran in, leaned on his dad's chair, and almost set his chin on Lee's head. But he wasn't quite brave enough. Lee could be a bit . . . testy. Yet so affectionate, tussling with the boys in the yard, tossing the football. At the moment, Dup didn't know which side of his pa sat at the table.

At sixteen, Dup was cute and charming, yet still awkwardly finding his way in his world. It didn't help he had to swim in his older brother's wake. At eighteen, LJ was a full-grown man, a chip off the Leroy block. Square-jawed, handsome, and star of every sport the school offered. Tuesday suspected his achievements were to spite his dad. *See, I didn't need you.*

But Tuesday knew different. He needed Lee's approval very much. She saw the letters he tucked into Leroy's bag on his way to bed or out the door for school. To her knowledge, Leroy never responded.

That being said, she was still Ma around this place. "Dup, you and LJ clear the table and wash the dishes," she said. "You can have dessert while listening to the *Lone Ranger*."

"You do it, LJ. I did it last night." Dupree casually reached for the last dinner roll, but Lee shot out of his chair and grabbed him by the collar. "Don't you mouth off to your ma. Ever."

Dup's eyes filled with tears and his cheeks burned red as he cut a glance at Doc.

"Hey, boy, you look at me when I'm talking to you." Lee was harsh because he wanted their respect. He'd forgotten it was earned.

"They're your sons, not one of the boys on your crew," she'd told him.

Tuesday gently touched Leroy's shoulder as she passed toward the pie safe. "It's all right. The boys and I sort of have a tradition. I tell them to do something, and they whine and complain, but they always mind. Isn't that right, boys?"

"Yes, ma'am." Dupree stepped back as Leroy released him. LJ stood with his arms folded, a defiant air about him.

"Got to be tough with boys, Doc. You had daughters, but with boys . . ." Leroy pounded his fist against his palm. "You got to make men out of them."

"I agree. Boys are different, but, Lee, sons need love and tenderness as much as girls, if not more. I've seen—"

Leroy laughed. "You're soft in your old age, Doc."

Leroy, please. Pie should sweeten him up, though. Always did. And she'd try to get ahead of things tonight, put on her lacy nightgown and see if she couldn't gentle him down, say some things that need saying. He took truth easier after lovemaking.

"Can I make the coffee, Tuesday?" Doc said. He'd become a regular at her table and knew how many scoops to put in the percolator.

After nursing Leroy's gunshot wound, Doc came around every other week or so. The other day, he showed the boys how to plow up a little garden in the sandy soil and told them which crops to plant. He instructed them how to properly stack firewood and fix a leak on the roof. All the things their daddy should've taught them.

In turn, they took Doc to the beach and taught him to fish in the surf. He provided the Knight household with a calming, stabilizing presence. He helped with dinner and homework and read to all of them from the Psalms and Proverbs before bed.

"Pardon me." Doc maneuvered behind her, his hand grazing her hip. He took the cups from the shelf and returned to the table, leaving his fragrance to cloud Tuesday's thoughts.

"I could join you in Montgomery," he said to Leroy. "If you need."

"Might be a good idea, Doc. There's bound to be some . . ." He shot a look at Tuesday.

"Don't stop on my account," she said. "You've been shot and sliced. I don't think you're a traveling salesman, Leroy."

"How's the rink, Tooz?" Leroy pulled her down to his lap when she set his pie in front of him. "I stopped by the bank. That new teller, Cletus, told me you're in the black. Good to know you're not squandering money at the beauty parlor and the dress shop."

"Do I look like I've been to the beauty parlor? And I've had this dress since before we were married." It still fit, thank God, even if the waist was a bit tight.

At the sink, the boys tossed suds at each other but managed to get the dishes washed, dried, and put away. "I'll do the pots," she said as she handed them each a large slice of pie and scoop of ice cream in white china bowls. These dishes were the only thing her grandmother left behind. "Hurry, or you'll miss your program."

"You should get them a new radio, Lee," Doc said. "That old thing takes twenty minutes to warm up."

Leroy shrugged and dug into his pie, thanked Doc for the coffee when he filled his cup, then made his way into the living room to listen to the *Lone Ranger*.

"Need any help with the pots?" Doc said.

"You best go in with the boys." For the hundredth time today, Tuesday noticed the small crack running down the side of the sink window. She flipped on the light as the last of the western sunset glowed above the horizon. "I don't want Leroy getting ideas something's up between us. He's not always rational."

"What ideas might those be?" Doc leaned against the counter with a damp dish towel slung over his shoulder.

"Well, nothing, of course, but like I said, Lee's not always rational."

"You know why I come around, Tooz?" Doc spoke low and gazed at his polished shoes.

The warm kitchen suddenly felt cold. "Why, you—you come around to help out. Which, you know, the boys and I really—"

"If you don't know, I'll leave it." He snapped the towel in the air and draped it over the rack by the door to dry. "I know I'm old enough to be your father, but I thought it was time to be honest."

"Sometimes honesty means we say nothing at all." She tipped her head toward the living room. "You best get in there, hear what the Lone Ranger is up to."

He squeezed her arm as he passed, and when she was alone in the kitchen, a deep sob broke her composure. *Oh, Doc.* Leaving the pot and pan in the now-tepid dishwater with fading suds, she made her way to the back stoop.

The North Florida air was fragrant with the hope of spring. The golden light along the horizon blended with the neon colors of the Starlight. Burt manned the rink tonight, and by the notes on the breeze, he'd raised the panels to release the music of a newly reborn Dirk.

She'd suspected Doc loved her. She'd seen it in his eyes a few times. But since he said nothing, nor made a move her direction, she'd let herself rely on him as a friend. Tonight's exchange changed things. Gazing at the Starlight, his words in her ears, she resented him slightly for telling her.

Every part of her was intertwined with the Starlight—her childhood, her teen years, meeting Leroy, raising the boys. If she left Lee, which *had* occurred to her on occasion, for the love of a good man, she'd lose everything that defined Tuesday Knight.

She jumped when the screen door creaked behind her. Leroy stepped down to the driveway and kicked at the thin gravel. "Doc's got a lot of nerve." He struck a match against the bottom of his shoe and lit his cigarette. "Telling me to buy the boys a new radio."

"Why don't you? You built the one we have now before we were married."

"It still works." He blew out a long stream of smoke toward the barn, which by now was really nothing more than an oversized shed that leaned too far left. "Don't want the boys to get spoiled."

Tuesday scoffed. "How you reckon? They wear hand-me-down clothes, live in a house that was once a fishing shack, and their mother cooks on a wood-burning stove." Lee gave her a hard look, which she returned. She'd not kowtow to him, and every word she spoke was true. "You talk big about making a better life for us, but you don't seem to mind the ribbed lines have worn off your sons' corduroys and the rubber's peeled away from their sneakers."

"You should tell me these things."

"When would that be?" Tuesday shifted from Doc's confession to Leroy's dereliction of duty. "When you breeze in town for a day? When you're laid up in bed with a wound? You scared the beans out of LJ when you were shot. Did you know that? Never mind that slice down your cheek."

"Boys need to learn life is hard."

"Lee, we're very aware life is hard and unfair. But some people add fuel to the fire. A lot of men go through life without getting shot or cut." She sank to sit on the porch steps. "Why *did* you get shot? Who cut you? Why, if you're working so hard, do I live in this shack with a stove from the last century, wearing dresses I bought before we were married?"

"You don't think I want to do better by you and the boys? What do you think I'm doing out there?"

"I have no earthly idea, Lee. That's the point. Did a lawman shoot you?"

He crushed his cigarette on the sun-bleached concrete walk. "Maybe."

"Have mercy, Lee. Will you stop this life? I won't have some lawman or mobster knocking down my door looking for you. This town talks. We know what men like Capone or the Trafficante gang do to folks they don't like."

A note hit the air. More music from the Starlight. Tuesday moved past Leroy to listen. Dirk was playing "Take Me Out to the Ball Game." She wished she was skating.

Lee wrapped his arms around her. "I'll get the boys a new radio."

"I'd rather you find a job around here and treat them with kindness."

"I don't mean to be harsh, Tooz." He kissed her neck. "I'll do better. I promise. But for now . . ." He kissed her lips. "I love you. You know I do."

"Then come home for good, Lee. Please. That's all I ask."

16

HARLOW

She was in the sound booth talking with Nora, the rink's best DJ, who wanted to know everything—*simply everything*—about being in a Bon Jovi music video, when Matt found her.

"Was he cool?" Nora perched on her stool, wide-eyed.

"Yeah, he was cool. Really cool." Harlow turned at Matt's touch, the morning's *Gazette* in hand.

"They ran the story. Not as favorable toward the rink as I'd like, but . . . Hey, Nora, how are you?"

"Amazing. I'm breathing the same air as someone who touched Jon Bon Jovi."

"What?" Matt said, his attention on the article. "I never met Bon Jovi."

"Not you, McFly." Nora tapped Matt's forehead. "I'm cuing up JBJ's greatest hits for this afternoon's session."

"Knock yourself out." Matt passed the Friday, April 3 *Gazette* to Harlow. "Rachel wrote the story herself, and by the way it reads, she's known about the eminent domain strategy for a while. When I talked to her, she acted like the *Gazette* was neutral, only reporting the news as it came. But clearly this is a well-written, well-researched piece in favor of progress. Which tells me the domain story was in the queue, waiting for the right time, probably alongside the Starlight's obituary."

"How long have you been dealing with the press, Matt? Of course she knew." Harlow reached for his hand. The one with the bruised knuckles. "Have you heard anything from the man you hit? Do you think he'll file charges?"

"Dale? No. He cares too much what people think. It's one thing to get punched in a near-empty diner. It's another to have it appear in the *Gazette* because he filed charges against a Hollywood star. Against *the* Lieutenant Striker."

"You didn't have to hit him on my account." Yet his passionate defense of her made her look at him, and even herself, in a new light.

"Yes, I did. I'd do it again, Harlow. Just call my name and—"

"I'll be there."

"I would." Matt said, eyes on the newspaper. "You can count on me."

There was a catch of emotion in his voice that popped the sound booth's atmosphere and filled Harlow with a confident warmth.

Nora made a small commotion with a stack of CDs, then hollered toward the door as she rushed out. "What? Spike, you need me?"

Harlow glanced at Matt with a laugh. "She thinks you're getting mushy."

"Mushy? Naw, just a guy talking to a girl. His friend."

"Exactly." Harlow reached for the newspaper with waves of the shy sixteen-year-old crushing on Logan Howard. "Do you think you should apologize? To Dale?"

She scanned the *Gazette's* bold headline: *THE STARLIGHT TO GIVE WAY FOR PROGRESS.*

"I'll apologize if he does," Matt said.

"It never hurts to go first, Matt. Hey, this article says he's one of the town councilmen." She looked up. "You might consider going first. He could make trouble for the petition."

"Maybe, but I'm not the only one who knows he's a jerk. As for the petition, Mary finally got them posted in the courthouse and the post office. Tyler finished the flyers. I'm going to pick them up." He leaned in and kissed her forehead. "See you later." He paused at the door. "Did I just kiss your forehead?"

"You did." He was doing it, drawing her in, gaining her trust, making her feel like she was wanted in his world.

"I don't know why," he said. "I can't say habit because I kiss no one that way. Not even Granny."

"It's fine. Let's not make a thing of it."

"You're acting weird." He exhaled. "Are things going to be weird?"

"Just go." She shooed him out the door. "Get the flyers. Forget it. And, Matt, for the record, I'd be there for you too."

When he'd gone, she tried to read the article, but she kept reliving that split-second kiss, the warmth of his lips radiating on her skin.

"Are you two a thing?" Nora returned to the sound booth.

"We're just friends. You didn't have to pretend Spike needed you."

"I felt like a third wheel."

"You weren't." Harlow slipped from her stool. "I'm going to open up."

Afterward, she perched at the ticket desk, skimming the last of the article.

Sea Blue Beach's founder, Prince Rein Titus Alexander Blue of Lauchtenland, a royal sovereign nation, was born in 1857. After his wife and son died during childbirth, the prince set sail around the world. The 1882 storm off the coast of Cuba sent his yacht into the Gulf, where he lost his crew. He, along with broken pieces of his ship, washed ashore. Prince Blue died a hero on the Somme in 1918.

He lost his wife and child. Founded this great town. Died on the Somme. A hero. And Harry Smith wanted to demolish his legacy. A man like the prince deserved to be remembered. Honored. In that moment, Harlow felt as if her journey and the prince's, no matter how improbable, landed both of them on these shores for a reason.

One by one, skaters trickled in. Friday afternoon was a fairly busy session, and Tuesday warned her it would be even more so during the summer. Around one thirty, a group of retirees from the Nickle High class reunion of 1920 and 1921 ventured into the Starlight. Tuesday came out from her office and greeted them like family, which Harlow was beginning to understand as the heart of the Starlight.

"I haven't seen a couple of them in years," Tuesday said, looking very young in her tan slacks and pale blue blouse, a black bow clipped in her silver hair. "Harriet will be disappointed she missed it. I told her not to move to Melbourne Beach."

"Who's Harriet again?" Harlow smiled at the young couple entering, who looked like they needed a break from the sun.

"I forget you've not lived here your whole life. Morris and Harriet Nickle used to own your place. Matt may have told you about them. Harriet was my best friend, and her son, Abel, was best friend to my boys. Her grandson Booker was Matt's best friend. For a while, anyway." Tuesday's light faded. "They've not talked in years. Sad shame, really."

"His sister Trinity was my cashier at Biggs. She gave Matt a cool greeting."

"I'm not surprised." Tuesday pointed the sunburned couple to the skate room, then picked up the *Gazette*. "I've not seen this yet. Matt said it favors eminent domain."

"I liked the last paragraph about the town founder. Seems like a fairy tale to think Sea Blue Beach was founded by a real prince."

"I knew him my whole life, but when my mamaw left me behind, he was my savior. Gave me a job and place to live." Her voice faded as she remembered. "He left a few months later for the war, and all these years later, I still miss him."

"So we have to save his Starlight," Harlow said.

"I knew you'd catch the vision." Tuesday gave her a knowing smile. "Yet in the end, the prince always said, the life of the rink belonged to Immanuel."

"The man on the wall?"

"He's more than a man, Harlow," Tuesday said. "He's God with us."

17

MATT

Small southern towns moved slow. He understood that, but for Tyler to put him off again was too much.

"You said the flyers were done," Matt said.

"No, I said I was doing them, but then a big order came in for Harry's business and—"

"Tyler, you see what he's doing."

"Yeah, yeah, I know. Stonewalling us."

Matt pulled out his credit card. "I'm paying for his order and adding extra to have ours done today. Come on, Ty, all you need is a photo of the rink and some text. 'Save the Starlight. Sign the petitions at the courthouse and post office.'"

Matt had checked both petition locations on his way to Copycat. So far, they had four signatures. Really three. Dominic Moreno signed in both places. And he felt sure Jeremy Chambers, a Nickle High basketball star, was not old enough to vote. So two. They had two signatures.

Come on, Sea Blue Beach. Let's save the Starlight.

Tyler promised to have the flyers done by five, and Matt headed back to the rink. When Harlow looked up from the ticket booth, he had that flip-flop feeling, the kind that made a man write poetry and croon a love song.

He'd not given much thought to why he kissed her, except he wanted to kiss her again . . . a few inches below her forehead.

"Did you get the flyers?" She tore at the cellophane around a new roll of tickets.

"Harry gave him a big job, so Tyler put ours on hold. I'm sure it's part of his strategy to get in our way." Matt checked to see how many skaters were on the floor. His goal for now was to save the rink. After that, he'd figure ways to improve business. A group of senior citizens slowly skated, clinging to one another. "Who's out there? Where's the floor guard?"

"A Nickle High reunion," Harlow said. "Class of Twenty and Twenty-one. Your granny was excited to see them. Craig was supposed to be floor guard but didn't show."

"Then let's just remove the Starlight from Craig's things-to-forget. I'll call his house, let him know his services are no longer needed. I'll be the floor guard." He started to walk off. "Unless you want to do it?"

"I don't skate."

"Hmmm, we'll see."

Matt called Craig's house, gave his mother the news. Then called Simon Caster, the kid who mowed Harlow's lawn and delivered pizza for Tony's. He was always hustling. "Simon, Matt Knight. You want a job at the Starlight?"

As Matt exchanged his Adidas for his skates and looped the whistle lanyard around his neck, his old high school buddy, Milo Patitucci, walked in, flashing his Sea Blue Beach PD badge.

"Got a minute?"

"Sure. What's up?" Matt peered toward the rink floor as Nora called for the Hokey Pokey. "Make it quick, Milo. Got no floor guard and a bunch of senior citizens about to put their right foot in and their left foot out. We might need to dial 9-1-1."

"What happened at the Blue Plate?" Milo crossed his arms and leaned against the sound booth wall.

"Is this about Dale Cranston?"

"You know it is, Matt. You hit him?"

Matt started to speak, then remembered the advice of his LA lawyer, Norman Lundquist III, who worked his legal magic for Matt a couple of times. *"Keep your mouth shut."*

"Is that what he's saying?"

"He's pressing charges, Matt. I'd like to punch his arrogant face too, but even in Sea Blue Beach, punching a man is a first-degree misdemeanor." Milo held up a slip of paper. "Right or wrong, Judge Hart signed a warrant for your arrest. He and Dale used to bowl together."

"At that old Tin Pins Alley? It shut down years ago, which is no surprise when you misspell the number ten."

"Also not a crime." Milo waved the warrant. "I got to haul you in, Matt. You'll see the judge tonight."

"Haul me in?" He laughed, but Milo did not. "Okay, fine, then I want to file charges against Dale Cranston for insulting the Starlight and Harlow."

"Fine, but first—" Officer Patitucci reached for his cuffs. "I can do this outside if you want."

"I don't need cuffs."

"Procedure. Also, Dale hired a lawyer. He's claiming your training with Chuck Norris makes you a life-threatening weapon. Did you really hit him with a jab, cross, uppercut?"

"I plead the Fifth, Milo. The Fifth."

"Okay, off with the skates, Matt. Let's go. By the way, who's the brownish-blonde at the ticket booth?"

"The woman Dale insulted." Matt jerked the skates' laces. "Harlow Hayes."

"*The* Harlow Hayes?"

"Yes, *the* Harlow Hayes." Matt tugged off the skates, returned them to the office, and reached for his sneakers. Unbelievable.

"She, uh, gained some weight."

"Which is what Dale so rudely commented on . . . among other things."

"What's she doing in Sea Blue Beach?"

"Apparently working at the Starlight."

Milo jiggled the cuffs and pointed to the door. "The squad car's right outside. I figured you'd want this on the DL, though I *did* see a reporter at the courthouse when I headed over here."

Perfect. And he'd truly believed Dale would never want that punch to go beyond the walls of the diner.

Matt asked for a minute to tell Spike where he was going.

The big man laughed. "Did you really punch him? Don't answer. I'll just say he's had it coming for decades. Want me to call Dup?"

"He's got one of those phones in his truck. The number's on the wall in the office."

Just outside the rink's side door, Milo cuffed Matt and helped him into the back seat.

"I loved *Flight Deck*, bro. Seen it three times."

"Don't try to flatter me when I'm handcuffed, Milo." Matt stared out the window. Harlow was right. He shouldn't have hit Dale. Watch. The state will offer a deal to drop the charges if Matt left town for six months. Which would mean he couldn't fight for the Starlight. Well, he'd not take it. He was going to see it through. Maybe, in some small way, redeem himself. Get rid of that thing eating him up inside.

"Can we stop at the Blue Plate for a burger? I'm starved. My treat."

"I'll call in an order once I book you." Milo glanced at him through the rearview mirror. "I tried to talk Dale out of it, Matt. I swear. That's why he went to the judge."

The jail was in the back of the courthouse, and if the world was in black-and-white, Matt would think he was in Mayberry. A reporter waited at the entrance.

"Matt Knight? Tebow Gains from the *Gazette*. Is it true you punched Dale Cranston for no reason?" He stuck a small tape recorder under Matt's chin.

"Tebow." Milo shoved him out of the way. "Do you really think he's going to confess? You have enough for your story."

Tebow refused to stand down. "Why'd you punch him?"

"Who said I punched him?"

That went on for a few minutes until Milo tossed young Tebow out the door. Thus the story began of how Matt Knight, Hollywood star and Sea Blue Beach hometown boy, was photographed, fingerprinted, and locked up for defending the honor of the Starlight, his granny, and the charming, exquisitely beautiful Harlow Hayes.

"What do you want on your burger? The works?" Milo angled back to see Matt in the cell, phone to his ear. "You want fries and a Coke?"

"And a slice of apple pie. When do I make my phone call?"

"As soon as I order. Audra, hey, Officer Patitucci here. . . . You heard already? On the radio? News travels fast. Yeah, a couple of burgers with the works and . . ." When he hung up, he released Matt to make his call.

Dad answered his truck phone on the first ring. "Spike called. Told me everything. I called a lawyer."

"Who'd you call? I have a lawyer in LA. His number is in my leather—"

"You don't want an LA lawyer for this, Matt. Besides, when could he even get here? Two, three days? A week?"

"He can call the judge."

"Bodie Nickle is on his way. He knows our legal system, every judge and lawyer."

"Bodie." Booker's older brother. Matt would've laughed except for the shock of it all. "Bodie Nickle is not going to defend me. He may actually volunteer to prosecute me."

"Like I said, he's on his way."

"I don't know, Dad. I saw Trinity at Biggs, and the look she gave me . . . even Harlow noticed."

"Well, I trust Bodie. Give him a chance."

Give him a chance? Matt hung up with a sense of doom. But he had it coming. He'd skirted the law a few times. Every once in a while, it got to win.

"I see justice has been served." Dale Cranston strolled in, puffed up and puffed out with a yellowish-blue bruise under his right eye.

Where'd he get that shiner? Matt had popped him on the chin, where admittedly there was a fading mark.

"Dale." Milo stepped between the two men. "You can't harass the prisoner. Go on home."

"I'm not harassing." He pointed at Matt. "You can't come into this town and act like one of them kids in the Hollywood brat pack. Nobody around here is going to kiss your fanny because you were in a few movies."

"You're just mad 'cause your theater is second run and can't get *Flight Deck* until everyone's seen it in Niceville," Milo said, steering Matt back to the cell. "Dale, scoot."

Stretched out on the cot, Matt listened to the sounds of the jail—Milo offering Dale his own cell if he didn't skedaddle. The door opening, then closing. The creak of Milo's chair. The click and slide of a desk drawer. The snap of a stapler and the sharp timbre of a ringing phone.

"Sea Blue Beach PD, Officer Patitucci here." He listened with an eye on Matt. "Who is this? Yeah, sure." He shoved his desk chair to the cell, dragging the receiver and the long cord with him. "It's your agent."

Matt reached between the bars for the phone and pressed it to his ear. "Cosmo?"

"Are you in jail?"

"Why? Is it in *Variety* already?"

"I called your dad, looking for you. Got him on his truck phone. I've got to get me one of those."

"You'd never have a moment of peace. The car is the one place clients can't get to you."

"Food for thought, food for thought. Listen, Cindy Canon doesn't like her new co-star."

"Who is it?"

"Conner Reid."

"Not surprised. I can see it. He can be a bit much, even though he has that British accent."

"So, this is your lucky day. Okay, maybe not since you're in jail, but you're back on the project. I told you getting out of town would improve your reputation."

"It's only been three weeks."

"In Hollywood, that's like three years. You in?"

"What do you think?" he said. "As soon as I get out of here, I'll head to LA. Oh, wait, Cos, I'm helping my granny save the Starlight."

"You got time. Roger Woods is working out the details with Conner's contract. My guess is he'll start rehearsals sometime in May."

"Then I'm in." He'd have to work out something with Dad and Harlow for the Starlight. "But, Cos, I'll need to fly home the end of May. Get it in my contract."

As much as he loved the idea of getting back to work, especially with Cindy, he felt sad about leaving Granny. And, to be honest, Harlow.

"I'll overnight an updated script. Why were you arrested anyway?"

"Punching someone."

"I don't get you, Matt. You're not *that* guy. But you keep trying to be *that* guy. One day I'd like to know why."

"Me and you both." But Matt had an inkling. Deep down.

As he handed the phone to Milo, the burgers arrived. He doled out the food, then pulled his chair over to the cell.

"Remember the homecoming touchdown your sophomore year?" Milo laughed through a big bite of his burger. "You smoked the Chipley secondary in a post route for an eighty-seven-yard pass. Secured the regional championship for us."

"I twisted my ankle on that play. Then the team piled on, and I limped off the field with an ankle sprain, three bruised ribs, and a dislocated shoulder. Had to sit out the state championship."

"Still a great game, man. When the guys get together, we still talk about it." Milo reached for his soda. "Dude, you should join us one night. We gather on the deck of the Fish Hook. They'd love to see you."

"Maybe." The placeholder answer for "probably not." In Matt's mind, it was just that kind of night, one of chest-thumping and bragging, that destroyed Booker's life. The aftermath tainted Matt's Sea Blue Beach and Nickle High memories. It was why he hated coming home. Why he let strangers crash his place and destroy it. Maybe even a factor in why he hit Dale Cranston.

"You ever talk to Booker?" Milo said, looking at Matt over the rim of his soda cup.

"Where'd that question come from?"

"The look on your face."

"No, I don't talk to him."

Thankfully, Milo changed the subject. Updated Matt on his latest girlfriend and how she might be the one. He'd bought a place in town and was fixing it up little by little. Then the side door opened, and the lovely Harlow walked in.

"Isn't this *The Life of Riley*?" she said with a big smile.

"Harlow, hey." Matt closed up his lunch container. The fries were already cold.

"I brought you something." She shoved a bag from Sweet Conversations through the bars as Milo exited the room, answering a call on his radio. "Be careful when you bite," she whispered. "There's a teeny-tiny file inside. You'll be out of here in six months, maybe a year."

He wanted to reach through the bars and kiss her. "Is it chocolate? 'Cause if it's not chocolate, I don't think I can—"

"Who do you take me for? Of course it's chocolate." She rested her head against the bars. "Matt, why didn't you tell me you were getting arrested? All because of me. I'm so sorry."

"I'm in here because of me." He raised her chin so he could see her eyes. "This may not be the right time to tell you, but . . ." Matt tested his confession, hungry to say something real and true. "Well, I think I'm falling for—"

"Matt." *Milo, you dumb lug.* "Your deliverer is here." He came around the courthouse entrance with Bodie Nickle, who was dressed in golf clothes.

"I should go." Harlow skirted around Milo and Bodie. "See you later, Matt."

Milo watched her go, then unlocked the cell. "Did we interrupt something?"

"Yep." Matt offered his hand to Bodie. "Thanks for coming."

He tugged off his golf glove. "It's been a long time."

"Are you sure you want to defend me?"

Bodie smirked. "I'm sure. Listen, we're going straight into the judge. We have Harris, not Hart, which is in our favor." Milo cuffed Matt again. "Let me do the talking. You only answer when spoken to, otherwise keep your mouth shut." Bodie gave him a long, hard look. "Think you can do that?"

"Yeah, I can."

In the courtroom, Bodie chatted up the state attorney. They laughed and mimed golf swings. When the clerk called his case number, Bodie motioned Matt forward.

The charges were read, and the judge asked, "How do you plea?"

Bodie answered. "Not guilty, Your Honor."

"So you're Matt Knight, the actor?" Judge Harris glared at him.

"Yes, Your Honor."

"Loved you in *Flight Deck*. Don't love you in my courtroom. What are you doing in Sea Blue Beach?"

"Visiting my grandmother. Trying to save the Starlight."

"I grew up skating there every weekend." He shuffled through papers, then addressed the state attorney, who recommended Matt be released on his own recognizance.

The judge agreed with the slap of his gavel and gave the state a month to bring charges or drop the case. At Dale's behest, his attorney requested a protective order. The judge all but rolled his eyes and told Matt to stay at least five feet away from the plaintiff.

Outside in the breezy cool of the April afternoon, freedom felt good.

"I'll see what I can do to make this go away, Matt," Bodie said. "This case will rely on eyewitness testimony, which can easily be refuted. Our memories are so deceptive. Also, I don't think training with Chuck Norris five years ago makes you lethal." He paused by a late-model Mercedes. "By the way, we're all sorry about what the town is doing to the Starlight. Granny Harriet can't believe it. Let me know if I can help in some way."

"Bodie . . ." Matt hesitated. "Thanks, I mean it. If Trinity was my lawyer, I'd still be in jail."

"Yeah, well Trinity needs to worry about herself. She's working through her second divorce." Bodie unlocked the driver's side door. "I signed the petition for the Starlight on my way here. I'll remind the rest of the family at Sunday dinner."

"Appreciate it. I'm staying at Dad's. Send my bill there."

Bodie slipped behind the wheel of the Mercedes and powered down the window. "You ever talk to Booker?"

"I think you know I don't."

"Darn shame," he said. "Darn shame."

18

HARLOW

She'd just carried out the Starlight's trash from last night when Matt met her at the back door with a new pair of brownies.

"Lace them up and follow me."

"I don't skate." Harlow stepped around him and into the safety of the rink. "What happened with your lawyer?"

"I'm ordered to give Dale a wide birth and the state has a month to make their case." He picked up two *Gazette* delivery sacks, grabbed her hand, and steered her toward the Beachwalk. "Tyler came through. We're plastering the town."

"With?" She peeked inside one of the canvas sacks to see a stack of flyers. "I'll walk."

The news from the big green scale motivated her, and this morning she jogged a mile and breakfasted on eggs and no-butter toast. She brought a salad with tuna for lunch and avoided Spike's Concession like the plague.

Even more troubling than concession food or Matt shoving

a pair of skates at her was her early morning dream of Xander. The image of him walking the shores of Cole Island, holding the hands of their beautiful, towheaded children was so real and clear.

The dream ended with a buzz of the Starlight sign, and when she stumbled into the bathroom, the shadow of the *T* crossed through the window and onto the tile.

"Babe, if you can catwalk down a runway in stilettos, you can skate, trust me." Matt took a seat at the first bench, kicked off his shoes, and pulled on his skates. "Skating around the town in defense of the Starlight is the best promo. Even my publicist—well, former publicist—couldn't come up with something so brilliant."

Babe? That's the second time this week he'd called her *babe*, and like the first time, they both pretended the word didn't linger between them.

"This," she said, motioning to her tall frame, "does *not* move on wheels."

He gave her a bit of a naughty grin, handed her a set of skates, and patted the space next to him. "Shoes off, skates on."

"You are so annoying." She'd not confess to Matt, but a small part of her wanted to try.

"We'll go down the Beachwalk, then up Third Street to Sea Blue Way, cross over to Marlin Avenue and up Pelican Bay. I want a flyer in every shop and business window that will allow it." He pulled a hammer from his canvas bag. "I'm personally nailing a dozen to the side of the Midnight Theater."

"Are you dying to be a lightning bolt of controversy?" She sat, cradling the skates in her arms. "He'll slap you with a vandalism charge."

"He'll have to catch me in the act." He knelt in front of her, pulled off her Keds, and shoved on a brownie. "Come on, HH, work with me here." He grunted and shoved. "Are you curling your toes?"

"Why would I help you force me into these ugly boots? I was a fashion model." She laughed and stomped her foot into the boot. "If I get photographed in these—"

"I'll buy you a pretty white pair once you discover the magic of roller skating. There. Now tie the laces. Not too loose or you'll twist your ankle."

"You have this vision of me skating merrily along, and I'm telling you, this is going to be tragic." She tugged on the laces while Matt shoved on another skate.

"We're starting by the beach, so if you start to fall, topple into the sand."

"Oh that's nice. Just fall into the sand. As if I'll have a choice." She laughed despite herself. "You're such a twit."

"But a good-looking twit." He peered up at her, his smile in his eyes. "You said so yourself."

Yes, *yes*, she did. Matt skated their shoes back to the rink, then returned to help her stand. Immediately, her feet flew out from under her. He caught her with his mighty-strong right arm.

"I get it now," she said. "You're trying to kill me. Death by roller skates."

"Or maybe I'm trying to hold you in my arms."

"Matt—"

"H, come on, j-just kidding." Yet it didn't feel like kidding. Neither did his comment in the jail yesterday. Something about falling and a trailing, wordless ellipsis . . . *Falling for you? Falling in love?* "Just glide," he said. "Don't resist the forward motion. The wheels know what to do."

"Oh really? Do they have a degree from Yale?" Harlow inched forward, arms flapping at her side.

"Graduated summa cum laude. H, you're doing great." Matt looped the smallest *Gazette* newspaper sack over her head. "Hand a flyer to anyone and everyone along the beach, and leave some at the food trucks. If you run out, there are more in Granny's office."

"Wait, aren't we doing this together?" She clung to the bag, yet it couldn't save her. If she went down, the bag went down.

"If we split up, we'll cover more ground." Matt skated backward, a big grin on his chiseled face. "Harlow Hayes, it's time to learn to skate."

"Is that a metaphor? Huh? Matt Knight, that better not be a metaphor."

"It's like walking the runway, HH."

"It's nothing like walking a runway."

Granted, walking a Paris runway hadn't been easy the first time either. Especially in six-inch spiked heels as her dress fell apart and she strutted all but naked. She was lauded for her professionalism. And to no one's surprise, that designer didn't make it.

Stiff-legged and angling forward, Harlow roll-walked toward the food carts. If she made it to Pete's Pretzels, she was getting one. Flat out. The flyer sack was awkward, and when she tried to adjust it, her feet moved farther and farther apart.

"Here." She handed a flyer to a couple walking their dog. "Sign the petition at the courthouse. If you do, Matt Knight, the A-list actor, will visit your house."

By some miracle, she inched her feet together and handed out another flyer. "Save the Starlight. Sign the petition. Matt Knight, the A-list actor will buy you a Lamborghini."

Her feet rolled apart again, and she painfully pulled them back together. Matt lied. The skates did *not* know what to do.

Next, she rolled into a group of women, grabbing the nearest arm as a brake. "Do you live in town? Voters? Go sign the Matt Knight A-list actor petition to save his grandmother's skating rink. He'll pay for your kids' college tuition."

She passed out a few more flyers, finally, barely getting the hang of rolling. Then the Beachwalk took a dip, and she went flying.

"Hey, slow down. Wheels, slow down!" *Faux Victorian lamp-post up ahead.* She hooked her arm around the post and spun, stopping all forward progress when her skates hit sand. "Matt!"

Crumpled in the sand, clinging to the *Gazette* sack, she spied him yukking it up with a group of clipped-haired men watching the waves and women. Pilots from Eglin. She'd seen them at the rink.

She pulled herself up and carefully, slowly, hitched forward onto the solid concrete of the Beachwalk. Sweat trickled down the side of her face. Her blue sundress clung to her back and torso.

Matt slapped one of them a high five. The real pilot and the fake one finding camaraderie. Matt spotted her and motioned her over. "Harlow, come say hello."

"I'm busy. Passing out flyers." As much progress as she'd made in recent weeks, she didn't need a stand of hunky men giving her the once-over, remarking how they used to have a poster of her on their bedroom wall.

Focusing on keeping her feet together, she managed to stay upright and moving, passing out flyers, promising Sea Blue Beach citizens and probably a handful of tourists dinner with Matt Knight.

"Harlow, hey, what're you doing?" Simon Caster steadied her as she started to trip.

"Passing out flyers." She freed herself from the sack as Simon introduced his brothers, Todd and Adam, who had the same ruddy cheeks and John Travolta hair as Simon. "Nice to meet you. Here, Simon, you work for the Starlight. Matt wants one in every business."

Simon took the bag while Adam—or was it Todd?—just stared. "You're Harlow Hayes."

"I told you I mowed her grass, Todd." Simon made a Bugs Bunny what-a-maroon face.

"Yep, he does." Harlow turned into the breeze. "I'll buy you all milkshakes from the Tasty Dip if you empty that sack for me."

That did the trick. Armed with flyers, Adam and Todd started off, but Simon hung back. "Hey, I was coming to find you. There's a man at your house," he said in a low voice. "Looking in the windows. When he saw me, he asked where to find you."

"That's weird." And creepy. She'd had a stalker in her early days. But maybe Dad drove down to surprise her. He'd flown to

New York after Xander kicked her to the curb. Sat with her on a friend's couch, watching movies, holding her hand when she started weeping, offering to have a talk with "that young man."

"He said he was your fiancé."

"My fiancé?" Harlow chilled in the sunlight. "Are you sure he said fiancé?"

"Yeah. I didn't know you even had a boyfriend."

"Simon, do you know Xander Cole? What he looks like? Dark hair, aristocratic face, New York accent?"

"Oh yeah, that's him." Simon grinned. "Didn't you two break up?"

"Yes, we did." Harlow started for the house, forgetting her feet had wheels and stumbling into Simon. "For crying out loud." Dropping down to the Beachwalk, she yanked off the skates and handed them to Simon. "Return these to the Starlight. Please."

She ran from the beach through town, her sock feet thumping across the asphalt, only slowing when she saw a dark sedan parked along the curb. Xander sat on the porch steps, watching her.

"When Simon told me . . . I didn't believe it." She patted her pocket for her keys and gathered her breath. "What are you doing here?" Shoot, her keys were at the Starlight.

"Looking for you." His posture and expression were utterly Xander Cole. Right down to his khakis and sockless feet sheathed in Italian leather loafers.

"W-where's Davina?"

"Can we talk? Inside?"

"I don't have my keys."

"There's a spare under that fake rock." Xander pointed to the one at the far end of the trimmed but neglected flower bed. "I remembered as you came running up."

"Well, that's nice to know." The fake rock, the key, her dream, his sudden appearance felt ominous, as if she should be paying attention to the unseen.

When she unlocked the door, Xander followed her in. There

were a few newspapers lying around, but the house was tidy, lived-in, and welcoming.

"The place looks great, H." Xander turned in a circle. "I've not been here since the remodel. You have exquisite taste."

"Except the chandelier. That was all you." She bristled a bit when he called her H. That was Matt's nickname. Xander picked it up on set but surrendered the right to use it when he locked her out of the penthouse.

"I rather like the chandelier. It fits the room." He smiled. "Strange being here with you standing so far away when my only night here we—"

"Xander, what do you want?" She resented his intimate inference. That he felt free to travel through her memories.

"To talk." He closed the distance between them. "Harlow, where are your shoes?"

"At the rink. I was passing out flyers on the beach."

"In socks?"

"I was wearing skates. Talk about what, Xander?"

He laughed softly. "You don't skate, Harlow. Remember my nephew's birthday party? When I rented Rockefeller Center? You fell a thousand times before making it halfway around."

"Don't tell me you came all the way to Sea Blue Beach to reminisce." She'd forgotten that night at Rockefeller Center and how he kept telling her, *"Everyone's watching, Harlow. Get it together."* The criticism seemed so unlike him.

He leaned against the back of the couch, crossing his arms and ankles. "This is harder than I thought." He raised his gaze to her. "I want to get this right. I want you to hear me."

Sweat trickled down her spine. Where was he going with this? "Xander, wait. I need to shower. I don't know why you're here, but I'm a mess. Give me fifteen."

"Yes, of course." He reached for her hand when she turned for the stairs. "For the record, you look really sweet, darling."

Darling? What was he doing?

Her thoughts ran wild as she showered and dressed, selecting a pale pink sundress. It clashed with her recent sunburn, so she changed into a green paisley number, wove her hair into a braid, then dropped to her knees to retrieve her white sneakers from the back of the closet.

As she did, one of the floorboards gave way, and Harlow's arm crashed through, grazing something cold and hard.

"Harlow, you okay?" Xander called up the stairs.

"Yeah, I fell through a loose floorboard." Harlow pulled her arm free, examining a red mark and small scrape. Why was there a loose floorboard in her newly restored home?

Grabbing her shoes, she peered into the hole, not seeing anything but floor joist, and fixed the board back into place. In the bathroom, she cleaned the small wound, then headed downstairs.

"You okay?" Xander ran his thumb over the red mark and the scrape and offered to call the contractor. "That might bruise. But you're not bleeding."

"I'm fine, Xander." She sat on the sofa to slip on her shoes—it just seemed proper to be completely dressed—and waited.

"I miss you, Harlow," he said, sitting next to her. "That's why I'm here."

"You *miss* me? What are you talking about? How did you know where to find me?"

"I gave you the place, didn't I?"

"You gave me—" She was on her feet. "Did you want me to come here? This wasn't some long-overdue apology for kicking me out of our home?"

"I wanted you to have the place, Harlow. Honest. You'd put a lot into the remodel, and I thought you deserved it. Also, Jinx told me you'd moved out."

"You talked to Jinx?"

"That's not the point, Harlow."

"It's entirely the point. Xander, you locked me out of the penthouse. You told security not to let me past the lobby. I couldn't get my clothes, my jewelry, makeup, or toiletries. Nothing." She glared at him.

"Davina said she sent you your things."

"Well, she didn't."

"I'm not surprised. More reason to give you this cottage." He sighed. "I'm sorry for how I treated you. Sorry for how it all went down. I miss you."

"Xander, you're on the cover of *People* with Davina. You're getting married. You can't miss me."

"But I do." With an exhale, he stood. "I might as well just say it. Harlow, I want you back. That's why I'm here. I'm deeply, passionately in love with you."

"Excuse me? You what? Xander, you can't . . . you can't . . . just . . . show up . . . and say . . . What? You're deeply, *passionately* in love with me? You've ignored me for two years. Do you know how much pain and humiliation you've caused me? Also, small detail here, you're engaged to your ex-wife."

She thundered into the kitchen. She needed water. And air. At the sink, she filled her glass from this morning and shoved open the window.

"This makes no sense. This makes no sense," she muttered.

"I know, and I'm sorry for everything." A calm, cool Xander moved slowly toward her. "I was a total jerk. I don't know *that* Xander Cole." He bent to look into her eyes, but she couldn't maintain contact. "Some alien possessed me, but I'm free of it now. Harlow, I'm not in love with Davina. I'm still *very* much in love with you." His voice softened with sincerity. "I never stopped loving you. I tried. I gave in to Davina's pleas to give our relationship—and, yes, we had a history—another chance, but now I know the only one for me is you. So, hat in hand, I'm here begging *you* to give *me* a second chance. Tell me what I need to do."

Harlow gulped down her glass of water. "I had a dream about you this morning. You were walking on Cole Island with our kids."

"Darling, forgive me, but isn't that a sign? You dreamt of us and here I am. The universe is telling you something." *But was it?* "You must miss me too. Listen, I won't deny or excuse my behavior, but know I'm sincere when I say I love you. I want to marry *you* and have *that* family walking on Cole Island."

Harlow set her glass on the counter with a thud. "Okay, what'd Davina do? Change her mind? That's why you're here? Davina doesn't want kids."

"*I* changed my mind, Harlow. Davina is gone. I'm over her. I'm free."

"But I'm not, Xander." Her loud reply could've been heard at the Starlight. "I came here to get free of you and here you stand. I don't want to ride this sick merry-go-round of she leaves you, you leave me, now you're leaving her."

"I know you love me. Why else would you dream of me?"

"Maybe it was more of a nightmare."

He laughed low. "Okay, fine, I get it. I showed up out of the blue. You need time to adjust. I think you're here in Sea Blue Beach because you still love me."

"That's a stretch. I came here to get back the power I let you have over me when you broke my heart."

"I'll go slow, win your trust. But I'm as real as I've ever been." He was saying all of his words but not listening to hers. A trait she'd overlooked before. "Come back to New York. I'll pay for you to get a place. We'll work on us while you get in shape for CCW."

"Jinx told you about CCW?"

"She knew I'd be proud of you. Darling, that's fantastic. You always wanted that gig. It's the perfect job while we raise our kids."

No, no, this was all wrong. "Can we just cut the crap? You're here because Davina's done something, right? Or you heard I might be the new CCW It Girl and wanted me on your arm?"

"Absolutely not. None of that, Harlow. I'm here for you alone. Davina and I have parted company for good. And take CCW off the table, I don't care. Be a wife and mom if that's what you want. I'll support you."

Harlow stepped onto the back porch and faced the Starlight. *Tell me what to do.*

"When did you decide this?" she asked.

"Probably six months ago."

"And you just now decided to tell me? But first you warmed me up with your generous gift. This house. Well, I'm not giving it back."

"I'm not asking you to give it back. It's yours free and clear. Harlow, believe me, I love you madly."

"Don't say *madly*. It doesn't suit you."

"You want more of the story?" Xander propped against the porch post. "About six months ago, I was on my way home from work, thinking about the evening ahead, and it hit me. I expected to see you on the other side of the door." He touched her chin and turned her to face his. "I expect you to be there when I wake up. I think of you all the time. I'm here to offer you what you want, Harlow. A family. The house, the white picket fence, children, dogs and cats. A hamster for all I care. I'll even clean the cage. I'm offering you all of me."

His presence, his tone, was the Xander she'd loved. "I'd never been in love before you," she said. "Never made love to anyone. You swept me off my feet. You were so charming and kind and generous, and I thought we had so much in common. A *Father Knows Best*, *Leave It to Beaver* future. When you proposed, I was the luckiest woman in the world."

Between Matt shoving her down the Beachwalk with a sack full of flyers and this conversation, she was spent. And starving. "My whole life was orchestrated by Mom. I trusted her. Leaned on her. Then I met you and transferred all my dependence on her to you. With Mom, I had this twisted idea that I had to make her happy. With you, I had some twisted idea that *you* would make *me* happy."

"I can't make you happy, Harlow. That's too tall of an order. But I can be there for all the ups and downs, loving you with all my heart and creating our own happiness. If I'm honest, the happiest I've ever been was with you. So give me a chance. Give *us* another chance."

She regarded him for a long moment, sinking into his petition. "I don't know. . . . This is so confusing."

"Then listen to your dream. Trust the vibes of the universe because they've been making me think about you like crazy, darling." He said *darling* with the patrician *H* of all blue blood New Englanders. "The question is do you still love me? Even a little?"

"Look at me, Xander." Harlow stepped back, allowing him to take in her body. "I'm not the Most Beautiful Woman in the World anymore. I'm not *the* Harlow Hayes, supermodel. What if this is me?" She struck a pose. "Can you love this girl?"

"Harlow, I will love you however, whenever. You are beautiful and sexy, clever and smart. I love the woman on the inside as much as—"

"I think you should go."

Xander hesitated, then took her hands. "Will you at least think about us? Please?" The gold flecks in his hazel eyes seemed to glow as he spoke. "Can I call you?"

"You can do what you like. No guarantee I'll answer."

"Fair enough," he said, stepping off the porch. "But I'm not giving up. When I want something, I go after it."

Which Harlow Hayes knew all too well. "Have a safe trip home, Xander."

"I'll call soon," he said. "I'll prove we belong together."

19

MATT

What happened to Harlow? Why were Simon Caster and his brothers passing out the Starlight flyers?

"Simon, hey, what are you doing?" Matt looked inside the sack looped across his body. "Where's Harlow? Are those her skates?"

So far the flyers were a huge success, with people taking several, promising to talk to friends, family, coworkers. Several admitted they'd not heard about the Starlight's demise or the chance to save it. Most of the businesses and shops sided with the Starlight. Salty, one of the assistant managers at Biggs Market, took a handful of flyers. "We'll stuff them into the grocery sacks."

As promised, Matt nailed several to the exterior of the theater, then headed to the bank. They rejected him. *"We're on the side of progress."* Figures.

"Harlow handed them to me when I told her some man was looking for her." Simon waved a flyer at a passing family. "Do you live in Sea Blue Beach? Cool, take a couple of these. Sign the petition to save the Starlight. Say, do you know this dude? He's Matt Knight. Yeah, from the movies."

"Hey, how're you doing?" Matt nodded at the family.

The woman who took the flyer grabbed her husband's arm. "Matt Knight. We heard you grew up here but never thought we'd see you. Honey, it's Matt Knight."

"I can see that," he said.

"I loved you in *Under the Lamplight*." Ah, his first rom-com. "Can I have your autograph? We just moved here last year. I'm Jenn. He's Bob." She dug out a Biggs receipt. "Bob, do you have a pen?"

"Why would I have a pen when you're the one with the Mary Poppins bag?" He focused on Matt. "Dug you in *Arizona*, man. Gutsy stuff. Heard you did all your own stunts."

"Aha. At last." Jenn speared the air with her ballpoint. Matt scribbled his name while reminding Bob and Jenn to sign the petition. Then it was back to Simon.

"Some man was at her house. Said he was her fiancé." Simon stopped outside of Suds Up Laundromat. "When I told her, she yanked off the skates and hightailed it, all heels and elbows. Miss Lucy, can we put some flyers in your window?"

Miss Lucy was more than eager. "I voted for that Harry Smith but never again. Move home, Matt. Run for mayor. You'd win in a landslide."

"Maybe one day."

"All sorts of celebrities are getting into politics. Our own president used to be an actor. Sonny Bono ran for office."

Miss Lucy was a hoot. She talked on as Matt taped a few flyers to the front window.

Then he went back to interrogating Simon. "Her fiancé? Xander Cole?"

"That's the dude."

Matt looped his *Gazette* sack over Simon's head. He had to find Harlow. "Take flyers to the library and the fishing museum.

And Alderman's Pharmacy." A blue truck eased alongside them. Dale Cranston rolled down the window and raised a fistful of ripped-up flyers.

"Aren't you supposed to stay away from me? I consider this breaking your protective order. I'll let this one slide, but don't let me catch you or any of your posse posting these gall dern flyers on the side of my theater or I'll have vandalism added to your list of offenses." Dale snorted and drove off.

More and more, he regretted punching that guy. But he had bigger concerns at the moment. Matt dashed toward Harlow's in his skates, all the while working up a speech for Xander Cole. But when he saw a dark sedan in front of the house, he stopped in the middle of Sea Blue Way.

What was he going to do, barge in and punch *him*? Get arrested again? Did he even have a right to get involved? This was Harlow's private business.

Still, what was Xander doing here? Did he want the house? Did he decide she needed to pay him for it? If so, Matt would gladly loan her the money. She must be free and clear of that lump of flesh.

He considered sneaking onto the porch and peeking in the windows just as Dad drove by.

"Hey, someone from *The David Letterman Show* left you a message at the house." Dad passed him a slip of paper with a New York area code. "The lady said Emilio Estevez canceled."

Matt tucked the paper in his pocket. "Do you think I should go in there?" He pointed toward Harlow's.

"Does it have anything to do with why you're standing in the middle of the street wearing skates?"

"Harlow's ex is here. I should see if she's okay."

"Leave her be, Matt. She can handle herself."

A car horn sounded and Dad drove on while Matt skated to the curb with a final glance at Harlow's front door. Dad was right. She could handle herself.

He hated when Dad was right.

TUESDAY

OCTOBER 1939

The Starlight was shining! The entire town buzzed about her Stars at the Starlight. LJ had proposed the idea one evening after dinner while perusing *Roller Skating* magazine.

"Ma, let's get the Van Horns or Heddy Stenuf to perform at the rink. Or Vivian Bell. She's the reigning speed skate champion."

"Now why would those stars want to come to the Starlight?"

LJ and his mischievous smile . . . *"'Cause we're the Starlight."*

He wrote to them via the magazine that night, and now the rink was the center of the Sea Blue Beach Fall Fair. Farmers, growers, pickers, fishermen, sailors from the naval ports, the boys from Eglin, and folks from across the growing Panhandle converged on Sea Blue Beach, expressly the Starlight, for a week of celebration from their harvesting labors and *to see the stars*.

Surely the Man on the Moon could see their festivities from his lofty perch. Shop doors were opened from seven in the morning until midnight. Beach vendors sold boiled peanuts and hot, buttery corn on the cob. With Burt's help, Tuesday set up a bonfire outside the Starlight and introduced folks to a newfangled idea—marshmallow roasting.

But that was nothing to the show going on inside the rink. Spectators lined the walls and filled the balcony, crowding together under the raised panels.

The Van Horns replied to LJ's inquiry first, then Heddy. Once the ball got rolling, Tuesday gave her heart and soul to this night. She made long-distance phone calls she couldn't afford and used the last penny in her account to pay for travel and lodging. The Fall Festival had always been good to her, but this year was her pièce de résistance.

And now, it was time for the show! Wearing her beautiful Richardson skates, Tuesday rolled through the crowd and onto the amber-colored wood floor, with the cord of the microphone rig she'd rented all the way from New Orleans trailing behind her.

"Ladies and gentlemen," Tuesday began, "tonight the Starlight presents"— LJ aimed the spotlight on her as her voice filled the rink and swirled around every man, woman, boy, and girl, across the sand and over the sea—"for the first time ever"—the band, positioned in the balcony around the Wurlitzer, blasted the first notes of "Goodnight My Love"—"the great acrobatic skating couple Earl and Inez Van Horn."

Tuesday faded from the light, coiling the microphone cord, as Earl and Inez swept past her in an artistic and acrobatic dance skate. The crowd ooh'd and aah'd. Tuesday watched for a few minutes thinking Prince Blue would be proud, then hurried to her office, where Heddy Stenuf waited to go next.

Jackpot, jackpot, jackpot. The money she'd shelled out for her stars, the band, the equipment and food, plus a few extra employees, had been worth it. The Starlight was shining, and after tonight, she'd be well in the black.

"Do you have everything you need, Miss Stenuf?"

"Sure do. Swell little joint you've got here, Tuesday Knight. Good for you."

"You don't know how much all of this means to us."

"I love to skate, and I love anyone who gives me a stage."

Tuesday refreshed Heddy's coffee, then found LJ in concession, boiling hot dogs and stirring up a large batch of hot cocoa.

"I know you'd rather be out watching the show with your friends," she said. "But I can't do this without you."

"I know," LJ said with a sly grin. "That's why you'll let me go flying tomorrow morning. Mr. Diamond is taking me up again in his crop duster. Then we're going to watch the training at the airbase."

"I don't suppose I could talk you out of this flying craze. It makes me nervous to have you up in the air with only God's breath keeping you afloat." She brushed her hand over his dark brown hair, which even Brylcreem couldn't tame. He wore a red-and-blue plaid shirt, the colors faded from washing and ironing, corduroys, and a pair of scuffed brown lace-ups.

"Ma, flying is freedom. Wait until I'm really good and I'll take you up. You'll see."

"Are you going to run away, join the circus? Become a wing walker?"

"No, I want to pilot the plane, not walk on it." He made a face. "Though if I found a pretty girl who wanted to walk on my wings . . ."

Tuesday laughed and kissed his cheek. "You will most definitely find a pretty girl. Hopefully one who makes you feel like *you* have wings without an airplane."

LJ blushed and shrugged off her hand. "Did Pa make you feel like you had wings?"

The older LJ became, the more keenly he noticed his parents' relationship. "Your pa made me feel grounded and protected. Which was what I wanted."

"Does he still?"

"What are all these questions?" She shoved LJ out of the minuscule kitchen. "I've decided you have the rest of the night off. Go find your friends. Have fun. Ginger, can you take over here with the hot dogs and cocoa?"

Back out to the rink, Tuesday worked the crowd and caught the rest of the Van Horns' show. They were spectacular. When she spied her youngest leaning against the ticket booth, arms folded, she made her way over to him. Dupree Knight had grown another two inches over the summer, matured a little, and became smitten with Mimi, a girl from school.

"I can do what they're doing," he said, scowling. At seventeen, he swam in young man pride. He believed he could fly to the moon if you gave him a rocket. "Me and the fellas turn tricks like that when we're not trying."

Dupree was a talented skater but hardly like the Van Horns. He couldn't toss a girl through the air like Earl just did Inez, catching her as she landed.

"Why not enjoy the magic, Dup? Don't compare, have fun. Where's Mimi?"

Dup jutted his chin toward the benches. "With her friends, gushing over the Van Horns."

"Well then, next time she comes to the Starlight with her skates, you show her what you can do."

Dup grinned as he lowered his arms and defenses. "Guess I'll go sit with her."

Tuesday watched him head over to the group of girls, passing Daisy and William Anderson, a lovely young couple, new to Sea Blue Beach. Tuesday started to say hello when Leroy appeared with several other men just beyond the lights. For a moment, everything stopped. There was no music, no skating sensation on the rink floor, no crowds filling every space. There was just Leroy.

He looked fine. Mighty fine. In his dark jacket over light gray slacks, his hat set jauntily on his head. The scar on his cheek had faded more since she'd last seen him.

Of the three men accompanying him, Doc was not among them. He'd not been around much since his near confession. Tuesday missed him but thought it was best he find comfort elsewhere. Leroy saw her and removed his hat. Doggone it, he melted her every time.

The sudden explosion of cheering and applause startled her. The Van Horns circled the rink, taking their bows.

"Tuesday, Miss Stenuf is up." Burt handed her the microphone and fed her the long cord. He jerked his head toward Leroy. "What's he want?"

"Don't know."

"Whatever it is, tell him no."

With Burt's advice riding in her chest, Tuesday skated to the center of the rink. "Thank you, Van Horns. Weren't they marvelous?

Simply marvelous. Three cheers. Hip hip hooray! Hip hip hooray! Hip hip hooray!"

Earl and Inez waved and shook a few hands before disappearing into the back room.

"Give another round of applause for the Van Horns. They'll be back later tonight. But now, ladies and gentlemen . . ."

Leroy and his boys were on the move. *Where are you going? What are you doing here tonight of all nights?*

"Give a Sea Blue Beach welcome to Miss Heddy Stenuf."

The beautiful blonde burst into the spotlight as the band begin to play. Tuesday hurried off the floor and handed the microphone to Burt with a sense of foreboding.

"They're in the office," he said.

"Bring four hot dogs, will you? And some coffee." At the door, Tuesday squared her shoulders, raised her chin, and stepped in. "Good evening, gents. Lee, I'm surprised to see you."

Leroy sat at her desk, while two others leaned against the wall, arms propped on her file cabinet. The third man watched her from under a dark, thick brow, possessing an air of authority. She didn't need introductions to know he was the one Lee worked for, the one who kept him away.

"Can I get you seats to the show?" she asked. "It's quite something."

"We've seen Heddy before," Leroy said. "Great gal."

"Really? You never said."

Leroy looked to the man in the corner, then reached into his pocket and tossed a roll of money onto her desk.

"What's this?" Even from a distance, she saw the bills were hundreds, not tens.

"Rent." This from the man in the corner.

"Rent for what? You could have a thousand private parties for that much money. We don't charge—"

"We want to use the Starlight for . . ." Leroy glanced at the boss. "Business."

"What kind of business?"

"Don't you trust your husband?" The boss man had a smooth, arrogant voice.

"I'm sorry, I don't believe we've met."

"Runner Jenkins." He offered his hand, but Tuesday didn't take it.

"Mr. Jenkins, the Starlight is mine and mine alone."

"Bought with my money." Leroy's tone was harsh, no doubt saving face before his colleagues.

"You gave it to me, and you cannot take back a gift unless it's surrendered. I am not surrendering the Starlight."

Burt kicked the door open, carrying a tray of hot dogs and coffee.

"Let's leave the room to Leroy, fellas. Go watch Heddy." Runner took a hot dog and cup of coffee. The others followed suit.

"You embarrassed me, Tooz," Leroy announced when they were alone. "If a man can't manage his own wife, then how—"

"*Manage?* I don't *work* for you, Lee. I'd give my right arm if you lived a life worth sacrificing for, but you don't." She stepped closer and tapped the desk with her finger. "How dare you come into my place, *my* sanctuary, and offer me dirty money to turn the beautiful Starlight into a thieves' den." She flicked her hand toward the bundle of money. "How much is that? A working man's annual wage?"

"Ten years' wage, Tuesday." He reached for the last hot dog on the tray. "Don't you see? This is my ship coming in."

"Your ship?"

"Our ship. The SS *Lee and Tooz*. Baby, with this money I can buy you the diamond ring you've always wanted and a gall dern new stove. Shoot, let's get a new house and a new car. We can send the boys to some fancy Yankee school."

"I'm comfy in the old house, thank you. LJ doesn't want to go to college, he wants to fly airplanes. Dup loves to work with his hands. But you'd know these things if you lived with your family."

"You're starting to sound like a broken record. Listen, doll, we're married. What's mine is yours, what's yours is mine." He offered her the money. "Take it. Get what you need. Go shopping. Get your hair done, order new clothes. All we want is the rink at night after closing." His eyes narrowed and expression darkened. "And we're going to have it."

She slapped the money away. "I don't know what kind of tomfoolery you've devoted your life to, but you're not the man I married." She'd never said those words out loud before. But there they were, stinging her heart. By the look on Lee's face, stinging his pride. "I'm not riding this train with you, and the only way you get the Starlight is over my dead body, Leroy George Knight."

He peered at her with fire in his eyes. "I can take the Starlight anytime I want. Don't forget it."

"Are you going to stab me? Huh? Are you?" She shoved his chest. "Maybe shoot me? Are you *that* greedy?"

"Pa, you're home." Dupree burst into the room and wrapped his arms around Leroy. Forget being seventeen and on the verge of manhood. He was a boy who adored his father.

"Um, yeah, Dup, I'm home." Leroy had sense enough to cool his ire and embrace his son, clap his hand on his back, tell him how tall and handsome he'd become and how he hoped he'd played the heck out of linebacker this year.

"You coming to see me play?"

"Of course he is. Aren't you, Lee?" Tuesday said, a rod of steel in her backbone.

"We play Chipley next week. It's going to be a whale of a game." Dupree started out the door. "Come see Heddy, Pa."

"Sure, right behind you." He leaned toward Tuesday. "We'll finish this later. I can do what I want with the Starlight, you know I can. The bank will trust me over you."

"Lee, you promised me you'd never touch the Starlight."

"Did you file the deed with the county? Or is it at the house?"

"I guess that's for me to know. Now, find your son and watch the show with him. Or have you given up keeping your word altogether?"

When he'd gone, Tuesday collapsed into her chair, trembling.

If he got a hold of the deed, he *could* do anything. All he had to do was inquire at county records to know she'd not filed it. She'd been nervous they'd require her married name. Maybe even Leroy's. Why he'd not insisted on his name being added remained a mystery. Maybe he was hoping the county would do it for him. Maybe he meant to keep his promise, but his hoodlum boss, Runner, got him thinking otherwise.

She trusted none of them. If he inquired at the county records, he'd probably try to search the house and the rink. The loose floorboard in the kitchen just might give her away.

"Tooz, Heddy's almost done." Burt leaned in. "You okay?"

"You were right, Burt. I had to tell him no."

She collected herself and headed out of the office. Lee stood at the front of the rink with his arm wrapped around Dup's shoulder. Overhead, the image of Immanuel looked down from the raised panels.

"What do I do?"

Then she spotted LJ in the balcony with his friends and waved him down.

"Go home, get the box under the kitchen floorboard," she whispered. "Take it, hide it, but don't tell anyone where, including me. But *you* remember, hear me?"

"Ma, what's going on?"

"You hear me?"

"Yeah, but what—" LJ caught sight of his pa from the corner of his eye. Without another word, he squeezed past the spectators and dashed out of the Starlight.

20

HARLOW

Who does he think he is?

The more she considered Xander's surprise visit, the more she fumed.

Sitting on the kitchen floor, back against the white shaker cabinets, leg in a V across the large square tile, she commiserated with her friends. Or what remained of her friends.

A Blue Plate takeout box once containing a cheeseburger, fries, and coleslaw, along with a smattering of squeezed ketchup packets. A slice of warm cherry pie from the bakery. A package of Oreos from Biggs.

Yes, siree, she swung for the fences this afternoon.

What she wanted right now was a large box of Hayes Cookies, but no one sold them in Sea Blue Beach, which she considered criminal.

She ripped the wrapper from a Reese's peanut butter cup and crumbled it on top of a pint of vanilla ice cream.

"I still love you."

Ha. Like a cat loves a mouse. Is that how he saw her? A mouse? Someone—no, some *thing*—to be toyed with according to his whims.

She rammed the crumbled candy pieces into the ice cream with a large spoon, catching the excess spillage with her tongue. When she had the proper mixture, she scooped a large bite.

You're a fool, Harlow. Admit it, you ignored the signs and broke your own heart.

So many things were becoming clear. Like when she learned he'd had lunch with Davina a month after their engagement. Which she'd never have known except Annis, the head of Icon, saw them together. *"Rather cozy scene for a divorced couple. Didn't she cheat on him?"*

She let it go that evening as they sat on their penthouse deck, cuddled under a mound of blankets, fragrant logs crackling in the fireplace, a winter sunset painting the Manhattan sky. Until he announced he wanted Davina at their wedding.

"After all, we were married for fifteen years."

"Xander, did you have lunch with her? Annis saw you. Said you looked rather cozy."

He could've won an Oscar for his reaction. Surprise, shock, contriteness, and repentance.

"Yeah, babe, I did. I meant to tell you. Does it matter? I didn't think . . . Wow, so sorry. Men are dolts."

Harlow shoveled a large dollop of ice cream, chocolate, and peanut butter into her mouth. It was cold and sweet, filling all the cracks Xander exposed.

The day after she asked about his lunch with Davina, he came home with a diamond necklace from Tiffany's.

"Forgive me, darling?"

"Of course I forgive you. But you don't have to buy me expensive jewelry."

She chose to believe Xander's lunch with Davina didn't mean

anything. Didn't want to rock the boat because she had an eye on *her* prize. A family of her own.

Sucker! Harlow breathed in all the lingering scents of her comfort and took another large bite of ice cream, which brought on the brain freeze. If only her brain *could* freeze out reality.

"I'm still very much in love with you."

No, Xander Cole, you're in love with yourself.

She washed down the ice cream with a swig of cold, watery Diet Coke. Now she needed something salty. Where was the bag of Lay's? Ripping it open, she dipped a large, perfectly fried potato chip into the ice cream. Gnarly to the max. Someone should invent salty, fried potato spoons for eating ice cream.

When the concoction of chips, ice cream, and peanut butter and chocolate was gone, Harlow Hayes crawled off the floor, rinsed her hands and face, then returned to her spot, the stupor of her consumption settling in.

Oh grody, she was supposed to be at work. What time was it—five thirty? No wonder the kitchen shadows were so long.

Sorry, Matt.

She should call him. The afternoon skate was over, but as of right now, she'd not make the evening shift either. Never mind that she abandoned the mission of passing out flyers. So if she called him, what would she say?

"Hey, um, I'm eating my emotions right now. Can't come to work."

The zig-zag-zing of shame split her in two. She'd been doing so well. Now her dress was stained with ketchup and mustard, ice cream and chocolate. Why did she let herself get out of control?

"Harlow Hayes, this is not how your mama raised you." Exactly. Which might be part of the problem. Nope, Dr. Tagg would tell her this was Harlow Hayes' mess.

Draining the last of her soda, she stood and surveyed the mound of food wrappers and decided to clean up tomorrow. As she entered the living room, the shadow of the *T* from the Starlight sign once again made a shadow on her floor.

Harlow curled up on the window seat and observed the entirety of the Starlight sign. What had been on Prince Blue's mind when he built such an extravagant rink?

"You were building your ship, weren't you?" He understood real heartache. "Only this time on land. A safe harbor for all. A place to sail through life."

The Starlight had become that for her in the last four weeks. She came down to claim the only possession she had, but instead Sea Blue Beach and the Starlight claimed her.

Though at the moment, she felt lost and confused, definitely a "woman overboard" moment. She was tired, so very tired. And sick. Why, why, *why* did she let Xander do this to her? Moving a three-thousand-calorie haul through her system required a fiery furnace, and the first drops of digestion sweat beaded up on her forehead, down her neck, and under her arms.

Harlow collapsed backward on the bench seat and stared at Xander's gaudy crystal chandelier swinging from a rustic beam. An eighty-thousand-dollar monstrosity.

"The house has to look like the *Xander Cole and* the *Harlow Hayes."*

He'd said that a lot, didn't he? The Xander Cole and the Harlow Hayes. Maybe that's why she thought of herself in third person.

When she told him she planned to change her name to Cole after they married, he'd said, *"No! You're Harlow Hayes,"* as if somehow changing her name, making them a family, would cause her to lose her identity.

Do I still love him?

The sweat beads thickened. No. Impossible. How could she after everything—No. Just . . . don't think about it.

"HH! You here?"

Harlow bolted upright. Matt. *Door, be locked, please be locked.*

"Are you okay?" Harlow shrank against the window and grabbed a few pillows for camouflage. "Harlow?"

The doorknob jiggled.

"Harlow, I'm worried. Look, I know Xander was here. Simon told me."

"It's open, Matt."

Matt walked past her into the kitchen, bringing the scent of the ocean and the rink, of fading soap, of a man's life. She smelled of sticky sweetness and perspiring underarms no longer guarded by her Secret.

"Harlow?"

"I'm here." Stains and all. "Sorry I missed work."

Matt propped against the kitchen archway. "I see you dined with variety this afternoon."

"I put the Reese's in the ice cream. Ate it with chips."

He looked impressed. "Nice touch. So, Xander?"

Her eyes brimmed over. "Xander said he loves me. Wants me to go home with him. Marry him." She sat up and gathered her dignity but kept her distance to separate her fragrance from his. "He claims Davina confused him, made him think their relationship deserved another chance but now he realizes he's"—she intoned his refined upper-crust accent—"deeply, passionately in love with me."

"What brought him to this revelation?"

"That he was thinking of me all the time, expected me to be there when he came home at night. My theory is Davina admitted she doesn't want a family."

The weight of his confession mingled with her extravagant lunch. Xander knew how to appeal to her with talk of a family. Fresh perspiration beaded over the old. Nevertheless, he sounded so sincere.

"Hey, what's churning behind your gorgeous eyes?"

She twisted her hands together, then wiped a dew of perspiration from her lip. Was the A/C working? "Just wondering if . . . maybe . . . he deserves a second chance."

"What? No, Harlow, he's a putz. Like you said, Davina's done something to make him realize she's a schmutz and when she turns up all repentant and batting her eyes, he'll go right back to her."

"I don't know, Matt. Putz aside, Xander is one of the most genuine people you'll ever meet. He wants a family. I want a family."

"There has to be more to a relationship than that, Harlow. I mean, what really happened between you two? What didn't you tell me at the diner the other day?"

She tossed off the pillows and focused on the shadow of the Starlight's *T*. "I didn't see it coming. The breakup. One day I lived in a Manhattan penthouse with my fiancé, the next day the security guard wouldn't let me past the lobby desk. I had no idea what was happening. I called the penthouse, Xander's work, no one would talk to me. The security guard who said hello to me every day and exchanged pleasantries, who I bought Christmas and birthday gifts for, walked me outside and said, 'I have orders not to let you in, Miss Hayes.'"

"He just kicked you out?"

"I took a cab to Icon and tried Xander's office all afternoon. He was in perpetual meetings."

"I suspected he was a snake, but he's really a monster."

"I checked into the Waldorf until we sorted it out, but a week later he still wasn't talking to me and then my financial advisor was arrested. All my money was gone, except for what I had in savings. Icon called me for work, but I couldn't, Matt. I just couldn't smile for the camera. The man I'd trusted with every fiber of my being, with my heart, even with my money, was no longer speaking to me." She dabbed a tear from the corner of her eye. "Pretty pitiful, huh?"

"Xander, yes. You, pretty darn courageous."

"I shouldn't have told you." She peered at him. "No one else knows. Please don't tell anyone what he did to me. I'd die of humiliation. People think our split was mutual."

He scooted closer and brushed a lock of hair from her eyes. "You can always count on me." He patted his chest. "Your story is right here. Locked in the vault. No one will know. I've made a few costly mistakes running my big mouth, H. But I think I've learned my lesson."

"What kind of mistakes?" She rested against the windowpane. "It might be nice to hear about someone else's troubles."

"Cindy Canon, for one. Told her I'd outshine her if she didn't watch it."

"Well, that's true. What else?"

"Said some things about Roger Woods."

"That's it? Doesn't seem that horrible. What else?"

"Plenty."

"Like what, Matt? Come on, tell me."

"There was this one incident. When I was a teenager."

"Anything to do with that cashier's brother? The former best friend?"

"I think I see a red light up ahead."

"Cheater." She smiled softly. "One day you'll tell me, right? I trusted you with my story. You can trust me. Also, and this will sound nuts, but I really love my job at the rink. I missed out on the high school, minimum-wage job thing. And the rink, wow. How can the town let it be destroyed?"

"I'm glad you're on my side."

She patted her chest. "Always."

"So Xander? What are you going to do?"

"I don't know. He bowled me over today. I mean, the nerve of him showing up and declaring he never stopped loving me."

"Look at it this way, H. You discovered his weak character before the vows and the children."

"I guess that's one consolation prize."

"Listen, you know what Granny would say to a girl with a broken heart?" Harlow glanced at him, waiting. "There's no better place to heal than the Starlight."

"Next thing you know, she'll have me in an ugly pair of brownies, dragging me around the rink."

"That's when the real healing begins," he said. "Look me in the eye and tell me you still love him. That you can trust him."

She breathed in and looked him square in the eye. "I don't know, Matt. I don't know."

"I'm not busting your chops, Harlow," he said. "But make sure you're not giving what's left of your broken heart to the man who swung the hammer."

21

SEA BLUE BEACH

Things are heating up around town. The flyers Matt, Harlow, and the Caster boys passed around caused quite a stir, and this morning, April 14, Matt Knight appeared on the Rollo on the Radio show. From the buzz we're picking up, folks called in from as far east as Tallahassee and west to Pensacola, north to Dothan and down south to Lake City. On a clear day, AM radio commands the airwaves.

Fans are slightly disappointed, though. Matt Knight mostly talked about Sea Blue Beach and the petition to save the Starlight, though Rollo insisted he tell some amusing and harrowing Hollywood anecdotes before letting him go.

In other news, a rather stunning bouquet of flowers arrived at 321 Sea Blue Way yesterday while Simon Caster ran his rusty little mower over Harlow Hayes' lawn.

Harlow still jogs faithfully three or four mornings a week. We watch as she heads to the Starlight a little after noon. As far as we know, she's not put on another pair of skates.

Mayor Harry Smith darts in and out of shops and establishments with a bit of determination, kicking up his campaign for progress.

Our secret is still out there. We believe there's one person who knows the truth. But we've not seen him in a long, long time.

TUESDAY

She listened to Matt on the Rollo on the Radio show in the Starlight's sound booth with Nora and Harlow. He was charming and entertaining until he told behind-the-scenes stories about the filming of *Flight Deck*, including how he fell overboard into a rather turbulent sea.

Her joy depleted as she pressed her hand over her thudding heart. She'd not lose another of her loves to war. Even a fake one.

Still, she swelled with hope when he talked about the Starlight. The townsfolk would get off their duffs and sign the petition now.

"What's next for you, Matt?" Rollo said. "After you save our Starlight?"

"Got an invite to join my buddy David Letterman on *Late Night*. Then I'm filming a rom-com with Cindy Canon this summer. Should be fun."

"Is it true Harlow Hayes lives in Sea Blue Beach these days? I've been stuck in this dark studio far too long."

"She is . . . has a home here. She's getting her life together after—" Matt stopped abruptly.

Tuesday took Harlow's hand. She seemed rather somber today.

Rollo smoothed over the dead air. "So, Sea Blue Beachers, get out, sign the petition to stop the ugly high-rises from obstructing our cerulean shores. Save the Starlight." Bumper music introed a commercial for First Federal Bank.

"Matt's going on Letterman?" Nora said. "How cool. I love him. Look at me, little Nora Kittle, surrounded by celebrities and friends of celebrities."

"Matt was swell, wasn't he?" Tuesday said, smiling at Harlow and Nora. "I think we've got the momentum. You know I've been getting calls from out-of-town folks wondering what the blazes is going on."

Harriet Nickle rang from Melbourne Beach to give her an earful about Harry Smith. Tuesday listened for a good twenty minutes before Harriet took a breath and said, *"I'm just preaching to the choir, aren't I?"*

Matt informed her there were a bunch of locals shocked to hear the news. Even more to learn such a thing as eminent domain existed in the United States of America.

Paul Holland was all fired up the other day, talking to Spike. *"Didn't we fight a war to keep the government from taking our property? Does President Reagan know about this?"* All politics aside, it seemed a shame that a handful of elected officials could make such a monumental decision.

Ever optimistic, Tuesday imagined they'd have the number of signatures required by now, but Matt informed her yesterday they only had fifty-three.

"I should get to work." Harlow slipped her hand from Tuesday's. "I didn't finish washing the front window yesterday."

"Harlow, is everything all right?" Tuesday said. "Is it about what Matt said on the radio? He does get to talking sometimes, forgets where he is, who he's talking to, and who's listening."

"No, no, he's fine. I'm fine."

"Before you wash windows, I was wondering if you could run the deposit to the bank for me this morning." Tuesday pressed her hand to her lower back. "My lumbago is acting up."

In the office, she unlocked the safe and took out the blue bank bag. "You know you can tell me if something's bothering you, Harlow. Matt mentioned your former fiancé stopped by for a visit. And that business on the radio, he's just chatting. When he was a boy, if Dup and I suspected him of any shenanigans, all we had to do was buy him an ice cream and sit with him on the beach. He'd tell on himself and half the kids in town."

Harlow reached for the bank bag. "Matt's been a good friend. And yes, my ex showed up. Rather took me by surprise. But I showed him. Ate myself into a stupor. Ask Matt, he saw the aftermath."

"Harlow," Tuesday said, "can I be bold with you? Go easy on yourself. You're healing. You'll achieve what you're after."

She sighed and fidgeted with the bag's zipper. "Xander says he still loves me, wants me back. That he made a mistake going back to Davina." She smiled softly. "I feel like an episode of *All My Children*."

"Chalk that one up for a lesson learned. Next time you feel like eating yourself into a stupor, come to the Starlight and skate. Always worked for me."

"Maybe." She slumped forward. "I don't know why Harlow Hayes hurts herself to get back at Xander Cole. Or if I'm honest, my mother—but let's not go there."

"You've given them too much power. No other human should have such control. You've got to love yourself, Harlow."

"I'm not sure I know how, Tuesday. My whole life has been about making others happy."

"Has Matt told you my story? I didn't have it easy growing up as an unwanted baby. But the Starlight gave me purpose. It became my vocation, my way to help my fellow man."

Harlow regarded her for a moment. "Is this your way of asking me to work more hours, Tuesday?"

She laughed. "Come, follow me." She walked Harlow out to the rink and pointed to the mural. "Immanuel here made sense of it all for me. After the rink had closed at night, I'd talk to him.

I didn't know if he was real or not, but Prince Blue sure thought he was, so when all was dark and quiet, I'd sit right here"—she stamped her foot against the polyurethane now covering the wood floor—"and talk to him. Call me crazy, but he talked back. Those glowing eyes sure took a minute to get used to, let me tell you. Especially being alone here in the dark. But know what I came to understand? Peace. Real peace. The kind no one could take. Not Leroy when he was off running with the thugs. Not war or death. And, most recently, not eminent domain. Though I've had my moments over the years."

Harlow glanced up at the man on the wall and breathed in. "I don't think I've ever felt any real peace. With Xander, some. I loved him so much I surrendered everything for him. Gladly."

"Harlow, that's what love does. That's what Immanuel, God with us, did."

Harlow studied the other pieces of the mural. "Who are the children?"

"You, me, anyone who's ever come to the Starlight." Tuesday linked her arm through Harlow's. "You know I do my best thinking and figuring on roller skates."

Harlow's laugh was melodic. "You and Matt . . . Harlow Hayes does not skate. She can barely run up and down Sea Blue Way." She held up the blue bank bag. "Do you need anything else while I'm out?"

"No, no, you go on. But I'm telling you, Harlow Hayes." Tuesday started for her office. "There's a skater inside, and she's dying to get out."

MARCH 1940

"Ma, I'm going with some of the fellas to Pensacola." LJ hovered over the newspaper spread across the Starlight's office desk, reading an article about airplanes. The boy was infatuated with them. "We want to see *Stagecoach* at the Saenger Theater."

"All the way to Pensacola? That's the third time this month. I know you like the Duke, but—"

"Abel hasn't seen it."

"LJ Knight, do you think I have my head in the sand? Harriet told me he went with you last month." Tuesday dropped the basket of dirty linens from concession on the floor. The Suds Up Laundromat had just opened, and Rupert, the owner, offered her a good deal on the rink linens. But until she decided to take him up on it, she still did the rink's washing. "Will you cart this home? Get the washer going?"

"So you don't mind if I go to the movies?" LJ reached for the basket.

"Isn't the Midnight showing anything you want to see?"

"Naw, old Mr. Cranston is running *Anna Karenina* again. It's almost like he doesn't want young folk in his theater. Dale's a teenager. Why don't he say something?"

"I've known the Cranstons all my life and found that none of them have much sense." Tuesday regarded her oldest with a sense of pride. "LJ, you've grown into a man now. You don't need my permission to go to the movies, but do be careful and try not to worry this mother's heart. Don't go off doing anything stupid."

"Why would I do anything stupid? I'd never worry you on purpose, Ma."

"No one ever does. Fill the car with gas on your way home. And find Dup, tell him to make sure we have enough wood to make dinner."

"Abel is driving." He hoisted up the laundry basket. "But I'll fill up the tank anyway. Need anything else?"

"Yes, there's a pair of brownies in the skate room needing repair. I think the bearings are going. I could ask Burt, but he takes forever and a day, and in the end you have to fix his fix."

"I'll do it now." LJ set the basket by the side door and returned a few moments later with the skates and the repair kit. "Ma, you know I love you, don't you?"

"Of course. Where's this coming from?"

"My heart, I reckon." LJ examined the skate in his hand. "Yep, it's the bearings."

What was that affectionate exchange about? She'd always tried to hug and kiss her sons, especially since she didn't have a mother's love growing up, but they usually scrunched up and grumbled something like, *"Ah, Ma, don't get all mushy."*

With the afternoon session fifteen minutes away, Dear Dirk began to warm up the Wurlitzer with "Amazing Grace" and "The Old Rugged Cross."

"Did you see this?" LJ nodded to the newspaper article as he removed the wheels of the skates. "Boeing is testing a pressurized aircraft cabin."

"What does that even mean?"

"Flight is the future, Ma." LJ smiled up at her. "I'm going to be a part of it."

His passion for flight consumed his free time. Every spare minute, he went up in an old Huff-Daland Duster and buzzed the beach, the treetops. Anything to get time in the air.

For all Leroy's plans to give his sons a better life—which never materialized—LJ made his own way. Even Dupree, in his final year of high school, had apprenticed himself to a carpenter, Mr. Day, who said he showed a real talent for it.

"LJ, Abel said y'all are going to the pictures." Dup barged into the office in his usual fashion—boisterous, energetic, overflowing with life. "What time? I want to go."

"You're working the Starlight, Dup." LJ's bass voice carried more authority than a big brother's usually would. "Ma needs you here."

"Can't Maggie or Jethro cover for me? *Stagecoach* is John Wayne. I got to see it."

"You've seen it three times," LJ said.

"So have you."

"Jethro is out on the boat with his father," Tuesday said. "And Maggie's manning the concession. I suppose I could—"

"Don't, Ma. Don't let him off the hook."

She brushed her hand over Dupree's wild curly hair. "You need to sit in Travis's chair, get this mop tamed. I'm surprised Principal Warner lets you walk the school halls."

"I'll go right now. Get all spiffed up for the pictures."

"You're not coming with us, Dup." LJ stood, forgetting the tools in his lap as they clattered to the floor. "Even if Ma covers your shift, which she shouldn't, you're not going with Abel and me."

"Abel is my friend too."

"You're working the Starlight. End of story."

Tuesday startled at the edge in LJ's voice. If something was up, he'd tell her soon enough. Meanwhile, Dup huffed off, slamming the office door so hard the light fixture over the desk swung.

"Are you sure you can't take him along? He admires you so much. I can work the Starlight with Maggie. If I need to, I can call Sylvia or Donny."

"You'd have tanned my hide for acting as rude as he does." LJ had completely disassembled the skate and lined up the worn wooden wheels on the floor. "At school he's all charm. 'Yes, ma'am' and 'no, sir.' With you, he gives lip."

Tuesday propped against the file cabinet and watched LJ work the skate. He was right, of course. She coddled Dupree, trying to make up for all the ways Leroy disappointed him. At the end of the day, she wasn't his father, and boys needed fathers. Girls too, if anyone was asking. She'd have liked to have known her father. Even his name would be something.

"LJ, do you . . . do you miss your pa?"

"Nope." He held up the skate to inspect the boot. The size 8R was burned into the leather sole. "Mr. Diamond is more of a pa to me than Leroy Knight. And Doc too."

"Doc? W-when do you see Doc?" Tuesday had seen him at

Thanksgiving but not since. He stayed a few days, eating leftovers and swapping stories from the Great War with Lee, captivating LJ and Dupree. One morning, she woke to learn he'd hopped a ride on an early-morning train. His absence always left a hole in the house. Maybe a little of her heart too.

"He comes by every few weeks. We go over to Eglin or Niceville. He says he don't want to come by the house with just you there. Said it might make Pa mad, but who gives a flying fig what Pa thinks?"

"I do, and so should you," Tuesday said. "What do you and Doc talk about?"

"Flying, mostly." LJ worked the delicate parts of the skate so skillfully.

"Do you want to fly as a vocation?"

"I hope so, yeah." He sighed and set down his tools. "I know you want me to stay here, take over the Starlight someday, but—"

"Someday, LJ. I know it's not your passion. You have dreams to chase." Tuesday brushed aside LJ's bangs. "You need to see Travis too. Whatever you do in life, LJ, I wish you happiness. I hope you find a nice girl, get married, settle down in Sea Blue Beach, and take over the Starlight while you work on giving me a passel of grandchildren."

"Ah, Ma . . ." LJ blushed at the idea of marriage and babies. "I will. One day. Promise."

It didn't seem so long ago she'd been the blushing bride, full of hope. "I can still see your pa sporting you around town in the crook of his arm, so proud. He was only a year older than you are now."

"Probably trying to figure out how to make a buck off me."

Word was spreading around town how Leroy Knight ran a small gambling ring through North Florida and southern Alabama. Along with it, he moved bootleg hooch, avoiding the Feds and their taxes.

"Not back then. You can't remember how he used to read you bedtime stories, then sing you to sleep."

"Well, he ain't that pa now." LJ dusted off his jeans and stepped around Tuesday. "I need to get a few parts for these skates." He paused at the door. "I *do* want to be an aviator, Ma. Some of the fellows at the air base say I got a knack for it."

"Then go fly, my boy. Go fly."

22

MATT

David Letterman: "Ladies and gentlemen, please welcome the star of *Flight Deck*, Matt Knight."

On a rainy April day in New York, movie star Matt Knight stepped around the giant fake column, into the lights and applause, and bowed to Paul Shaffer and the World's Most Dangerous Band, and to the audience members who were on their feet, applauding and whistling.

Letterman: "You got more applause than I did."

Matt: "I thought that's why you had me on the show?"

Letterman laughed. Matt adjusted his tie.

Letterman: "It's good to see you, man."

Matt: "It's good to be here. Thank you for asking me to fill in for your preferred guest, Emilio Estevez."

> *Matt sensed the audience leaning into their banter as Dave tried to explain how Emilio couldn't make it due to filming delays. There was a collective, feminine sigh, which Matt reacted to and got a laugh. Brat Packer Emilio* **was** *a hot ticket these days.*

Matt: "Sure, rub it in. He's working and I got fired."

Letterman: "Come on, you got fired. But who cares, *Flight Deck* is still killing it at the box office. Are you cashing all your checks? Buying a yacht? A small European country?"

Matt: [chuckling] "I'm taking time off, visiting family." No need to spoil the shtick by confessing he'd been rehired for the Cindy Canon movie.

Letterman: "And where is that? San Tropez? You're so tan!"

Matt: "A small town in North Florida. My grandmother owns an iconic skating rink there. I'm on a quest to save it from 'progress.' Some of the locals want to tear it down and put up a parking lot."

Letterman: "We'd heard you grew up roller skating. It's still somewhat of a craze but I thought *Xanadu* killed the sport. [Laughter mingled with boos.] So, how do you plan on saving this rink?"

Matt: "The old-fashioned way, a ***Mr. Smith Goes to Washington*** sort of thing. We're getting up a petition for the locals to sign so we can put it to a vote."

Letterman: "You're not using your star power, getting some of your buddies to come to town? I mean, I might be willing–"

Matt: "No, man, this is for the hometown folks. I'm just a regular Joe there."

That got a light sigh and applause, and Matt soaked it up. From the moment he'd walked on set, the showman in him yawned and stretched awake. He sensed the crowd clinging to him, and he needed it. He was eager to please. Bring on the wow factor.

Letterman: "So you're having fun in your hometown. So, what, what else are you doing?"

Hint: Entertain us, Matt.

Matt: "Well, it's a lot of work saving a hundred-year-old rink built by a prince."

Letterman: "A prince. What kind of town is this? Host to a prince and the great Matt Knight."

Matt: "Don't forget Harlow Hayes. She recently moved to Sea Blue Beach and is working at the Starlight, helping my grandmother and me."

The mention of Harlow sparked Dave and the audience.

Letterman: "Harlow Hayes? *The* Harlow Hayes? What's her reaction to Xander Cole and Davina breaking up again? I just heard about it today."

Matt: "Dude, he flew down to see her." [Matt

shifted in his chair and the set became his living room.]

Letterman: "Really? So the romance isn't over?"

Matt: "Who knows? Harlow's smart. I don't think she wants to be with a man who broke up with her by locking her out of their penthouse. Cole wouldn't even let her go up to get her things. Security escorted her out and left her on the street. What a putz."

Matt, what did you just say? *He tried to replay it in his mind but the lights, the audience, Dave's voice jammed his concentration.*

Letterman: "He locked her out? Dang. So Harlow's in Sea Blue Beach. Are you two an item?"

The audience leaned into the question, tugging on the actor, Matt Knight.

Matt: "No, no, we're just friends." [He winked at the crowd.] "For now. But yeah, she's doing great, getting on a diet plan, working toward being the new CCW It Girl."

Dude, what are you doing? Stop talking. Take it back. Say you're joking. Call cut!

Letterman: "So the Billionaire and the Beauty *could* get back together, but the Bad Boy might give him a run for his money." He turned to the audience. "Remember you heard it here first!"

Matt: [pushing a big laugh from his gut] "Haha, no, no, we're friends. Y'all, I'm just kidding . . . about everything. Made it up. Ha. I'm an actor, I lie for a living.

I don't know anything about Harlow's life. Nothing at all."

The audience deflated. Letterman's expression hardened. No one believed him.

Matt: "So, are we doing Stupid Human Tricks or what?"

His adrenaline shut down so fast he couldn't move. It was Booker Nickle all over again. Only worse, if possible. What was wrong with him? He'd patted his chest and promised her no one would ever know.

He just told millions of people Xander Cole treated her like toilet paper on the bottom of his shoe. Tomorrow it would be in the newspapers. Harlow, I'm sorry. *He pictured her sitting on the window seat, so vulnerable and honest. Sorry wouldn't be enough. He'd betrayed her. Fool. Stupid. The studio began to spin. His skin was on fire.* ***Fix it. Fix it.*** How, how, how?

While he sat there in a pit of panic and self-loathing, someone shoved a pair of skates at him and pointed to the obstacle course. Matt tried to focus, but he felt like he was going to implode. Somehow, he managed to speak.

Matt: "Dave, what are we doing? Last time I did a Stupid Human Trick I almost broke my nose."

The audience aah'd with sympathy as he removed his shoes and tugged on the skates. Anything to distract from his big, fat mouth. Why did he do it?

He managed not to kill himself during the Stupid Human Trick—which involved skates, ping-pong balls, a bungee cord, and Velcro—though death might have been mercy.

Afterward, he cornered the producer and begged him to cut out the Harlow segment. "She'll be humiliated. Please don't air it. Please." The guy smiled, promising to give it a look.

Matt sat like death-warmed-over through a dinner meeting Cosmo set up last minute with the producers of a spy-thriller in development. Why didn't he blow that *secret instead of the one about Harlow?*

On his way back to the hotel, he rehearsed a groveling apology, but nothing—no words—came close to fixing the damage. So, he resigned himself to the truth: Harlow Hayes would probably never speak to him again.

HARLOW

The rink had been closed for thirty minutes, but she remained at the ticket booth, flipping through a book that had arrived from Dad in the morning mail. *High Output Management*. He'd stuck a note inside.

Har,

Take a look at this. I think you'd like it. You've got a business mind. Let me know what you think.

Love, Dad

"You hanging out for a while, Harlow?" Spike quietly set a hot dog and Diet Coke on the booth. "The dog's all beef."

She smiled. "You spoil me."

He winked and nodded. "We all need a bit of spoiling now and then."

Nora also stopped by on her way out. "I left the sound on for Tooz." She motioned to Harlow's book. "Aren't you going home?"

"In a minute." She closed the book and tucked it under her handbag, ready to go home. "Spike brought me a hot dog."

She took a small bite, but she really wasn't hungry. Ever since Xander and her binge, food and home didn't feel so cozy. She replayed that day over and over, how she barged out of the house, a woman on a mission. Then Matt witnessing her disgrace. Yet he'd been so gracious and sweet, acting like it was no big deal.

"I want you back." What was she to do with Xander's confession? Did she love him enough to overlook his betrayal?

I don't know, I don't know, I don't know!

"Harlow, you're still here." Tuesday paused by the booth. "Did Matt tell you to stay? Keep an eye on me?"

"No, I just . . ." She gave her a soft smile. "Didn't want to go home yet."

"Put on your skates. Join me on the floor."

"I don't have skates." She moved from behind the booth. "I'm interrupting your tradition. Tuesday Knight at the Starlight."

"I'd like a little company." There was a weight in her words, as if some royal command had to be obeyed. "Look in my office, in the cupboard. Bottom shelf."

"Really, Tuesday, no. Harlow Hayes can't skate."

"Harlow Hayes can do whatever she wants to do. Tonight, it's skating." Her smile smoothed the lines on her face. "Come on, what are you afraid of, really? Get out there with me. It'll do you good. Besides, I've always wanted a daughter. A granddaughter will do."

Tuesday had played the trump card. "Okay, you win, but you

have to promise not to laugh." She'd spent so many years traveling, posing, and being viewed only for her exterior that being wanted for herself was irresistible.

In the office cupboard, Harlow found a large, battered box imprinted with the word *Richardson*. Inside was a beautiful pair of white, well-worn boots.

"Tuesday," she said, carrying them out to the floor, "aren't these yours? I'll just get a pair of brownies."

"Those were the first pair I ever owned. Leroy bought them for me and the boys one Christmas. Weren't we something with our Richardsons, skating at the Starlight, in a Depression-era small town."

"I'm sorry the town wants to knock it down." Harlow joined Tuesday on the bench under the image of Immanuel and kicked off her shoes.

"All my life, people tried to knock me down, but Immanuel saw me through."

"It's sort of hard to trust in an image on the wall, Tuesday." Harlow tugged on the first skate.

"Give it time. He'll be the image in your heart soon enough." Tuesday pointed to the skates. "Lace 'em up good. I'll fire up the music."

Working the rink night after night, Harlow had fallen in love with the fashion of skates—well, not the rentals, let's be real—but the beautiful white boots the girls wore, accented with pom-poms. Still, she must be aware of the skates' trickery—luring her in only to drop her to the ground the moment she moved.

Remember the day she passed out flyers? Exactly.

On the floor, Tuesday skated gracefully to "Clair de Lune," arms wide, one leg raised gracefully behind her. "Come on, HH," she called. "You can't learn without effort."

Harlow shoved up from the bench, grabbed the pony wall, and stepped her way onto the rink. She wanted to skate to the music. It was so lovely and peaceful. But for now, she'd be grateful to not fall. Glancing toward Tuesday, who was on the other side, turning in gentle circles, Harlow pushed off.

"I want to be like you when I'm eighty-seven," she hollered.

"Then you're in the right place."

"What did you want at twenty-nine?" Glide right, left, trip, stumble, right, left, wheels clattering against the floor, then smack on the ground, face-first.

Tuesday rolled up and offered Harlow a hand. "What all women want. To be loved, give love. I wanted to be a family with Lee and the boys."

"If anyone ever asked me," she said, shoving onto her feet, trying not to use Tuesday for balance, "I would've told them all I wanted in life was a family. What's better than being a mom, raising the next generation? Talk about a legacy."

"You know, I think deep down Matty wants a wife and kids as much as anything."

"Are you matchmaking, Tuesday?"

"Now why would an old woman like me try matchmaking?" With that, she skated off.

"Yeah, I hear you." Harlow glanced back at Immanuel, who seemed remarkably and unrealistically alive for a painting. "Hey, are you going to help me learn to skate or what?"

First Tuesday got her into skates, and now she had her talking to a wall. Still, for a split second, she felt him smile. But since he wasn't real—she didn't care what Tuesday said—it had to be in her imagination.

For the next hour, she inched around the rink, arms like wings, braving a move away from the wall only to go down hard. All the while, Tuesday Knight skated freely around her.

Two women facing the end of everything they'd lived and worked for were leaving it all on the rink.

By the time they'd removed their skates, shut off the music and lights, and headed into the Starlight's parking lot, Harlow had made it around the rink a dozen times without falling or reaching for the wall.

"You did well," Tuesday said.

"Did I?" Harlow rubbed her butt bone. "I'll be bruised in the morning."

Tuesday glanced at the night sky, dotted with the stars, like a celestial Morse Code, then juggled her old pocketbook for a set of car keys. "What more evidence do we need than this night sky? God is with us, and that's a great, great comfort." She walked toward her car. "Are you going to watch Matt on Letterman?"

"I stopped watching late-night talk shows when I became a punch line."

"Matt wouldn't allow that to happen, Harlow."

"Even so, good intentions can get lost. Matt can tell me about it when he gets home."

"Well, you know best. Can I give you a lift?"

"Thank you, but I'll walk. It's a beautiful night."

Harlow waited until Tuesday was in her car and driving off before making her way across the Starlight's parking lot toward Sea Blue Way, feeling lucky, even a bit proud, to have skated with Tuesday. Wouldn't Matt be surprised when he got home?

She'd just walked through the door when the phone rang. "Harlow, it's Matt." He sounded funny, like he was weak and far off. "I have to tell you something."

23

MATT

He arrived home early Thursday evening, and as he made his way down the hall to drop off his bag, Dad greeted him from the kitchen.

"Did you mean to say that stuff on Letterman? About Harlow?"

"What do you think?" He changed from jeans to shorts and exchanged his button-down for a T-shirt. "Have you seen Harlow or Granny? Is there any buzz in town?"

"Not that I can tell. Saw Granny this morning and Harlow walking toward the rink this afternoon. How'd your movie meeting go?"

"I don't remember half of what they said. I've not slept since the taping. I called Harlow, Dad. Warned her." Matt retrieved a cereal bowl and joined Dad at the table.

"That was smart. What'd she say?"

"Nothing. I apologized, and I think she thanked me for the heads-up, but . . . Dad, she told me that stuff about the breakup in confidence."

The producers not only kept the Harlow segment in the show but also used a clip of it as a teaser during prime time. Wired with guilt, Matt had monitored the news. Checked the newsstands outside his hotel and at the airport, but so far the headline of the day was the USSR's nuclear testing, Wayne Gretzky breaking the all-time scoring record, a seventh-inning comeback for the Yankees, the upcoming premiere of *Beverly Hills Cop II*, and a British MP being charged with gross indecency.

Then he saw a daily tabloid headline in the airport newsstand. *THE BILLIONAIRE LOCKED OUT THE BEAUTY.*

"You have a bunch of messages on the machine."

"Do I want to hear them?"

"One of these days you're going to have to figure out what gives you diarrhea of the mouth, Matt. Didn't you listen to yourself?"

"Yeah, after it was too late. I was trying to defend her, not expose her. I wanted Xander Cole to look like the bad boy, not me. But sitting on the set, I become someone else. Not your son, or Harlow's friend, or the kid from Sea Blue Beach. I'm Matt Knight, the big-time actor, the entertainer. You've seen the great actors or singers who go on a talk show and bore everyone to death. Letterman calls me because I'm entertaining."

"Then learn to tell your own stories, not other people's." Dad poured another bowl of Frosted Flakes. "You've got to keep your head about you, Matt. Couldn't you cut and refilm the show or something? You'd think after Booker—"

"I asked them to delete that segment. Instead they made a promo out of it. I called my publicist the next morning. Woke her up. Asked if she could get ahead of it, call in some favors or something, but she laughed at me. Said the billionaire locking out the beauty was PR gold. Even better if the romance isn't over. It will be the hottest story. The alliteration alone makes it a headline. The Billionaire, the Beauty, and the Bad Boy."

"You don't need a publicist to get in front of this, Matt. It's already out there. You might want to check in with Harlow before you hit the hay tonight." Dad added a little more cereal to his bowl of milk. "In other news, Harry's going around to businesses, offering perks with Murdock, even a break in taxes, if they stand with progress."

"Taxes? He can't unilaterally cut taxes."

"He can within a certain percent. He managed to get that passed in the last two years."

"He's a piece of work." Matt's spoonful of cereal tasted like cardboard. "Have you seen our signature count? Any more come in while I was gone?"

"I checked this morning. Looks like you have a little over a hundred." Dad slurped the last of his cereal and carried his bowl to the sink. "Matt, why didn't you talk about *Flight Deck*? Or your new movie with Cindy what's-her-name?"

"I've talked about *Flight Deck* for months on Letterman and every other talk show. The movie with Cindy Canon . . . I don't know. It was a better script to say I was still fired. And the story of me leaving Cindy at a seedy bar is old news. But the Billionaire booting the Beauty? That's tantalizing. No one knew that story." Matt shoved his cereal bowl aside and peered at his father. "How evil do I look in all of this?"

"Not evil. Just unwise. Selfish. Maybe a tad foolish." Dad returned to the table with a microwaved cup of decaf. "Some collateral good might have come from you running your mouth. A couple of newspapers called Granny wanting to do a story on the 'iconic' roller-skating rink with connections to the Royal House of Blue. One was the *New York Times*."

"Won't change Harry's mind, but it might get us more signatures. I've been racking my brain to understand why I blabbed about Harlow. I honestly thought I was talking about Xander Cole, not her. I wanted him to get demerits for treating her that way."

"I suppose in some twisted way, I see your logic." Dad sipped his coffee. "The messages on the machine for you are reporters wanting to know about our special rink and town. Mostly they want to know about Harlow."

Matt shoved away from the table. "I'm going to see her. Wish me luck."

"She's a good woman. She may not want to talk, but she'll listen. At least for a second."

"That's more than I deserve."

Jogging toward the rink, Matt fumbled for a fresh apology. But his words only sounded like excuses. He entered the side door into an electric atmosphere. The evening session was far from over. The floor was crowded with skaters, and in the foyer, Granny talked with reporters.

"Hey, what's going on?" Matt gently tugged on her arm.

"I'm telling these kind folks about the Starlight." She grabbed his arm and shoved him toward her office. "Will you all excuse us?"

"Matt, Hammel Porter from the *Miami Herald*. We met on the *Flight Deck* junket. Is it true Harlow Hayes—"

"No comment." This from Granny, who had a death grip on Matt's arm until she closed her office door. "Harlow hid in the back room when the reporters and photographers showed up. Matt, what happened on that show?"

"My big mouth. Stay in here. Don't talk to any more reporters." Matt crossed the crowded rink with determination, sensing Immanuel's gaze on his back. *If you're real, help me out, will you?*

"Matt Knight! Hey . . ."

"Matt Knight, OMG!"

"Lieutenant Striker, can we get a picture?"

Hands grabbed at his T-shirt, his hair, his shorts, but he powered through until he arrived at the blue door marked *Private*. Four strides in, and he stood at the back room, knocking softly. "H, it's me. Can we talk? Please." Matt rested his forehead against the doorframe. "I don't deserve it, but forgive me. I'm sorry. So, so sorry."

After a painful, weighty moment, the door swung open with such vigor, he almost toppled over. A pale, exhausted Harlow fired off a couple of visual daggers, then slammed the door shut.

Fair enough. "Harlow, you have every right to be mad. I'm mad at myself. Livid. I don't know what came over me. I heard myself talking, but it's like all the words had a mind of their own. That guy, *that* Matt Knight, wasn't me. He's an arrogant windbag. I promise I did not intend to tell your secret. Never, ever." He gently slapped his hand against the door. "Please open up. I want to apologize to your face. You can slap me, kick me, spit on me."

The door swung open again. "What good will that do? It's out there. You can't take it back." Her blue eyes blazed. "Worse, you sound like Xander. Do I have something on my forehead that says, *Betray Harlow*? I'm starting to think my personal agency doesn't mean anything to anyone. I'm just a pawn."

"I'm sick about this, Harlow. I can't sleep. I can't eat." Matt eased into the room and shut the door. "I am so, so sorry. And you're not a pawn."

"Why didn't you talk about yourself? There's plenty of juicy stuff there."

"Everyone knows my juicy stuff. I mentioned you were in Sea Blue Beach, and Dave asked about you."

"Tell me, were you drunk? High?"

"No. That was just the actor Matt Knight, entertaining. I should call Dale Cranston. Tell him to come punch me."

"How about if I punch you?" She gave his arm a sharp jab. "Thanks to you my answering machine is loaded with messages like, 'Harlow, we had no idea.' 'Harlow, how could you let him do you that way?' 'Harlow, I thought we were friends. Why didn't you tell me?' 'Harlow, how awful for you.'" She paused and shook her head. "My mother's message was the best, though. She asked where she went wrong and why didn't I tell her? 'Wasn't I always there for you?' So on top of being the pity of the world, I'm now guilty for not confiding in my friends and family. But you—" She stabbed him in the chest. "I confided in you. You said it was in the vault. That no one would know."

"I tried to get the producer to edit it out." He leaned against the wall.

"By the way, Xander thanks you. He's telling the press how much he loves me. That the Billionaire treated the Beauty poorly but he's going to make it up to me."

"Is that what you want?"

She sank down onto the old, shredded, soft quilt on the bed and brushed a tear from her cheek. "I started to feel at home in Sea Blue Beach, like I'd found my life, not the one belonging to everyone else, and the supermodel Harlow Hayes." She peered up at him. "Even wondered if you and I might . . ." She waved off the thought. "Never mind. I'm leaving. Going to Buckhead. I can't do this on my own. Mom wants to help, and—"

"I'll help, Harlow." He knelt next to her. "I know you can't trust me but . . . Remember when you brought me the cupcake? In jail? I started to tell you something."

"We got interrupted."

"You're not wrong wondering about you and me. Yet, considering my utter failure with your trust, I'll keep my thoughts to myself. But one day I'd like to tell you—"

"Matt, we should just call it a day."

Once again his careless speech wounded a precious thing. "Can you at least forgive me? Please."

"I'd have felt less betrayed if you told them I was a fat, burger-binging slob who invented the potato-chip spoon for ice cream. Or that when we met in Sea Blue, I was tucked under my steering wheel, eating a slice of pizza." She smiled softly. "As embarrassed as I am by that, it was a pretty funny scene."

"You had me the moment I saw you crouching down." Matt sat next to her on the bed. "Remember Trinity from Biggs?"

"The red light. Second red light, actually."

"Yours isn't the first life I've ruined." Matt rose up to sit next to her.

"Aren't you being a bit dramatic? You've not ruined my life. My trust, yes. Not my life."

"Well, I ruined Booker's, and he was my best friend. We grew up together. Bodie, the lawyer who got me out of jail, is his older brother. Granny and his Granny Harriet are best friends. When Booker and I got our licenses, we used to sneak out and go drag racing down Highway 20."

"So that's a thing with you."

"Granny gave me a sweet '70 Cuda when I turned seventeen. Booker, Bodie, and I souped it up with headers, carburetor, intake manifold, mag wheels. No one could beat us. Booker got cocky one night. Ended up smashing the car and breaking his leg. He missed our entire football season."

"And people worry about girls using too much toilet paper and spending hours on the phone."

Matt laughed, hoping she listened to his story in the name of forgiveness. "Booker was crazy smart and was up for every scholarship known to man. USC had offered me a full ride to play football, so going into our senior year, we felt like we had it made in the shade. Then Booker got hurt, and Coach benched me a few games for being reckless. Our dads made us watch videos of tragic car wrecks. Once Booker got out of his cast, Grandpa Nickle had him working every Saturday for the rest of the year. Said if he had time to sneak out and drag race, he had time to work. Dad hauled me to work with him. I had three jobs besides football and school."

"Sounds reasonable." She cut him a side glance. "So Booker's sister is mad at you because he missed a football season?"

"Booker was a four-point-oh student. Bs were not acceptable. Cs, devastating. He came skating one night. I was the floor guard, so we chilled and skated, talked. He confessed he was flunking an advanced Calc Two course. I laughed because Booker never failed anything. But he was serious. Really panicked. The wreck had messed with him. I jokingly suggested he should steal the answer key to the fall final. The transom over the gym door never latched, and the math teacher, Ellison, never locked his file cabinet."

"Ah, I see. He stole the test and you blabbed?"

"He aced the test, and no one was the wiser until my loose lips sank his ship. Let's just say teenage boys and beer don't go together. Booker got expelled. No leniency at all. The principal was a hard-nose, old-school, by-the-book kind of guy. No amount of persuasion made him change his mind.

"Booker didn't graduate. He lost his scholarships. He accused me of blabbing because he'd wrecked my car, but I promise that was not the reason. It was just a bunch of guys drinking cheap beer trying to one-up each other. And I had the story to top all the stories. By Monday morning, it was all over school.

"Booker's parents made him finish up at night school, but nothing was the same. He planned to go to law school like Bodie. But because I couldn't keep a secret, because I wanted to entertain the guys, I ruined his life and lost my best friend."

HARLOW

Harlow felt Matt's regret in his apology to her. Heard it in his story of Booker Nickle.

"Your friend cheated, Matt, and got found out. You played a part, but he ruined his own life. Xander broke my heart, but I'm the one who ate my way out of a career."

"Maybe, but that was his cross to bear. I betrayed him. Let him down. Worse, I didn't really know if he stole the test. He could've studied hard and aced it on his own."

"But the school believed he cheated. Has Booker forgiven you?"

"We've only spoken once in fifteen years. And that was eight years ago when he cussed me up one side and down the other. He's in New Mexico somewhere, I think. He's sent me a couple of letters the last few years but I can't bring myself to read them."

"With a story like that, I almost have to forgive you. Can't have you bearing the burden of *ruining* two people's lives."

Matt bumped her with his shoulder. "I wish I could take it all back, Harlow."

"Me too. Not just the Letterman show. But the last two years. I'm not sure why I'm so scared to let people know how Xander treated me. Maybe it's years of projecting this perfect image of myself. If I confessed what really happened, everyone would pity me, or see me as weak. Ordinary. Yet I've loved being *ordinary* in Sea Blue Beach. Now that my story is out there, I don't have to hold it in anymore."

"Xander looks far worse in that scenario than you, Harlow," Matt said. "So, am I forgiven?"

She peered at him. "Okay, I'll forgive you. But . . . let's call it a day. Just leave things as they are right now. We had a few fun weeks, right? We'll always have the Starlight."

A knock rattled the door, and Dad's voice bled through. "Har, kiddo. It's Mom and Dad."

"It's open." She sighed. "I told them not to come. I can drive home on my own."

Matt greeted her parents. Dad was gallant and pleasant. Mom not so much. She barely acknowledged him.

"Let's go, Harlow. Dad parked right outside."

"I'm driving my car, Mom."

"Okay, then I'll ride with you so we can strategize." Mom glared at Matt. "I'm grateful for one thing. Your big mouth caused my girl to come home. So I'm happy about that."

There it was again. Mom's happiness.

Dr. Tagg asked her not to use those words, but Mom had no

other channel to tune in. Harlow ignored a sense of unease. She could handle Mom. She was more aware of herself now. More in command of her destiny.

Telling her parents to meet her at 321 Sea Blue Way to get her things, Harlow paused at the door, glancing back at Matt.

"I am grateful for the Starlight. I skated with your granny on Tuesday night."

"All right, H. I knew you could do it." His smile touched her. "The Starlight will miss you."

"Harlow?" Mom called. "I'd like to get on the road soon, make it home before two a.m."

"I should go." Harlow picked up her handbag and motioned for the door. "I already said good-bye to Tuesday." Her tears started to sting. "Good luck with the petition. And tell Spike, and Simon and Nora . . . well, tell them I love them. They accepted me so easily."

"You're easy to accept."

"Harlow Anne," Mom called. "While I'm still young."

"She's a bit of a drama queen." The longer she lingered, the harder it was to break his gaze. "Bye, Matt."

"See you, Harlow."

"Yep, see you too, Matt Knight." *Don't go*. "Thanks for waking me up that morning to run. I'm starting to like it."

"I hate running," he said with a laugh. "I just like being in shape more."

"Okay, I really should—" She gave a small wave, slightly irritated by her thumping heart. *Just go already. You're calling it a day.* "Bye, Matt."

"Bye, HH. Go get 'em."

24

TUESDAY

1940

This was curious. She'd not seen LJ in two days. Since he went to the pictures with Abel. She noticed his bed was made, which almost never happened. No socks or underwear were on the floor. And the bathroom was unusually tidy.

He'd missed work at the rink, which was very odd. When she asked Dupree, he shrugged and said he wasn't his brother's keeper. Harriet asked Abel, who claimed LJ had gone to Dothan to play some baseball. Baseball? He'd not played ball since he discovered flying. And why wouldn't he tell his ma?

At the rink, she waded through a crowd of teens on the newly established tradition of spring break. Dupree worked as floor guard and was showing off, flirting with a group of girls. He'd grown another couple of inches this past winter. The hem of his pants sat right at his ankles.

From the balcony, Dirk played his jaunty tunes, and at the end of his sessions, he played a hymn. Tuesday had grown partial to "I Come to the Garden."

She exchanged her shoes for her skates and made her way to the floor, half expecting to see LJ saunter in.

"Ma!" Dupree tugged on her arm. "Doc's here to see you."

He stood against the ticket booth, and she nearly slumped to her knees.

"Is Leroy dead?" Tuesday said when she reached him. "Is that why you're here?"

"Let's talk in your office." Doc closed the door as she entered, taking the nearest chair.

"Tell me straight up. I can take it."

"Lee's alive and well, though I don't know where. Maybe Memphis, maybe Chicago. I cut ties when he started running with the Rossi gang. They're not a big outfit, too weak to survive the big guns, but it makes Lee a big fish in a small pond."

"And he always told me he hated fishing." Tuesday eased her grip on the arm of the chair. Lee was alive. "Why aren't we enough? Me and the boys?"

Leroy Knight needed something besides her love and their family. Just like her mother and granny.

"I couldn't tell you. He and I don't see eye-to-eye on how he treats you." By his tone, the look on his face, he still carried a torch for her. "He's one of the smartest yet most foolish men I know."

Tuesday loosened her laces and removed her skates. "Have you eaten? I made a roast last night and bought a fresh loaf of bread from Good Pickens this morning. Roast beef sandwich with a glass of milk strike your fancy? Burt and Dup can look after things for a while."

"It sure does, but we need to talk first, Tooz."

She glanced up at him as she tucked her skates back in the Richardson box. "Why do I have a feeling I'm not going to like what you have to say? It's about LJ, isn't it?"

"He's fine, Tooz." Doc tugged at his slacks and gently sat back in the chair. "He made me promise not to tell until he got on the train, and now I'm regretting my part in this."

"Train? What train?"

"He's run off to join the RAF."

"The RAF? Doc, what are you talking about?"

"The Royal Air Force." Dear Dirk's rendition of Ethel Waters' "Stormy Weather" wafted through the closed door. "He took the train out of Birmingham to New York. He boards the *Queen Mary* Monday morning. He's written you a letter. You should get it soon."

"He wrote me a letter? Why how kind. I only lived in the same house with him. What possessed him to join the RAF?"

"He says war's coming and he wants to fly. He's afraid FDR will keep America out of this one."

"Afraid? He better be afraid. Flying a warplane isn't like dusting crops or buzzing a few trees. FDR be darned if he doesn't keep us out." A few blue words toppled from her ruby lips. "LJ's an American citizen. How can he join England's air force? He'd have to know someone—" She regarded Doc. "You. You helped him."

"He wanted to go, Tooz. He was heading to Canada with another kid when I got wind of the story."

"What wind is this? Why didn't it blow my way?"

"I hear things. Out there. Word is Leroy gave him the money."

"Leroy?" She moved about the office trying to take it all in. "He gave him . . . That's a whole new low, Doc. Sending my son off to a foreign war without bringing me in. Not letting me say good-bye. Or even better, giving me a chance to knock some sense into him. Oh, that man!"

"I don't regret helping him. But I do regret keeping it a secret. I need you to know I tried to talk LJ out of it. But if the Canadians figured out what he was really doing entering their country, he could've landed in prison. At least with my connections, he's under a good commander for now. I hear there's already an American unit under a chap named Charles Sweeney. LJ may end up in his squadron." Doc tried to take her hand, but she twisted away. "I know you're upset."

"Upset? I'm furious."

"Well, then." Doc stood to go. "I'll be off. If you need anything, just—"

"Wait." He was her last link to LJ. "Why didn't he tell me?"

"Why do you think?"

"What's wrong with our Air Force? Eglin is just down the road. Why didn't he just enlist?"

"Like I said, he thought FDR would keep us out. He's a young man, Tooz. He wants to test his mettle. Have an adventure. He's more Leroy than you want to admit," Doc said. "You raised a good man. Be proud of him, of his courage. To be honest, LJ may end up without a war anyway. Chamberlain wants to negotiate peace with Hitler."

"Peace? That maniac invaded Poland." Just then, Dupree looked in. "Did you know too?" she asked. "Did you know your brother was planning to run off?"

"I didn't think he'd do it. And we're out of oil for the popcorn."

"Run 'round to Biggs and buy more. I'll call the supplier in the morning."

Dupree lingered a second, then said, "Sorry about LJ, Ma."

"You don't have to be strong all the time, Tuesday." Doc took her hand. "You can depend on others."

"But I do have to be strong, Doc." If she let herself feel weak—*be* weak—she'd fall apart completely, never to be assembled again. She could sense her joints and bones rattling, about to snap. "I have to be strong for Dupree and the Starlight."

Doc released her hand. "Not much has changed about how I feel, Tuesday, right or wrong. But my heart demands I be your friend first and foremost. So if you—"

"W-when do you think I'll get his letter?" She ached to hear from him, to read his handwriting, to know that he was okay.

"Soon, I reckon. LJ told me to tell you to keep the Starlight on and he'll be home as soon as it's over."

"Then I guess that's something, isn't it?"

25

HARLOW

The Sunday morning golf routine remained a strong tradition in the Cookie and Anne Hayes household. Harlow lay in bed, listening to them bustle about.

"Have you seen my gloves, Anne?"

"In the closet, top drawer. Cook, Marge is on the phone, wants to know if we want to have lunch after."

"Only if Wayne buys. That skinflint wormed his way out of the last five lunches."

"You kept count?"

"Yes, I kept count. Anne, where are my shoes?"

Harlow snickered and realized something about home she'd forgotten. Mom and Dad's morning chatter always felt like love to her.

However, after a week of being in her pink bedroom with the Rick Springfield poster, she knew Buckhead wasn't where she belonged. Nor New York.

Sea Blue Beach was home.

She'd get back there once she got on her feet, dealt with Xander, and landed the CCW job. By then, Matt would be back in Hollywood.

Kicking off the covers and getting out of bed, Harlow slipped into her cut-off sweats and ratty T-shirt with a glance at her old homework desk. A fragrant and stunning bouquet of roses arrived Friday morning from Xander with a handwritten note.

Roses are red, violets are blue, I might be rich, but I'm so poor without you.

His corny little ditty dripped with his signature sincerity. He'd always been self-deprecating about his wealth, careful to realize his privilege came from the hard work of his ancestors.

To her relief, the stir from Matt's faux pas on Letterman died down rather quickly. There were a few clips on entertainment news and stories in the tabloids but not much else. Mom wondered if Xander had something to do with it, but Harlow surmised even the heir of American aristocrats didn't have that sort of clout.

He'd called Friday night, and they talked for an hour.

"People seem to accept Davina and I are over, and I'm still in love with you. Have you thought any more about us?"

"Not much, no. Now that Matt told the world my story, can you answer why you locked me out of the penthouse without a word, Xander? Why you wouldn't take my calls? Why I learned you were back with Davina on Entertainment Tonight*?"*

"I told you, I don't know that Xander Cole. But, darling, I'll spend my life making it up to you. And you and I did talk eventually."

"That doesn't answer my question." Harlow felt as if she channeled a bit of Tuesday's courage. *"You're a forty-four-year-old man, Xander, in command of your own person. You treated me like an enemy."*

"Fair enough, fair enough. I've no excuse. But I'm all in, Harlow. I'll do whatever it takes to win you back."

When they hung up, she thought of Matt. His apology. His expression as she left the Starlight. So genuine and unassuming. For the first time since she met Xander, his sincerity didn't seem as pure as she remembered.

Mom caught her daydreaming several times, and her Yoda-like senses suspected something amiss, worried something might topple her goal of seeing Harlow back on top of the modeling game.

Saturday morning, Harlow braved the scale. She was down ten pounds from the big green machine at Biggs. With Mom's hovering, she knew she'd keep on track.

Saturday afternoon, she joined Dad for lunch at the cookie plant. They had an invigorating discussion about the business book he'd sent to her.

"With your name and reputation, you could start a business, build your own brand in cosmetics or fashion," he said.

"So you're telling me I have options."

"You have options."

"Harlow?" Mom came in as Harlow tied on her running shoes. "We're off to the club. Do you want to come?"

"Mr. Fernsby banned me in 1975."

"I don't think that still stands." Mom walked over to inspect the roses, and Dad leaned against the doorframe. "Fernsby would be groveling at your feet if you showed up."

"Probably not."

Her hook shot on the ninth hole a dozen years ago had sailed over the sand trap and landed smack-dab on the middle of Stu Willingham's bald head. Of course he made a big stink and threatened to sue—who and for what no one knew—but the club acquiesced. Harlow was banned.

However, to this day, the shot was legend, and no matter how much Stu complained, it was part of club lore.

"Nonsense. You're the Harlow Hayes."

"Oh yes, my free pass in life. Mom, I'm sleeping in my teenage bedroom. Not the image most people have of *the* Harlow Hayes."

"It's a step up from sleeping on couches all over Manhattan." Mom straightened the edge of Harlow's covers.

"But not my own place in Sea Blue Beach."

"You had to get away from that monster."

"Matt?" Harlow laughed. "Outing me on national television isn't much worse than what Xander did. The more I think about it, I'm grateful it's out there. No more holding in that secret."

"I still want to know why you never told me he locked you out. Why I had to learn about it on a late-night talk show."

"Anne, let's go." Dad gently steered Mom out the door with a compassionate glance at Harlow. "We're late."

As her parents drove off in one direction, Harlow ran in the other, through the morning sun, sweating out her thoughts. Should she—could she—return to Xander? After seeing a darker side of his character, could she trust him?

She ran two miles in record time, then grabbed a glass of water from Mom's gourmet kitchen.

She'd planned an egg white omelet with toast for breakfast, but being as she was alone, and knowing Dad kept a stash of Hayes Cookies in his desk, she wandered toward his office. How many times had she stared at that drawer, aching to open it but never gave in?

Dad's office of wood and leather overlooked the trees and flower gardens of the backyard and the kidney-shaped pool. Papers, letters, and notes written on scrap paper littered his antique mahogany desk. She studied a drawing of a new cookie package with the ingredients written in a lovely script. Caramel, crushed almonds, chocolate swirls.

A brilliant businessman, Dad worked with eclectic organization.

The wall above the wainscoting was dark blue and mounted with the history of the Hayes Cookie Co., founded by her great-great-grandfather, along with a recipe, a dollar, and two bits. She leaned closer to the large black-and-white print of the first batch of Hayes Cookies. 1887.

"Same year the Starlight was built."

The phone rang, and Harlow let the machine get it. Mom was probably calling to tell her what she could have for breakfast. Or it was Xander, who she didn't want to talk to at the moment.

However, the machine didn't pick up and on the sixth ring, Harlow answered.

"Hayes residence." She flopped into Dad's big comfy chair.

"Hey, it's me."

She fumbled forward, nearly spilling her water. "Matt."

"I just want to say—"

"You don't have to apologize again. You're forgiven. I think it's blown over, really."

"I feel like I can't stop apologizing. But we're cool?"

"Yes, Matt, we're cool. How are the signatures coming?"

"We're getting there. I'm going on the Rollo on the Radio show again. Simon took flyers to the houses on the northwest side of town. A lot of those folks work in Fort Walton and are on the edge of Sea Blue Beach happenings. But we're down to the wire. Last day is Thursday."

"Well, good luck. Tell Tuesday I'm sorry I'm not there to help."

"You're where you're supposed to be. How's it going? Granny and Spike say hi," he said. "Nora and Simon too. Well, everyone at the rink. Audra asked about you."

Twelve years in the world fashion scene and no one had called her in the last two years. Jinx had only reached out once since she left Manhattan. "Tell everyone hi for me. I miss them."

"I'm heading to LA for a week," Matt said. "I'm up for a spy-thriller, and the producers finally settled with the Conner Reid ousting from the Cindy Canon movie. Roger Woods wants to start rehearsals. Not sure I'll be able to make it back for the signature validation."

"Try. Tuesday counts on you."

"She told me to tell you to keep skating."

"Is that a metaphor? It feels like a metaphor." Harlow reached for one of Dad's mechanical pencils and added her doodles to his desk calendar.

Milk chocolate instead of semi-sweet.

Harlow Hayes.

The Starlight.

Matt Knight.

Roller skating.

"Probably. She knew there was a skater in you."

"When she asked me to skate with her, I couldn't say no. Your granny is hard to resist."

"Tell me about it. I've got a story about peas, Saturday morning cartoons, and Cap'n Crunch that'll curl your hair."

"Yeah, well, I've got stories about Anne Hayes that will make your granny look like Santa Claus, the Easter Bunny, and the Tooth Fairy rolled into one."

He was so easy to laugh with. Harlow yanked open Dad's lower desk drawer to see his stash of Hayes Cookies. She dug out a handful.

"Hey, I should let you go," Matt said. "It was good to talk to you."

"Oh, okay. Well, thanks for calling," she said, munching on a small round cookie, craving milk.

"I'll call again, H. I lost one important relationship in my life. I don't want to lose another." *Important?* She was important to him?

"You didn't lose me. I'm glad the world knows. The secret was weighing me down. I'm free of it now." She popped another cookie in her mouth and washed it down with her water.

"Good luck, Harlow."

"S-same to you, Matt. And hey, maybe Booker isn't so mad at you anymore. If I forgave you, maybe he has too."

Harlow settled the receiver on the cradle, wondering why she'd left Sea Blue Beach in such a huff. Maybe she should've stayed. Worked it out with Matt.

Yet, there was Xander and CCW and . . . She grabbed another

handful of cookies and walked to the kitchen for a glass of milk. At the counter, she considered her omelet fixings while licking the cookie dust from her fingers.

Harlow Hayes. What would it take? Every time she made it on the weight-loss bandwagon, she ended up falling off.

Draining the last of the milk, she put her glass in the dishwasher and vowed to be on her guard the rest of the day. She returned to Dad's office, cleaned the crumbs from his desk, and put the almost-empty box back in the drawer with an IOU.

On her way to shower, she detoured into Mom's office. Dad's door was always open but not Mom's. It was her domain, a dark paneled cave with thick carpet, curtained windows, and in Harlow's mind, secrets.

Mom's desk, unlike Dad's, was neat and organized, with her Day-Timer open to today's date. Harlow flipped through her schedule of dinners and meetings. She had a note to call Jinx, with *CCW update* circled in red.

Mom, oh, Mom. She needed a life beside Harlow's. The office had no personal or private photos of their family life. No family vacations. No Christmas mornings or Thanksgiving dinners. The frames on the credenza were of Harlow on the runway. Harlow's first *Vogue*. Mom and Harlow during Fashion Week. Dad, Mom, and Harlow at the *Talk to Me Sweetly* premiere. A half dozen Harlow headshots from various photo shoots.

Mom, oh, Mom. A stranger would think she merely kept the stock photo that came with the frame. It all felt so cold. It reminded her of Xander's office, also with very few personal photos.

He had two, actually. Both formal, shot by Princess Diana's favorite photographer, Patrick Demarchelier. One from their engagement, which Harlow had loved. It was a stunning black-and-white taken at the family's Montauk house. And the other at the Coles' private island.

Harlow thought of her own house. Why hadn't she set out pictures? Next time she went to 321 Sea Blue Way, she was going to take a lot of pictures, frame them, and fill the barren part of the wall going into the kitchen. She had a top-of-the-line Nikon upstairs in her bedroom.

Thinking of Sea Blue Beach made her smile. She'd framed a few mental pictures in the last few months. Tripping down the Beachwalk in a pair of brownies. Falling across the Starlight floor in Tuesday's skates. Matt's alluring, teasing smile—that's his real crime, being so darn handsome—the morning he banged on her door at five a.m. to go for a jog.

She also felt a bit energized about her goals to undo the last two years, regain her reputation, and have a future with CCW. Also, Harlow Hayes needed money. After that, she could decide the rest of her life. Viewing options from on top of the world were far better than the ones at rock bottom.

She peeked in Mom's cherrywood filing cabinet, which was full of meeting minutes, and travel agendas from Harlow's early days in modeling. In the closet, she found a couple of sweaters and Mom's UGA cheerleading outfit. Classic long skirt, saddle oxfords, and a sweater sporting a big *G*. On the top shelf was Dad's old projector and tucked into the back corner was Grandma's trunk. She'd never looked in the large leather thing before. She wasn't even sure why Mom had kept it. She had very few mementoes from her impoverished childhood, least of all anything Grandma owned.

A red-and-cream-colored paper with pastoral scenes lined the inside. The top drawer held several dull brass medals on faded ribbons from Mom's college days, a picture of Dad's first day at Hayes Cookie Co., when he was, like, twelve, and a frame with his college diploma.

Harlow removed the drawer to find an old photo album she'd never seen before. When she dug it out, a musty, ephemeral odor floated into the closet. The album was thick with images of Anne Hayes, née Greensly, as the Miss Georgia first runner-up, 1955. Mom! Harlow knew this room had secrets.

What else was hidden in this treasure trove? Dad's high school letterman sweater and a pair of very tired-looking leather roller skates. Beneath those things Harlow found Mom's senior yearbook. 1953.

"You told me you lost this." Harlow settled with her back against the wall and flipped it open. Mom was beautiful with her fifties hairstyle and fixed smile. The pages were loaded with signatures.

To Anne, the most beautiful girl in school. Good luck. Harvey. '54.

Anne, will you marry me? Har! Fred Posey. '56.

Anne, we had so much fun in Mrs. Wallace's Home Ec. class but you're going to be a star in New York. Remember me when you're famous! Always, Lucy DeMarco. '53.

Famous? Mom never wanted to be famous. She just wanted to marry "the Cookie Monster," her nickname for Dad.

At the page titled *1953 Trojan Ambitions*, Harlow scanned for Mom's name. Anne Greensly, Anne Greensly.

I'm going to be a famous model and actress.

Harlow read the words over and over. Since when? Scouring through the yearbook, Harlow learned Mom had been homecoming queen and star of the high school play, *Junior Miss*.

She never! When Harlow adjusted the book to crawl out of the closet into a better light, a manila envelope fell out.

At Mom's desk, she dumped the envelope's contents. Eight-by-ten headshots of Mom, eight-by-tens of her walking down Madison Avenue with two very beautiful women. Harlow recognized both of them: Winnie Hart, now famous under her real name, Wilhelmina, and the gorgeous Sunny Harnett. The date on the white edge was May 1957.

The last picture was a snapshot in a quintessential midtown office with long windows overlooking the city. Mom stood by the corner of a desk, arms folded, her gaze fixed on a man talking to a statuesque beauty with artisan features.

Annis Miller, founder of the Icon Agency. This looked like some sort of meeting, not a photo shoot. Mom wore a suit and heels, her brownish-gold hair styled in a simple flip. Why was she so fixed on the man, the one who pointed to the papers in Annis's hand? He looked familiar. Dashing smile, dashing jaunt in his stance, his hair in a dashing ducktail probably held in place with a good *dash* of tonic.

Whoever held the camera captured a private moment. Mom definitely had eyes only for him. Her expression was . . . love.

In that moment, the past and the present collided, and Harlow jumped up. The man. She knew him.

"Oh my gosh—"

"Harlow?" Mom dropped her clubs against the wall. "What in the world are you doing in here?"

26

MATT

Night had long since settled over Sea Blue Beach as he joined Dad on the back porch steps after the Starlight's Tuesday evening session.

"Is Granny skating?" Dad reached into his mini cooler and passed Matt a beer.

"She's carrying on like nothing's changing." The bubbles of the beer felt good on his tired throat. As the evening DJ, he'd mixed things up, resurrecting some of the old racing and tag games, which involved a lot of shouting and whistle blowing, but what a blast. Who could stay depressed trying to Hokey Pokey on wheels? Or feel angry while relay racing to the Jackson 5's "Rockin' Robin"?

"I'd expect no less," Dad said. "She's been my rock all my life. I'd not be here without her. Without that crazy Starlight."

"You should tell her that, Dad. She thinks you gave up your dreams for her. Thinks you resent the Starlight."

"Maybe. I thought she'd get the picture, what with me building my business and raising you here. Though she's not entirely wrong. Growing up, I had it in my head I was fourth in line behind LJ, the Starlight, and Pa. Maybe even Doc." Dad set aside his empty beer bottle. "Then we all went to war . . ."

"Who's Doc again?"

"The older gentleman who ran with Pa's crew for a while. We met him when he dug a bullet out of Pa's shoulder one night." Dad pointed toward the rink. "In the back room. I think he had a thing for Ma. But for her, there was only Pa. Who didn't deserve her." He looked over at Matt. "Just so you know, there's nothing out there more valuable than family, friends, a good town, and a solid job that allows you to go to your kid's ball games. When your mom died, that's when I saw how great your granny was, and I gave up some of my young man foolishness."

"Hark, Sea Blue Beach! Dupree Knight is expressing tenderness for his ma and son."

"Don't be a wise guy." But there was a layer of affection in Dad's voice. "I'm not sure I can sleep without the Starlight sign casting its colorful glow over the town. Sometimes even makes me want to skate."

"If you showed up with skates, Granny would keel over."

"Probably," Dad said. "So, you're going to LA? Any word from Harlow?"

"I'll be back in a couple of weeks. The petitions come down Thursday for verification. Spike and Mary are going to take care of it. I called Harlow, and she's forgiven me, but we've 'called it a day,' as she said. Besides, I'm not sure I can compete with Xander Cole anyway."

"You're ten times better than Xander Cole. What about your misdemeanor charge? Any word from Bodie?"

"The state attorney has to decide if they have a case. I'm hoping they consider a misdemeanor charge involving a Hollywood star is not worth the hassle. I'd be happy to pay a fine. Even apologize to Cranston."

"I've been thinking about your diarrhea-of-the-mouth issue."

"You got some Pepto-Bismol wisdom for me?"

"Matt, I think you should call Booker."

As he chewed on Dad's advice, the Starlight sign cut through the dark horizon. The wind rose and fell. Somewhere on the next street over, an engine revved.

"I think that's what's been eating you up inside all these years. Why you let people walk all over you, crash at your place, trash it. You don't think you deserve your success because you ruined Booker's life. Or so you believe."

"And I'm still messing up people's lives. Look, Dad, Book blasted me in front of everyone that one Christmas we were both home. He made it clear he never wanted to talk to or see me again."

"Then you stopped coming home for holidays."

"I flew you and Granny to my place a couple of times." Though nothing compared to Christmas at the Starlight. Not even Tinseltown.

"I've been thinking about the night you blabbed," Dad said. "You were supposed to meet him at the Starlight, right? Then you ran into Ricky and Jonas. You never showed."

"Yeah, so? He was off stealing the test."

"I wonder if he wanted you to talk him out of it."

"It's a decent theory, Pop, but I'm still the one who blabbed. Would Principal Conroy have been more lenient if the whole school didn't know?"

Matt distracted himself from the familiar sense of guilt by breaking off the twigs and peeling the loose bark from a stick he found at the bottom of the steps.

"Booker is responsible for his own actions. Even his daddy Abel said so. But your friend needed you that night, Matt," Dad said, "and you never showed. Did you ever apologize to him for *that*?"

TUESDAY

SEPTEMBER 1940

A girl did the best she could, you know, after her son ran off to join a foreign military. As promised, LJ sent a letter from New York before boarding the Queen Mary.

> *I'm sorry I didn't tell you, Ma, but I was afraid you'd talk me out of it, and I wanted to go. Doc says I'll be well cared for, and there's a group of American fellas flying for a Charles Sweeney. I promise to be careful. You know I'm good for it. I never lied to you except this. Don't let Dup get away with anything. I've written to him too, told him to help you without giving you lip. I think he's good for it. Well, the train's pulling into the station. That's why my writing is so wobbly. I'll get this in the nearest postbox. I love you, Ma.*

In the first few months he was gone, he wrote often, promised he was thriving, excelling in his training, and learning the ways of the British.

But now England was in the fight. Chamberlain did *not* broker peace with Herr Hitler, who American journalists called a caricature and a clown. Yet that *clown* amassed an army, invaded Czechoslovakia after Poland, and, in July, bombed London. As far as Tuesday Knight was concerned, he bombed her boy.

In August, Leroy started showing up. He looked old and worn out, like a man carrying on in sinful living. He puttered around the house, fixing things like the rotted posts on the porch and leaks in the roof. Even fixed the loose floorboard in the kitchen. Thank goodness LJ had removed the deed box. Tuesday made a note to ask him where he'd hidden it in her next letter.

Lee painted the house a pretty blue and hammered new white shutters by the front window. He mowed the lawn and plowed up the front flower bed for perennials. He bought her a new washing machine and showed her plans to expand the kitchen and add on a family room.

Wasn't that peachy? Yet every night as Leroy mopped the gravy from his plate with her homemade bread, he never said a word about why he was home or about her old potbelly stove.

In September, he showed up with workers and technicians to install central air conditioning at the Starlight. Central. Air. Conditioning. Land sakes alive. At the Starlight! It was practically unheard of in these parts, except for movie theaters, but the old Midnight didn't have A/C. Dale Cranston Sr., who just remodeled the place with his granddaddy's inheritance but decided against central air, turned every shade of green.

Tuesday asked Lee a hundred times, "Where did you get the money?"

"Someone owed me a favor," he answered a hundred times in return.

He pulled out his Richardsons and joined her at the rink several nights a week, and even took a turn playing the Wurlitzer. He only knew one song, but my, how her heart overflowed.

The boss man with the thick brow and beady eyes came around once in a while, inspecting the Starlight with a hungry look in his eyes, talking in low tones to Lee.

Once, after skating and devouring ice cream cones on the porch, Lee dared to ask if she still kept the deed to the rink at the house. And if she'd filed it with the county.

She scooted closer to him, kissed his full, ice cream–sweetened lips. "You know what I said, Lee. If you ever asked about the rink again, I'll kick you out of my house for the rest of your born days. Hear me?"

By the look on his face, he heard.

Even better than all the buying, skating, loving, and sprucing up, Lee and Dupree talked like men. A high school graduate now, Dup worked for Mr. Day's carpentry company full-time. In the evenings, he and Leroy listened to the radio and talked sports and war.

It took some time, but Tuesday grew accustomed to her husband being home, though she knew better than to hope this was the new way of things. Lee carried a faraway look in his eyes, and his shoulders sagged under a heaviness known only to him.

One night, as she washed dishes and he rolled a cigarette, she said, "I don't like you talking to Dup about war, Lee. He's a dreamer. He'll get wild ideas in his head, try to join up like his brother did. LJ's going to lose his citizenship over this. I don't want Dupree following the same path."

"LJ will be fine. Once we're in this thing, the American government will do something for the boys who fought for England. As for Dup, I told him to stick near Sea Blue Beach." Leroy struck a match, and the fragrance of tobacco filled the kitchen. "Until he gets called up. Though he should be going off to college."

"What?" Tuesday exclaimed. "Called up?"

"There's something else too, baby. I talked to my old commander." Lee moved to the porch door to release a plume of smoke. "I can reenlist, go in at my former rank of sergeant."

"Reenlist?" Tuesday flung water and suds to the floor as she whirled around. "You're thinking of going back in the army? You're forty-two years old. Why would they want you? Why do you want to go? What happened to FDR keeping us out of this?"

"When you see rain clouds gathering . . ." Leroy took a long drag of his cigarette. "The army wants experienced men. Besides, I done some things I ain't proud of, Tooz." Regret tainted his confession. "I told myself I was doing it for you and the boys, getting us to a better life. After all, how can a common working man climb the ladder of success when greedy politicians make laws for their own benefit and hike up the taxes?"

"You don't have to join the army to redeem yourself, Lee. Just start doing honest work."

"I ain't cut out to run a skating rink, Tuesday. Or sack groceries or sweep floors. The boss is after me to run gambling in the back room at the Starlight after closing." Leroy's cigarette perfumed the kitchen with tobacco. "I want out of the racket. This ain't my game, never was, but I tried. Doc said it best. 'Lee, you're a fighter.' He's right. Ever since the Great War, I ain't found my place." He looked into her eyes. "Except with you." He dropped his cigarette to the porch boards and stamped it out. "I liked soldiering. It was honorable. Compared to what I do now, it's downright noble."

Tuesday dried her hands, wrapped her arms about his waist, and rested her head against his chest. "You do what you have to do, Leroy Knight. And when you're done, I'll be here, waiting for you."

He tipped her face up to his with a soft touch on her chin. "*You* are my starlight, Tuesday Knight. I loved you the first moment I saw you." His kiss was tender and full of love. "I'm sorry I've let you down."

"You gave me two beautiful boys, a home—"

"Lonely nights."

"The Starlight."

"Raising our boys on your own."

"Yet here we are with two healthy, *good* sons, a business I love and can run on my own. You may have run around too much for my taste, but you never abandoned me like my mama and granny. You gave me what no one else saw fit to do. You gave me love. Lee, I've felt it from the first time you held my hand."

He wrapped her in his arms and together they faced the cool wind as the first raindrops fell. "I'll be around for a little while," he said. "I'll fix up the house and anything else you need at the Starlight." He tugged a piece of paper from his pocket. "This is a bank account in New Orleans. Never, ever show it to anyone, hear me? But if you need anything, you call this number and ask for Monte."

"Lee, I don't want blood money."

"It ain't blood money. In fact, I've probably saved it from being blood money."

"You stole it?"

"From thieves, crooks, murderers, and liars, yes."

"Then I can't." She tried to shove the note away, but Lee folded it into her hand.

"I won't sleep at night unless you have this, Tooz. You don't have to use it if you don't want, but just in case . . ."

She relented and tucked the paper in her pocket. "Dup's manning the rink tonight with Treader. How about we drive over to Niceville and see the new Roy Rogers picture, *Colorado*?"

"You just want to see if the newsreels will update you on the battle in Britain."

"We might get a glimpse of LJ."

"How long since you've had a letter?"

"Three weeks, maybe more."

"He'll write, baby. He loves his mama too much to let her worry."

"He's doing a poor job of it at the moment."

Leroy laughed and patted her bottom. "You get dolled up, Tooz. I'll finish here."

Lee doing the dishes? Sakes a'mighty. Miracles happened in Sea Blue Beach. She liked to think the Starlight had a part to play.

At the bathroom sink, she washed her face, put on a bit of rouge and lipstick, then fluffed the curls on the ends of her hair. She slipped from her housedress to the new frock she'd ordered from Montgomery Ward and exchanged her everyday shoes for a pair of low-heeled pumps usually reserved for church, weddings, and funerals. Clipping on a pair of earrings, she glanced out the window toward the Starlight.

When she came down, Leroy had dried and put away the dishes, hung the towel on its rack, combed his hair, and tied his tie.

"I checked the mail." He motioned to the table. "A couple of bills. I'll pay those." He reached for a yellowish envelope. "LJ."

"A letter? Not a telegram?" Tuesday tore at the flap, but she was shaking so hard, Leroy took over and read aloud. "'Dear Ma . . .'"

Just a short note to say I'm fine. Don't worry. Your boy LJ knows how to take care of himself. I can't pretend you don't know how rotten it is over here. The Huns are really giving it to us. I'd like to say the blitzkriegs are propaganda, but we hear the Messerschmidts day and night. Us chaps on base are all right. We play cards and listen to Glen Miller, but everyone in England, especially London, is pretty jacked. They're sending all the kids to the country. I'm glad I'm here, Ma. Glad to do my bit. It's not just about flying—though no lie, I dig it—but to fight for the good guys. I think of Pa and the Great War. Maybe I'll help save the world like he did.

She glanced at Lee, whose eyes glistened.

I miss you and the Starlight. Even that little pest Dupree. How is he? I'll drop him a line soon. Is he wanting to join up yet? He won't have to wait long 'cause most of us don't think the president can keep the good ol' US of A out. Best get some shut eye. Signing off and hoping to dream of you, Sea Blue Beach, and the Starlight.

Your loving son,
LJ

She pressed the letter to her face and tried to breathe in the scent of her son. "He's all right, he's all right."

"Of course he is." Leroy said. "He's a Knight. Let's get to the movies and maybe catch a glimpse of him on the newsreels."

"I like what he wrote about you, Lee." Tuesday tucked the letter inside her purse. She'd read it ten more times before closing her eyes tonight.

"Maybe he'll stop hating me so much."

Tuesday slipped her hand into her husband's. "You know the line between love and hate is thin. So very, very thin."

27

HARLOW

"You told me you lost your senior yearbook." Harlow handed the yellow-and-black book to Mom, who dropped it to her desk without a second glance.

"I did. For a while. Now it's found. I don't understand what you're doing in here, Harlow."

"Snooping, Mom. Like all good daughters do. You're supposed to be golfing."

"Marge hurt her back, so Wayne took her home. Then it looked like it might rain, so we thought we'd have a nice brunch with you."

Harlow picked up the yearbook and flipped to Mom's senior ambition page. "'I'm going to be a famous model and actress.'"

"I had to write something." Mom pressed one hand to her forehead and anchored the other on her hip. "Everyone knows those things are all hype."

"What about these?" Harlow held up the black-and-whites. "These are professional photos, Mom. This is a headshot. This is a stroll down Madison Avenue with Sunny Harnett and Winnie Hart."

"I know who they are, Harlow."

"Me too. You made sure of it. What I don't know is why you're with them or why you didn't tell me any of this. You were Miss Georgia runner-up? A model?"

"It didn't seem important. I was focused on you."

"Our trips to New York, the networking, the pushing and shoving is finally making sense. You knew all the right people, didn't you?" Harlow held up the picture of Mom sitting in the office. "But here's my real question. What are you doing with Devier Cole, now one of the most powerful men in Hollywood and the *uncle* of my former fiancé?"

"Anne, Harlow?" Dad appeared at the door. "What's going on?"

"Harlow snooped through my things." Mom shot Dad a pointed look.

He glanced down at the photos and yearbook. "She found your trunk."

"I asked you to throw it out," Mom said. "But you insisted on keeping it."

"I thought you might want the contents someday."

"I don't, and now Harlow is in my business."

"Mom, why the big secret? So you modeled. Why didn't you tell me? It would've helped me make sense of my life. Dad, what's your part in all of this?"

"You."

"Me? What do you—" Harlow fell against the desk with a glance at her mother. "You got pregnant with me." More shadows peeled away.

"Well, now she knows, Cookie. All the years of hiding it were for nothing."

"I never wanted to hide it, Anne."

"Oh my gosh . . . wait. I don't understand. I thought you married right after college. Mom, what's the look you're giving Devier?" Harlow examined the photo again. "Were you in love with him?"

"Very much, but he wasn't in love with me." Mom tugged off

her golf gloves. "Fell for him the moment I met him. Sort of like you did Xander. But it wasn't two-sided. After my year as a Miss Georgia runner-up ended, I took a semester off, went to New York, and signed with Icon. Annis wanted me to meet him. Dev was older, charming, and the most marvelous man I'd ever seen. We had a few dates—probably for publicity's sake—but there was no spark for him. He left for Hollywood right after that picture was taken. I came home to finish school the fall of '57. I ran into your dad at a football game and—"

"Eventually made me," Harlow said. "You wanted a career in modeling and acting, but you got me instead. Which you didn't want. So I became your puppet, the kid who fulfilled your lost dream. Do you know when I was seven, I sat on the stairs one night, listening to you cry, telling Dad how you grew up poor and never had anything of your own. How you just wanted a chance. You were crying so much it scared me. Mom, I thought something had happened to you, or that Grandma pulled her tricks again. Little did I know it was because of me. From that moment on, all I ever wanted was for you *not* to be sad."

"That's ridiculous. Why didn't you say something?"

"I was seven. I didn't know to say anything."

"So because you eavesdropped, misunderstood a complicated conversation, and made some childish assumptions, I'm the bad guy here?"

"No, Mom, that's not—I mean . . . From that day on, I made a promise to myself to make you happy. Didn't it seem weird to you I never rebelled, never said no, loved everything you loved?"

"I just thought—"

"Did it ever occur to you to ask *me* what I wanted? Man, it all makes sense now. I grow up with an ambition to make you happy, but you had no intention of making *me* happy."

"Harlow, that's not fair," Dad said. "Your mother loves you. She—"

"Saw an opportunity with her above-average-looking little girl?

Made some calls to all the right people? Entered me in fashion shows here and there? Enrolled me in charm school." Harlow tucked the photos in the envelope and returned them to the yearbook. "I was with Xander for two years and you never once told me about Devier. Is he the reason I got the part in *Talk to Me Sweetly*? He is the studio head."

"Your mom was only trying to help you get into acting."

"Did I want to be in acting? Not really. But, Mom, you did, didn't you? Star of the school play."

"Harlow, I understand you are angry," Dad said. "But watch your tone."

"You're darn right I am angry. Why didn't you stick up for me, Dad? Why did you let her do it? You say I have a head for business, but you never stepped in, never let me work at the cookie plant."

"Your mom didn't want you around all the cookies."

"Afraid I'd be a *chip* off the old Cookie Monster block? That I'd like Dad's world more than yours? That I'd turn into who—*what*—I am now?"

"Harlow, that's enough," Mom said. "Neither one of us deserves your attitude."

"Don't you? I've felt unwanted and empty before, but I really feel it now. I didn't think anything could top Xander locking me out of the penthouse and not speaking to me for months. Or Matt blabbing my private life on Letterman. But this?" She held up the yearbook. "Tops the two worst days of my life."

"I find that harsh." Mom squared up, chin raised, eyes narrowed. "I never imagined you'd be so ungrateful. I steer you toward untold opportunities and fame, and what do I get in return? Lip. Sour grapes. I'm hurt, Harlow. I'll not deny it." She sniffed and wiped under her eyes.

For the first time in her life, Mom's tears did not move Harlow. "That makes two of us. You weren't helping me find opportunities and fame—you were helping yourself. I finished your dream because I was the one who interrupted it."

"That's nonsense. Your gain does not return my loss."

"Do you hear yourself? You count me as a loss. Not that you gained a child, or built on the Hayes family legacy, but an interruption to your ambitions. Do you two even love each other?"

"Of course we do." Mom paced the office, one hand on her back, one on her forehead. "Is this Dr. Tagg's wisdom? Some psychobabble? Blame all your woes on your parents?"

"No, Mom, this is my wisdom. Believe it or not, I can think for myself. I have ideas about who Harlow Hayes wants—no, no more referring to myself in third person. Who *I* want to be."

Mom huffed and faced the window, arms folded tight. "So sue me, I made a few calls. Isn't it enough that I could see you were something special?"

"I wish it was but, Mom, I felt more like your project than your daughter."

Mom turned from the window as Harlow picked up the yearbook and headed out of the office. "Where are you going?" Mom followed her. "Bring that back."

"I'm going home, and this is coming with me." Tasting freedom trumped all the junk food she'd ever consumed. Including Tony's pizza and a potato-chip spoon dipped in ice cream.

"Home? You are home. Harlow?"

TUESDAY

OCTOBER 1940

Fall, such as it was in the Florida Panhandle, descended on Sea Blue Beach. The humidity thinned, making an eighty degree day almost cool.

Hauling a small load of laundry from her new Maytag wringer washer, Tuesday made her way through the morning sun to the clothesline, pausing to look up at the sound of an airplane engine.

Some of the boys at Eglin had taken to waving a wing as they flew over the Starlight and the house on their way to maneuvers. She'd lift her hand and wave, hoping some British mother did the same for her son, if perhaps he flew over her yard while she hung the family laundry.

She clipped the towels and sheets to the line, humming to herself. Imagine, men flying like birds. When she was born in 1900, no one had ever flown anything motorized. She'd seen an air balloon at a fair when she was ten, but those pilots had little control. They could never outrun a hail of enemy bullets.

She tried to enjoy the beautiful morning, but she worried. The last letter she'd received from LJ was the day she went to the movies with Leroy. They sat through *Colorado* twice, hoping for a glance of their son in the newsreel, but no such luck.

She also had a list of chores on her mind. The staff was giving the Starlight a good cleaning, and Walt Marrs was mending the wood floor damaged by a skater who strapped on a pair of metal street skates. The accounts needed to be updated and the staff scheduled for the Halloween All Night Skate.

While President Roosevelt's fireside chats continued to assure Americans he "hoped the United States will keep out of this war," more and more flyboys showed up at the Starlight on the weekends, which was where LJ should be. But why dredge it all up again? Just be proud of him.

Leroy was away at boot camp. In his last letter, he said he'd be home in mid to late October.

We've a lot of work to do if we want to be ready to fight. The president is being political, Tooz, but we're going in one way or another. I know this means I'm away from you again, but it feels right to be here and take a stand for something good and decent. Believe it or not, I'm doing it for you.

This time, she believed him.

Dupree remained at his job and excelled. In the evening, he was glued to the radio for war news, bragging what he'd do when called up and shipped "over there."

Tuesday prayed every night the call would never come.

She'd hung the last of the washing on the line when she saw Doc's car turning down the drive. A splinter of dread stuck in her craw. While she counted him a trusted friend, he was so often the bearer of bad news.

He parked his Deuce under a shade tree trying to turn green into gold.

"Just in time for some breakfast." Tuesday met him in the yard, the empty basket resting against her hip. "Coffee's still hot."

"Here, let me." He took the basket, set it on the back porch by the washer, and followed her inside. "Lee said he'd done some sprucing up."

"You've talked to Leroy?" She settled the iron skillet on the stove, added wood to the fire, and reached for the can of bacon grease. "Prop that door open, will you?" Her ol' wood-burning stove still turned the kitchen into a furnace.

"He's doing well." Doc set his hat on the hook, then did as she asked. "He's a soldier. I think that's why and how he ended up with the Memphis mob. He needed a cause." There was sympathy in his eyes as he took a seat at the table. "All your boys will be in Europe before it's said and done. Best prepare yourself."

"Then I'll keep the Starlight shining."

He smiled softly. "Tuesday, leave that and sit down with me."

"W-why?" Her legs weakened as she moved to the nearest chair. "You're scaring me."

He reached into his shirt pocket and produced a telegram. "I got this the other day. LJ put me down as his next of kin."

"No." He pressed it into her trembling hand, but she stood, jerking away. "Do not come in here again as the Doctor of Doom. I won't have it. Whatever that telegram says, it's a lie."

She slammed the skillet on top of the stove, then flung it against the wall. Melting grease puddled on the floor, and the hot handle had marked her palm. "This is your fault. *You* let him go. You gave into his wild ideas. You fixed it with your old commander or your wife's family." She ran her hand under cool water, sobbing. "*Noooooo!* No, no, no!"

Doc took her into his arms. "At some point, every boy becoming a man must test himself. Am I brave enough? Am I strong enough? Am I honorable enough? He must find something to believe in that's bigger than himself. God. Country. Family. A war against evil. He died a hero, Tooz. He'd want you to be proud. He shot—"

"I don't want to hear it. I. Don't. Want. To. Hear. It."

"—down a Junker headed for London. But when he dove away, he crashed into a Messerschmitt. They both went down."

She slumped into him with one hammer of her fist against his chest. He braced her with his hand around her waist, but after a moment, they sank to the floor together.

"I want . . . I want . . . him . . . I want him back, Doc." Shaking, she washed his shirt with her tears. "Get him back!"

"I wish I could, Tooz."

The fire blazed in the stove while the kitchen turned dark and cold as she wept and remembered.

The sweet, dimply, curly-headed baby with the roly-poly thighs. The toddler trying to run before he could walk, banging into furniture, falling down and getting up again. The six-year-old determined to do it all by himself. The ten-year-old who shot up four inches in one year. The big brother who wrestled in the yard with Dupree, laughing. The teenager who kicked a can down the street as he walked to school with his buddies, his books slung over his shoulder, bundled by a leather strap. The boy who became a man and said to her, *"I want to fly, Ma. I want to fly."*

"Doc." Tuesday dried her face with the hem of her apron. "It was *me*. I'm the one who told him to go." She pushed to her feet and walked out to the porch, faced the Starlight, and dried her cheeks. "He said to me, 'I want to fly, Ma.' And I told him, 'Then go fly.'"

"That's the best thing you could've ever done for him." Doc stood beside her. "We're going to need an army of LJs in the days ahead."

"They have Lee. He's worth ten men."

"True enough, from what I've observed." Doc glanced down at her. "You're worth a thousand women, Tuesday."

She brushed his shirt where her tears had left a stain. "You're worth quite a bit yourself, but you absolutely must stop delivering bad news." The wind snapped the clothes on the line. She'd forgotten all about the laundry or the chores needing to be done. "What happens now?"

"He'll receive the Distinguished Flying Cross, I'm sure, possibly other medals as well, and the heartfelt thanks of the British people."

"His body?"

"The bottom of the Channel."

She swiped away fresh tears. "He loved the water as much as the air, so rest in peace, Leroy Jr." She wondered if she'd break again, rattled by tears and grief, but the view of the Starlight anchored her.

Life and death were assured, but the Starlight would remain because Immanuel watched over it. He watched over them all.

"Does Lee know?"

A car stopped at the end of the drive, and a man in uniform stepped out.

"He knows," Doc said.

Tuesday ran down the slippery sand-and-shell driveway and launched into her husband's arms. "He's gone, Lee. He's gone."

"I know, baby, but I'm here now. I'm here."

TUESDAY

MAY 1987

She'd heard it said, "You can't fight city hall." Well, you can't rush them either. Which was exactly what she told Matt when he called for the umpteenth time.

"Nothing yet, Matty. I've lived in Sea Blue Beach for eighty-seven years, and no one has ever rushed the council."

The petition-gathering window had closed two weeks ago. The supervisor of elections had the lists and was verifying that every signature belonged to a Sea Blue Beach registered voter. After Matt's stint on Letterman and his second appearance on Rollo on the Radio, they'd collected almost four hundred names. Fifty more than needed.

Well done, Sea Blue Beach. Tuesday suspected Immanuel's hand in it as well.

"I'm calling Harry," Matt said. "They don't need two weeks to verify the signatures, Granny."

"Let this matter play out. City hall can't defeat the Starlight. I'm declaring it now. She's built on the rock." Her voice rose with a preacher vibe. "Let the waves roll. Either Immanuel's got this or he doesn't."

"Granny, Immanuel is a painted man on a Starlight mural."

"He's God with us, and whether you like it or not, He's all we got, Matt. We've seen what man can do, now let's see what God can do. How's the movie business?"

"Great. We're rehearsing the rom-com. Filming starts in June. Last night Cosmo told me I landed the role of Luke Orman in a spy-thriller called *Cloak of Darkness*. It's not big money up front, but if the film does what they expect, it'll be my biggest role and paycheck ever."

"Money doesn't buy happiness, Matty. In fact, in my life, money—or the quest for it—only brought pain."

Simon entered with a pair of brownies that had seen better days and added them to the donation box. Recently, a man in Pensacola had contacted her about restoring old skates. He fixed them up with outdoor wheels and donated them to city kids.

In moments like these, it seemed the Starlight would go on forever and ever. It must. Surely the prince and Immanuel worked something out all those years ago.

"Granny, did you hear me?"

"Sorry, Simon came in the office. What did you say?"

"Have you heard from Harlow? I thought she'd keep in touch with you, but—"

"Why would she, Matty? She's off living her life, just like you. As all kids should. Pretty soon things will get back to normal around here, and all this talk of destroying the Starlight will be put to bed and we'll chug along like always."

"I miss her, Granny," Matt said.

"Then go after her."

"She made her feelings known. Called it a day. I hurt her like I did Booker. She forgave me, but . . ." Matt's hesitation told her he wasn't convinced. "I think she'll go back to Cole. Why not? Handsome. Rich. The Beauty and the Billionaire."

"Poppycock, Matt. Harlow may have a wounded wing, but that billionaire isn't the one to mend it. With all his money and privilege, he lacks one thing."

"What? A royal title?"

"Wits. He don't have your wits. And I'll tell you something else, you see Harlow in a way no one else does. I've seen the way you two interact. Peas in a pod."

"I don't think so, Granny. Besides, you're biased. Judging by Harlow's reaction to Xander's visit, she still has feelings for him."

"You never knew your Grandpa Lee, but even with all of his shenanigans, we were connected in a way words couldn't explain. I guess you'd say soulmates these days. That's what you and Harlow are, Matty. Soulmates." Truth timely spoken felt like gold to her. Honestly, people should try it.

He laughed. "Granny, you old romantic."

"Matt, you have some regrets. We all do. Don't let Harlow be one."

Tuesday felt a twinge of regret not telling him Harlow was right here, at the Starlight, but it was at her request. *"I got some things to figure out. So I'll just be a regular gal around Sea Blue Beach and the Starlight."* Though with the supermodel back at the rink, Matt would find out soon enough.

The beauty returned almost two weeks ago. Came asking for her job on a Tuesday morning and started that afternoon. She looked softer than before, as if something transpired to let the light inside out, though a shadow or two still flickered through her famous blue eyes from time to time.

"What do you hear from Bodie on your case?" Tuesday said.

"The State Attorney's office asked for an extension. Bodie is sure they don't have enough to prosecute. Dale's probably trying to pressure them. He thinks he has more clout than he does."

"I hope you've learned a thing or two in this process, Matt. Like your dad says, figure out what's eating you." Tuesday sensed a presence at the office door. Harry. "Matty, let me call you back. The mayor is here."

"Great, put me on speaker—"

She pressed the end button on the portable phone. "Harry, what brings you around to the Starlight?"

28

HARLOW

The cool May morning pushed her to run a little farther, a little faster. She'd have to measure the distance with her car, but she figured two and a quarter miles.

She worked the afternoon and evening shifts at the rink, so she used her morning for chores. She balanced her bank account, tossed in a load of laundry, unloaded the dishwasher, manhandled the trash can out to the street just as the garbage truck went by, and watered the plants she'd potted in the kitchen and living room. And framed what personal photos she could find before leaving Buckhead.

One of her at a friend's birthday party. She was probably ten. It was blurry, but she loved it.

One of Dad working the batter machine at Hayes Cookie Co.

One of Harlow reading through her lines on the set of *Talk to Me Sweetly*.

One of Mom's modeling headshots.

She almost called Matt to dish about her Mom discovery, but she'd made it clear they were done. It didn't seem fair to stir things up.

With her Nikon, Harlow explored Sea Blue Beach, finding all the quaint corners and old buildings for her creative lens. One roll was entirely of sunsets, sunrises, and the Starlight. She had three rolls at Alderman's Pharmacy for development and planned to frame the best of the best. More and more, 321 Sea Blue Way became Harlow Hayes's—no, it became *her* home.

Tucking her keys and some money in her pocket, she headed out the door. First stop Alderman's to see if her photos were back, then to the library to pick up a stack of business books, then the Blue Plate for lunch. During her run, she'd used her mental energy to psych herself up for a big garden salad with grilled shrimp. But lettuce and tomato never measured up to the breakfast platter of eggs, bacon, fried potatoes, and pancakes. During the whole two-plus miles, she feared she'd cave. The struggle was real.

A couple of teen girls across the street hollered at her. "Harlow, we're coming to skate tonight." Another woman stopped her in the middle of the sidewalk with a gentle tap on her arm. "Any word on the signature verification? I got my whole family to sign the petition."

"Still waiting." She started to say Tuesday was anxiously waiting, but now that she thought about it, the older woman seemed remarkably calm.

The rest of the town buzzed with anxiety, though. Would there be a Starlight or a Murdock monstrosity this time next year? Tension mounted as dissenting opinions debated in the public square.

The photos weren't back yet at Alderman's. So she headed to the Blue Plate's back deck by way of the Beachwalk.

"Harlow, hello." Xander popped out of nowhere and stood in front of her.

"Xander!" She jumped back, taking him in. Dressed in a blue pullover and pressed khakis with Top-Siders, his thick black hair lightly touched with silver and tousled by the wind, he seemed larger than life. And so oddly out of place.

"Sorry, did I scare you?" He laughed low.

Since she left Buckhead, he'd called her a half dozen times and sent a box of her clothes and shoes Davina had stuffed in the back of a closet. All perfect for the life she *used* to lead. Not for Sea Blue Beach.

Their conversations were a complicated two-step of his *"Give me a second chance"* and her *"I don't know."*

During one call, she asked if he was aware his Uncle Devier knew her mother in another life. He did not. Well, hadn't until *Talk to Me Sweetly* filming started.

"And you didn't tell me?"

"Sorry, didn't think it was important."

Was anything important enough for him to tell her? *I'm dining with my ex-wife? My uncle knew your mother when she was a model? I'm breaking up with you?*

"What are you doing here?" she asked.

"Come on, Harlow. You know why I'm here. You." He tipped his head toward the yacht moored offshore. "I had to see you. So I gathered the crew and sailed down. Arrived last night. I went to your place, but you weren't there. The kid mowing the lawn said you might be at the diner."

"I was about to grab a late breakfast," she said, thinking again of the platter she'd dreamed about on her run.

"I was just about to have breakfast on the yacht. My new chef, Baptiste, makes wicked scrambled egg whites with spinach and mushrooms."

Egg whites. A diet plate. On the SS *Spirit of Fortune.*

"I have to work in a couple of hours."

"I'll have you back in time, I promise. Please."

Being on time wasn't her concern. It was more that she'd be an emotional mess. But she was hungry, and he did sail all this way to see her.

At the end of the dock, a crew member waited with a tender to drive them out to the *Fortune*. A steward led them to the Portuguese deck, where a table was set with a linen cloth, bone china, and crystal glasses. The morning sun glinted off the pitcher of mimosas.

It was lovely. And classic Xander. Harlow sat with some trepidation as he filled her glass.

"I remembered these are your favorite."

"Yes, but they have a lot of calories."

"Cheers." Xander tapped her glass with his. "And who cares about calories?"

"Me." She'd come to the conclusion food must not rule her one way or the other.

"So," he said after a moment, "are you at least thinking about coming home? What about us?"

"There is no us, Xander. And I am home. I like it here. I'm not sure I want to leave."

"Okay, okay, I think I can accommodate that, Harlow. Work something out." He sipped from his glass and gazed toward the water. "But if we both want children—"

She unrolled the linen napkin ring and lined up the cutlery by her plate. "Is that what this is about? Children? You know I want a family, so you're using it against me? Or you're feeling your own biological clock ticking? You want an heir? It will take too long if you go after some other long-legged model or actress."

He glared at her. "Is that what you think? That I'm executing some master manipulation?"

"You are goal oriented, aren't you? And *children* was the first thing out of your mouth, Xander."

"No, the first thing out of my mouth was 'I love you.' I mention children because it's what we both want, Harlow. Give me a break here. I know, I was a jerk to you. I hurt you, and I'm sorry. I just want to get back to who we were before."

"Who were we before? I was moony-eyed for you and completely unaware Davina had returned to your life." Harlow had been thinking about this a lot lately. "I'm not some business deal to renegotiate. I'm flesh and blood." She raised her arm and pinched the skin. "How could you block me like a common criminal from our home? How could you in good conscious ignore my calls?" She swigged her mimosa, fired up. "In fact, how dare you treat me that way? I was your fiancée."

"Yes, and again, I'm sorry."

"It's not about being sorry, Xander. It's about the man inside." She stretched to poke his chest. "A good man, an honorable man, would've talked to me, given me a chance to fight for us. He would've made provision for me, especially after his financial recommendation emptied my accounts."

"I told you, Davina—"

"No, Xander, stop blaming her. You allowed yourself to be duped. You. All you."

"Fine, it was all me. I was stupid and blind—"

"Excuses."

Xander launched out of his chair. "What do you want me to say? That I'm a selfish, evil man who didn't care if I hurt you?"

"That's what it felt like to me."

"I thought . . ." He sighed and faced away. "I thought if we cut it cleanly without a bunch of drama, we could both move on." He knelt beside her chair. "But I was wrong, darling. Very, very wrong."

"Once upon a time, I thought hearing that would make me feel better, but it doesn't."

"Now you're just punishing me. How long are you going to make me pay? Another year? You'll be thirty going on thirty-one. I'll be forty-five in two months. I'd like to have children while I have the energy."

The conversation quieted as a steward carried out their breakfast.

"I'm not punishing you, Xander," she said when they were alone again. "But you can't come in here, crook your finger, and expect me to come running." She stirred her eggs with her fork but didn't take a bite. "My whole life has been one big manipulation."

"What do you mean?"

"Nothing." She took a forkful of eggs. They were creamy and cheesy. Very good.

"I promise that is not what I'm doing. I just want the woman I love to come home."

"Xander, do you really love me? Or am I just filling the hole left by Davina?" That felt good. "I walked straight from Mom's world into yours. I loved you, but I see life differently now. I'm not *that* Harlow Hayes. I love Sea Blue Beach. I love working at the Starlight. I'm reading business books."

"You want to start a business?" He raised his glass to her. "I have it on good authority, I'm a brilliant businessman. So you're not going to take the CCW job?"

"I'd be crazy to pass it up. Jinx said the money is amazing. But I have to lose the weight." She shoved her mimosa aside. "Otherwise, I can do that job in my sleep."

"No doubt. You're *the* Harlow Hayes, Most Beautiful Woman in the World."

"I'm starting to resent that title."

Xander regarded her for a moment. "How's the diet going?"

"It's going."

"Since we're being honest, Harlow . . ." He sighed and glanced toward the Starlight sign. "I may have been the reason you turned to food for comfort two years ago, but now you're just stonewalling yourself."

"Yet you served me orange juice and champagne." Harlow leaned toward him. "Do you want me or the beauty? Am I okay like this, Xander? When I gain weight with each pregnancy, will you still want me? I can't live under that false standard anymore. Maybe I am being rebellious because I was always *the* Harlow Hayes and never plain ol' me. I grew up on rabbit food and powdered drinks, diet soda and bread that tasted like cardboard."

"I'm not saying what the industry demands is fair, but I am saying if you want to go on with it, you have to fit the mold. The same will apply to your business. I don't hire an engineer to be my accountant."

"But you hired a crook to be mine."

"I was as surprised as you." He took a bite of his omelet. "And yes, I will love you no matter what. But, Harlow, even you can't fight how extraordinarily beautiful you are. Even now, you captivate everyone around you. I mean, when they were deciding on the Most Beau—" He stopped suddenly. "Oh, hey, did I tell you I finally closed on the new plant in China?"

"Don't change the subject. When they were deciding on what? Finish the sentence."

"Harlow, it's not . . ." He glanced away. "Nothing."

"You know your eyes twitch when you lie, Xander." Sounds from the shore drew Harlow's attention to the tourists on the beach and a couple of buff dudes hustling to the water with surfboards under their arms.

Suddenly, she saw Matt in her mind's eye, lacing on a pair of skates so she could pass out flyers, telling her she could do it, then shoving her down the Beachwalk while he chatted up the pilots on the beach.

Boldness welled up inside of her. "Xander, finish your sentence. What were they deciding? Don't tell me it was about a plant in China or some financial portfolio because you said it on the heels of me somehow being extraordinarily beautiful."

"You know how the world works, Harlow. Figure it out." Xander moved to the edge of the deck with his mimosa in hand.

The first time he took her out on the *Fortune*, Harlow leapt from the deck without hesitation. While she hated the sensation of falling, falling, falling, then hitting the water and sinking down without restraint, she loved kicking to the surface and inhaling the first glorious gulp of air. Once upon a time, she loved doing things that scared her a little.

"Why don't you tell me how the world works, Xander?" She moved next to him.

"Networking. Relationships. Favors. You scratch my back, I'll scratch yours."

"Is that how I got the part in the movie?"

"No," he said sharply. "I had nothing to do with the movie. Though I think Anne had been in touch with Devier. But you earned the part. Those five auditions weren't fake."

"Then what? What were you deciding about my extraordinary . . ." A white fluffy cloud drifted past the sun and shaded the yacht. "Xander, you manipulated the Most Beautiful Woman title. Oh my gosh, how is that even possible?"

"I didn't manipulate. But they called—"

"Who called?"

"People, Harlow. The ones deciding. Influencing."

"The ones deciding?"

"How do you not know this?" He sighed. "Yes, there's a final consensus. People talk. Your name was in the top five, and a few influential people called, asked if I'd like to get you to number one."

"You bribed them?"

"Not a bribe exactly, but I contributed to a couple of things. Maybe helped with some jobs."

"You bought me the title? I really wasn't the most beautiful. I had to be helped to the top?" She was a fraud. Everything about her was orchestrated by someone else. "I thought I'd earned that one. On my own. A reward for all the magazine covers, the runway shows, the early days of go-sees, and going from one photo shoot to another. For the hours I spent strutting in front of mirrors, practicing my expressions, starving myself half to death so I could do the job well. But I didn't earn that title. Your money bought it."

"I'm not denying your hard work, but being named the most beautiful is, well, subjective. Sometimes the decision makers need a little shove."

"Then the title is yours, not mine."

"Darling, come on. Be reasonable. You did earn it. I just nudged. Geez, I'm sorry I opened my mouth."

"It's a condition men get when I'm around. They say things they don't mean. But you know what I think? You've been dying to tell me the truth. That somehow it makes me beholden to you."

"You're not so naïve as to think the world is fair. We were—we are—the Billionaire and the Beauty. I merely added the exclamation point. And why would I want you beholden to me? That's ridiculous." Xander sipped his drink. "There were a lot of beautiful women in the running that year, Harlow."

"Well, then, why don't you marry one of them?"

She walked to the edge of the yacht, secured her keys in her hand, and jumped. Falling, falling, falling, and she had never felt so free.

TUESDAY

JUNE 1944

"I can't shake it, Harriet. The fear." Tuesday finished her iced tea and set it on Harriet's counter. "I lost LJ. Who's next? Dup? Lee?" Tuesday slipped on her gloves. She always felt like dressing up a bit when Harriet invited her over. She was a lady's lady. "What do you hear from Abel?"

"Same as you. He's on the USS *Mason* now. He doesn't say much other than the chow ain't nothing to write home about." Harriet laughed. "Then he goes on for another page about breakfast, lunch, and dinner. He got to see Morris when they docked last month. Didn't I tell you? They went out on the town. Morris said Twain was right: 'The coldest winter I ever spent was a summer in San Francisco.' He says California is fine, but loading bombs on ships is hard work. He's made a good friend, though. A Jimmy Fausnaugh from Columbus, Ohio. Says we're going to visit them when the war is over."

"I suppose that will be the case for a lot of us when it's all said and done. Now, why don't you come to me for dinner? I've not cooked for you in ages. I'm not working the Starlight tomorrow night."

"My dear friend, I love you like a sister but you're an average cook at best, and in your hot kitchen, I'd roast right along with the meat. Stick a fork in me, I'm done. No, you come here, where everything is electric." Harriet laughed and walked her to the door. "Surely you can buy a new stove by now."

The Nickle place at 321 Sea Blue Way was bright and airy, even cool on a June day with all the windows open and the ceiling fans turning.

"You're right. But I've gotten a bit sentimental about the old thing. I love the smell of the wood in that potbelly, and nothing beats the way it cooks the food. And I can heat up a can of beans with the best of them, Harriet Nickle, so mind yourself."

Harriet pulled Tuesday into a hug. "Our men will come home. I've been talking to Immanuel, asking Him to look over them."

"He can't do anything less."

They set a time for dinner tomorrow, and Tuesday walked home. She wanted to change into slacks before heading to the rink. So many women wore them these days.

As she neared her place, an old man in a civil uniform rode up on a bicycle. Ransom, from the telegraph office.

"Mrs. Knight. I'm so terribly sorry." He stretched the yellow telegram envelope toward her.

Tuesday kept walking toward her porch. "I don't want it, Ransom. You just take that and go on. It's not for me."

"Mrs. Knight, I . . ." He dropped his bicycle and ran after her. "My condolences."

"Get away from me." When he tried to press it into her hand, she tossed her purse at him. "I said I don't want it!" She thought Doc was the only bearer of bad news until he came along.

"I understand." There was a sadness in his voice. Of course everyone in town despised the man who brought telegrams of death. "The Scotts over on Calhoun Street done lost three sons. But, Mrs. Knight, wounded telegrams don't look no different than killed. Read it first."

She yanked it from his hand. Maybe Dupree was merely wounded. Or missing. Getting wounded wasn't Leroy's style. He was all or nothing. Her fingers trembled as she tore away the flap. A thin Western Union note slipped out as Ransom rode off.

> The Secretary of War sends his deepest regret that your husband, Master Sergeant Leroy Knight, was killed in action on June 6, 1944, on the beaches of Normandy. Letter to follow. Sincerely, the Adjutant General.

She collapsed to the gravel, her body swollen with a cry she could not release. Crumpling forward until the gravel pierced her cheek, she curled her fingers into the rocks and dug into the dust. Voices sounded around her. A car door slammed. Shouts volleyed over her. This was her end. She could give no more.

Immanuel! *Where are you?* How could He allow it? Hadn't she been through enough? Abandoned enough? Had she failed in her devotion in minding the Starlight?

She woke fitfully when thunder rumbled through her room and a gust of wind rattled the cottage. Heavy blackout curtains cut off the light of the heavens and stifled the air.

Still in her dress from tea with Harriet, Tuesday peeled off her torn stockings and lit the candle she kept on the nightstand for when blackouts were called. Down the hall, she paused by Dupree's room. Harriet slept, curled up in her tea dress.

Down the narrow stairs to the kitchen, she found Doc sitting at the table, nursing a cup of coffee, his thick gray hair bearing the ring of his hat. He looked tired in the cold kitchen light. Tuesday tugged the blackout curtains on the kitchen window closed.

"The warden will come by if we let light out." She cut off the overhead light and set the candle on the table. "So you know?"

"Ransom called. I told him to if you got a telegram. You know Lee asked me to look out for you."

"I didn't know you were in any one place long enough for a phone call."

"I've been staying over in Fort Walton. Volunteering where I can." He nodded toward his cup of coffee and gave Tuesday a half smile. "It's cold. But I'm starting to like it."

Tuesday pushed past the creaking screen door to the porch. An inky sky hung over the dark town. Even the Starlight was subjected to blackout regulations. But God's lightning didn't care about man's rules and lit up the whole sky with long, zigzagging electricity. Tuesday liked to think it was just for her because today her world changed forever. She was a war widow.

The screen door creaked again, and Doc stood beside her. "Normandy was a victory for the Allied forces."

"Is that your version of a pep talk? That I should be glad my husband gave his life for freedom?"

"You know that's what he'd want. If his number was up, Leroy Knight wanted to go out fighting."

A single tear ran down her cheek. "How I hate that you are right."

"If you need me to do anything, Tuesday, just tell me."

She stepped off the porch without a word and started toward the Starlight, which stood tall against the strobes of lightning.

Only when she arrived at the rink did she realize it was locked up tight. She fell against the wall and slid down to the walkway. Thirty yards away, waves rolled against the shore.

She was void and numb, like one of those cartoon robots at the movies. She screamed, wanting to cry, but her eyes were dry. When a figure emerged from the blackness, swinging a lantern, she knew it was Immanuel. She'd had this dream before. When Granny abandoned her.

He set the lantern by her feet and joined her on the ground. Tuesday slowly slumped sideways and rested her head on his shoulder. "Why does everyone leave me?"

"I'll never leave you."

Breathing in the fragrance of the holy man, she whispered, "Watch over Dupree. Please."

When she woke up again, she was in her room, the blackout curtains pushed aside so the morning light and sea breeze gushed through the open window.

One floor below, someone fried up some bacon and eggs, and the aroma of toast and coffee rose through the floorboards. Tuesday hustled from bed, peeled off her sticky clothes, and stepped into the shower. Then she tied her hair with a ribbon and slipped into Leroy's favorite dress.

"Harriet, you stayed all night?" The table was set for two. "Is Doc here?"

"He shoved off this morning. He waited to say good-bye, but you were still sleeping. Doc was terrified you'd died of a broken heart."

Tuesday gazed toward the Starlight. She'd had the dream again. Of running to the rink, of seeing Immanuel.

"I won't die or give up. I'm not leaving Dupree. It's the two of us against the world now. Who's running the rink?"

"No one. We're all in mourning, Tooz."

"All the more reason we need to open."

Burt was too old for military service, but Dear Dirk tried several times to join up. His eyesight and a few missing teeth earned him a solid 4F.

"Now come on, sit down. You need some sustenance." Harriet

brought a skillet of fried eggs over to the table. "I owe you an apology, Tooz. This wood-burning stove is marvelous. Still makes the house hot as blazes, but I declare the food tastes delicious and the house smells like hickory."

"What would I do without you?"

"Friends don't ask that question. You'd do the same for me. Don't got no animals to tend these days. Just as easy for me to sleep here." She retrieved the bacon and toast. "Coffee?"

"Please." Tuesday took a mug from the counter. "I dreamed about Immanuel. The same dream when Granny left me. I was here, in the house, saw you and Doc as plain as I see you now. I ran to the Starlight but it was locked, so I slumped down by the door. Immanuel appeared out of darkness, swinging a lantern."

"You're making me jealous. Let's bless this here food." Harriet offered a short prayer, then took up her fork. "What'd Immanuel say?"

"That He'd never leave me. Harriet, there was so much peace. I put my head on His shoulder and drifted away. But it was just a dream." Tuesday cut into her eggs and reached for the butter.

"You think so?" Harriet stepped onto the porch and returned with a lantern. "Doc found you by the Starlight, all curled up, with this by your side."

"The lantern?" She looked up at Harriet. "Immanuel carried this in the dream."

"You still think it was a dream, Tooz?" Harried said. "I'd say you saw God and He left you a piece of heaven."

29

SEA BLUE BEACH

We suppose you're wondering what Harry said to Tuesday when he walked into her office. We're not really sure. Town whispers only go so far.

Some think his memories of the Starlight finally got a hold of him and he toasted the Murdock deal.

Others say, *"Surely he remembers how his drunk daddy got born again at a revival meeting hosted by the Starlight."*

Dale Cranston was overheard saying at Sweet Conversations that Harry went to negotiate with Tuesday. Had a check in hand, but she flat refused to take it. There's still a lot of fight in that woman.

The petition signature verification is still in the works. Seems Marie Turner, the office manager, went into an early labor, which threw town hall into chaos. She delivered a beautiful baby boy, and Harry ordered blue balloons to fly from the radio antenna.

Since there's no deadline on the signature verification, folks know darn well Harry is stalling, indicating a victory for Matt Knight and his five-person committee.

Dupree has been seen around town with a photographer, taking photos of the Starlight. He's also had his crew working on a Starlight museum. Demolition or not, that would be nice.

Gazette editor-in-chief Rachel Kirby is making the rounds, talking to old-timers, going in and out of the courthouse and the library. Sooner or later, the *Gazette* will tell us what she's working on.

Matt Knight is off to Hollywood. Harlow seems settled at 321 Sea Blue Way. She had Simon Caster digging up her flower beds and planting new shrubs and a bougainvillea.

We see her jogging about town, still in her old sweats, and hope she's going to stay. She's one of us.

As we all wait for the verdict on the petition, the Murdock people come and go. Something's brewing. We all feel it.

MATT

HOLLYWOOD

"We're ready for you, Matt." The assistant director, a go-getter named Snow Snowden, handed him notes on the scene. "From Roger."

"Is Cindy ready?" He folded up the edition of the *Gazette* that arrived last night and reached for the notes. While there was no news of the petition, the newsprint was full of Sea Blue Beach anecdotes. Like how Marie Turner, who'd just had a baby, sent her teenage sons to Suds Up, and they used too much detergent which flooded the whole place. So . . . "Suds Up!"

Why did he spend so many years avoiding home? Because of

what happened with Booker. Then why didn't he try to mend things? Why not read his next letter? If he ever sent one.

"Cindy's ready," Snow said. "So, lights, camera, action."

Matt smiled. "Check the gate and we're good to go?"

"The camera gate has been checked."

Matt liked the old-time movie references, like checking the film gate to make sure it was clear of lint or hair or a bug.

He flipped open Roger's note. *Bro, get your head in the game.* He made a face. His head *was* in the game. Sort of. Occasionally he was distracted with thoughts of the Starlight. With images of Harlow.

He'd not talked to her since that one Sunday. He'd picked up the phone to call her a few times but backed out. She'd forgiven him, they were on solid ground. Just let it go.

In other news, he called Bodie for an update on his case. *"No word yet,"* he said. *"I think it's going to blow over."*

"Matt, go to one, please." Roger motioned him to the heroine's living room. They'd been filming *Date for My Daughter* the last two weeks in a 1930s Hollywood Hills home.

And there had been issues. It started when one of the grips tripped over a lamp cord, which blew an electrical fuse, which started a small fire. Roger looked exactly like Doc Brown in *Back to the Future*, when his test of creating one-point-twenty-one gigawatts caught a tarp on fire.

After the fire brouhaha, the set and costume designer got into an argument over the color of the couch clashing with Cindy's outfits. You'd think it would be an easy fix, but no. Last but not least, every time Roger called "Action," the eighty-pound German Shepherd next door barked. So, Roger had them filming this evening scene at four a.m. because the dog was still inside, sleeping with its owners.

Matt portrayed Mitchell Davidson, a brilliant architect who believed in old-fashioned love and traditional American values. He played him upright and clean-cut, channeling his dad.

Cindy played Clementine Sparks, an avant-garde interior designer, who believed in nothing traditional, especially love. Cindy owned the role. She was Clem. The girl from Midwest America who wanted to shed her family's values.

The script was sort of an eighties version of *The Goodbye Girl* but with two young, urban professionals. Clem had just been kicked to the curb by her boyfriend and business partner. Mitch, the architect, just happened to be there when she found out.

Gradually, he felt more like Mitchell than Lt. Striker. Yesterday, as he read another back copy of the *Gazette*, Cindy smacked down the top of the page and peered at him.

"You're such a square."

"Why, thank you." He meant it too. What's wrong with being square? Foundations were square. Bricks were square. Dashing, rugged men sported jaws that were square. Boxes were square! Really, how much could one pack in a circle?

"Let's get this shot before the sun comes up and the dog is out," Roger said, clapping his hands. "Snow, are we ready? Someone fix the blackout curtain on the southern window."

Matt moved under the lights of the small living room that was Clementine's apartment and became Mitchell Davidson. He enjoyed this film. Enjoyed being busy. He felt lonely and empty in his big, lonely, and empty house. He spent most of his nights flipping through cable channels until he fell asleep.

A couple of nights ago, a former frequent guest, Groove, came around, looking to crash for a few days, but he was drunk and high. Matt gave him money for a hotel instead. He had to stop assuaging his guilt over his past by letting people crash and trash his place. He had to stop despising his success. If he could manage those things, maybe he'd find the courage to call Booker.

On his way home last night, he'd spotted a *For Sale* sign in the yard of a really cute cottage in the Hills that overlooked the city. He peeked inside and fell in love. The place felt like home. Like Sea Blue Beach. He called his Realtor first thing this morning.

"Matt, you with us?" Roger looked around the camera, where he confirmed the shot. "Cindy, love, how are you?"

"Call action, Roger," she said. "Don't talk to us like we're children."

"Action."

The scene was Mitchell and Clem's first kiss, and even though they'd filmed the happily-ever-after ending on the beach two days ago, Matt had to play Mitchell as a square, awkward yet eager man wooing Clem for the first time. The script called for Mitchell to dance around the kiss, but Matt could just hear the guys watching in the movie theater with their girlfriends, shouting, "Just kiss her!"

So he did. Mitchell snatched Clem to his chest, and without so much as a by-your-leave and the scripted romantic line, he tipped her chin up and kissed her. No hesitation. No waiting. No games. Eyes closed, Matt—er, Mitchell—became the guy who wanted to fall passionately, madly, *squarely* in love. Cindy—er, Clem—somehow became Harlow, and he was back at the Starlight. Desperately wanting to kiss her.

Matt broke away, stepping back.

"Cut! Wow, Matt, that was spectacular. Even I felt that one."

Cindy bristled. "That wasn't in the script. Clem is supposed to be the one—"

"Cindy, doll," Roger said, "we're leaving it in. Fantastic. Matt, your instincts are spot-on. Ellie, bring me the next pages. Let's see if we have to tweak some dialogue. Take thirty, everyone."

Matt retreated to the green room, and Cindy followed. "What was that?"

"Sorry, I suddenly envisioned all the guys in the movie theater, arm around their girl, holding their breath, begging this square dude to kiss this crazy, beautiful vixen. So I went for it."

"Fine, your instincts are good, but—" Cindy touched her finger to her lips. "That was a real kiss, Matt. Not for Clem. Or me. Who were you kissing?"

"It was Mitchell kissing Clem." Matt made a plate of cheese and crackers. "I'm just that good." Bluffing, bluffing . . .

"I've been kissed as a character by a man playing a character, and that was not what just happened in there." She grabbed a small plate, choosing slices of apples and a couple of carrots. "Are you in love with Harlow Hayes? Did she forgive you for Letterman?"

Matt choked on his cracker, spewing Townhouse dust all over. "What? No. I mean, yes, she forgave me, but I'm not in love. We're barely friends."

"Then why do you talk about her every day?"

"What? You're crazy. I think Clem's gotten under your skin." He never talked about Harlow. Not even when one of the crew mentioned Matt's blabbermouth appearance on Letterman.

A few others came in for sodas and snacks. Snow popped in for some grapes. "We're almost done with the changes. Brush your teeth and get ready for the next scene."

"Snow," Cindy said, "I was just telling Matt how much he talks about Harlow."

"Which is ridiculous," Matt added. "Back me up, Snow. Tell her. I never talk about Harlow. Ever."

"You talk about her all the time," Snow said. "Okay, not all the time, but at least once a day."

"More like three, four times a day." This from Jenny, one of the makeup artists, who pulled a cold soda from the cooler.

"You keep count?"

"Oh yeah, we have a running pool. It's up to two hundred bucks on how many times you'll mention her during the shoot."

Back on set, Roger said, "Matt, the kiss actually plays perfectly into the character development. I don't know how we missed it. Ellie has the new pages ready."

Matt studied the changes. This particular scene is a few weeks into the relationship, with Mitch and Clem cooking together and more than the food was heating up.

"Let's get this in one take." Roger perched behind the camera.

"Cross your fingers that the dog stays asleep. Matt, stay on script this time. Quiet! Lights. Speed. Rolling *annnnnddd* . . ." The clapper snapped, and Roger called, "Action."

Mitchell was supposed to wrap his arms around Clem as she stirred her Italian grandmother's tomato sauce. Instead, Mitchell-slash-Matt moved next to Clem-slash-Cindy and said, "When have I ever mentioned Harlow? Give me an example."

"Cut!" Roger shot from behind the camera. "All right, who told him? Does he know about the Harlow pool?"

"He knows," Cindy said. "He kissed me like he was kissing someone he loves."

"I do not love her. We called it a day."

"Harlow this and Harlow that." Cindy poked Matt's chest. "Especially when we're going over a scene. I'm trying not to be insulted, but you act like she's a better actress than I am. 'When Harlow played Bryn in *Talk to Me Sweetly*, she was so honest and sincere.' Or 'Her house in Sea Blue Beach is a lot like this place—it'd make a great set. It's a remodeled 1902 cottage.' Now, how would I know the year Harlow's house was built if you didn't tell me, Matt? We also know she's not a roller skater, but she finally got out on the Starburst floor with your granny."

"Starlight."

"Whatever. Am I right, everybody?" Heads bobbed. Every last one of them.

"Thank you, Matt and Cindy. Can we please shoot this scene? The sun is coming up and that dog will cost us another day of shooting. Our budget is shot." Roger was starting to sweat. "Back to one. Brandi, touches, please."

The makeup artist ran from behind the lights, checked Matt and Cindy for shine, smoothed their hair, then ducked back into the shadows.

"Action."

"So what if I mention her?" Matt said. "It doesn't mean I'm in love with her. I mean, we're friends. Sort of. She's a really special—"

"Cut! That's not the line, Matt."

"Matt, why so defensive?" Cindy said. "It's okay to admit you're falling for her. You have a lot in common. Fame. Sea Blue Beach. Wanting a family. Saving the Starburst from demolition."

"The Starlight. Geez, Cindy, how hard is that to remember?"

"All I'm saying is if you love Harlow Hayes . . . " More poking on Matt's chest. "Go. Get. Her. You know Xander Cole will pull out all the stops. I've met him. He's a force to be reckoned with, and he has a history with her. You win points in the better-looking category, but he's got *way* more money."

"Clearly you don't know Harlow at all. She's not some opportunistic fortune hunter." Matt paced around the set, thinking . . . thinking . . . "Okay, let's say I wanted to talk to her. What would I say?"

The entire crew chorused, "I. Love. You."

Giovani, the craft caterer, shouted, "Will you marry me?"

"There you go, Matt." Cindy punched his arm. "Don't *play* a romantic hero—*be* a romantic hero."

"But I humiliated her. I don't think she can trust me."

"Then earn it back."

"Please, Matt, Cindy, let me know when I can film my movie." Roger collapsed into his director's chair.

"Sorry, Roger. I'm good to go." Now Matt was starting to sweat. Could he admit it? That he loved Harlow even if she didn't love him?

Roger called action, and as the scene started, the phone chimed through the tiny house.

"Don't stop, keep going!" Roger said. "And who was supposed to disconnect the ringer? You're fired."

"Matt, it's for you." One of the crew handed him the portable receiver.

"Unbelievable." Roger hung his head and spewed a few finely chiseled words.

It was Harlow. Matt stepped outside and faced the view of Hollywood.

"Hey, what's going on? How'd you get this number?"

"Cosmo. Matt, they've verified the signatures. There's a town hall meeting tomorrow night."

"How'd we do? Any indication? Wait, Harlow, you're in Sea Blue Beach?"

"Buckhead wasn't home. Sea Blue Beach is home. I didn't tell you because . . . well, anyway, I'm working at the Starlight, helping Tuesday."

"Oh, okay, good. Great. Are you back with Xander?"

"Matt, did you hear me? Town hall, tomorrow night. And no, I'm not with Xander."

"I'm on my way." He tossed the phone to the nearest grip. "Roger, I'm off. Be back in a few days."

"Matt, where are you going? We're filming a movie here . . . Matt!" Roger followed him out the door. "Matt Knight, you're fired!"

"No, you're not, Matt," Cindy called. "You go! Get Harlow!"

TUESDAY

OCTOBER 1967

Groovy was the "vibe" at the Starlight tonight. From the bell-bottoms and long hair to the USA and USSR outer space treaty to the music where the Beatles reminded everyone that all we need is love.

Spike, who'd just taken over the Starlight's concession business, had grown out his afro and sideburns, and wore bright colored bell bottoms.

Manning the ticket booth, Tuesday watched over her kingdom,

dressed pretty hip for a gal of her age, wearing an orange-and-pink polka blouse with brown slacks and Keds. Out on the floor, her new gal, Darcy, got after a couple of hoodlums who crashed one another into a corner.

It seemed to Tuesday that kids today were angsty and full of themselves. Baby boomers, they called them. Every day she heard stories of how this younger generation made their demands, expecting more for less.

With sound systems replacing the Wurlitzer for skating music, Dirk played for churches and social gatherings. He'd amassed quite a fan base along the North Florida coast and lower Alabama. Tuesday still had him come in on Monday and Thursday mornings for the older crowd.

Back to the young ones. The war in Vietnam made them angry. Their parents made them angry. It seemed they longed for something more meaningful than the old traditions and a steady paycheck. When they found no answers, they smoked weed, snorted cocaine, and gathered en masse for the Summer of Love.

The airmen from Eglin still called the Starlight their home away from home and raced around the rink like daredevils, doing backflips and leapfrogging over each other. She saw LJ in all of them. He'd been gone twenty-seven years, but she missed him like it was yesterday.

The British government recognized his contribution to the war with the Distinguished Flying Cross. Leroy also earned a few medals posthumously. She added them to the collection he'd amassed from the first world war.

From the stories she'd heard over the years, Leroy had landed smack in the middle of a fight when he hit the shores of Normandy. The letter she received from his commander said he died while taking out a hill of Germans. Well, didn't that sound like her man.

She missed him. Not in the everyday way. She'd lived so much of her life without his presence. She missed the anticipation of seeing him, of hearing his voice. Sometimes while standing at the kitchen sink, she'd glance up, expecting to see him. But it was nothing more than a phantom memory. With all the goings-on in the world today, she'd sure like to hear his opinion.

In his honor and LJ's, the boys from Eglin skated for free, and Spike gave them half off. On this particular Saturday afternoon, the rink was full of young men in their jumpsuits or jeans and a button-down, demonstrating why they'd been selected to fly. One young man in particular, Gene, showed up at the Starlight every spare moment.

"Evening, Miss Tuesday." He set his skates on the front desk and looked toward the rink and his fellow aviators. "Boy oh boy, this place reminds me so much of my rink back home."

"So you've said." Gene was a repeater. Told his stories over and over. But Tuesday didn't mind. She hoped some British mama had listened to her son talk about home all those years ago. Gene's ruddy cheeks and peach-fuzz mustache told her he was probably LJ's age when he ran off. "I know your mama is proud of you."

The music changed from the Four Tops to Simon & Garfunkel. "Everybody's feeling groovy." A half dozen airmen lined up to sling one another from the back of a line to the front. From the lobby, a group of teen girls with bright blue eye shadow, pink lips, and hair teased to the ceiling entered with their skates dangling over their shoulders by the long laces.

The session only had an hour left, so Tuesday charged them half price, then tapped Dominic, the kid who spun the records, to keep an eye on the ticket booth.

Back in the office, she straightened her desk, inspected a pair of old skates, and accepted a hamburger from Spike.

"I was thinking of replacing the tables and chairs, Tuesday."

"It's your concession, Spike. Let me know if I can help."

Burt, who now only worked part time, brought in the mail and gave a little hip swing to the start of Little Eva's "The Loco-Motion" on his way out.

Seeing how the mail consisted of bills, she opened her accounting ledgers and fished the checkbook from the bottom desk drawer. Might as well pay the piper.

She'd just written the last one when Dupree came in with ten-year-old Matty and dropped a manila envelope on her desk. Matt gave her a big hug, then grabbed his skates from the cupboard.

"Can he stay with you tonight, Ma?" Dupree said. "I've got to finish up a job in Fort Walton tomorrow, and I want an early start."

"Of course he can, Dup. Anytime. Matty, I saw Booker on the floor a few minutes ago." He shot out of the office, skates clattering. "Two peas in a pod, those two."

"Yeah, they're good buddies." Dup kicked out the chair in the corner and sat with a thump. "You think I should find a girl to marry, Ma? Give him a mother?"

"What about the gal you took to dinner last week?"

"Eh," he said with a shrug. "She was sweet. Pretty. But not Mimi." He cut her a grin. "Or you."

"Well, you're going to have to cast a wider net than Mimi and me, Dup. There's a gal out there for you. Until then, we're getting along all right, aren't we? The three of us."

"Sure, but I think Matt feels it, you know? That the other boys have a mother, and he doesn't."

"He has a mother. She's in heaven." She held up the manila envelope. "Now where did this come from?"

"Your mailbox. I stopped by on my way here. I put the rest of your mail on the kitchen table but thought you might want this one."

"You mean you wanted to know what's inside."

There were two letters inside. One was from a Mrs. Mary Lou Brodbeck. And one from . . . Leroy.

The thin, soiled envelope had yellowed with time. Yet somehow, when Tuesday's trembling fingers brought it to her nose, she could have sworn it bore the fragrance of his cologne and hair tonic.

"Ma, what is it?"

"It's from your pa." She passed over Mrs. Brodbeck's letter. "Here, read this. I'm shaking."

Dear Mrs. Knight,

I can only imagine your surprise to find a letter from your husband more than twenty years after he wrote it. Apparently, he'd given it to my husband, who stored it with his things. They were together in Normandy, and after the war, Julius didn't talk much about D-Day or any of it, only that he'd fought alongside some of the best men on earth.

Julius recently passed, and I found this letter to you from your husband among his things. No matter how delayed, I pray you will find it a comfort. I know I would.

Yours sincerely,
Mary Lou

Dupree lowered the letter. "A lot of the fellas wrote home before a big offensive. Even me. But thankfully, you never had to read it."

All these years, she'd longed for a final word from Leroy, but when the military returned his things, almost no personal effects were included. Dupree surmised they'd been lost along the way. Typical army. Leroy was buried in Normandy with his brothers-in-arms.

But *this* . . . this letter finally brought him home.

"You read it." She offered Dup the letter, then pulled back. "No, I will." Tears filled every part of her as she unfolded the army-issued stationery.

My darling Tooz,

Slowly, she lowered the letter and slipped it back into the envelope.

"Ma, don't you want to read it?" Dupree pointed to the door. "I'll step out if you want."

"You know, I think I'll save it for later." She stood, tucking the letter into her pocket. "What's another couple of hours when it's been twenty-three years? Now, I should make my rounds, make sure we're shipshape."

Dupree pulled her close as she passed. "You deserved better from him, Ma. But I've reckoned with my anger toward him over the years. He loved us. He sure as heck loved you."

"Don't feel sorry for me, Dupree. I've had such a life." She rested against his thick chest that held the heart of a loving, kind man. "A man who loved me, two swell boys, the prince, and the Starlight. Still the best part?" She leaned back to see her son's face. "Immanuel, Dupree. Life and the devil tried to take me down, but Immanuel raised me up. What's better than knowing a prince, I ask you? Knowing a God who knows me."

Her son rested his cheek on her head. "You're the strongest person I know, Ma. Matty and I . . . Where would we be without you?"

For a moment, when Dupree smiled down on her, it was Leroy, and Tuesday Knight had zero regrets.

She made her rounds as the last session ended, locked up the money bag in the safe, then found Spike closing up concession. When she was alone, Tuesday tied on her skates and cued up Jim Reeves on the hi-fi. His melodic voice echoed through the empty rink. "I come to the garden alone."

Except she wasn't really alone. Immanuel was with her. And tonight, so was Leroy.

When the song finished, Tuesday sat in the middle of the quiet rink and read the letter.

June 4, 1944

My darling Tooz,

I'm writing to you with a dull pencil on a piece of paper I borrowed from Lt. Durban. We've been in the thick of it, but I'm fine. I told you I'm too ornery to die. I survived the Great War and being a thug for the mob, so the Huns don't scare me.

I miss you more than ever. When I was running all over God's creation before this mess, I knew I could get to you anytime I wanted. I don't have that luxury now, and I regret every moment I was away.

I dreamed about you and the Starlight. Guess it was a few nights ago. I'm going to make it up to you, Tooz. I mean it. I'm done disappointing you. I'll live like a regular Joe so we can grow old together. Maybe spoil a few grandkids. What do you think?

Anyhow, being as I am in a war, there's something I need to get off my chest. If the worst happens, I don't want to take this business to my grave.

Tuesday closed her eyes. Was this where he confessed his affairs? Murders? Did she want to read on?

I didn't buy the Starlight for you. The prince gave it to you when he went to fight the Great War. Maybe he knew he wasn't coming back. Hoboth was the caretaker until your thirty-second birthday. Guess age is the way they do things in royal families. So there it is. The Starlight was always yours. Hoboth was coming up the drive with the deed when I pulled in.

You're probably wondering why I told you I bought the Starlight. I wanted you to be proud of me. I knew the men I'd worked for weren't honorable, and I wanted to do one thing you could hold onto all your life. Yet sitting here now in the middle of a world war, I wish I'd done things differently. Can you forgive a slob like me? I'd like one less sin on my account should I face the Almighty sooner than expected.

If I don't come back, remember how much I love you. I never strayed, Tuesday. Not once. With that, I'll sign off. Give my love to everyone there, and keep the Starlight on for me.

Your loving,
Lee

30

HARLOW

She gazed toward the back door. So far, Matt had not arrived. Yet it seemed half of Sea Blue Beach filled city hall for this special town council meeting. If the room had rafters, people would be swinging from them.

Harlow sat up front with Tuesday, Dupree, and Spike. Where was Matt? He'd called from LAX to say he'd booked a flight, but she'd not heard from him since.

Audra from the Blue Plate tapped her on the shoulder. "Hey, Harlow, some of us are getting up a weekly girls' night. Want to join us?"

"Um, yeah, sure. I'd love to if I'm not working."

Audra smiled. "I'll talk to you next time you're at the diner."

Harlow whispered to Tuesday, "Audra just invited me to a girls' night. You think she's sincere? Like they don't want to mock me or something. Take pictures and sell to the tabloids."

"Listen to yourself. Of course she's sincere. Harlow, you're more than a pretty face," Tuesday said. "People around here see that."

"Can we settle down?" Harry gaveled the meeting to order. "This is a special session of the Sea Blue Beach town council on the matter of the petition requesting a vote on the eminent domain action against the Starlight roller skating rink."

"I'm going to have to buy me a food truck, aren't I?" Spike muttered. "Join the trucks on the beach. Doggone, I like working out of the Starlight."

"Just wait and see, Spike," Tuesday said, who remained remarkably calm. Harlow squeezed her hand. For her own sake more than Tuesday's.

"I'm going to cut to the chase," Harry said. The room stirred, restless. "We've carefully reviewed the signatures."

"Harry, just get on with it." The demand came from somewhere in the middle. "Are we getting a vote or not?"

"Hold on, Martin. I want to assure Sea Blue Beach citizens that the utmost care and integrity was used to verify every signature."

"Harry, I could've verified the names in an afternoon. You've taken a month."

"As you know, Marie was out with her new baby, and Lynn had been scheduled for vacation to Disney World with her grandchildren. We got to the petition when we could." Harry raised a piece of paper. Tuesday freed her hand from Harlow's and leaned forward. "Forty-one of the signatures were not valid registered voters."

"That leaves us with three fifty-nine," someone shouted. "That's more than enough."

"Yes, but we also had five Donald Ducks, six Lieutenant Strikers, and four Cinderellas." He glanced at Harlow. "More than likely, the celebrities attached to the cause inspired tourists to sign. And two people signed twice. In the end, three hundred and forty-two signatures were valid, which falls short of the requirement." Everyone talked at once, and Harry banged his gavel until

Harlow felt the pounding in her chest. "The petition has failed," he shouted. "Eminent domain proceedings for the Starlight will commence next week, with demolition sometime after Labor Day."

In the middle of the chaos, the double doors opened, and Matt Knight walked into city hall like George Bailey, Superman, and Han Solo rolled into one, with a touch of Clint Eastwood's steely grit.

"Matt Knight to save the day."

"Take that, Harry Smith. Lieutenant Striker just walked in."

"My Matty boy," Tuesday said.

Harlow rose up to see him cutting through the crowded center aisle, speaking to folks, shaking hands.

"Matt, save your breath, there's nothing you can do." Harry waved the gavel over his head. "We've done our due diligence and—"

"Not here to see you, Harry." Matt exited the crowded center aisle, eyes on Harlow. "Granny, you okay? We'll figure this out."

"I'm fine, but you do what you got to do." She tipped her head toward Harlow.

What's going on?

Matt grabbed Harlow's hand and spun her into his arms, his debonair expression like one from Hollywood's Golden Age. His gaze lingered on her lips, and for a moment she watched the scene from those would-be rafters along with the rest of the room.

He said nothing. Then, "Can I kiss you?"

"Yes." Here. Now. Please.

His warm, full lips touched hers as he wrapped her in his arms. She surrendered to the pure pleasure of it all—to every firing nerve and luscious tingle. Yet she felt more than pleasure. She felt love.

Cheers erupted to the beat of ol' Harry's gavel.

The kiss lingered until he rested his forehead against hers. He whispered something, but the cheering was so loud, she couldn't make out a word. She just laughed and drew him back for a second round.

"This meeting is adjourned," Harry said. "The petition failed. The Starlight will be demolished." He brought his gavel down so hard the face flew off and hit Carny Albert on the head.

"Let's get out of here." Matt gripped Harlow's hand and dashed down the center aisle, with Dupree helping Tuesday through the crowd as Spike hollered, "Gangway, folks, gangway."

When they got to the double doors, Tuesday turned back to the crowded room. "Everyone who wants . . . meet me at the Starlight."

"Good job, Granny," Matt said just before he pulled Harlow into his arms on the steps of city hall and kissed her again.

"Matt," she said, "didn't you hear? The petition failed."

"Did you hear *me*?" Matt asked Harlow.

"With all the loud cheering? No."

"I said I love you, Harlow Hayes. What do you think about that?"

TUESDAY

Sea Blue Beach without the Starlight. How would the world make sense? Despite the music and skaters still rounding the floor, the somber band of citizens gathered in concession foreshadowed the days ahead.

Yet seeing Matty and Harlow in love cheered her to no end. About time.

"Okay, citizens of Sea Blue Beach." Audra's voice needed no magnification. She could be heard into next week. "What are we going to do? We're losing our Starlight. Don't think you're safe and this won't impact you. With Harry having eminent domain power, any one of us could be next."

"I don't own a business, Audra," someone said. "I work in Fort Walton."

"Fine, Grady, but your old neighborhood could be at risk." Audra wagged her finger at the lot standing about, arms folded. "It's unconstitutional what Harry's doing."

"Federal law allows it." This from another voice in the crowd.

"Well, it shouldn't. Let's start a second revolution."

The crowd stirred, and a debate followed until Matty calmed everyone down. "We wouldn't be in this mess if everyone had signed the petition."

"We need to double-check the signatures, make sure Harry's on the level."

"I signed the petition."

"Me too."

"All right," Matt said. "I'll talk to him tomorrow, see what else we can—"

"You can do nothing." Harry barged into the Starlight, along with the town council, Chief Grant, and Officer Patitucci. "We submitted to the process and our side won." Harry held up a small stack of papers. "Tuesday, can we talk in your office?"

"Here I thought you came to ask me to couple's skate." Tuesday gazed toward Immanuel. Didn't He have a plan? The peace and confidence she possessed earlier quickly evaporated. "We can talk here."

She glanced at the crowd, then Matt—who nodded his approval—and Dupree, who remained stone-faced.

"I'd like to hear what you have to say too, Harry." Audra stood next to Tuesday.

"All right. Well, here are the signatures." He held up the papers, and Matt reached for them. "You can check for yourself. And here's a check for the Starlight. It's more than generous. We had it appraised, and Murdock kindly chipped in additional funds."

Dupree took the check and skimmed the amount.

"Dup, hand that back. I'm refusing the money." Harry might be the mayor, but to her he was still the little runt hobbling around on eight wheels.

A few weeks ago, when he came into her office to talk, he'd tried to hand her that check—with some condition she refused to hear. She'd been so confident when she turned him down. So sure Immanuel would save the rink.

"It's a good offer, Ma." Dupree tried to show her, but Tuesday refused to touch that devil money.

"You can't turn it down, Tuesday. We're taking the Starlight." Dale Cranston shoved in beside Harry, chest puffed out for no good reason. "Chief Grant here and Officer Patitucci are hammering up the notice of demolition tonight."

A sheepish-looking Milo held up the orange paper with bold black letters. Tuesday stumbled back, reaching for Dupree.

"Dale, simmer down," Harry said with a soft glance toward Tuesday. "This town owes you a debt of gratitude, Tuesday, for keeping the Starlight shining. Prince Blue would be proud. However, before we pay out so much money, we'd like to see the deed, establish ownership." He took the check from Dupree. "I'm sure you understand. We have a fiscal responsibility to the town. We've checked with the county records, and it seems the deed is missing. Perhaps it was never filed in the first place."

Tuesday stepped toward him, done with decorum. "Harry, do you truly want to see the Starlight smashed with a wrecking ball?" Yes, she heard herself, pleading, like she did when Mamaw loaded up the wagon, climbed on the buckboard, and told the driver to get going.

"It's a done deal, Tuesday." Dale forced himself forward. "You lost."

She glanced toward her son and grandson, then Immanuel. Her whole life, she believed the mural was the image of a real God who came to this world as a man. She'd seen and touched Him, but in this moment, Immanuel was nothing more than a figment of Prince Blue's imagination. A Lauchtenland fairy tale. The night after Leroy died? It was a dream, re-creating the prince's story of Immanuel appearing to him on the beach. Maybe she wanted to see Him so much, her subconscious delivered.

"I'm sorry, Tuesday," Harry said, "but we're moving forward with progress."

"Then if you don't mind," she said, "we'd all like to skate tonight. Nora, put on some music. Everyone, free rentals. Spike, can you serve up some popcorn and sodas?"

"Tuesday." Harry gently touched her arm. "I suggest you start packing up, holding your auction. We'll give you the summer, but that's the best I can do. Dup, talk to her. Can you scare up the deed for me?"

"First you're taking the rink and now you're trying to get out of paying." Dupree stepped nose to nose with the mayor. "If one brick is harmed before she is paid—"

"She'll be paid, Dup. I just want to see the deed. If not—" Darn if Harry didn't look a bit nervous with Dupree staring him down. "She'll be paid."

"You do what you have to do, Mayor Smith," Tuesday said. "We'll do what we have to do." A flash caught her attention, and she glanced at Immanuel, high on the rolling panels, with a twinkle in His eye. "Come on, people, let's skate. Harlow, you can wear my old Richardsons."

The bass of "You Dropped a Bomb on Me" filled the rink. Tuesday laughed. Nora, that girl . . . well done.

"Tuesday, there's nothing you can do." Dale simmered like a teakettle on her old wood-burning stove. "The Starlight is coming down."

"Dale," Matt said, "back off. Give her a minute."

"I don't care to hear from you, Hollywood." Dale was riled up tonight. "I'll see you in court."

"Dale Cranston, if your mama was here, she'd be ashamed." Tuesday wagged her finger at him. "She'd expect bigger things of you."

"Don't talk about my mama."

"She was a good woman and a good friend. We all know you're still angry Dupree got the girl you wanted, and that Matt won't bring his movie premieres to the Midnight. Which, by the way, you've still not shown *Flight Deck*."

What happened next will forever be one big blur. Dale's face flamed red, and he lunged at Tuesday, his hands like claws. Harry moved forward, stumbled and tripped, causing Tuesday to fall backward. "Dupree!" The last thing she saw before hitting the carpet was Matt's fist connecting with Dale's chin.

31

MATT

Milo charged a buck a person to let tourists walk through the jail and take pictures of *the* Matt Knight behind bars, reclining on a narrow cot, hands locked behind his head, legs stretched out, crossed at the ankles.

Imagine, in all that kerfuffle, he was the only one arrested. Harry's testimony was he moved to calm down Dale, tripped on the Starlight's old carpet and into Granny.

Dale insisted he had no intention of harming Granny. His I'm-appalled-at-this-accusation expression was worthy of the big screen.

However, Matt's testimony that he never intended to hit Dale was refuted by so-called eyewitnesses and he was arrested.

Word spread through the night to the morning Rollo on the Radio show that Matt Knight was behind bars. When folks began to visit the Sea Blue Beach jail, Milo started charging. If Matt retained any ego while sitting behind bars, Milo's scheme put him in check.

"This is fantastic. Matt Knight. I had no idea when I booked our vacation here we'd see a movie star." A woman with a camera in hand waited as her husband paid the admission for a family of four. "Is Harlow Hayes here? Can we see her?"

"All you get is Matt Knight," Milo said. "Thank you for your donation to the Sea Blue Beach Police Benevolence League."

The little girl, around nine or ten, pressed her face between the cell bars. "Do you need some water?"

Matt sat up, touched by her sweet offer. "No, thank you. I just had breakfast."

"What'd you do to get in here?"

"Do you know what it means to plead the Fifth?" He didn't mean to put his fist between Dale, Harry, and Granny, but instinct kicked in. And maybe his loathing for Dale Cranston. Just a little.

"Yeah, my brother says it all the time when he's in trouble." The little girl cut Matt a side grin. "Me too."

"Atta girl."

"Jackie, smile for Mama." The woman snapped a photo of her daughter talking to Matt before Milo hustled the family along.

"Any more tourists out there?" Matt stretched back out on the cot. "How much have you made? Twenty bucks? You'll answer to God for this, you know."

"I'm up to seventy-eight big ones. I let a few people pass through while you were sleeping."

"Andy Griffith would never do this, you know. Never."

"I couldn't resist, Matt. You're going into the judge any minute now. Look at it this way, I'm building public sympathy." He glanced toward the door as more tourists entered. "Come on in. See Lieutenant Striker behind bars. Step this way. That's a dollar per person. Even kids."

Matt smiled and waved, wondering when Bodie would get him out of here. He seemed rather irritated last night when Matt called. *"Please stop allegedly hitting people. The state was just about to drop your case. They won't now."*

The morning passed with one court delay after another, so he remained the main attraction in Milo's little circus. As the day wore on, more and more folks filed through the jailhouse door.

"My sister and I called off work to drive down from Thomasville, Georgia."

"I was just happening through and stopped for a bite at the Blue Plate."

"Can I have your autograph?" A young woman stuck a pen and autograph book through the bars. Matt obliged.

He smiled for the cameras and signed autographs, imagining this to be one of the more interesting chapters for his autobiography. The women flirted. The girls giggled and blushed. The men shook his hand, cleared their throats, and delivered lines like, "Dug you in *Flight Deck* and *Cochise County*." Boys passed by with bored expressions and said, "Cool."

Matt picked up bits and pieces of conversation.

"The Starlight is being demolished? I'd love to live in Sea Blue Beach. I'd skate there all the time."

"Our skating rink back home closed."

"Have you seen Harlow Hayes? I heard she lives here."

"I was hoping to get a glimpse of Harlow Hayes. Supposedly she gained a lot of weight. Welcome to my world."

The midafternoon rush faded, and Matt stretched out on his cot again. Milo left to answer a call from dispatch. He came back with Dad in tow.

"You want me to bring some of your things from home?" Dad stood at his cell. "Make this feel more like your room?"

"Very funny." Matt scrambled off the bunk. "How's Granny?"

"Home, resting. Dr. Peters took a look at her. She hit her head pretty hard, bruised her right arm, but no concussion. No broken bones."

"I want to file charges against Dale."

"Actually, Harry's saying it's all his fault. He feels horrible. Bodie is on his way to see the judge. Dale is blaming you for everything and pushing for jail time."

Matt leaned against the cell door. "I'm sorry for all this mess."

"Don't be," Dad said. "I've been dying to punch Dale Cranston since high school. But your granny would've given me the business. I will say this about you, son, never a dull moment when you're around. Can we talk about your dramatic entrance and kiss with Harlow. . . ?"

"I was wondering the same thing." Harlow stood in the doorway.

"Hey, HH." Matt gripped the bars. "Dad, can you give us a moment?"

"Seems we've played this scene before," Harlow said when Dad had gone. "Me out here, you in there."

"This wasn't how I saw things going."

"You're an actor. Play out the real scene for me." She perched on the edge of Milo's desk. "Does this theater have popcorn?"

"Harlow, that wasn't *the* Matt Knight kissing *the* Harlow Hayes. It was regular Matt kissing a girl he's crazy about."

"Hey, Matt, I was thinking about ordering from the taco truck. Do you—" Milo glanced between the cell and his desk and turned around. "That's right, I forgot I have lunch with the chief."

"Milo, man, can you let her into the cell? Please?"

"No can do. It's against regulations to allow a civilian in a cell with a perp."

"Milo, you turned the jail into a tourist attraction. I think you can let Harlow in for a few minutes. Please."

"Five minutes." He unlocked the door. "If Chief finds out, I'm in deep doo-doo."

The lock clicked, and a rather shy Harlow joined him on the cot. "Now we're both on the inside."

Matt was unsure if he should hold her hand or just go for it and hold all of her. His buzzing lips made their preference known.

"Xander was here," she said. "A few weeks ago. He sailed down on his yacht."

"I see." Matt's lips buzzed a little less.

"Xander's influence played a role in me being named Most

Beautiful Woman in the World." She shifted around so her back rested against the cold, brick wall. "He didn't mean to tell me, but in his zeal to prove he loved me, he leaked a few details."

"Influenced? How?"

Harlow made a face.

Of course he knew how. "Money."

"I'm a fraud, Matt. An Anne Hayes/Xander Cole composite. Fulfilling Mom's dreams to rub elbows with the rich and famous, to touch the beautiful people, Hollywood. For Xander, being the envy of every man in the world. Makes me wonder if Harlow Hayes can actually do anything on her own. Does she have any ambition other than to keep her mother from crying? Think, Matt, a childhood perception has informed my whole life." She smacked the wall with her hand. "This, *this* place—ha, a metaphor for Harlow Hayes. A prisoner of someone else's doing. No, her own doing."

"HH, slow down, back up. What's this about your mom? I'm missing some details here."

"That Sunday after you called me, I went snooping." She told him what she'd discovered, a story of a secret pregnancy and unrequited ambition.

"So that's what your mom was crying about when you were seven years old? Because she never got the chance to be a model and actress?"

"Pretty much. She saw potential in me. Had the connections. Dad went along with it to make her happy. To make up for his part in ruining her dream. He also thought I wanted to model because I never protested. Never rebelled. Oh my word, just listening to this story sounds like a *Dynasty* plot."

"Write me into the script, will you? I'm a successful actor carrying around guilt for his part in ruining his best friend's life, stumbling into an unbelievable career, which he doesn't deserve because of what he did to his friend. And to be honest, wondering if acting is really his life's calling."

"Aren't we a pretty pair?"

"Well, you are," he said with a wink.

"Stop." But Harlow blushed a little, and his lips buzzed again. "What's the magic formula?" she said. "How do we find out what we were put on this earth to do? Dad knew he was the cookie monster of Hayes Cookies Company when he was a kid."

"Granny became the keeper of the Starlight, which fit her perfectly. Dad apprenticed with a construction company before the war and found his calling."

"If it's any consolation, you're a fabulous actor, Matt. Maybe you're so successful because you were born to do it."

"You, Harlow, are an amazing model. And a good actress. Maybe you're successful because you were born to do it. Granted, your folks went about it the wrong way."

"Yet here we are, two famous and beautiful people, sitting in a jail cell. The metaphor continues." There was a bit of sarcasm in her voice. "Wonder what it would feel like to be free. On the inside. No more guilt. No more eating my pain." Harlow walked over to the cell bars. "No more not liking myself."

"My former publicist said I should figure out what's eating me. Dad said the same thing, suggested I call Booker, try to make amends. But even thinking about it makes me queasy. I can't shake it. I'm still the guy who came home for Christmas right after my first movie, saw Booker at the Starlight, and got torn to shreds. In front of everyone. He blamed me for everything wrong in his life right down to his latest relationship flop. Said my big mouth ruined his life." Matt joined Harlow at the cell door.

"I get it. I've borne the weight of Mom's tears all these years. Maybe that's what my weight is all about—Mom's tears. Yet we're all responsible for our own actions. I can blame Mom or Xander all day long for why I ate myself out of a career, but no one put the food in my mouth. Just me." Harlow lifted her gaze to Matt. "Seems we're prisoners of our choices."

"Maybe I hit Dale because I see myself in him. I wish someone would punch me."

"Look at us, a couple of philosophers. Maybe what appears to be random events or accidents is just part of the journey to our destiny." Harlow lightly touched his arm. "I wouldn't have had such an amazing kiss last night if Xander hadn't broken my heart. If I'd not lost my job."

"You think the kiss was amazing?"

"You couldn't tell?"

He pulled her into him. "About that kiss . . ."

"And your declaration." She rested her hands on his chest.

"I meant it." He held her a bit closer. "I'm in love with you, Harlow, but since you didn't answer me—"

"Matt, I really need to get clear of Xander first," she said. "And work some things out with my mom. When I tell you what's in my heart, I want there to be nothing weighing me down."

"See, there's the HH I knew on set. Wise, reasonable, in command, and breaking my heart."

"Oh, gag me with a spoon, why don't you?" She laughed. "On set you were gaga for your real co-star, Hazel Rosen."

"Only because I didn't stand a chance with you."

"You have a chance with me now, Matt. But do you really want me?" She broke free of his embrace and motioned to her tall frame and full figure. "I'm not the girl on the cover of a *Sports Illustrated* swimsuit edition. I never will be again."

"I want the girl on the inside, and just so you know, the girl on the outside is darn sexy. Though it might be good to stop sabotaging yourself."

"Fair enough. I'd like you to get rid of the guilt over Booker. Call him, Matt."

"Ah, Harlow Hayes negotiates. Deal. Should we seal it with a kiss?"

"Matt Knight." *Daggum Milo*. "Bodie's here. You're going to see the judge."

"Officer Patitucci, bro, your timing . . ." Matt sighed and pressed his forehead against Harlow's. "I'll take an IOU."

"I gave you two extra minutes." Milo swung open the cell door. "Not my fault you couldn't get it done. I'd have kissed her a half dozen times already."

So Matt stood before the judge on a Wednesday afternoon, a bit bleary-eyed and disheveled, with Harlow vibes thumping in his chest. He was released on his own recognizance while the state investigated additional charges.

"Matt," Bodie said as they walked out of the courthouse, "stay away from Dale Cranston. This is two misdemeanor counts now." He clapped him on the shoulder. "I'll talk to the assistant state attorney when I get to the office."

On his way home, Matt stopped to see Granny. She was sweeping up the kitchen, declaring there was no need for folks to make such a fuss over her.

"It's just a bump and a bruise. What's going on with you?"

"You mean besides spending the night in jail?"

"Matty, do me a favor. Don't stay angry at yourself. Don't hold anything against Dale for what he says. Let's show kindness and mercy. It's the way of Immanuel."

"Harlow was saying perhaps moments like these actually lead us to our destiny."

"She's a wise woman."

Matt walked home by way of the Starlight. The orange Notification of Demolition signs glinted in the afternoon sun, and he felt as if the Starlight had lost a little piece of its soul.

Inside, the music played but the atmosphere was subdued.

"The joy seems gone, Matt," Harlow said.

Since he was flying back to LA on Friday, hopefully he wasn't really fired, he and Harlow made plans for tomorrow— breakfast, lunch, and dinner.

At home, Dad had scrambled up some eggs and laid thick slices of bacon in the cast-iron skillet for dinner.

"I've been thinking," Dad said, getting up to pour another cup of coffee from the old percolator, a wedding present from when he married Mom. "What if I bring Granny out to Hollywood in August? Get her away from the demolition talk and the death of the Starlight. I can take time off. I'll be finishing a big job next month, and the crew will have finishing work to keep them busy. Noble Haney can run things for me."

"If you can get her to leave, sure. By the way, I'm selling the beach house and buying a sweet place I saw in the Hills. It's small but homey." Matt motioned to the kitchen. "Like this. There's plenty of room for you and Granny. The back deck has a great view of the city."

"I'll talk to her." Dad doctored his coffee with a scoop of sugar. "Say, do you think I could meet the Duke? The last movie I ever saw with your Uncle LJ was *Stagecoach*."

"Dad, the Duke died ten years ago."

"Then I'll go by that theater with all the footprints." A shadow of sadness passed over his face. "LJ and I sure loved that movie."

"I wish I'd met him."

"Me too. And your grandpa. He was a son-of-a-gun but a warrior. I see a bit of him in you—and not because you keep decking Dale Cranston."

The conversation moved to town happenings, how to get Granny to California, Matt telling Dad he was buying him a dishwasher as he hung up the dishrag and dried his hands on a terry cloth towel.

They both turned at the knock on the kitchen door. A grim-faced Bodie stood on the other side.

"They're bringing charges." He set his briefcase on the table and accepted a cup of coffee from Dad. "We're going to trial."

32

SEA BLUE BEACH

JUNE

A-LISTER MATT KNIGHT GOING TO TRIAL

WRECKING BALL SKATE TO BE THE LAST NIGHT AT THE STARLIGHT

These two salacious *Gazette* headlines have the whole town talking. Gossip fills our streets. Matt's upcoming trial made national news. ABC, NBC, *Entertainment Tonight*. A new network called CNN had trucks lined up outside the Starlight for a week.

For now, he's headed back to LA, leaving his defense up to his crackerjack lawyer, Bodie Nickle. Folks are still awaiting the trial date. What's taking so long?

Harlow has remained in town, and we couldn't be happier to see her jogging Sea Blue Way every other morning. Trina Bevel noticed the supermodel stepping up on the big green scale in Biggs yesterday. We've also noticed her on the skating rink floor now and then, toddling along in Tuesday's old skates. HH, we're all with you.

Spike told Audra at the Blue Plate that the Starlight's phone is ringing off the hook.

"Tuesday, say it isn't so! The rink is closing? What . . . demolished?"

"I told my family we're headed to Sea Blue Beach. My kids have never skated there!"

Every day, more and more cars line our streets and avenues. Old-timers, former Sea Blue Beach citizens, and children of deceased former Starlighters who'd heard the stories of the rink built by a prince on a rock by the ocean but had never visited.

The cottages at Sands Motor Motel announced a waiting list, and every beach cabin and summer-only home is rented out. Even the dilapidated fishing shacks have lodgers. Tents pop up in yards and along the beach.

Phil, the postman, disappears every other day inside the Starlight with bags of letters from all over the world, from former tourists passing through, to those who'd booked a week's vacation, to spring breakers across the Panhandle and LA—that is, lower Alabama.

Then, to our delight, Harriet Nickle and her sister Jubilee arrived. What a treat. We almost think it's worth the ruckus over the Starlight to see those gals back home.

Most nights, the rink bursts at the seams, with lines snaking around the octagon-shaped building. Spike convinced Tuesday to add a ten o'clock to midnight session just to accommodate everyone.

We'll get all the life we can out of our dear Starlight until the mayor calls for the wrecking ball. Wrecking ball. Two words that make some of us want to cry.

In this time of sentiment, we remember our friend Doc, who'd settled down in Sea Blue Beach after the second war. Said his old bones were too weary to keep on trucking. He told Dear Dirk he dreamt his wife was talking to "the man on the wall of the Starlight" and took it to mean he needed to roost near the rink for his final days.

However, he got restless, and at the age of eighty, bought a boat, christened it the *Betsy*, and set out to sail the path of the *Titanic*. We stood by the dock as he shoved off, saying, "I'll be back after I drop flowers over my wife and daughters' graves. It's long overdue."

Word came back how the Coast Guard found him and the *Betsy* adrift over the site of the wreck, Doc gone peacefully in his sleep, a nautical map and a picture of his girls on his chest.

It tore Tuesday up something fierce, but she put on a memorial at the Starlight worthy of her friend. All of Sea Blue Beach turned out.

In light of our memories, the orange demolition sign seems a slap in the face. But we know, deep down, that all small towns have a secret. Ours might just save the Starlight.

HARLOW

June flowed into July, with Harlow's days anchored by the rink. She marveled at how Tuesday rebounded from the demolition news to reign as queen over her kingdom, paying no mind to surveyors and contractors milling around inside and out.

"Tuesday, can I borrow some of your mojo?" Harlow said one afternoon.

After her prison cell conversation with Matt, she was determined not to sabotage herself. Especially when Jinx called to say Charlotte Winthrop was still committed to Harlow being her next CCW It Girl.

So, she told Blaire and Miss Beulah at the Blue Plate not to let her order tater tots with her spinach and tomato omelet and lightly buttered toast.

Matt called every morning and evening. "How's Granny doing?"

"Like the rink will go on forever. Any final word on your court date? Have you called Booker?"

"No."

"That's it? No?"

"It answers both questions."

"Matt, call your friend. Get it over with. Rip off the Band-Aid."

"I miss you," he said. "The crew says I talk about you all the time." His tone made her feel all squishy and warm. Like she belonged to him.

Thoughts of him cruised through her all day. Her heart skipped when the phone rang just as she returned from her jog—three a.m. Pacific time—and then again at night, as she crawled into bed.

The Xander situation took care of itself. After he sailed away, she called him once and he called twice. Both conversations died quickly after their hellos.

When she said good-bye the last time, she knew they were both done.

"Be well, Xander."

"You too, Harlow."

Mom called a few weeks after the confrontation in her office, insisting her choices for Harlow were spot-on and she didn't owe her an apology or explanation. *"I've given you a life most girls can only dream about, and sometimes not even their dreams are enough."*

After that rough call, Harlow ached for a candy bar, but she didn't have one in the house, and she refused to run out to Biggs or Alderman's to buy one in defiance of her stubborn mother. After a few minutes, the impulse died, and shew, progress. Three months ago, she'd have been out the door in a New York minute.

She worked the rink tonight, happy to see Dupree show up with his skates, which brought Tuesday to tears. They went around for a good long while together, mother and son holding hands.

He'd been helping Tuesday go through all the boxes in her office and the back room, carrying out several garbage bags in the evening, leaving more than enough memorabilia for the coming Starlight museum.

Over in concession, Spike flipped burgers and grilled hot dogs. Simon ran back and forth to the back room storage for napkins, serving trays, and soda syrup.

Nora cued up Peaches & Herb's "Reunited" and called for a couple's skate, though no one ever left the floor these days.

"Here." Tuesday shoved her old skates at Harlow. "I can't live with myself if you don't master skating. Now get out there. Dupree will help you. Trust me, you'll have fond memories after the wrecking ball knocks this place down."

"How do you do it?" Harlow hugged the skates to her chest. "Stay so calm? This mess is breaking my heart and I'm a new kid around here."

"Immanuel." She pointed to the mural. "I was disappointed in Him, even doubted He existed the night they hammered up the demolition signs, but I've had time to reflect, do a bit of talking to Him, and I know I can trust Him. If He doesn't save us, He must have a better plan."

Nora announced an all skate with Earth, Wind & Fire's "Shining Star." No one could stay off the floor once the beat filled the rink, including Harlow.

"Hey, Harlow." A group of teen girls rolled past her, so smooth and in control of their feet. "You hanging around town? Could you give us some pointers with our makeup?"

"Absolutely." She walk-rolled-stumbled while hanging onto the wall, her back stiff, her feet at awkward angles.

Another skater swooshed passed with a greeting, but she only caught the back of his head. "Are you staying in town after the demolition?" he called when he passed her again. He was a Starlight regular, but she never got his name.

Another skater, one of the Biggs managers, rolled next to her.

"Harlow, I'd really love to stock Hayes Cookies, but I'm having trouble connecting with the distributor. Any ideas?"

"I'll give my dad a call." Whoa, she almost face-planted.

"Doing okay, Harlow?" Dupree gently grabbed her arm.

"You tell me." She clung to him until she stopped wobbling and tried to absorb the skating tips he offered.

She continued around the rink with him until Nora called all the dancers and shufflers to the floor. The bass riff of Madonna's "Into the Groove" shook the Starlight as the disco ball began to spin. Every skater bopped to the rhythm like a choreographed music video. Even Dupree—a man in his sixties—got into it and headed a long line of shufflers.

Harlow clung to the wall until the group of girls interested in makeup linked their arms through hers and pulled her along.

That Friday night, she never left the floor. When Nora announced the final song, Harlow was hot, sweaty, and exhilarated.

"That was amazing." She wrapped Tuesday in a hug as she surveyed her kingdom. "Did you see me? I made it all the way around without touching the wall, and I went backward for maybe three feet before I ran into Andrea Fuller, but she was really nice about it." She yanked off her skates and looked out over the thinning crowd. "Gosh, I feel like I'm twelve. I think. I never really got to be twelve."

"I knew you'd love it." Tuesday smoothed her hand over Harlow's hair. "Simon covered your chores. Why don't you go on home?"

"I'm too jazzed to go home." So she stored her skates—hers now, not Tuesday's—and headed down the Beachwalk. The air under a bright moon was thick and warm. The Gulf lapped lazily against the shore, as if switching the tide might require too much effort.

The aroma of cinnamon and baking dough drew Harlow toward the pretzel truck. She paused. Did she need a pretzel? She'd eaten a good dinner. Roller-skated her heart out. She was a little hungry, sure, but wouldn't it be better to go home, shower, and go to bed?

Yet she'd roller-skated! Didn't that deserve a celebration? She was almost to Pete's Pretzels when the heart-stopping fragrance of roasting meat wrapped around her. Just past the food trucks and beyond the Beachwalk lights, a fire burned. A man looked up and beckoned her.

Me?

She glanced around. Several families and groups walked along the shore, so she'd not be alone out there. She cut across the sand toward the firepit. Maybe he was a friend of Dupree or Matt. Or Tuesday. She knew everyone. As she drew near, the sound of the waves and the wind in her hair stilled.

"Would you like some fish?" The man looked familiar. Felt known. "Sea bass is very good." He drew a pan from the coals. "I made some bread as well. Sit, please." He pointed to the rough-hewn bench on the other side.

"Begging your pardon, you don't appear to be a licensed vendor. I'm not inclined to eat with strangers."

"If you dine with me, then we won't be strangers. Please—"

Call her crazy, but she wanted to sit, to talk with him. Her belly rumbled for the fish and bread. "Are you sure you have enough?"

H, stop this. Go home. But oh, the fragrance—like real, nourishing food. One bite and she'd be whole.

"More than enough."

She sat across from him, hugging her handbag to her chest. "So, is this a new business? Fish over an open firepit? Should I call some more people over?"

"This is just for you and me." He handed her a plate with a slice of sizzling fish and warm bread. Their eyes met, and she stood abruptly, dumping her plate in the sand. "Immanuel."

"Yes," he said with a laugh, picking up her plate. "I've got more." When he spoke, the evening stars seemed to swoop low and listen in. They were brilliant and alive, and so close she could touch them.

"Y-you're real."

"Didn't Tuesday tell you I was real?"

"You're a painting. A mural. A story." He wore the same long coat with his burnished brown hair flowing over the collar. His hat rested next to him.

His voice was soft yet booming. The mural depicted a man among men from another era, but the image didn't do him justice. He was more alive than anyone she'd ever known. The flames of the fire paled in comparison to his eyes.

"The mural is just a representation. The prince insisted, thinking it would preserve the story of the Starlight and Sea Blue Beach. Of me."

"Why don't you keep the Starlight from being demolished? Tuesday's putting on a good show, but—"

"Let's talk about you, Harlow." He offered her another plate of bread and fish.

"Must we? If you're really God, then you know everything. I certainly know myself."

"Do you? Then why do you believe you're not worth loving?"

She choked on her bite of bread. "Excuse me?"

"You don't think you're worth loving because the ones you should've been able to trust let you down. Your parents, Xander, people in your career, even Sea Blue Beach by taking the Starlight. You think I've let Tuesday down."

She stared at her plate, afraid to look up. Afraid of what else He'd see. "I, um—"

"Do you know my story, Harlow?"

"No. Some. Not much."

Immanuel stirred the fire, turned the roasting sea bass, and settled in with his own plate, telling her from the beginning how God, who is love, paid a ransom for Harlow Hayes. If He loved her that much, then she must be worth loving.

Immanuel set his plate aside. "Harlow, I came to tell you I'm the bread of life. If you eat of me, you'll never go hungry again."

"Something tells me you're not talking about what's on my plate."

"You won't need Tony's Pizza to feel satisfied in your soul again. Believe in Me. God with *you*."

33

MATT

JULY
SEA BLUE BEACH

Between long days of filming, putting his house on the market and moving to his new-old Hollywood Hills place, Matt had yet to call Booker. Not to worry, Harlow gently reminded every few calls.

She was doing killer with her weight loss. Down twenty-five pounds since early May.

Now, after umpteen delays, Matt was in Sea Blue Beach for his court date. "What's our play here, bugsy?" Matt's weak James Cagney imitation did not amuse Bodie.

"Our play here is you being cool," Bodie whispered as the jurors filed into the jury box. "Humble."

"Pass me a fork and a plate of crow."

"Don't play up your celebrity. Look sober and dignified."

"And a side of humble pie."

"Judge Harris is serious but fair. The state believes they have an open-and-shut case, having so many eyewitnesses between the diner and rink. But I'll make them doubt what they saw."

The case continued to make news, but more in a Matt-Knight-defends-his-grandmother's-honor kind of way. He'd suspected his former publicist Amelia had a hand in spinning the details. She always had a soft spot for him. This morning, fans gathered outside the courthouse with *Free Matt Knight* signs.

"We're cheering for you, Matt."

"We love you, Matt Knight."

"Justice will prevail!"

"Free Matt Knight. Free Matt Knight."

Dad entered the courtroom, wearing his blue work shirt and jeans, his hair combed back, his shoulders square. Next to him, Granny sat straight with her chin raised, and gave Matt two thumbs up. Where was Harlow? She said she'd be here.

Seeing Dad and Granny messed with him more than he thought it would. They deserved better from him. He deserved better for himself. This wasn't the set of a movie, a role to play. This was his real life. With real consequences.

"Remember, Matt," Bodie said. "Sober and dignified."

There was no need to remind him. James Cagney joking aside, sobriety wrapped every part of him.

Matt's original approach had been to pretend he was on the set of a police drama, playing the part of a man unjustly accused. But seeing Dad and Granny, the judge, the somber faces of the jurors, he could be nothing but regular Matt Knight, vulnerable and a bit scared. Honestly, he'd earned his way into this mess fair and square.

Tapping Bodie's arm, he leaned in. "I'm going to confess."

"No, you're not. With a first-degree misdemeanor charge, you could get up to a year in jail. Don't you listen to anything I tell you? Now sit back and be quiet."

The judge entered, and the case of the State of Florida versus Matt Knight was in session. He glanced back at Dad. *Where's Harlow?* He shook his head with a shrug.

The assistant state attorney, Marvin Moore, delivered impassioned opening remarks about allowing those who think they are above the law to get away with small infractions while the common man pays the price. "A misdemeanor today means a felony tomorrow. Before you know it, a punch turns into aggravated battery, which turns into murder."

Bodie shot to his feet. "Objection. The ASA is implying my client is a murderer."

"Sustained."

"The state will prove that Mr. Knight's actions toward Dale Cranston were deliberate and violent. You will have no choice but to render a guilty verdict." Marvin Moore returned to his table with a glib look of satisfaction.

Bodie approached the jury box. "My client does not believe he's above the law," he began in a deep, collected, even voice. "He cares about this community, the people, and traditions. The state will try to paint him as a cold, egotistic Hollywood star who lives for his own glory. Matt Knight is the exact opposite, which we will prove. Don't see a celebrity in this courtroom today. See a man, an ordinary citizen, trying to do what's right. Just like you and I would."

One by one, the state called their witnesses.

Moore: "Did you see Mr. Knight strike the victim?"

Mrs. Philpott of 2020 Ocean Front Lane: "Yes, I did. Smack. Right in the kisser."

One by one, Bodie challenged their testimony.

Bodie: "Mrs. Philpott, you saw the defendant hit the victim in the kisser?"

Mrs. Philpott: "Yes, sir, I did."

Bodie: "Can you define *kisser*?"

Mrs. Philpott: "The lips. The mouth."

Bodie: "Your sworn testimony is you saw my client hit Dale Cranston in the mouth?"

Mrs. Philpott: "Yes, I did."

Bodie: "I have here a photograph of Dale Cranston taken after the so-called altercation." He handed it to the judge, then to Mrs. Philpott. "Can you describe where you see a bruise on this man's face?"

Mrs. Philpott: "Oh, yes, I see. He has a bruise around his eye."

Bodie: "Is that the kisser, Mrs. Philpott?"

Mrs. Philpott: "Well, no. Dale, how'd you get that black eye?"

Male Voice: "He ran into one of the projectors."

Judge Harris: "No shouting from the gallery and the witness will not address the plaintiff."

Bodie: "Mrs. Philpott, did you actually see Mr. Knight hit Dale Cranston?"

Mrs. Philpott: "I saw him fall over. Right into Blaire. Made a mess of everything."

Bodie: "The waitress Blaire?"

Mrs. Philpott: "Yes."

Bodie: "Blaire was in the kitchen." He offered verified evidence from Audra at the diner that Blaire was in the kitchen, helping her unload a shipment of napkins and Styrofoam cups. "Mr. Cranston fell into Rachelle Dickenson."

Mrs. Philpott: [hand to her lips] "Well, those girls look so much alike from behind."

Bodie: "Mrs. Philpott, can you say beyond reasonable doubt that the defendant gave Dale Cranston this black eye?"

Mrs. Philpott: "I guess not. Gee whiz, sorry, Matt."

Moore: "Objection! Let the apology be stricken from the record."

"Overruled."

And so it went. Moore produced his eyewitnesses, and Bodie challenged every one of them. Even Milo couldn't swear Matt actually swung at Dale that night in the rink.

Bodie: "Is it your sworn testimony, Officer Patitucci, that Dale Cranston was poised to lunge at the defendant's grandmother, Tuesday Knight?"

Milo: "Looked like it, but then Mayor Smith fell into Mrs. Knight and things got chaotic."

Bodie: "Did you see the defendant strike Dale Cranston?"

Milo: "Not exactly."

Bodie: "Yes or no, Officer Patitucci."

Milo: "No."

Moore tried to eviscerate Milo's testimony, but he recited the details exactly the same, no matter how Moore tried to twist up the facts.

Sensing his case shredding, Moore called two character witnesses on behalf of Dale Cranston: Harry Smith, mayor of Sea

Blue Beach, and Lloyd Boyd, head of the chamber of commerce. Moore's questions and their answers were perfunctory and boring. Expected.

"The state rests, Your Honor."

Judge Harris glanced down at Bodie over the top of his spectacles. "Mr. Nickle, call your character witness. Let's get this done. All this talk of the Blue Plate is making me hungry."

"The defense calls Harlow Hayes to the stand."

Harlow?

The courtroom doors opened, and she strutted into the courtroom and down the aisle like it was a Paris runway. She owned the walls, the ceiling, the floor, and every breathing person in the room. She moved gracefully, eliciting a chorus of oohs and aahs. Her hair with golden highlights flowed over her shoulder in loose curls. She wore slacks and heels, with a blue jacket that turned her eyes into a cloudless sky.

Hubba hubba. Matt was a goner. No way back. Guilty of heart-palpitating love, Your Honor. Give him life without parole.

After the bailiff swore her in, Harlow glanced his way for the first time.

"Bodie," he whispered, "why'd you call Harlow? She was at the diner. She can't lie."

Bodie scribbled on his legal pad. *HUSH!*

If asked outright, "Did Matt Knight hit Dale Cranston in the Blue Plate Diner?" she'd have to say yes. He didn't know what she saw at the rink, but at the diner she had a front row seat.

Don't lie under oath for me, H.

Bodie went to work. "You're Harlow Hayes of 321 Sea Blue Way and formerly of 432 Park Avenue, Manhattan, New York?"

"Yes."

"Can you tell us about your career?"

"I was a model with the Icon Agency for twelve years. More recently, I have been employed at the Starlight."

"Objection." Marvin Moore was a hot poker fresh from the

fire. "What is the purpose of this line of questioning? The state concedes Ms. Hayes is a famous model who owns a residence here in Sea Blue Beach. Can we move on?"

"Sustained," Judge Harris said. "Move on, Mr. Nickle."

"Harlow, can you tell us about the day at the diner and the punch in question?"

Her eyes glistened as she swiveled toward the jurors. *Oh, H, brilliant move.* "Life is never easy, is it?" The women nodded, and the men stared. She was composed, confident, exuding all of her HH qualities.

"I'm sure everyone knows my big heartbreak of '85." The redhead with freckles on the end wiped her eyes. "All my life I wanted to be a mom. Not very hip these days, right? Today women are supposed to want careers, to break glass ceilings, but I wanted to be a mom with a bunch of kids. My mom started me young in modeling, and while I'm grateful for the opportunities it gave me, I missed being a part of a family. I never felt my life was my own."

Moore slowly stood, adjusting his tie and jacket. "Ms. Hayes is not on trial here. Must we continue with the world's smallest violin playing 'My Heart Bleeds for You' in this emotional manipulation?"

Marvin Moore had just made a fatal mistake. The women scorned him, and the men appeared perturbed. For sure Amos Luckenbach, at seventy-eight, had never heard Harlow's story. The man lived on a boat.

"Overruled," Judge Harris said. "Go on, Ms. Hayes, but do get to the part about the defendant."

"Yes, Your Honor." She couldn't be more sincere and humble. Something had happened to her. Matt leaned for a deeper look. She was different. Brighter. "Anyway, I first met Matt on the set of *Talk to Me Sweetly*, and—"

"I loved that movie."

Judge Harris slapped his gavel. "Juror Number Four, please refrain from speaking."

Harlow detailed her friendship with Matt on the set and their surprising meet-cute at Tony's Pizza, depicting the scene quite accurately, recounting her embarrassment. "My dress was hiked up to kingdom come, showing off my underwear."

"Oh mercy, ain't that the worst? Had something similar happened to me when—"

Judge Harris slapped his gavel. "Juror Number Four, one more outburst and I'll remove you from the room."

"Anyway," Harlow said, "there I am with a mouth full of pizza and *the* Matt Knight kneels down in front of me and says, 'H, what are you doing here? Wow, it's so good to see you.' He didn't stare or gawk. He didn't laugh or curl a lip. He made me feel . . ." She glanced down at her hands. "Special. And I hadn't felt special in a really, really long time. Maybe not ever."

Oh, Harlow . . . Matt's lips buzzed something fierce.

"He hired me to work at the Starlight before I even applied. I didn't even know how to skate, but Tuesday taught me. Though I secretly think she wanted me to dust the floor, because I spent a lot of time on my backside."

Marvin Moore moaned and slumped down in his seat.

"Ms. Hayes, let's move on to the day in question. Did Dale Cranston stop by your table as you dined with Mr. Knight?" Bodie said.

"He did. He ridiculed the Starlight and me. Matt told him who I was, but Mr. Cranston said I was too fat to be Harlow Hayes. However, he did suggest I was pretty enough to be used for a one-night stand or two."

The jurors and every spectator in the courtroom gasped.

Moore was on his feet. "Objection, Your Honor. Dale Cranston is not on trial. Insulting someone does not warrant being assaulted."

"Well, it should." Juror Number Four again.

The atmosphere exploded with shouts and gavel banging.

"Order!" Judge Harris said. "I will have order in my courtroom. Mr. Nickle, get to the point. Now."

"Ms. Hayes," Bodie said, "did you see Matt Knight punch Dale Cranston?"

"Actually, no, I didn't. I was staring at my plate. Because of what Mr. Cranston said about me. I was ashamed."

A collective gasp was followed by a low din of spectators talking among themselves. The jurors leaned together in a discussion accented with wild gestures. Outside, the "Free Matt Knight" mantra continued.

"Did you see Mr. Knight strike Dale Cranston at the Starlight on the night of May 26?" Bodie continued.

"No, I did not. I only saw Mr. Cranston lunging at Tuesday, but the mayor got in the way. I tried to keep Tuesday from falling."

Bodie glanced back at Matt and mouthed, "Boom."

Boom was right. Once again, Judge Harris banged his gavel, trying to bring order. Everyone talked at once.

Through the noise and chatter and the "Free Matt Knight" chants, Harlow glanced his way, and her eyes pulled him from his chair like a scene from *Close Encounters of the Third Kind*. He passed through the chaos and stepped into the witness box.

"Is this going to be a thing with you? Kissing me in crowded public forums?" she said.

"Maybe, but I have one question, and remember, you're under oath."

"I'm listening."

"Marry me, Harlow."

"That's not a question."

He grinned through all of his buzzy, fuzzy sensations. "Will you marry me, Harlow Hayes? I know what we said in the jail cell, but something has changed. You're free. I can see it in your eyes, and I want what you have."

"It was Immanuel."

"Granny's Immanuel?"

"My Immanuel."

He brushed her lips with his. "Marry me, HH."

She gripped his shirt. "Better believe I will, Matt Knight, and have a passel of babies."

Pulling her into his arms, he knew he was holding his heart and his future. Her kiss unfurled a vision of laughter, tears, arguments, late colicky nights, diaper changes, school plays and sports, birthday parties and exhausting family vacations, and mad lovemaking, even when they were too tired. Every movement of her body against his said it was so.

When they broke apart, the courtroom was silent, every eye on them. The redhead in the jurors' box gushed, breathless, "Not guilty, Your Honor. Not guilty."

At that point, the judge gave up on any sort of order as Mr. Moore shouted, "The state withdraws the charges" and Judge Harris brought his gavel down.

"Matt Knight, you're free to go."

34

HARLOW

AUGUST

If she heard it once after the trial, she'd heard it a thousand times.

"Meet me at the Starlight. Late session."

"Are you going to the Starlight? Meet you there."

The *Gazette* published a special issue detailing the history of the Starlight. Tuesday didn't love the name "Wrecking Ball Skate" for Labor Weekend. She preferred "Last Night at the Starlight."

Harlow was old hat around the place these days. Just a regular Sea Blue Beacher, who attended a girls' night at the Fish Hook and hosted a book club at her house.

Skates laced up, she entered the rink to Boston's "More Than a Feeling." The shufflers were cruising around the outside of the rink, and she ached to join them. But first, she had to make it a whole session without stumbling.

After her dinner with Immanuel three weeks ago, she became more peaceful. The stride of her morning jog was longer. Even more surprising, she'd not rolled off the diet bandwagon once. Temptation still existed, but after Immanuel's bread and fish, her emotions changed.

She took to asking Him for help when she felt weak. Last night, while closing the rink, the stragglers informed her the vending machine dispensed candy bars if you bumped it just right. Got to be honest, the Snickers bars were calling her name. She peered up at Immanuel's mural and said, "Can you help a girl out?"

A second later, Simon said he was good to go and asked if he could walk her home. She forgot all about the Snickers.

Even more miraculous, she told Mom she'd forgiven her. To which she replied, *"For what?"* Even if Anne Hayes didn't get it, Harlow needed to say it. She ended the call with a soft "I love you." For the first time in her life, she was inching along her personal rink, free to fall and get up again.

Dad wanted to know if she'd like to open a Hayes Cookie retail space in Sea Blue Beach. As it happened, she'd jogged by an empty space next to the future Starlight museum that same day.

Matt's firm, warm hand landed on her back. "Look at you, skating." He'd come home for the weekend. More and more, she knew she belonged with him. He drew her close for a couple's skate.

"Don't look at your feet," he said. "Look at me. Feel the music. Don't overthink it. Roll, push, roll, push. There you go. Glide, glide, glide."

She curled her right hand around his and settled her left on his thick shoulder. The rink lights dimmed, and the disco ball cast a romantic prism across the floor. The melodic sound of a piano, guitar, and drums preceded the velvet voice of Elvis. "For I can't help falling in love with you."

"They're playing our song," Matt said.

Harlow scooted into him and breathed him in. Then bump, her skate rammed into his. Stumbling backward, Matt's foot kicked hers, which launched her tripping and stumbling, arms pinwheeling, toward the half-wall.

"Help, I'm doing the splits. Dial 9-1-1."

"Work your feet together," Matt called.

"You work *your* feet together." She shooed away the six-year-olds hobbling along. "Pardon me, excuse me. So sorry." She crashed into the wall, arms and legs flailing.

Matt rescued her, trying very hard not to laugh as she straightened her shirt, squared the waist of her jeans, and tossed her hair over her shoulder.

"Well, that was fun," she said, sweat trickling down her back. "Where's a video camera when you need one?"

"Guess we got tangled up." Matt took her hand as Nora continued the couple's skate with the Eagles' "Best of My Love."

"You're laughing," she said, settling into Matt's movements, thinking about how goofy she must've looked.

"No, not laughing."

"Then you're over-smiling."

Now he laughed and kissed her. "We're going to be great together, Harlow."

"We'd better be, or I'm telling Immanuel on you." She adjusted her feet and rolled along, smiling, feeling all the shy yet glorious sensations of being so close to someone who saw through her.

Harlow enjoyed her unhindered free fall into love. When she'd fallen in love with Xander, she wasn't free on the inside. Now she was.

On his first day back in LA after the trial, Matt met a man on set who knew a lot about Immanuel, and he started teaching Matt from the Good Book.

Harlow's skate ran into Matt's again, and she fell against his chest. He kissed her cheek and eased his hand around to her hip. As awkward as it was to skate so close, she stayed against him, swaying side to side.

After his courtroom victory, Matt bought steaks and corn on the cob from Biggs and grilled out at Dupree's, who carried home an apple pie from Sweet Conversations. Tuesday tossed a lovely garden salad, and they ate that night with Bodie and his family at Dupree's dining room table.

"Harlow, welcome to the family," Dupree said when he'd poured the wine. *"If you ever need any help at your place, something fixed or looked at, just call Ma."*

"Tuesday?"

His laugh rang through the kitchen. *"Naw, just pulling your leg. Call me. If I can't come, I'll send one of my guys."*

"Don't pull my leg, Dupree. I'm tall enough as it is."

Laughter was truly a healing balm.

The techno dance beat of Shannon's "Let the Music Play" revved up the rink.

"Babe, I got to skate!" Matt shoved off to join a couple of teens in the shuffle line, and in his haste, kind of, sort of, gave Harlow a little push.

"Matt, hey . . ." She flailed, again, teetering, then tottering, skates clicking and clacking against the floor. "What happened to Elvis and take my hand? Remember the half-wall incident of 1987?" Harlow grabbed at the air, straining to stay on her feet. "Somebody, anybody . . . hey . . . take my hand."

Matt zoomed by, miming a dropped bomb on his heart.

"I'm going to bomb you with these skates when I take them off. No, I'm not *even* going to take them off."

Suddenly, a gaggle of girls swarmed around her. One of them grabbed her right hand, and another her left, and they held her steady as she worked her skates into alignment.

They talked like she was part of their crowd, ignoring the beat of the music, leisurely skating with one foot extended and tipped up to roll on the back wheels. Round and round she went, finding a smoothness in it all, even managed to do that thing with one foot forward, rolling on the back wheels. Did the Starlight pass out gold medals?

They chatted about the upcoming school year and how so-and-so was the predicted homecoming queen. Two of the girls were going out for volleyball, while the other two planned to audition for the school play.

When the Commodores' "Brick House" poured through the speakers, the girls came to life and skated away, singing and pointing to one another. "She's mighty, mighty . . ."

They motioned for Harlow to join them, but she wasn't quite ready for "Brick House" tomfoolery.

"Well, well, we meet again." Simon skated next to her. "Know what I was thinking, Harlow? The first day you came to Sea Blue Beach, you seemed sort of broken."

"I thought I was hiding it so well."

"But look at you now. Learning to skate. Getting married. Even prettier. You've changed."

"Okay, flatterer, did Matt send you over here?"

"No, this is me talking."

"Thank you, Simon. I mean it."

"Just so you know, I like this you better than the Harlow Hayes in the poster on my brother's wall." He nudged her with his elbow.

"Me too, Simon. Me too."

TUESDAY

Wrecking Ball Skate at the Starlight turned into Wrecking Ball Month.

Audra had a line outside the Blue Plate Diner, and the food trucks on the beaches closed up in the afternoon, completely out of food for the day.

Folks she'd not seen in years, decades, arrived on the hour. The Starlight hosted a reunion every night.

Two of the old-timers, sisters Georgia and Maria from '73, '74, and '75, had rushed in. "Miss Tuesday! We had to come back. We're here to help. What can we do?" Spike handed them aprons and now they baked pizza and doctored hot dogs, alongside Ernie, another old-timer from—oh, let's see, '68 and '69—yes, because he'd fried half his brain in San Francisco during the Summer of Love. His parents yanked him back home and asked Tuesday to give him a job. *"He needs responsibility. Don't go easy on him. Make him do his job, show up on time."*

Ernie turned out to be one of the best hires in her Starlight career. Then the war in 'Nam got him for a year, but he'd matured, became a leader, graduated college, and now ran a successful cleaning business in Jackson, Mississippi.

"I got my work ethic from the Starlight, Tuesday, mopping and sweeping. Spike, hand me a broom! Is that little Georgia Zimmerman? Hey, and Maria!"

Tuesday added a ten a.m. session and still had skaters lined around the rink all day. Dupree came every night, laced up his old black boots, donned a whistle, and served as floor guard.

"Ma, did you see?" Dupree rolled behind the ticket booth for a sip of his drink. "Griff and Joannie are here, and Dennis too." Classmates of Dup's from high school and some of his best friends.

Griff and Joannie were proof the Starlight was a place for miracles. High school sweethearts who broke up for good right before graduation, then loathed each other all through college. One summer, while home on vacation, they met up at the rink. He asked her to couple's skate, and since he was the only boy in the place that night who knew how to do more than hold hands and go 'round and 'round, she said yes, eager to refresh her dance skills.

He kissed her when the song ended—Tuesday witnessed the whole thing—and now they were the parents of three, grandparents of ten.

Dennis never married, but Dup said, "He's skated with Kathleen

DiMarco three times, and I saw them at the Blue Plate the other night."

"What about you, son? Is there a love for you?" Tuesday said.

"Don't know, Ma. It might take a miracle, but if she's out there, she'll come to the Starlight." With that, he returned to the floor, blowing his whistle on a couple of speedsters.

"She better come before Labor Day weekend," Tuesday whispered to herself with a glance at Immanuel. If He planned on saving the Starlight, He was taking His sweet time.

Harry stopped asking Tuesday for the deed. Yesterday he asked her to sign some papers so he could *"just go ahead and give you the money for the rink."*

"No thanks," she'd said. *"I'll wait until the bitter end."*

She wished she had the deed just to show off how how fancy and regal it was bearing the prince's signature. But LJ had taken its whereabouts to a watery grave.

A man and a woman about Dupree's age approached the ticket booth. "We're looking for Tuesday Knight."

"You're talking to her, but I'm afraid we're at capacity for this session, and the line for the next is a mile long."

"No, no, we don't want tickets. Not right now. We're Sissy and Mikey, children of a couple you helped out during the Depression, Norvel and Elise Brandley. You put us up in the back room and fed us for a week."

"My mother was on the verge of a nervous breakdown," Sissy added, "and my father, well, he may have walked into the ocean if you'd not let us harbor at the Starlight."

"I remember you." Tuesday came around the booth and embraced them. Sissy held her tight, and Mikey, a big strapping man in his fifties, rested his head on her shoulder for a long, long moment. "Look at you now," Tuesday said. "Are you married, with children and grandchildren?"

They were, as was their youngest sibling, Elias, who lived in South Dakota and planned to come next week, if at all possible.

Married with eleven children between them and fourteen grandchildren.

"All our lives, our parents pointed to you, Tuesday Knight, as an example of how to love, how to be generous. We know we weren't the first family to ask for your help or the last. We came all this way to tell you our family never forgot you."

"You have to skate. Come through the back door next session."

"We accept, if you accept this from our parents." Mikey pressed an envelope into Tuesday's hand. "Dad invented an electrical component used in radar during the war. He went on to work for GE and NASA, then started his own business. He's retired now, but"—he squeezed her hand—"he wanted you to have this. He thought it might help save the Starlight."

"There's no saving the Starlight. I can't accept." She could not take the man's money. "The city has made the decision. You see the demolition signs." She held out the envelope, but no one reached for it. "The wrecking crew comes next week, so it won't be used for what your father intended."

"Doesn't matter, Tuesday. It's a gift from our parents. They never, ever forgot you, Sea Blue Beach, the Starlight, or that image of Immanuel." Sissy pointed to the mural. "So please, keep the money, use it for yourself and your family."

"Dad will disown us if we come back with that check," Mikey said.

Tuesday brushed away tears. "I don't know what to say—"

The Brandley kids left for the Blue Plate to grab a bite before the evening skate.

"Who were you talking to, Ma?" Dupree grabbed his soda again.

"Children of a family I helped during the Depression." She handed the envelope to her son. "Their parents sent this to help save the Starlight. I tried to give it back, but they insist it was a gift. I'm so overwhelmed with all the folks coming home only to say good-bye. So much joy in the sadness."

Dupree tore the back flap and read the check. His expression told her nothing. "It's for twenty grand, Ma."

"Let me see." Sure enough, handwritten by Norvel Brandley. Two zero, zero, zero, zero. "I can't take this. How preposterous."

"You can if it's a gift."

"Dup, I gave them a bed and bath for a week, a couple of meals, nothing much fancier than bean soup. That doesn't merit twenty thousand dollars."

"What is it you say? 'Who knew so much could come from so little'? It's the story of the Starlight, Ma." He pressed the check into her hand. "All the years you stuck with it, hung in there, fought for the rink, survived storms and economic crashes. You warded off Pa and his gambling goons. You stood up for what was right. So much came from your small efforts."

"All right, get out onto the floor. You're making me cry." She yanked open the center drawer for a tissue, finding nothing but her old shears—the ones she used to cut up linens for Doc to bandage Leroy.

Dupree had one thing wrong. All of this wasn't because of her. Not even the Starlight. This was the handiwork of Immanuel of the Starlight.

He was sending her out in style.

35

MATT

He spent the last week of August in LA. Roger wanted to reshoot a couple of scenes, and while he was there, his beach house sold. He felt like a weight had been cut away.

Then he flew home Labor Day weekend for the Last Night at the Starlight. He took a Saturday night redeye to New Orleans, arriving as the Sunday sunrise broke through scattered clouds. A puddle jumper landed him in Fort Walton, where he whistled down a cab, arriving at the Starlight just in time for the noon session. He planned to skate until the final song.

Entering the rink, he waved to Dad and Granny, then greeted Harlow, who manned the ticket booth, with an all-consuming kiss. He didn't care about the gawking skaters waiting in line or the clicks of the instant cameras.

Let the world know! Matt Knight found his better half.

"Hey, babe," he whispered in her ear. With her hair in a ponytail and just a touch of makeup, her high cheeks seemed more pronounced than a week ago, and the blue sundress that matched her eyes hung loose.

"Matt Knight, let us in, man!" Fan alert. *Smile. Be cool.* He glanced toward the door. Ricky Lanter and Jonas Tucker! His old high school football buddies. They greeted one another with a "long time no see" and the requisite handshake-hug combo. Matt's bittersweet memories of Booker surfaced.

He'd almost called him twice, but between the reshoot and packing up the house, giving away some of the so-called treasures he no longer needed, he didn't have the emotional energy.

"Can you believe no more Starlight?" Jonas said. "Ol' Sea Blue won't be the same ever. How's Granny taking it?"

"She's holding out for a miracle, but—hey, let me introduce you to Harlow Hayes. H, two of my friends from Nickle High."

Ricky and Jonas went all starry-eyed and lost their bravado, shyly shaking Harlow's hand. Jonas managed to get a hold of himself and make a joke. "Y-you sure you want to hang around this scallywag?"

"Why not? You did."

Ricky slapped Matt on the back with a loud hoot. "I like her even more now." He leaned toward the supermodel, who continued to pass out tickets. Three hundred per session and no more. Every brownie in the skate room got a turn on someone's feet.

"Well, Harlow, see, we were the ones who made Matt cool, *soooo* . . ." Ricky motioned between him and Jonas. "That means you're going to have to hang around us."

Harlow passed five tickets to a waiting family. "Here you go. Welcome to the Starlight." Then she turned to Ricky and Jonas. "To be honest, boys, I'm cooler than all of you put together, including Rob Stone and Steve Hilliard."

They laughed while the husband of the entering family got stuck between gawking at Harlow and grinning at Matt. His wife moved him along with chagrin. "Pardon him," she said. "He doesn't get out much."

Matt always loved Harlow's demeanor, her broken kind of confidence, but this version of her was totally . . . tubular. Okay, so he spent last Sunday morning before work with a bunch of surfers.

With a light kiss for Harlow, he walked Ricky and Jonas to skate rental. They drilled him about *Flight Deck*. Did he really fly in a P-51?

More Nickle High alum breezed into the rink. Burke and Chambers, Caffey and McCord, followed by several faces Matt recognized from his elementary days.

Bodie Nickle arrived with his family. "Matt Knight, my favorite client." They slapped hands, bumped shoulders. "Did you get my bill? Hey, Harlow, thanks for winning the case for us. I'd like you to meet my wife, Latisha, and this is Morris, named for my grandpa. We call him Deuce. Our daughter, DeShawn, whom we call Dish."

"Matt." Dad tapped him on the shoulder and held out a whistle. "Want to help on the floor? It's really crowded."

As he headed for his skates, someone called his name. The older, more mature voice of Booker Nickle.

"Booker, hey, man."

"Don't worry, I'm not going to bite your head off this time," he said, offering to shake Matt's hand.

The years peeled away, and when the first sob hit, Matt locked him in a hug. "Book, I'm sorry. So, so, sorry."

"No, man, I'm sorry."

"Me and my big mouth. You were right to hate me all these years. Look what I did to Harlow on Letterman."

"Matt, look I need to tell you—" Booker paused. "Can we talk someplace quiet?"

Harlow appeared from behind him. "We're at capacity, so no more ticket sales. I'll work the floor. I've been dying to blow one of these whistles. You two grab a beer or something. Hi, Booker, I'm—"

"Harlow Hayes." He cut Matt a glance. "You always had the best luck with girls."

"Girls?" she said toward Matt. "You mean there's more than Patti Evans? Tell more."

"Book, don't get me in trouble already." Matt roped the whistle lanyard around Harlow's neck. "He's exaggerating."

"Booker, you and I will talk later." She grinned and whispered to Matt as she shoved him toward the door. "See? That wasn't so bad, was it?"

He suggested the Fish Hook at the opposite end of Sea Blue Way. Small talk melted a bit more of the ice between them. Booker, who wore the plaid shirt, jeans, and boots of a rancher, was still in New Mexico.

"I bought the place, so now I'm the one with all the headaches."

"Do you love it?"

"This beach boy *loves* the land. The bookworm loves his horses and cows. Give me a hot, dusty day and a cold, dry night, my favorite horse, a couple of cows, and a pretty girl . . ."

"There's a girl? Okay, now it's all making sense."

"Cassidy." They stepped onto the Fish Hook's back deck. "She wanted to be here, but someone had to watch the ranch. Literally. We've been married three years. Bodie didn't tell you? I sent you a wedding invitation."

Matt took a seat at the nearest picnic table. "I couldn't bring myself to open anything you sent."

The whirling fans cooled the warm air of the deck. Their server, Maisy, blushed when she saw Matt.

"I'll have a Coke and a basket of fried pickles," he said.

"Same for me," Booker said.

More small talk about Sea Blue Beach, the weather, and if VP George Bush would run for president filled the space until the drinks arrived.

"Here we are." Maisy held up a camera. "Matt, could we please have a picture for our wall?"

"Of course."

She hollered into the dining room. "He said yes, y'all. Come on." The entire place spilled onto the deck, staff and patrons alike.

Booker played photographer.

"Do you like it?" Booker said. "Celebrity life?"

"I like acting. I like the money. I like the open doors. But celebrity comes with a burden. And it sure didn't help save the Starlight."

"One of my cowgirls recently found out I knew you and went bonkers. Wanted me to invite you to the ranch, maybe film a movie there so she could be in it."

Matt grinned and tipped his Coke. "How'd she find out you knew me?"

"I told her, didn't I?" Booker thanked Maisy for his Coke and took a long drink. "Matt, I was already caught cheating before you blabbed."

"What?"

"Based on my performance in class, there was no way I could've aced the test. Mr. Ellison called Dad. Your big mouth just told the whole school. Ellison was going to give me another chance, but when Principal Conroy got involved . . . you know the rest of the story."

"That doesn't excuse me, Booker. I made it worse. But why didn't you tell me this?"

"I was mad and hurt. Thought maybe you did it on purpose because I wrecked your car. I was humiliated, kicked out of the school named for my ancestors. I let myself and the family down."

"Then why did you lay into me that Christmas at the Starlight?"

"Because I didn't get to do it when we were seventeen. Eight years of seething came to the surface. I'd just started working on a ranch too, which felt beneath me at the time. Then I started learning about black ranchers and cowboys, their contribution to the west, and got good at my job—really good. Last year, when the owner, who sort of adopted me as his own, offered to sell me the business, I took it."

Maisy arrived with their fried pickles and refilled their sodas.

"Want to know the irony?" Booker said. "When I got in trouble and Grandpa Morris took me on all his jobs. I learned welding, plumbing, electrical. I can build or fix anything on the ranch. He also told me stories, Matt."

"What kind of stories?"

"The history of our family, of Sea Blue Beach. How Grandpa Malachi saved Prince Blue on a dark and stormy night. How Sea Blue Beach was built. He knew more history of the Starlight than your granny. He told me about your dad and Uncle LJ growing up with my dad. He'd say, 'You and Matt best work things out 'cause the Knights and the Nickles go way back.' Made me realize that history didn't begin the day I was born, but I was responsible to write the next chapter. I knew I'd forgive you one day. Just not *that* day."

"I get it, man."

"I do have one question, Matt. Why *did* you tell?"

Matt dipped a fried pickle into the horseradish sauce. "We were in Caffey's barn drinking beer and one-upping each other."

"You hated losing that game."

"And I had the story of all stories. The guys thought it was great. But the girls didn't understand our little game. They told. Book, if I could, I'd take it all back."

"I wouldn't." Booker laughed softly. "My life turned out for the better. I look at Bodie and think there's no way I'd want to be a lawyer. Ranching is physical, but it also takes a lot of creativity. I go to bed tired in a good way. My wife is brilliant at gardening and canning. We can survive the coming nuclear holocaust."

"Harlow said something similar. How our journey is full of events that led to our destiny. I'm glad you're happy with how things turned out. I've spent a lot of years loathing myself over this, and I want to let go but it's hard."

"Matt," Booker said, leaning over his fried pickles. "You're forgiven. Debt paid. Bodie's been bugging me for years to get this over with, so please say we're good so I can visit you in Hollywood."

Matt laughed. "Absolutely, I mean, if you're sure."

"It's time."

"Then we're good." They slapped hands, sealing the deal. "I'd love to host you in Hollywood."

"We got to get back the decade we've wasted over a situation that a cold Coke, fried pickles, and a bit of humility fixed in fifteen minutes," Booker said. "So what's with you and Harlow?"

"Ladies and gentlemen, the man goes for the jugular. I asked her to marry me."

"Probably the smartest thing you've ever done," Booker said. "Who, um, you asking to be best man? Your dad would be honored, I'm sure."

"He would, but I already picked a guy."

"Oh, well, good. Send me and Cassidy an invite. We'd love to—"

"You big dolt, it's you."

Booker cleared his throat before chomping on a fried pickle. "Name the day" was all he could manage.

Matt tried to speak, but since the space between them crackled with the unspoken, he held onto his craggy sentiment. Sometimes words got in the way.

After a few more pickles and throat clearings, Booker said, "Hey, I've been thinking about the Starlight and the town enacting eminent domain."

"I suppose Bodie told you our petition for a vote failed."

"You didn't need a petition, Matt. The town needs permission from the Royal House of Blue to do anything to the Starlight."

"The House of Blue? What are you talking about?"

"The Starlight and the rock it sits on belongs to the sovereign, royal House of Blue. The land and rink are deeded to Lauchtenland. Grandpa Morris told me because Grandpa Malachi told him. If Harry demolishes the Starlight without proper authority, Sea Blue Beach might be embroiled in an international incident."

"Booker, are you serious?"

"Grandpa Morris assured me the land and rink are all but official members of the royal family. Tuesday couldn't even sell it without their approval." Booker made a face. "He looked me in the eye and said, 'No one can touch the Starlight without royal permission.'"

36

TUESDAY

There were two sessions on this Labor Day evening. Seven to eight-thirty. Nine to ten-thirty. By then, she'd be spent. Nothing left to do but grieve with all who came to mourn.

"Have you eaten?" Harlow peered into the office with a box from the Blue Plate. "Audra sent this over. I think it's the turkey dinner. She said you loved her mashed potatoes and gravy."

"She uses real potatoes." Tuesday smiled and reached for the Styrofoam container. "It was good to see Matt talking to Booker. Warmed this old girl's heart." She sighed and stared toward the wall. "Is it wrong for me to be so exhausted and want to go home? I could sleep for a week."

Harlow took the chair next to the desk. "It's been an emotional summer and even more emotional weekend." She cupped her hand over Tuesday's. "It was good to see your friend Harriet and her sister Jubilee."

"They want me to visit them in Melbourne Beach. Harriet suggested a trip to New York City. I always wanted to see a Broadway play. But . . ." She exhaled the last of her energy. "Maybe I am too old for living life."

"Why not get some sleep before deciding your life is over? Which it's not. If you want to see a Broadway play, I might be able to help. I know people." She winked. "Matt knows people. We could treat the three of you to a tour of the city. Dine at the best restaurants, see a few shows from the good seats, get backstage passes."

"Harriet said there's a show called *Dreamgirls* about Motown and the Supremes. Could we see that one, Harlow?"

"Absolutely. We can hire a car to drive us around and play the tourist. Go shopping."

"Dupree wants to take me to California." She opened her dinner from Audra. "I think everyone's trying to tell me there's life after the Starlight."

"Though it doesn't make it any easier, does it?"

"There's one thing I'm grateful for, Harlow," Tuesday said, "and that's you. You came here broken and discouraged, but look at you now."

"Granny, where's the deed to the rink?" Matt and Booker banged through the door like they were boys again. "Is it here or at home?" He started opening cupboards and cabinet, the filing drawers.

"What's going on? Why do you want the deed?"

"Miss Tuesday," Booker said in such an urgent breath, "the deed to the Starlight shows ownership."

"We've been over this, Booker. While I'm the owner, the law gives Harry the right to take the land."

"Yes, under the US Constitution. But not under Lauchtenland rule. The rink belongs to the Royal House of Blue. Not Sea Blue Beach."

"Slow down, Booker." She glanced from him to Matt. "Are you two friends again?"

"Turns out we were both to blame," Matt said. "And I'll regale you with that story after we save the Starlight. Granny, where's the deed?"

"Miss Tuesday, if the rink and the land belong to the royal family, Harry can do nothing without their permission."

Tuesday pushed away from her desk. "This is news to me, Booker. How do you know?" She could just burst seeing him teamed up with Matt like the old days. "Do they own all of Sea Blue Beach?"

"Grandpa Morris only talked about the Starlight."

"God bless your grandpapa. That man was a wealth of Sea Blue knowledge."

"Granny, we can reminisce later. Where's the deed?"

"Matt, I don't know." She dropped down onto her chair. "The only one who did is buried in the English Channel."

MATT

"Okay, humor me, Granny. Map out all the places Uncle LJ might have hidden the box."

"I have no idea, Matty. He was hiding it from your grandpa. So, discount the Starlight or the house, even the barn."

"We discount nothing." He took a pen from the holder and pointed to the legal pad centered on her desk. "Sometimes hiding in plain sight is the best. What did he love to do, where did he hang out?"

"He loved to skate and fly. He spent all his free time watching the boys at Eglin and flying an old crop duster."

"Let's hope he didn't hide it at the airbase. We'll never get it back."

"Or in an old crop duster." Booker paced, thinking.

"I know this is a crazy idea," Harlow said, "but what if we

reach out to Lauchtenland and the House of Blue?" Matt loved his beautiful fiancée—for whom he had yet to buy a ring. He'd not found the right one.

"Great idea, babe, but how? Do you know anyone with connections?"

She winced. "Xander. He attended Princess Catherine's twenty-first birthday party right after he dumped me. It was all over the news."

"Then never mind. We'll find what we need another way."

"I'll call him. I have one more guilt-trip point to spend."

"That's my girl." He gave her a quick kiss, loving that he could do that any time he wanted. "Even if he agrees, we may not cut through the diplomatic red tape in time."

"We have to try." Booker leaned over Granny's shoulder to read her list. "The back room, the barn, under your bed and back of the closet, the school, my grandparents house."

Granny tore off the list and handed it to Book. "We have until morning. Harry assured me the wrecking ball crew would arrive first thing."

While Harlow returned to manning the Starlight, Matt and Booker searched from the back room to concession just to be sure. Even gave the Wurlitzer the once-over.

The barn really had no hiding place, but they struck gold in Granny's closet, finding a small box tucked away in the corner.

It was empty except for a note inside.

Dear Tooz,

In case you throw away the slip of paper I gave you, 'cause I'm figuring you will, here's the name of the bank in New Orleans.

He listed an account number, safe-deposit box, and the name Monte.

Just so you know, everything in the bank box I earned honest. I was going to surprise you, but Herr Hitler had other plans for the world. I hope one day we're reading this together and laughing about the good ol' days, eating dinner from your new electric stove. For now, I'm off to war.

Yours always,
Sgt. Leroy Knight

Matt found Granny watching the afternoon session, smiling at the skaters with a sadness in her eyes.

"We found this in an old metal box on the top shelf of your closet." He handed her his grandpa's note. "Did you know about this?"

"Yes." Granny sniffed the note before reading. "I never intended to use the money so I stored the note in the box. It smelled like Leroy's aftershave."

From concession, Spike hollered something to Simon Caster as they served the last ever Starlight session. He'd landed well. Purchased a premier spot on the Beachwalk. Pete's Pretzels upgraded to a franchise in Tallahassee. He sold Spike his trailer for a song.

"Did you ever call the bank?" Matt said.

"Never." She tucked the note into her pocket. "I didn't trust Leroy earned the money honestly."

"Booker and I are road-tripping to New Orleans in the morning. In the meantime, let's visit Harry. Buy some time from him."

"Matt, the deed isn't at the bank in New Orleans. LJ hid it long before Lee went to war. He'd have never told where."

"Still, I want to see what's in the safe-deposit box, Granny. Leave no stone unturned. Wonder if Harlow got anywhere with Xander."

She rounded the office door as he spoke. "He said he'd make a few calls."

"Excellent. I'm off to find Harry."

"Knock, knock." *Gazette* editor Rachel Kirby walked in with a story in hand. "I'm running this piece tomorrow. I thought you'd like a sneak piece. All this talk of the Starlight, Prince Blue, and Malachi Nickle got me digging about our history, see if I could do a series on our founders and key citizens. I spent weeks in city hall going over all the records, births and deaths, land deeds, who had what and did what and for how long, talking to old-timers. Even learned a few things about the newspaper I didn't know. And a couple more of our buildings can go on the historical register. Harlow, your house qualifies. Anyway, trouble is, I can't find anything on the rink. There's literally no record of it. It's crazy." She looked at Granny. "Do you know why?"

"The land and rink belong to the Royal House of Blue," Booker said. "I think if we had the deed, we'd be able to prove it."

"Rachel, didn't you work for the AP in London?" Matt said. "Got any connections in Lauchtenland? The House of Blue? Harlow made some calls, but let's try more than one approach."

"A royal mystery? I'm going to need more to the story, but yeah, I know a few people in the Royal Rota. Let me make a few calls."

Matt and Booker headed over to Harry's, who was tearing down after his Labor Day bash.

"I'd have invited you," he said, shaking Matt's hand, "but given the current situation . . . Booker, it's good to see you back in town."

"Came to say good-bye to the Starlight. And mend a few fences."

"Harry, we need you to delay the wrecking ball."

"Can't. The bulldozer and cranes are already here and the crew is scheduled for the morning. Delays will only cost the town money. Look, we've given you the summer to—"

"I'll pay for the delay. I need a day or two."

"What are you up to, Matt? I put up with your petition, listened to the arguments. It's time to let it go."

"Two days, tops, Harry. Maybe three. I'll cover the cost."

The mayor sighed. "Two days, then the Starlight is coming down. End of story."

HARLOW

When Tuesday closed up the rink for the last time in her life, it was all Harlow could do not to break down. She waited with Matt and Dupree outside, under the glow of the neon sign, letting Tuesday have her final moments alone.

Then with a loud ca-chunk, the Starlight went dark. In fact, the whole world went dark. No Beachwalk lights. No downtown glimmer. No moon. No stars. Just darkness.

To think, when she first came here, she wanted to block the neon sign from glowing into her living room.

Harlow fell against Matt, her ear listening to his thudding heart.

While he had extracted a stay of execution from Harry, Harlow didn't hold out much hope.

Xander laughed when she called in her favor. A detail she didn't pass on to the others.

"Could you ask King Rein's equerry about the Starlight?"

"You can't be serious? Call the royal family of Blue about a skating rink?"

Fine. She played her final trump card. "Xander, when you were on the cover of People with Davina, did my eyes deceive me or was she wearing the Van Cleef and Arpels Pont des Amoureux diamond watch you gave me on our first anniversary? You told me it was lost."

"I'll give him a call."

Dupree offered to drive Tuesday down to see Harriet Nickle in the morning, before the cranes and bulldozers fired up, but she refused.

"I can't leave the Starlight in its darkest hour."

There was a minuscule possibility of a Xander call. Even less for Rachel Kirby and her connections. Unless Matt discovered something unbelievable in the safe-deposit box, Harry would execute his plan. Tuesday reassured them Leroy never had the deed.

"I don't know what you'll find in the safe-deposit box, Matt, but it won't be the deed."

Matt walked her home and kissed her good night on the porch. "Are you as sad as I am?"

"I'm sad, but you grew up here. I can't image how I'd feel if I were you."

"Do you want to join me and Booker at the diner?"

"No, you two have some catching up to do. I'll see you tomorrow."

"I'll stop by on our way to New Orleans." Matt held her close for a final kiss. "I love you."

She watched him go, then sat in her window seat that faced the rink. "Immanuel, can't you help?"

She showered and slipped into her nightshirt, the one that was too big, and her sweatpants, and just before she shut off the closet light, she glanced toward the corner.

Wasn't there a loose floorboard in here? Wasn't this once the home of Morris and Harriet Nickle? Wasn't their son Abel Uncle LJ's best friend?

Harlow dropped to her knees and crawled across the floor, tapping every board until one gave way. *Eureka!*

Plunging her arm below the deck, she felt around until her fingers grazed something hard and cold. It wasn't a floor joist. It was a box. A metal box.

She ran to the kitchen for her newly purchased hammer and tore up floorboards until the box was free. Setting it under the light, she popped the latch and peered inside to find a rolled-up parchment-like paper.

Prince Rein Titus Alexander Blue, of the House of Blue, to Miss Tuesday Morrow, on this day, the Twelfth of June, 1916 AD.

The prince's titled signature along with a royal seal anchored the bottom right corner.

This was no ordinary county deed. This was a deed from the House of Blue and nation of Lauchtenland. "Oh my gosh. I found it. It was here all along."

Down the stairs and out the front door, she shouted to the night. "I found it! The deed! The deed. Matt, Dupree! Tuesday! Everyone!"

She ran back inside for her favorite running togs and sprinted toward Dupree's.

"Matt, hey! Booker? I found it. The deed. I have the deed. Dupree!" She banged on the door, then took off toward the diner. "We're saved. We're saved."

SEA BLUE BEACH

THE STARLIGHT IS SAVED. MAYBE.

This is better than Christmas morning. Everyone in town is reading the *Gazette*, huddled together in front of the Blue Plate or outside of Sweet Conversations, and gradually making their way to the Starlight.

From what we gather, the deed to the Starlight was no ordinary deed but one linking it to the Royal House of Blue in Lauchtenland under a Royal Charter.

Sort of like a little piece of their kingdom on our earth. The moment was worthy of a Hollywood soundtrack.

Bodie Nickle is talking. "As far as I can tell, the rink and the rock do not belong to the town. Harry, you'll have to buy the rink and land from them if you want to clear this area for progress. If not, you could risk the wrath of two state departments. The print on the bottom of the deed is clear. Tuesday is the caretaker until she gives it to someone else. Even then, she'll need a new document with a royal seal."

There you have it. The Starlight belongs to another kingdom, and Tuesday believes Immanuel knew all along.

TUESDAY

When all was said and done, Tuesday Knight had few regrets. She'd loved her husband, her sons, her friends, her town, and her Starlight.

Well, she regretted one thing.

When Matt returned with the contents of Leroy's safe-deposit box—a cashier's check for a ten thousand dollars and the most stunning diamond engagement ring—she wished she'd trusted Immanuel more.

Use the money to buy your gall dern electric stove. Wear the ring to remember Leroy Knight keeps his promises.

After a bit of rigmarole and posturing, Harry deflated like a stuck balloon. "Well, I wondered what was going on when we couldn't find any records of the deed. I'd heard rumors about the royal family owning the place, but it seemed rather outlandish, and since we've not seen a Royal Blue on these shores in my lifetime, I figured it was a fairy tale."

Then Rachel Kirby delivered detailed findings about Murdock's crooked ways. "I think we dodged a bullet, Mayor Smith."

Dupree offered to sell the town some land he owned toward the west with Knight Construction as head of development.

The Starlight officially reopened the first of October. With the windfall provided by Leroy—that man kept speaking from the grave—and the generous gift from the Brandley's, Tuesday paid Dup and his crew to redo the floor, fix up all the benches, remodel concession for Spike, and buy all new equipment since he already fitted out his food truck. She upgraded the sound system, painted over the scuff marks, mended the balcony railing, updated the bathrooms, and bought a whole new stock of brownies.

This Friday was the first All-Night Skate at the refreshed and updated Starlight.

Spike's Concession ran at full tilt, with Simon Caster at the helm until Spike closed up his food truck for the night. Even Harry Smith came by to shake hands and put on a pair of brownies. On the house, of course.

Matt announced his future plans. "I'm running for mayor of Sea Blue Beach." He started campaigning, even though elections weren't until next year and he had a new movie to shoot. Booker reminded him he had to film one on his ranch too.

Harlow sat at the ticket booth for a while, going through a couple of bridal magazines sent down by her mother.

Now, as the sun rose over Sea Blue Beach, Tuesday made her way to the office exhilarated but exhausted. Maybe she'd let the kids handle the next all night skate.

At her desk, she reached for the velvet ring box and inspected her once-young fingers that were now covered with spots and wrinkles. Yet it was the hand Leroy held and kissed.

"Are you going to wear it?"

She looked around to see Dupree at the door. "You should go home. Get some sleep."

"I'm taking you home first. And you didn't answer my question."

"The ring is lovely, but the moment I put it on, Leroy will have spoken his last. Why didn't he just give it to me? Get down on one knee and slip it on my finger?"

"You're asking why Pa wasn't traditional, Ma?"

She laughed softly. "He lived by his own rules, didn't he?"

"The ring will speak to you every day."

The beautiful, *large* diamond surrounded by smaller ones still surprised her.

"What was he thinking? I've never had anything so grand in my life."

"That's exactly what he was thinking, Ma." Dupree covered her hand. "All my life, I saw how much Pa loved you, despite his reckless career. He'd want you to wear it. He kept his promise. Now, since I'm about to choke up, I'll go to see if Spike needs help cleaning the grease traps. Then we're going home. How about a bite of breakfast at the Blue Plate on the way?"

37

HARLOW

MANHATTAN
OCTOBER 1987

About a month ago, she'd started thinking of herself as whole. Not the broken, rejected girl who dulled her pain with food.

She was loved. By the adorable Matt Knight, who proposed again, this time with his granny's ring. But she was also loved by Immanuel. A fact she realized more every day.

"So you saved the Starlight and now are opening a cookie store in Sea Blue Beach." Mom waited with her outside Charlotte Winthrop's office. "Have you and Matt set a date? Did you go through the magazines I sent you?"

"Yes, and we've picked a date at the end of December." Matt was in LA, doing studio work for the rom-com and prepping for the spy-thriller, which began shooting in February.

"Seems rather rushed."

"When you know, you know." Harlow squeezed Mom's hand. "I know I'm a disappointment to you."

"Harlow." Mom finally glanced her way. "You have *never* been a disappointment. And you may think you weren't a wanted child, but you were. Very much. Your dad and I have been talking quite a bit lately, saying things that needed to be said. And we're planning a vacation to Europe."

"I knew you had it in you."

In September, Dad spent a lot of time in Sea Blue Beach, helping Harlow purchase the retail space for her Hayes Cookie Shop. He hired Knight Construction to finish the build-out. In the evenings, father and daughter talked business and Immanuel.

"What do you think they're doing in there?" Mom adjusted her position to peek through the glass of Charlotte Winthrop's office.

"They'll come for us when they're ready."

"I can't believe they are keeping you—of all people—waiting. Like some intern applying for a job."

Charlotte's door opened, and she apologized for the delay. "We had an issue with our Port Fressa office in Lauchtenland. Please, come in. Harlow, at last. How lovely you look."

Charlotte led them to the position of honor and introduced her team. Jinx, of course, then Michele Brown, the CEO, and Emmitt, VP of Marketing and Sales, and on around the table. There were eight in all, looking very serious and more like Xander's crowd than Harlow's.

"I'll cut to the chase," Michele said. "We'd like you to lose twenty pounds, Harlow." She held up her hands. "Yes, you look fantastic. We know you've lost a good deal of weight already, and we are sympathetic, but I don't have to tell you how this business works. If it was just about advertising, there'd be no problem. We can airbrush you however we like. But it's the commercials and live events. It's our reputation in the fashion world."

"I'm happy with you as you are, Harlow," Charlotte said. "But

I must also work with my team. We've built a strong brand, so if they feel we need a thinner you, then we have to ask."

"We agree." Mom piped up as if Harlow were seventeen again. "Harlow can easily—"

"Thank you for considering me as your brand face, Charlotte." *Sit down, Mom.* "But I'm not losing another twenty. I'm not losing another ten. I'm happy with where I am now. I lost weight for me, not CCW." She reached for her handbag. "It was lovely to meet all of you. I will always be a CCW girl." Harlow walked around the table, shaking everyone's hand. "Jinx, let's talk soon."

She'd find another way to end her career on a high note. Matt had mentioned Cosmo "wanted a word." Maybe he could find her a movie role.

"Excuse me?" Jinx said. "You're just walking out? No discussion?"

"You made your position clear, and I've made mine. What's to discuss? Not to brag, but I think I look pretty freaking fantastic right now. If I lose another ten, never mind twenty, I'll be on the edge of skin and bones. I hate that look."

"This business is about skin and bones. You know that, Harlow," Jinx said.

"And I'm over it. Not going to do it."

"Good for you," Charlotte said. "I started CCW because I didn't like how things were done in the cosmetic industry. You're pioneering your own path, and I wish you all the best."

"Harlow, can we talk this over?" Mom remained in her seat, siding with those in the room. "This opportunity is—"

"Mom, I'm leaving. You can stay, but I think these people have work to do."

Jinx walked them to the elevator. "I was right, you know," she said, reaching around Harlow to press the down button. "When you got the key from Xander. I said, 'Go to the beach, it will do you good.'"

The elevator doors opened, and Harlow stepped inside with Mom. "Our wedding is at the end of December, Jinx. Mark your calendar."

"I'll be there. And oh, Anne, call me next week," she said. "We may have a job for you in our Atlanta office."

"Really?" Mom slapped her hand against the closing doors. "In what capacity? How? I do have some ideas. . . ."

"We'll talk next week." Jinx winked at Harlow as the doors closed.

They descended a few floors before Mom grabbed Harlow's hand and whispered, "Thank you."

SEA BLUE BEACH

MARCH 1991

We lost our beloved Tuesday in January. We mourned her death all winter, but somehow we understood she wanted to start her new year on the other side of the Starlight.

Her final years were her best. A direct quote. She saw her grandson marry the love of his life, and ten months later, she rocked her first great-grandchild to sleep. A girl. Tuesday Anne Knight, who recently started walking and goes by the nickname Little Toot. Two years later another little one arrived, Leroy Hayes, nicknamed Hazy.

Xander's call to the House of Blue made some interesting connections, and Tuesday, along with Dupree, Matt, and Harlow, flew to Lauchtenland for an audience with King Rein IV and the Crown Princess Catherine.

The king was most appreciative of Tuesday and the rest of us fighting to preserve Prince Blue's legacy. So much so, they gave Tuesday an honorary title, Lady Tuesday Knight, and Sea Blue Beach a Key to Lauchtenland. Rachel Kirby tagged along and filed a daily update for the *Gazette*, which we buzzed about over breakfast or while going about our day.

Taking a cue from Doc, the family sailed the English Channel and said good-bye to LJ, then visited Leroy's marker in Normandy. Upon coming home, Tuesday collected Harriet and Jubilee and flew to New York with a very pregnant Harlow for a few Broadway plays. Then she visited Hollywood.

What a storied life, Tuesday Knight.

While in Lauchtenland, she deeded the Starlight to Spike, with an official seal from the House of Blue, and as the first of the Knight Construction hotels were completed on the west end of town—we knew Dupree couldn't retire—vacationers booked their holiday at Sea Blue Beach and skated at the now-famous *royal* skating rink.

After the spy-thriller, which actually earned Matt an Oscar nomination, his career skyrocketed, so he decided to run for mayor "next time," and threw his support behind Harry. Forgiveness was a powerful tool.

Between babies, Harlow won the lead in a romantic comedy with a British chap, Hugh Grant, and no one said a word about her losing another pound, let alone twenty.

She has never worn the Jane Fonda workout gear.

These days, we see Matt and Harlow at home at 321 Sea Blue Way, running down the street with Little Toot and Hazy in a stroller. On sunny days, Harlow dons her hat from Biggs.

The Hayes Cookie Shop does a swift business with Cookie himself coming down to look things over and mentor Simon Caster, the manager. The kid is one sharp cookie. (Yes, we know . . . *punny*.)

Dupree met a lovely gal from LA—that is, lower Alabama—and we saw sparks flying from under his porch roof the other night.

Every now and then, if we look real close, we catch a glimpse of Immanuel walking among the streetlamps, between the homes and shops, and we remember the first night He walked onto our shore.

Perhaps you too will see Him one day. Until then, we'll keep the Starlight on for you.

AUTHOR'S NOTE

Like so many children of the '70s and '80s, I grew up roller-skating. For a season in my teen years, if I wasn't working, I was at the Skate Inn East in Tallahassee every weekend. My brother Danny could shuffle, which impressed me. I never mastered it. But I could dance-skate a bit.

My Uncle Porky (his high-school nickname stuck) gave me a hundred dollars during one visit, and I headed straight to the rink for my own pair of white boots with fuzzy blue accessories. I still have those skates.

Prince Rein Blue's home country of Lauchtenland, and the character of Immanuel, are from my True Blue Royal series. I love using characters from other books to make them come alive. You almost believe they are real.

I hope you enjoyed visiting the Starlight and Sea Blue Beach and will perhaps take a stroll down memory lane—or maybe even take a ride to your local roller rink.

Blessings,
Rachel

ACKNOWLEDGMENTS

Stories aren't written. They are rewritten. In my case, many times. Thanks to my editors, Dave Long and Jennifer Veilleux, for your insights into the Starlight. I think Jennifer read the story more times than I did. Blessings to you! Also, a shout-out to Kate Jameson, who took on the task of copy editing and double-checking many details.

Many thanks to Beth Vogt, who answered FaceTime calls with me on the other end saying, "I'm not sure I know what I'm doing." Her wisdom and advice kept me and the story going. She is the sole reason the Starlight became a skating rink. Brilliant, my friend.

Along the way, Susie Warren and I invented "condiment plotting," which involved tiny cups of cream, salt and pepper shakers, jelly packets, and sweeteners to work though plot issues while breakfasting at the Beachside Café. I'm starting a new book, so let's break out the jelly packets!

Michael Gross's book *Model: The Ugly Business of Beautiful Women* provided insight into the twentieth-century modeling world. Also, eighties supermodel Kim Alexis took some of her valuable time to talk to me. Thank you, Kim. Any deviation from reality is on me. Some aspects may have changed for the sake of the story.

Thanks to Judge John Harris for insights into Florida's legal system. I may have bent a few things to bring life to Matt's scenes, but Judge Harris's insights and ideas got me unstuck.

Thanks to author and Brit Debb Hackett for information about the British Air Force. I'm not sure all of that story line made the final cut, but I appreciated her and her husband's answers from across the pond.

To all my readers, thank you. I appreciate you so very much.

To my husband, who's survived life with a working writer and lived to tell about it *again*, thanks for all the encouragement for the past thirty-two years to be all God called me to be.

To Jesus. For all the reasons. He makes this life so worth it.

DISCUSSION QUESTIONS

1. When the story opens, we see Tuesday at war in her heart because of her husband's career. What do you think of her response to him? Do you consider her strong?

2. In today's culture, we talk a lot about strong women. Who did you feel was stronger in this story: Harlow or Tuesday? Discuss qualities of a strong woman. Who in your life represents strength?

3. Harlow crumbled when her heart was broken. Have you ever faced a broken heart or a huge disappointment? How did you come through it?

4. Why do you think it took Harlow time to stand up to Xander? Have you ever been in a relationship that tangled up your thinking and emotions? How did you free yourself?

5. Matt hates himself for what he did. He doesn't recognize some aspects of his life reflect his feelings about himself and the past. How can we let go of those things that hold us back?

6. Were you surprised when Booker showed up at the end? What do you think about his reconciliation with Matt?

Forgiving ourselves, as well as forgiving others, is a key to health and life. Do you have something you need to forgive in yourself or someone else?

7. What does the Starlight represent in the story? To you?

8. Did you roller-skate as a kid? What was your favorite roller-skating moment? Your favorite song? Is your hometown rink still in operation? Did you ever do the Hokey Pokey while on skates?

9. If you could tell yourself "learn to skate" about an issue in your life, what would it be? What steps could you take moving forward to see it realized?

10. The character Immanuel sets up on the beach to speak truth to Harlow. Did you recognize His truth? What truth has Immanuel spoken into your life?

FOR MORE FROM RACHEL HAUCK,

read on for an excerpt from

The Best Summer of Our Lives

The summer of '77 was supposed to be the best summer of Summer Wilde's life. But those plans never had a chance. After a teenage prank gone awry, she and her best friends found themselves on a bus to Tumbleweed, "Nowhere," Oklahoma, to spend eight weeks as camp counselors, and those two months changed their friendships and their lives. Now, thirty-something, Summer is at a crossroads. Returning to the place where everything changed, she soon learns Tumbleweed is more than a town she never wanted to see again. It's a place for healing, for reconciliation, and for finally listening to love's voice.

Available now wherever books are sold.

TURN, TURN, TURN

SUMMER

JUNE '97

The second Summer tumbled into Tumbleweed, Oklahoma, she'd arrived in the middle of the end. The beginning started three hours ago, when her manager, Clark, showed up at her Route 66 motel.

"The band left in the middle of the night," he'd said. "The Sparrows flitted. And I might as well tell you, I'm moving to LA. Got a job with the Bergman Agency. So, here." He handed her the keys to his '87 Ford F-150 as some sort of redneck consolation prize. "To get you home. And you can have it. Pink slip's in the glove box."

Sure enough, the minibus Summer had rented for her band, the Sparrows Fly, was gone, and her gear was piled up outside her Shady Rest Motor Court door.

Son of a gun. So it'd come to this? Her bandmates escaping in the night? At least her previous bands respected her enough to tell her to her face *"we're done."*

"Am I so horrible? So mean? That they sneak off in the night?" She'd tried to live "all for one, one for all," but she was really about herself. Besides, she should've let that phrase die twenty years ago. She could never recapture what had once been.

"Mean? No, I prefer terse," Clark had confessed. "Look, Summer, you *are* the show—the heart and soul of every band you've created. Why don't you just go it alone?"

Because she didn't want to go it alone. She'd grown up with best friends, the Four Seasons, and being part of a team was in her blood.

She also didn't want to be a one-hit wonder. But she was, even though technically "The Preacher" was Tracey Blue's. The country great heard the demo Summer recorded and turned it into a hit of Bobbie Gentry proportions, winning Song of the Year and Artist of the Year. Summer got a nod in the songwriter category but lost to Lori McKenna.

Four years after Tracey's release, country queen Aubrey James covered "The Preacher" because "she loved it," and the song rode Billboard's Top Ten once again.

Summer wrote fifteen new songs, formed Sparrows Fly, and hit the road again. At thirty-eight, dillydallying over *any* success was wasted success. But she failed, didn't she?

Then, as a parting gift, along with his truck keys, Clark handed her a coffee and the morning newspaper.

"Did you see the headline? Twenty years since the Girl Scouts at Camp Scott were murdered. Wasn't Tumbleweed near there? Where you were a camp counselor?"

Summer glanced at the headline and handed back the paper. Yeah, she was a camp counselor the year those girls were killed. Scared the heck out of the entire state.

After Clark said his good-byes, she sat on the edge of her bed and sipped the coffee. This was it. She quit. No more girl bands. No more this-is-my-shot-and-I-know-it business.

Face it, she couldn't make it in country music if Chet Atkins himself took her into the studio and laid down his classic Nashville Sound licks.

She'd gone eighteen years and over a million miles only to find herself driving from Tulsa to Tumbleweed. The last town she ever wanted to see again.

Up ahead, a sign came into view. *Tumbleweed. Population 2,883*. The *3* was hand-painted on the sign above a crossed-out 2. A new millennium on the horizon and the folks of Tumbleweed were still adding their newborns one by one.

Tumbleweed, what am I doing here?

Except for in the theme of "The Preacher," Summer didn't even visit Tumbleweed in her memories or dreams.

It's just that when Clark dropped all his bombs, then took a taxi to the airport, she didn't know what to do besides stand in the motor court parking lot and look pitiful.

She'd hauled her stuff inside, called Bryson at the Broken Barrel to tell him she'd be a solo act for the night's gig, and to keep occupied, she hopped into the white Ford and headed northwest. Her head did not want to return to Tumbleweed, but maybe, sort of, kind of her heart did.

Was she looking for *him*? Or the pieces of herself she left at Camp Tumbleweed on Skiatook Lake?

Arriving in town, Summer eased down the brick-laden Main Street and ached for the girl she used to be. The one who didn't need a drink to fall asleep. The one who hadn't had more lovers than she had fingers and toes. The one who didn't believe a record contract and an Academy of Country Music Award would give her life meaning. The one who didn't secretly yearn to impress people she'd left behind long, long ago.

She wanted to be the girl who loved her parents, who had three of the best friends in the world. A girl with hope, promise, and a future. A girl whose worst decision was a bad movie or crazy haircut. A girl who laughed at the memory of dumping concentrated car wash soap into the Florida State pool. A girl who spent a court-mandated summer with her friends as camp counselors at Camp Tumbleweed.

She missed the girl who'd so easily, so truly, fallen in love.

But it was too late, too late, too late. The emotional effort to even remember those days cost more than she wanted to pay.

Summer angled the truck into an open parking spot on Main Street and cut the engine. In the quiet cab, she glanced down the street. Tumbleweed had not changed in twenty years, except for new signs on the storefronts and a little more color on the façades.

At eleven in the morning, the town was alive with business. The pole at the old barber shop spun red, white, and blue, and a young man walked out, settling a hat on his newly shorn hair.

The hardware store advertised a sale, and Sue's Cut-n-Curl—Sue *had* to be going on eighty—displayed a row of wigs on a sidewalk table with the sign *Free to a Good Home*.

The door to the laundromat—oh, good ol' Tumble Time—was propped open, and a woman went in with her young son.

"Wellllll, you get the soap, I'll get the washer, honey. You get the soap, I'll get the washer, babe."

The song played from way back in Summer's memories. A sound from a time gone by. Eight weeks, eight Saturdays, and the summer of '77 still defined her. Maybe because the summer of '77 had broken her.

Had broken all of them.

Maybe she should just head back to the Shady Rest, get a nap—what a luxury—and redo her set list for the Broken Barrel.

Still, she was here, wasn't she? Might as well grab some lunch from the best diner ever, O'Sullivan's Diner & Drugstore.

If God cared about her one wit, O'Sullivan's would still have the Number Five on the menu and Tank Tilly would be behind the counter. He'd be, what, in his sixties?

Summer jerked at the call of her cell phone. She'd never get used to the beck and call of a personal phone. She pulled the device from the truck's console.

It was Clark. "You okay?"

"I'm sitting in Tumbleweed. You tell me."

"Come on, Summer, it's not that bad."

"Yet here I am. After my life fell apart this morning, I thought Tumbleweed might be a step up."

"Summer, don't be so dramatic—"

"I had a hankering for a good burger, fries, and a shake. I've been all over the country, and nothing beats O'Sullivan's."

"I'm sorry, all right?" he said, his voice cracking from a weak connection. "But I had to take this opportunity with the Bergman Agency."

"And you couldn't take me with you?"

"I tried, but—"

"They don't want me."

"It's just . . ." He sighed to the soundtrack of the airport. "No one doubts your talent. Everyone I talk to tells me you should write another 'The Preacher.'"

"That song was special, Clark. The lyrics were raw and personal, birthed from a place I didn't go to often." In fact, she'd not revisited *that* place since the night she wrote "The Preacher." The tune was simple but melodic with minor-seventh chords. "But after eighteen years in the biz with nothing to show for it but one song, I'm more of a liability than a possibility. Is that right?"

"You had more than a hit, Summer. You penned a future classic."

"Never feel guilty for going for your dreams, Clark. I should've said this at the Shady Rest, but thanks for everything you did for me. You stuck around when everyone else left."

She should be used to people leaving her. But the pain of it always felt fresh and sharp.

"I talked to Lucy Carter at Music Bomb. She said to give her a call and—"

"We'd kill each other. She's lightning, and I'm thunder. She only said to call her out of pity. Or because she likes you."

"Can I give you some advice, Summer?" She teared up at the tenderness in his voice. "Find a way to fix what broke you all those years ago. I have a feeling *that* girl will know exactly what to do with her life."

"I have a feeling that girl is more confused than this one."

"Trust yourself, that's all I'm saying. You'll be all right. You've got 'The Preacher' royalties, so there's no need to rush into something else. Take the summer off. You've been touring nonstop for eons. Whatever you're looking for ain't out there, Summer. It's in you. Sit still and listen."

It wasn't like her manager and friend to wax sentimental or personal, so his words hit hard and sank deep.

"I've got to go, Clark." Summer ended the call and popped open the truck door. She'd driven to Tumbleweed for a good burger, not to rehash what went wrong in the past. She knew what went wrong. Lies and betrayal, like all good tragedies.

A car horn sounded as a late-model Cadillac pulled into a parking spot next to her. An older gentleman in a ten-gallon hat rose out of the car like a cowboy superhero. He wore a bolo tie under his button-down collar, crisp blue jeans, and a pair of dark, shiny boots that came to a sharp point at the toe. His blue gaze lingered on Summer for a nanosecond before someone called hello to him.

Levi? Levi Foley? Of course not. This man was her father's age. Without a second glance, he disappeared through a glass door labeled *Life, Health, Home, and Auto Insurance*.

Is this what you're doing here, Summer Wilde? Looking for Levi?

Because if she was, she'd best hop into the truck right now and head back to Tulsa. Besides, the cute cowboy from the summer of '77 lived in California.

Hurrying across Main, she pushed her way inside O'Sullivan's and stepped into the past. A piece of her burden lifted.

Built in the early 1900s, when the Dalton gang ran through the territory, O'Sullivan's used to be the place where cowboys gathered. The decor of saddles, saddlebags, bullhorns, worn-out boots, spurs, cowboy hats, and a row of wagon-wheel chandeliers spoke of pioneers, of courage, of people not afraid to face the unknown to make a better life. She could use a bit of their courage and blind hope.

On her left was the drugstore. In front of her were the diner's red leather booths with red-checked Formica tables and the eat-in counter with no fewer than twenty stools. Behind the counter, the kitchen.

A man in a white chef's hat, black shirt, and large apron polished the countertop while Garth Brooks sang from the jukebox about a river of dreams. Tank Tilly. He was still here. A bit of gray showed from under his beanie, and Summer hoped for her sake he still dispensed unsolicited wisdom. She needed a dose.

She picked a stool and, without looking up, the man asked, "What'll it be?"

"I'd love the Number Five, Tank." She leaned back to review the chalkboard menu suspended above her on two fat chains. It'd been a while; the order of things might have changed. But no, the Number Five was still a cheeseburger with the works, fries, and a milkshake.

Tank scribbled on a pad of paper, then gave her a quick look before turning toward the kitchen. Summer sat up. *Remember me?*

He clipped the order ticket to the wheel at the service window, then slapped the bell. "Sooner, step lively, we got a special guest. Summer Wilde, famous country singer." He greeted her with a warm smile and took her hand in his. "I knew it was you. Pretty as ever."

"Ha. I don't know about that, Tank." The road life took a toll.

"I do. Know what I see? Some wisdom, some humility in those eyes." Add stupidity and hurt and he'd have her whole number. "I bought your record when you were with Wilde, Heart, and Landon. Keep the CD in my truck for long drives. You got a voice, girl, you do."

Wilde, Heart, and Landon was her second band, the one before the Sparrows. She tried to capitalize on her first success of "The Preacher" and drove the band hard. Toured nonstop. They almost strung her up and left her for the coyotes.

"So, your friends, what'd y'all call yourselves?"

"The Four Seasons."

"That's right." He rapped the counter with his fist. "Summer, Autumn, Winter, and Spring."

"Snow. Not Winter. Margaret Snowden, but everyone called her Snow." Snow's name felt weird on her tongue. She'd not spoken of her, or any of them, in ages. Eight, ten years?

"That's right, that's right. You'd think I'd remember that one. Anyway, I remember she had pale blue eyes. Y'all keep in touch?" He turned to the service window. "Sooner, how's the Number Five coming? Don't take all day, and give this girl your best."

Sooner's frowning face appeared in the window. "What in the world are you talking about? I always give my best."

"Just checking, simmer down." Tank turned back to Summer. "Can I get you a soda while you wait?"

"Diet Coke?"

Tank grabbed a glass and filled it with ice and soda. "So, you gals still in touch?"

"Um, yes, we, um, are." So she fibbed a little. That was the least of her sins. It was what Tank wanted to hear. He seemed pleased to have remembered them. "Tumbleweed hasn't changed much," she said.

"Girl, we'll go into the new millennium same way as we went into the last. A one-horse town. Folks like it that way."

"Some things have changed from 1900. O'Sullivan's has electricity and indoor plumbing." Summer tipped her head toward the jukebox. "If I'm not mistaken, that's Trisha Yearwood singing, not Kitty Wells."

Tank's laughter caused her to drop another one of her morning burdens. She'd not felt like pleasant company in a long time. She *might* have treated the Sparrows like her employees. Or servants. It's just she—no, they—were so close to a record deal.

"You got me there, Summer. But we do like to stay the same 'round here. We only got rid of all party lines two years ago, and some folks fought that, especially those out a ways on the ranches and farms. Said listening in on other people's conversations was the only way to keep up with the news."

"More like keep up with the gossip."

"Gossip, news . . ." He shrugged his big shoulders. "Six of one."

Sooner appeared at the window. "Phone for you, Tank."

When he'd gone, Summer glanced toward the phone booth in the front left corner between the drugstore and the diner. The same one she'd ducked into twenty years ago to call Dad. His assistant, Sandy, had answered. *Sandee*, who Summer hoped snorted like a pig when she laughed. She didn't. She was beautiful, ambitious, smart, and cunning, but not the reason her parents' marriage fell apart.

"Here we are, and as they say in France, 'Good eating.'" Tank set a plate heaped with a burger and fries in front of her. The aroma was pure heaven. She shoved the soda aside for the chocolate shake, which was so thick the straw stood up and saluted.

She was three bites into her burger, five bites into the crispy golden pile of fries, and one cold, creamy, delicious sip into her shake when the bells on the front door clattered against the cloudy glass pane. Soft footsteps skipped over the hardwood toward the counter.

"Summer? Summer Wilde?" A pretty face peered around at her. The woman wore pink scrubs, and her chestnut hair was pulled back into a neat ponytail.

Summer choked down her bite. "Yes?" Did she have a fan in Tumbleweed? Tank aside.

"It is you. I can't believe it. When I called Tank to place my lunch order, he said, 'You'll never guess what the cat dragged in.'" The woman lunged at her, wrapping her in an affectionate hug. "I never thought I'd see you again. It's been twenty years."

Okay, who was this beauty from 1977?

She moved back to let Summer study her, holding her smile wide.

"Oh my gosh, Greta? Greta Henderson?" Summer grabbed her

into a tight hug, as if to fill herself with everything sweet and wonderful about the girls she met that long-ago summer. "Look at you. You're a nurse or—"

"A doctor, actually." Well, that deserved a high five. "My husband and I have a general practice over on Fifth Street. We're cradle-to-grave, so we put Band-Aids on boo-boos, deliver babies, and take care of the aging. And I'm a Yeager now. My husband is Darrian."

"Girl, I'm so stinking proud of you." Summer sat back on her stool. Greta, a doctor. "Weren't you the doctor in the camp play?"

"I was, and I still have the cheap plastic stethoscope Snow found in the drugstore toy aisle. It hangs in my office."

"I knew you'd do great things, Greta. I knew it." Summer squeezed her hand and tried not to feel like a complete and utter failure. Riding the self-pity train rattled her bones.

But honestly, what had she done to help her fellow man? Written a bunch of sappy, crappy country songs so a room full of drunks could cry in their beers?

"I owe it all to the Four Seasons, Summer."

"You owe it all to Spring. She was your counselor." Greta got dropped off by her parents on their way to Europe. She was the only Camp Tumbleweed Tumbler who didn't rotate out every weekend. In fact, they'd inducted her into their unique friendship, dubbing her Baby Season.

"It was all of you." Greta's eyes brimmed with emotion. "First, you made me feel loved and accepted. Second, you showed me how to be a friend. I was a Tumbler until I was sixteen, then became a counselor. Lily did a great job running the camp. She was—"

"The best," Summer said. Mom restarted the camp she'd attended as a girl that summer of '77 and went on to run it for ten years. Summer would have to give her a call sometime. Soon.

"Yeah, the best." Greta held her gaze. "I'm sorry about your parents' divorce. I know how much you loved your dad."

"It was a long time ago."

The beat of silence held them for a moment, the past and present connecting with memories and affection.

"Here you go, Doctor." Tank set down two brown paper bags and a drink carrier.

"Thanks, Tank." Greta dropped a couple of bills on the counter, then turned to Summer. "I'd stay and eat with you, but I left Ned Banks on the exam table in a paper gown." She pulled a pen from her scrubs pocket and reached for a napkin. "You have to come to dinner." She scribbled her address and phone number on the napkin and slid the info to Summer. "Please. Darrian would love to meet you, and I really, really want to catch up."

A bit of dew collected in the corners of her eyes. "I can't tell you how much y'all impacted my life. I think of you all the time. Especially when I listen to your music or watch one of Snow's movies. I still hear from Spring. She's married, and a partner in a large law firm. Happy." Greta gathered her lunch. "Please, Summer, come to dinner. We have a lovely place on the lake. Tank here sold us a tract of land so we could build our dream house."

"Greta, go, you've got an important job." Summer held up the napkin. "I'll see what I can do." Lie. She was leaving town in an hour for one last gig. Then where? She didn't really know, but not here.

"Ain't it great to see her again?" Tank set another lunch box on the counter with the name *Foley* on the side. "Thanks to you gals and Camp Tumbleweed, we got two of the best doctors. Everybody says so."

"She's amazing. Seems content, happy, successful."

She and the Four Seasons had felt sorry for Greta the summer of '77 when her parents dropped her off at Camp Tumbleweed while they headed to Europe. The camp was run-down and overgrown, abandoned for twenty years. Who knew then how impactful those eight weeks would turn out to be?

"You hanging around long enough to take her up on dinner?" Tank said, giving the counter a wipe. "She's sincere in wanting to see you. I've heard her mention you girls around town. And I'm sure you know Camp Tumbleweed has taken another long nap. Going on ten years now."

"I'd heard." Summer peered up at him. She'd been here one summer twenty years ago, yet she felt like he knew her. "But I can't stay. I've got a gig in Tulsa tonight at the Broken Barrel."

"Then what? Going back to Nashville? Maybe you could come back here, hang around for a while," Tank said. "I always thought you fit with Tumbleweed. You're one of us."

"I'm not sure whether to laugh or cry, Tank."

"I know, I know. You got your dreams, your music, but life can be good here in Tumbleweed."

"And what would I do in Tumbleweed? Wait tables?"

"You could sing. I've been meaning to take out that old phone booth, put it in the front corner with the jukebox. Just never had anything put a fire under me to do it."

"Tank, I done told you to do it a thousand times." Sooner's voice boomed from the back. "If I ain't fire, don't know what is."

"Hush up, old man." Tank winked at Summer. "I could put a stage where the phone booth is now."

"Good luck with that, Tank. I mean it. It's a great idea." She pulled a twenty from her pocket. "I should get going. You still have the best burgers anywhere."

"On the house." He pushed back her money. "I'm happy to see you again."

Summer hesitated, then tucked the money into her pocket. "You reminded me life is full of good people, Tank."

He reached for her hands. "Sweet darling, I don't know what's happened between then and now, but—"

"An extreme lack of sleep."

"Then get you some rest. Tumbleweed is a good town for sleeping. Just saying . . ." He released her hands. "One more thing, Summer." Tank lowered his voice. "He's back, you know."

"Who's back?"

"Levi Foley. Took over his daddy's ranch. Mac Foley runs the insurance biz across the street."

"Levi's running the ranch? I thought he was a CPA in an air-conditioned office in LA."

"Found out he weren't built for the office, or for California. He's built for the ranch life. Ain't married, neither. And no kids."

"Well, good for him." Summer backed toward the door. "I'll see you around. Thanks for lunch. Best I've had in a long, long time."

"Should I tell him I saw you? Tell him about your show tonight?"

"No, Tank, do *not* tell Levi Foley you saw me."

Please don't tell him. She'd drown herself in someone's beer if Levi saw her at the Broken Barrel. The place was a dive. Where bands, or singers, went to die.

"Summer," Tank said, coming around the counter. "Whatever it is, you can—"

"I don't know what you mean." But her weak smile gave her away. "See ya."

Summer stepped outside and gazed west, toward the camp, to where she'd left chunks of her heart. It was amazing she had any left to live on.

What am I doing here?

The answer came, so clear, as if announced by the town crier. *Coming home.*

RACHEL HAUCK is a *New York Times*, *USA Today*, and *Wall Street Journal* bestselling author. She is a double RITA finalist, and a Christy and Carol Award winner. Rachel was awarded the prestigious Career Achievement Award for her body of original work by *Romantic Times* Book Reviews. Her book *Once Upon a Prince*, first in the Royal Wedding series, was filmed for an Original Hallmark movie. Two more of her titles are under film contract. A graduate of Ohio State University (Go Bucks!) with a degree in journalism, Rachel is a former sorority girl and a devoted Ohio State football fan. Her bucket list is to stand on the sidelines with Ryan Day. Rachel lives in sunny central Florida with her husband and ornery cat.

Sign Up for Rachel's Newsletter

Keep up to date with Rachel's latest news on book releases and events by signing up for her email list at the link below.

RachelHauck.com

FOLLOW RACHEL ON SOCIAL MEDIA

Rachel Hauck

@RachelHauck

@RachelHauck

More from Rachel Hauck

The summer of '77 was supposed to be the best summer of Summer Wilde's life. But after a teenage prank gone awry, she and her best friends found themselves on a bus to Tumbleweed, "Nowhere," Oklahoma, to be camp counselors, and those two months changed their friendships. Now, thirty-something, Summer is at a crossroads. Returning to the place where everything changed, she learns Tumbleweed is more than a town she never wanted to see again. It's a place for healing, reconciliation, and for finally listening to love's voice.

The Best Summer of Our Lives